USA TODAY BESTSELLING AUTHOR

DALE MAYER

A Psychic Visions Novel

SEED OF MALICE

SEEDS OF MALICE
Beverly Dale Mayer
Valley Publishing Ltd.

Copyright © 2017

ISBN-13: 978-1-773360-16-4
Print Edition

Books in This Series:

Insanity

Soul Legacy

Coveted

Boxed Sets and Bundles

https://geni.us/Bundlepage

About This Book

Charged with murder. Betrayed by her lover. Shunned by her friends.

After being acquitted of the murder, botanist Fern Geller runs from her past to learn everything she can about poisonous plants. She ends up doing a six month contract at the Garden of Death before finding the answer she's seeking…

When she returns to the same conservatory where she'd worked before, the new boss is missing and several other men are dead. Once again, all eyes turn her way.

FBI agent, London Behring hadn't expected Fern to look like she does now. Ethereal. Gorgeous. Gentle. Why and how had she been a murder suspect? Even more intriguing, how had she been acquitted of all charges? And more mysteriously, she'd come back to the scene of the crime… at the perfect time to fall under suspicion – again.

What magic did she possess to walk away from such crimes? And how can he stay free of her charms… a lure he's finding impossible to resist.

Sign up to be notified of all Dale's releases here!

https://geni.us/DaleNews

CHAPTER 1

BOTANIST FERN GELLER pushed open the door to the Milton conservatory, one of Portland's brightest tourist spots, and took a deep breath of fresh humid air. She preferred to work outside when given a chance, but, if not an option, she enjoyed working here. She used to come on a regular basis, but that was before...

There was a slight nip to the spring air. In contrast, inside it resembled the moist tropics. She loved them both, but going from one to the other was a little rough. She took her long braid and twisted it atop her head as she stood in place and took several more inhales, letting her lungs adjust to the shift in humidity. Also calming herself, shoving back the worry.

Loosening the top two buttons of her jacket, she strode through the main pathway toward the tour group ahead of her. The last thing she wanted was to get embroiled in a multitude of questions if she met the wrong people here, but she needed to know where the head of the department had hidden himself. It was a bit of a joke, but Reginald Drover preferred to be where no one could find him. A fascinating man to talk to—incredibly intelligent and extremely knowledgeable about his specialties—but the dispensing of his knowledge or the offering of any assistance was just not his forte.

1

How he maintained his position here was a mystery.

At least everyone else in the place was responsible.

The tour stopped to look at the orchids, and she caught sight of the tour guide.

Brittany. Good. She'd help. Fern stood in the back of the group and waited until Brittany's glance landed on her. She smiled as Brittany's face lit up. Brittany was a good kid, in her second year at the university, working on her own botany degree while helping at the conservatory on a part-time basis. Excusing herself from the group for a moment, Brittany walked toward Fern.

"Hey, I didn't realize you were back in town." Brittany opened her arms and hugged Fern. Stepping back, Brittany studied Fern's face. "You don't look too bad for someone who's been working in the Garden of Death."

Fern shook her head. "And I'm trying not to let anybody know I've returned," she said drily. "I'm looking for Reggie. Any idea where he is?"

"No, today is my first shift in a couple days. I haven't seen him yet. I suppose you checked all the usual places?" Brittany asked with a big smile. "It's early enough he won't have skipped out for the day yet."

"Or so you'd assume," Fern murmured. "In the months I've been gone, has he found any new hiding spots?"

Brittany shook her head. "I don't think so, but then I'm only here a few hours a week now, so anything's possible.

"Why only a few hours?" That wasn't good.

Brittany shrugged, her eyes downcast. "I almost lost my job. Reggie said I could stay for four hours maximum. I know the budget costs have overrun, and, with the latest news, the donations and grants have almost dried up. I'm lucky to get even this much."

"Interesting. Last I heard the conservatory was doing well."

"Oh, it was," Brittany said earnestly. "But, since you've been gone, you may not have heard all the rumors."

"Rumors?" Fern shoved her hands in her pockets to keep her fists hidden away. Rumors were deadly. They could destroy anybody and everything in their vicinity, and were often created without a grain of truth.

"Two deaths in the last couple months. One was a maintenance man, the other a visitor. Apparently unrelated. Now people are saying the place is haunted," Brittany added with avid horror. "Everyone is saying they've been murdered."

Fern's eyes widened in shock. That couldn't be good. "Haunted? Murders?"

That was the last thing she'd expected Brittany to say. Fern knew a little too much fraternizing went on between the staff employees, causing some rumor trouble, and although they happened everywhere, when it came to grant money, nobody could afford to have the faintest whisper of wrongdoing.

"Yes." Brittany leaned forward so none of the tour participants could hear. "And nobody knows what killed either of them." She took a step back, hurriedly twisting around to look at her group, as if to ensure they weren't listening in. "Be careful," she told Fern. Brittany glanced again at the gathering of guests, shifting restlessly. "I have to go. Bye." With a little finger wave, Brittany returned to the front of the tour group and said in a loud voice, "Okay, everyone, let's move on to the cactus gardens."

With happy murmurs they followed along.

Fern watched for several moments. This conservatory

was one of the largest in the world, split up into multiple themes. It had always been a favorite of the public, and even housed a special plant that only bloomed once every twenty years. People flocked in to see that rare occurrence. All these efforts brought in a lot of extra funding.

Like any grant-run institute, keeping the money flowing was always a difficult job. Any suspicious deaths would dry up the funding quickly. And that couldn't be allowed to happen.

With a frown, Fern retreated the way she'd entered.

Why two deaths now? Unless they were connected. Yet Brittany said they weren't. But then Brittany was a student, not a detective.

Surely somebody would have more information. That somebody should be Reggie. Something else to ask him about. If Fern could find him... His admin should know his whereabouts.

Fern hurried toward the office building, and, pulling out her ID card, swiped it to gain entrance. Only it wouldn't open the doors. She swiped a second time, and it still didn't work.

Through the double glass entryway doors, she saw someone inside, walking toward the exit. She stepped back out of the way, waiting until he opened the door. She flashed her card, and he held the door for her to enter.

Inside she headed down the long hallway to the stairwell. She took the stairs over an elevator any day. She studied her card, wondering if it had been damaged. Or had enough change occurred in her absence that her rights and access had been revoked, and no one had told her?

But then why would anyone do that? She was on the board, an active member in good standing. Sure, she'd been gone for six months. That was likely the cause of the problem. Maybe they'd been forced to upgrade the security system, and, as she hadn't been around, her access may not have been sorted out.

Feeling better for that explanation, she picked up the pace and almost ran up the last set of stairs. A lot of research was done here. Although they were listed as office buildings, the main offices were at the back behind a separate locked entryway altogether. She'd phoned Reggie's earlier this morning and left a message, telling him that she'd be coming to see him. It was foolish in that she doubted he ever listened to them.

Rebecca Ferguson wasn't at her desk out front like she normally was.

Finally reaching Reggie's office, Fern knocked gently on the wooden door. She gazed through the window beside the door, and it appeared dark inside, empty. Getting no answer, she knocked harder, then reached for the doorknob and turned it. It was unlocked. She pushed open the door.

She could tell it was empty with one glance. Exactly as she had figured. Damn.

She walked through the larger outer office and into the inner one in the back. If he was here, he'd be in the back corner. But it was empty too. His desk was cleaned off. Walking back out, she closed both doors and headed to the little coffee room at the end of the hall.

There she found two people, both strangers in official-looking business suits, their backs to her as they faced the huge wall-to-ceiling window.

"Have either of you seen Reggie?"

The two men pivoted her way.

She gave them a casual nod.

She couldn't see the second man as he now stood slightly behind the first, who stepped toward her and asked, "No. Why do you want to see him?" The other man straightened but remained silent.

She gave the first guy a startled look. Not what she'd been expecting. She followed up with a noncommittal answer. "I was hoping to talk with him this morning." She shrugged. "Only he's not in his office."

She turned to leave, but the first man called back, "Why would you expect him to be?"

She froze. Then very slowly she turned around to stare at the two men studying her. She still couldn't see the second man. "Why wouldn't I? It's his office."

The first man's lips tilted in a sneer.

She studied him, then asked, "Who are you? And just what the hell is going on here?"

"Maybe we should be asking you that question. Dr. Death, isn't it?"

Her heart froze. That name. Dear God. When would she ever be able to discard it? She kept her face blank as her spine stiffened and her blood pumped through her veins at triple the normal rate. If she could just get one breath out…

The first man stepped closer and pulled out a badge that he held up for her to see.

FBI. She stared at it with a horrible sense of déjà vu. Like hell she wanted anything to do with these two. Ripples snaked down her spine, but at least her chest moved properly. And she breathed.

She shook her head and took a step back. "Why is the FBI at the conservatory?"

"We'd like to see your ID," the first man said with a hard smile. "A nickname is not the same as proper identification. If you don't mind…"

"And, if I do, particularly as you seem to think you know who I am," she snapped, "what then?"

He took one more step toward her, conveniently in front of the second man, blocking her view again. "Then we'll have to insist."

She snorted in disgust. "Of course you will. After all, that's how you deal with people, isn't it? Manhandle your way into places where you're not welcome and through situations without any finesse or care for someone else. Especially not for the truth. Typical," she said in a waspish tone.

She was instantly sorry for spouting out her wrath, but she had no love for the FBI—or any law enforcement. The FBI just topped the list. It was hard to forgive them for the treatment she'd received at their hands. At least Derek, London's brother, wasn't here—her ex-fiancé who'd betrayed her in the worst way. That would just be the icing on the cake. She'd be running like hell back to England and the proffered extension on her contract at Alnwick Garden.

Still, antagonizing these men right off the bat wasn't the smartest move. "Look, I'm just trying to find Reggie. Do you know where he is?" She pulled her card from her pocket and handed it over. The agent took it and read her name. Instantly a frown whispered across his face. And she knew he'd heard her name before. At least the family name. Damn, she didn't need this. "So where is he?" she asked quietly.

"We don't know. He's gone missing."

She raised both hands. "Why not just say that from the beginning? He loves to do that, it's what he does. We spend half our days looking for him just so we can get a few problems solved around this place." She turned back to the door. "Thanks for nothing but wasting more of my time."

As she walked through the door, the first man called out, "We mean, he's gone missing, not just unavailable for a few hours or a day."

She froze.

"That is, of course, one of the reasons we wanted to speak with you."

She bowed her head. Of course it was.

She pivoted, her emotions carefully removed from her expression. "And why would there be an 'of course' in there?" She waited a long moment for one of the two men to speak. When they stayed silent, she gave a gentle sniff. "I thought so."

With a hard spin, she headed out the door once again.

And heard the first man ask in a low tone, "Did you kill him?"

The pain ricocheted inside through her gut and bounced off her bones before shooting a rod up her spine. "No. I didn't." And she took another step, the ache deep inside almost too much to bear.

"How can we believe you? You killed the previous head of the department."

She stood stock-still and closed her eyes, shaking her head. This would never go away. It didn't matter how many times she denied it or held up the acquittal for all to see. As far as anyone else was concerned, she'd killed Ben Kimball, the former head of the conservatory. The man Reginald Drover had replaced. It didn't matter to anyone that Ben needed killing in the worst way.

She kept her eyes closed, even when she heard movement. One of the men stood before her now.

When she lifted her eyelids, her body jolted with the

shock of recognition. Her heart, well, it knew her mate—and the pain of losing him. No, it wasn't Derek—it was someone much worse.

It was London Behring, Derek's hardass and way-too-sexy brother.

Shit.

CHAPTER 2

"HELLO, FERN." LONDON'S voice was hard, cold. She'd never known it to be otherwise, except in the very beginning when he'd been the complete opposite. But she'd been fooled by one brother, and it hadn't taken long to see through the second. Both untrustworthy. Both played with women's hearts. Both would do anything to make their own agenda happen. It didn't matter who got hurt.

She gave him a hard look right back and said, "London." Her breath still caught at the sight of him, at his name on her lips—and at the hint of color around him ... and his partner. She blinked, and the green tinge disappeared. She shook her head. That had to be her imagination.

The first man looked from London to her and said, "You two know each other?"

"Not really," Fern said. "Interesting, London, how you can now work a case you're personally involved in. I thought that wasn't allowed."

The first man looked briefly confused, shrugged and said, "The bosses put him on this case, so, whatever trouble you cause, it won't wash."

"Of course not. The FBI does whatever it wants with whomever it wants, right?"

London said, "Cut the crap. What do you know about

what's going on here?"

"Nothing. I just got back into town. I came to see Reginald. I left a message on his answering machine this morning. I expected him to be around today." She waited a few moments, getting nothing but silence in return, and then said, "So, unless you're arresting me, taking me to FBI headquarters, or to the local police station, I really must go. Always a pleasure." Fern spun on her heels and walked out, shutting the door very quietly behind her. She wanted to slam it but knew it would just make London happy.

Derek had been an asshole, but London, well, his actions had hurt her more than she could say. London was a bastard. Apparently she was a slow learner. She'd thought she'd gotten that message by now. It was just hard to accept. Even though her heart had taken a quivering jump of joy at the sight of him, at the sound of his voice, once that emotional jolt had calmed down, she faced reality.

The man was lethal. And not in a good way.

Where the hell was Reggie? If he was truly missing—as in, involuntarily—it would be bad for the conservatory. They couldn't weather another suspicious incident. The possibility that something could have happened to him made it that much worse. He was both friend and colleague. She lifted a hand, wincing to see the tremors, not just in her fingers but throughout her whole arm.

Confrontation always gave her the shakes. Her childhood hadn't given her the social skills to handle conflict with others.

She headed to the cafeteria. It was a faint hope, but Reginald had been known to sit in the backroom to work. His theory being that, if he couldn't be found, he couldn't be asked questions, and that was the only way he'd get work done. She wandered through the cafeteria, looking over the many tables and into the little nooks and crannies where the staff came for their breaks. But so far found no sign of Reggie. With eyes on the manager, she walked over to Denise and asked, "Have you seen Reggie today?"

Denise shook her head. "No, not at all. I hadn't expected to see you today either." She wore a big smile. "Welcome back."

"Thanks. I just got home yesterday. I was supposed to meet with Reggie as soon as I landed. He never did confirm, and I haven't seen him yet. I figured I'd better come in today anyway and find him."

Denise nodded. "As always, who knows where he is?"

The two women exchanged knowing looks, Fern hiding her growing concern. Thanking Denise, Fern turned and headed out the back door. People sat outside in some nice sunny spots, but Reggie wasn't one of them. It was also possible Reggie hadn't shown up for work; in which case, he could be at his house, although no one seemed to be there last night as she left the airport to drive by it, with no lights on inside or out and no cars in the driveway.

She resumed her quick tour of the conservatory property. No Reggie. She returned to her vehicle. Inside, dread piled up. She sat in her car for a long moment and then decided she had to find out for sure.

She left the parking lot and drove to Reggie's home. She still wasn't sure he lived in the same place. She'd kept in contact with him for the last six months, and he hadn't said anything about moving, but that didn't mean anything. Reginald was just as forgetful as he was good at avoiding people. She pulled into his driveway, happy to see it looked the same as it had late last night. She got out and checked the side garage door. She recognized Reggie's vehicle inside. That was a good sign, right? Although, last night she hadn't exited her vehicle to check Reggie's garage. The car may have been there even then. She walked up to the front door and knocked.

No answer. She pressed the doorbell and waited. And waited. Nothing. She was afraid to open the front door. She looked in through the windows but couldn't see anything. Not quite knowing what else to do, she walked around to the back door where the kitchen veranda was. As she neared the porch, she froze.

She saw no sign of anyone. It was quiet. However, there was a smell, not of death or decay—although both were here.

But of poison.

She slowly backtracked and came up against a hard body. She screamed and bolted. Only to get snagged and held firm. She twisted in hard arms to glare at London. Of course it was him. "What the hell are you doing scaring me like that?"

He raised an eyebrow and stared at her. "What the hell are you doing here?"

"I told you at the conservatory, I'm looking for Reggie. You say he's missing. Well, I'm worried. Did you get a warrant to go in?"

He just stared at her, as uncompromising and unhelpful as always. "Why were you backing up?"

"Because I didn't like the smell," she snapped. She didn't know if he understood. Probably not. In London's case, it was way too confusing to know what he thought.

He raised his head and sniffed the air. Shrugged. "I don't smell anything."

"Of course you don't." She shook her head, freed herself

of his hands that he still hadn't dropped and turned to walk around the house to her car.

"Where are you going now?"

"Home."

"What about this smell you were talking about?" he asked in a mocking voice.

She shrugged. "The only thing I can do is tell law enforcement. Since I've told you, I've taken care of my civic duty."

She picked up speed. She didn't know if he would continue to follow her or not, but she wasn't hanging around. She had no idea if Reginald lay inside the house, but now that more suspicious circumstances had been encountered, she hoped London would do the right thing.

LONDON WATCHED THE craziest, wildest, most passionate woman he'd ever met flee from him. *Again.* No love was lost between the two of them. Not now. Maybe not ever. But given the circumstances surrounding their association, that was probably a damn good thing.

She had been charged with multiple murders; the case had gone to trial, and she'd been acquitted. He hadn't been a part of that circus, yanked off the investigation by his bosses, although he knew she blamed him. If only for not stopping the police and FBI on their trumped-up charges against her. Maybe if their positions had been reversed, he'd have felt the same. He hadn't had a chance to explain his side of the issue, and he wasn't sure he could say much. All the evidence had pointed to her, but had it? He knew the cops were pissed when she'd walked.

But, for him, it had been a huge relief. She was a powerful narcotic, and, when around her, he'd struggled to kick the addiction. Before the trial, she'd been alive with laughter and joy. So beautiful, ethereal, as if not of this world. He'd been fascinated. But, during it, she'd been exhausted and terrorized, proclaiming her innocence. Thankfully, the jurors had agreed.

She had left the country soon afterward without saying a word to him.

Those months apart had helped him get his life together after his parents' death, just one month before the trial. His brother was still a mess today. And, for some of that, London placed the blame squarely on Fern. She had a lot to atone for, even if she hadn't been involved in the murder of the former department head or the other three people who had died.

That another department head was missing... Well, that was something to think about. The conservatory had had two suspicious deaths in the last six months. He knew the local cops were desperately trying to put her at the scene at the right time. But, according to everything they'd found, she'd been in England and firmly off their list of suspects.

Except on her days off when she'd traveled the countryside. In the cops' minds, she'd sneaked back into the States somehow. More frustrated and angrier than ever, the cops still waited for her to make a mistake. As London considered Reginald's unknown whereabouts, he had to wonder if that had just happened.

Steve, his partner for the last five months, walked up. "What the hell's going on?"

London gave him a quick glance. "Not a whole lot to tell. She was acquitted of the murder of the previous head of the department. And, according to her, just arrived stateside."

"Well, I doubt she's stupid enough to immediately murder the second one."

London shrugged. "As we well know, murderers aren't always logical."

"Sounds like she's been set up to me," Steve said.

"I considered that. And, if there's one thing this woman has, it's enemies."

"Including you?" Steve asked. "If you were involved with her, I wonder why you were assigned to this case. Crossing lines like that is not the smartest."

London nodded. "Sometimes you must do everything you can to put the past behind you."

"How is your brother?"

"The same." With that he turned toward Reginald's kitchen door. "She said she smelled something. I have to admit she looked terrified."

Steve walked up to the back door and sniffed. "I can't smell anything."

London nodded. "She's always had a nose for danger, and for death. If she said she smelled something, I believe her." London motioned to the kitchen door. "Let's check."

Steve turned the handle and pushed open the door silently. They didn't have to step any closer to recognize the odor. The smell of death.

"Shit," London whispered.

Both pulled their weapons and entered cautiously, calling out to identify who they were, and slowly walked into the kitchen.

The room was empty, but a definite odor came from the right side. London motioned at his partner and slipped into the other room. He stopped at the doorway.

There was a body all right. But not the one he had expected. Instead of Reginald, London found a middle-aged woman in jeans and a sweatshirt. He approached carefully but found no visible sign of trauma. She lay crumpled on the floor, her face twisted, her hands at her side as if clutching her belly.

Considering the earlier look on Fern's face and that nose of hers, poison would be an easy guess. But they'd have to wait for the autopsy. London searched the room for more victims. Then he and his partner searched the main floor and found nothing. They moved upstairs to check all the rooms on the top floor. No sign of Reginald. They silently made their way to the basement. And again found nothing out of the ordinary.

Beside the victim once more, London called it in. He turned toward his partner. "So, we have a dead woman in Reginald's house. He wasn't married, but he did have a long-time partner."

Steve looked around. "So was he kidnapped from here, or is he still missing on purpose?"

"Meaning?"

"Is he just avoiding his duties at the conservatory and has no idea what happened here? Did he kill this woman? Did he see who did? Did he interrupt something, then ran for his life? Or did he pull a disappearing act and left his partner to face whatever trouble he alone got himself into?"

"Was he the kind of man to do that? We need to know more about him," London said, quietly studying the orderly room. Outside of the body, there was little disturbance to the home.

"I'll run a background check on him. And her. Canvass his neighborhood and interview his coworkers. According to the staff we've spoken with so far, he's likely hiding somewhere, hoping the rumors will die down over the two recent deaths. But now, with this"—Steve pointed at the dead body—"I'll ask around some more."

London nodded. "The forensics crew will be here soon." He turned in a slow circle. "We need to find anything here before this place becomes so damn crowded we can't even walk through it."

"Also my run on the license plates confirms his car is here. If he's intentionally missing, wouldn't he have taken his own wheels?"

"Or he drove off with hers…" London cast a look at Steve. "Or he left on foot. Or he's been driven by someone else, either willingly or not."

Steve nodded. "Logical assumptions."

London snorted. "Which just means we're probably wrong on all counts about what happened, and we haven't considered everything yet."

The two grinned. They'd worked enough cases to know how true that often was.

"Anything to the rumors about her?" Steve asked.

Her. Fern. London shrugged and gave as neutral an answer as he could. And failed. "No idea. I just know I fell hard, but she was charged soon after, and I didn't know which way was up for a long time." And he hadn't had enough time in their relationship to learn who she really was on the inside, but he kept that to himself.

"Interesting woman."

"No. Secretive. Reticent. Lethal in so many ways. *Interesting* is way too mild a term."

THE BITCH WAS back. He couldn't believe it. He'd been waiting for this day for months. Talk about great timing. He'd driven past her house, as he always did, when he saw her. For a long moment, he froze in place, unable to even breathe. When he finally could, joy took over. It was all he could do to curtail a crazy dance.

Now he could put his plans in motion. He would make her pay. Like she should've the last time. Now he wouldn't give the courts a chance to let her walk. He would make certain she suffered forever. If the cops didn't pick her up and charge her within days, he'd hold his own personal tribunal. And he'd ensure she was found guilty.

It was hard to contain his joy, to believe that the time was now.

He'd put so much effort into his last attempt only to have it all blow up into nothing.

When he'd watched her burst into tears of joy at her acquittal, he'd been ready to kill her right then and there— just reaching out, snapping her neck in front of everyone.

But then *he'd* have paid the price, and that was not acceptable. Only one person here would pay, and that was her.

CHAPTER 3

FERN DROVE HOME with careful precision, her fingers locked on the steering wheel as she tried to control the panic rising inside once more. She'd calmed down after seeing London again, although her mind still struggled with the green hue she'd seen. She didn't see auras. These were warning cues to her. And witnessing the hardened wariness in London's gaze... Regardless of what she'd been through, his months hadn't been easy either. She didn't want to sympathize. She wanted to stamp down her happy emotions and use her hate to keep him at bay.

But it wasn't working.

The smell of poison at Reginald's house was the same one she couldn't get anybody else to detect at her trial because the participants' senses weren't that acute.

She'd had no idea hers was that discriminating, so definitive that she could detect toxins. She hadn't known how to convince anybody else poison was involved. Thankfully, her lawyer had, and that trick had turned the tide in the trial. She still had nightmares, thinking about what could have happened if he hadn't set up those tests for her—ones done right in the courtroom in front of the jurors' eyes.

Home now, she parked, got out and walked to the rear of her house. She'd left it empty while in England.

And she was more than ready to leave the country again.

Particularly knowing a job—and friends—waited for her across the pond. Inside she put on the teakettle, walked to her laptop and turned it on. She could return to Alnwick Garden and do another six months there. Put all this behind her. Walk away before she was embroiled to a level she couldn't get out of. She knew full well that the chances of getting through another court case with a second acquittal were almost nonexistent. Some people were determined to see her behind bars even now—and could manufacture evidence to keep her there. She knew that firsthand.

So many people believed she'd been a killer. They were wrong. And, if not for some unique friends, Fern would have gone down. The hardest thing about leaving the country the last time had been leaving her few, but true, friends behind. Yet they could communicate on a level she'd barely accessed. She'd worked hard to gain it though and hadn't been lonely once her skills had increased. In fact, while keeping in touch with her special friends here, she'd met several telepathically similar ones in England. According to them, an entire underworld of people existed with the ability to communicate on different levels. Fern wasn't sure exactly how much of it she believed, but they had stood by her in her darkest of times. For that she'd be forever grateful.

Considering everyone else had ditched her.

Girlfriends, coworkers, family, friends, and London. Derek had been worse. Even her extended family hadn't believed in her.

And that had hurt, and still did, a lot. Then again, they didn't know her. She'd just assumed family stood behind one another. Where she'd gotten that idea, she didn't know. But the dream had blown up in her face. Again.

She had been well-respected in her field until charged

with murder. She was a botanist, following in her parents' footsteps—only they'd been interested in herbs that healed, whereas hers lie in cultivating those that killed.

In many cases, there was a lot of overlap.

Her fascination had started in childhood and never stopped. Her grandfather, also a botanist, had died from an accidental overdose from picking tea leaves, something he did all the time. But this time, he'd mixed a lethal concoction. She'd often wondered if it had been an accident or intentional. He'd died while she was a child. Her parents rarely spoke of him. It captivated her that something so green and lovely looking could be lethal in so many forms. It had taken her decades to get where she was today. The last six months at the Garden of Death, as it was called, had been an eye-opener. She knew most of the toxic plants; but, to see the precautions necessary to grow these particular ones, especially in such close confines to each other, well, she'd been hooked.

The experience had also been a welcome breather after her nightmare trial.

Still, Ben Kimball, the former head of the Portland conservatory, had been poisoned. With Fern a specialist in her field, well published on the subject, all interests had been on her. It didn't matter how stupid it was to kill somebody with your own specialty. Better to kill using somebody else's.

But, when she had tried to convince the police of that, she'd gotten nowhere. So she tried to convince the FBI. No luck. Such was life when people feared you, distrusted what you had to say or just didn't want to look too close. Particularly when London's brother was involved. Derek had a lot of pull, and a lot of friends. He'd spread a great deal of poison, sowed numerous seeds of doubt.

She'd survived. But she wasn't a masochist. She couldn't go through that again.

With her laptop up and running, she quickly checked her email. One from Brent in England, asking her to please return. He didn't feel good about her trip home. She gave a strangled laugh.

And he didn't know about the email threatening Reggie that had sent her running home. The timing had been too perfect. Her six-month contract was over, and she'd been considering this trip already.

She hit Reply and typed an answer to Brent's email.

Glad you said that because I don't either. Now the new head of the department has gone missing. Of course, the FBI wants to talk to me. They were involved last time too with Ben's death as he'd consulted for them on several high profile cases.

Tears filled her eyes as she tried to explain. She'd spent many a long afternoon telling Brent about the case. A concerned stranger, he had helped her by letting her talk things through. He'd instinctively trusted her. She didn't want him to think that was unfounded. When she finally finished her message, she sent it to him.

Just then her email dinged, signaling a new arrival in her in-box.

It was from Reginald. Excited, she opened the email and froze.

If you are getting this, it means I'm dead.

She sank slowly back in her chair as she continued to read.

Every day an alert comes up, to Send or Not Send. Every day up until now I could say, no, don't send. Therefore, if you're getting this, I'm in no condition to stop it from being sent. In that case, you're in danger. Last time was a witch hunt. You survived, and got out. I was so happy for you, so proud of you. I never believed you were guilty.

At the same time, I haven't been completely honest. Not sure it's possible anymore. Things got very distorted, so completely confused. I wanted to call you back several times to help me. Two people have died here over the last six months. The cops said the deaths were accidental. They are wrong.

Thankfully, you were out of the country at the time, so nobody could pin them on you. But I suspect someone. I just don't know how to find out the truth without stirring up more problems. For you. For me. For the conservatory.

The worst-case scenario is that the killer found me. Trust me, he knows I'm looking at him. In which case... well, I couldn't stop this email, so draw your own conclusion.

The best-case scenario is that I've had a heart attack after a long-lived happy life, and it's forty years in the future, and you're wondering why the hell I sent this to you. But I know better. Also, I received several threats. I'm not a fool, no matter how much I give that impression, but I saw things in my life I didn't really care for, and I like most people even less. What I really do love is this conservatory. I'd tell you to run the hell away, but I know you won't do that either. I hope we get a chance to meet again. But, if not, you'll know why.

There the message ended.

She stared at it for a long moment, shaking her head. Into the quiet room around her, she whispered, "Why Reggie? Why?"

This was so not what she needed.

Her phone rang. She answered, her mind still consumed with the email. And then she saw the name. She gave a broken sob and said, "Hello, Stefan."

"You're transmitting very loudly again."

"I'm sorry." She tried to shut down the amplification of her thoughts.

He sighed. "Did you tell anyone about the letter that brought you home?"

"I just had some shocking news on top of a shocking day."

"Yes, it's been growing until about two o'clock this afternoon." His voice gentled. "Right now, though, whatever you just saw or did vibrated off the charts."

She sniffled, trying hard to stop crying. "You could tell? Without knowing the source?"

"I would explain if I could, but it's not always possible. So what's going on?"

She told him of the events leading to today's email from Reggie, ending with, "It's déjà vu. The letter-writer didn't even watch or care that I had followed the instructions. I came home in the twenty-four-hour time frame, but Reggie is missing now, as of yesterday morning."

"No, it's not déjà vu," he snapped. "What happened last time shouldn't have. It sure as hell is not about to repeat itself."

"I couldn't stop it then either," she reminded him.

"No, but the killer has been active since, while you were

in a totally different country. I heard another two died at the conservatory…" he let this voice trail off then added in a stronger tone, "We need to consider that the threatening letter was more about getting you to return than harming Reggie."

"I heard about that today as well, since I deliberately didn't follow the US news while I was gone." She took a deep breath and added, "And speaking of bringing me home to the US, somebody's dead inside Reggie's house."

She winced at Stefan's sharp inhale.

"But I don't know who."

"Let me check," he said, his voice fading.

She waited. If there was ever an odd couple, she and Stefan were it. She didn't even know who he was until she had been charged with murder. He had walked into the police station, stepped up to her and said, "I believe in you. Don't give up." She'd never seen him before—and he was too gorgeous to forget.

She was so desperately in need of a friend then that it hadn't mattered he was strange, possibly crazy, or that the stories he told her had all the same nuttiness to them. For some reason, she trusted him. Felt like she knew him. He certainly did her. The things he said about her, well, they'd all been true. Except for one. She had no psychic ability at all. She had a great sense of smell; that was it.

Stefan came back on the phone and said, "Yes, somebody is dead in that house. However, it's a female. The energy clinging to the dining room is that of a middle-aged woman."

She slumped in her chair. "Maybe Reginald's partner, Pam? If that's the case, where is Reggie?" The unknown was making her crazy too.

"No idea," Stefan said in a low voice. "Are you going to tell London why you came back?"

She shivered. "That would be the last thing I'd want to do."

"You tried to handle this on your own then. Are you sure you want to do it that way again? London could be a huge help if he wanted to."

"And there's the trick. *If* he wants to. Remember he blames me for his brother's condition? He's thinks I'm guilty of killing Ben and three others from my trial."

"He's also had some time to think. Maybe enough to realize things weren't as they appeared."

"He's also had time to reconsider and reaffirm my guilt. He wasn't friendly today, Stefan."

"No. It probably shocked him to see you," he said. "He wasn't part of that original circus."

"But we've always known he was in the background. His brother pointing the 'evidence' at me, keeping everyone directed at me, focused on me."

"But we never clarified Derek's motivation for that. Easy to say he's guilty. A killer himself because of that. But it could just be because he's jealous about you and London."

"Sure, but who else could be doing this? I'm as much in the dark now as I was then. But it's happening all over again."

"Did London say anything to you, implicating that you were involved?"

"No, not in so many words. His partner just loved the coincidence that I'm back in town and that Reginald's gone missing."

"Yes, wonderful timing, isn't it? That should help us sort this out."

"Why on earth do you trust London? I've never understood that." Stefan had been a staunch supporter of London since the beginning.

"I don't have proof to justify it, but I can read his energy. He cares about you, yet is conflicted because of his brother's statements."

She shook her head. "I hate it when you talk like that. What do I do? Leave the country again?"

"That'll just make you look guilty."

"As far as everyone is concerned, I *am*. Already tried and convicted. I wouldn't be surprised to see the police at my door this evening. Or in the next hour."

"Remember your thoughts are important, so don't send out negative energy."

She snorted. "London saw me. He's got everything all mapped out and sees me as guilty already."

"No, he doesn't," Stefan said quietly. "I'll check out a few things and get back to you. Stay calm, and take care of yourself."

LONDON MADE AN excuse to slip away from Reginald's house. The forensic team had arrived, and he was in their way. The coroner was en route, and the place swarmed with people already. London didn't object to the process, but he had somebody he needed to keep in the loop. Saying goodbye to Steve, London headed for his vehicle.

Instead of returning to FBI headquarters or the police station, he took a circuitous route and drove around the winding driveway at a huge private mansion. He parked around back and got out. The rear doors to the house opened before he ever got to them.

Bruno, the manservant, inclined his head and said, "He's waiting for you in the office."

London nodded. "Thanks." He walked straight down the main tiled hallway and took a left, heading into the office. He stopped in the doorway and rapped on the doorjamb.

Dr. Sartain looked up, then smiled and motioned for him to come in. "You have news, I presume?"

London glanced around—saw his boss standing in the corner and felt reassured, even though the director said nothing. London walked to the closest chair and sat. Sartain dealt with poisons and chemicals on a global level. He often consulted with the FBI on terrorists' cases. London didn't understand the connection to this one except that Dr. Death had been on their private watch list for a long time. Unfortunately.

"Some." London gave a brief edited version of what they'd found so far. He was uncomfortable with the duplicity involved in his job now. He wasn't as much undercover as checking out the process and the people involved, as well as Fern's involvement.

"Any idea if she's actually guilty?" Dr. Sartain asked.

London strummed his fingers on the armchair. "No, she isn't. Which means someone is setting her up."

His boss raised his eyebrows.

Dr. Sartain's gaze was piercing and dark as he stared at London. "Any idea who?"

London shook his head. "I think we're back to the same problem we had last time."

The doctor leaned back, tossed his pen on the desk and interlocked his fingers in front of him. "There have been a lot of deaths. All suspicious, pointing at her. Somebody must really hate her or thinks she's the easiest one to throw suspicion on to keep himself safe."

"I can't argue with either of those statements," London said.

"And what is your intuition telling you?"

London turned to stare at the window.

The doctor laughed. "I know you're uncomfortable with the question, but I've never met anybody with a stronger one."

"My intuition is also not unbiased."

"Of course not. Not only was your brother involved, but you were hung up on her yourself."

London pinched back the words threatening to burst free. This wasn't the time or the place.

"Did you sleep with her?" the doctor asked. "Sorry for the personal question, but it's part of your history, and we must know if it plays into this investigation."

London shook his head. "It didn't get that far."

Dr. Sartain nodded his head in a regal motion. "It's probably just as well. She was your brother's girlfriend, correct?"

"Earlier." London nodded. "They'd broken it off months before she and I got together. Still, I've often wondered how much him turning her in had to do with finding her in my arms."

"I imagine a lot."

An air of quiet contemplation followed, then his boss added, "People will do all kinds of things for reasons that have nothing to do with the obvious. If Derek thought you two were screwing around on him, then it's possible he would throw her under the bus."

"He's a mess now," London said. "So, whatever he did

back then triggered a series of events that affected him. Of course, he says she tried to kill him, but he survived the attack."

"Your brother is not the most stable person," Dr. Sartain said shrewdly. "All kinds of reasons could be going on in the back of his head for his actions."

London rose. He had done what he was supposed to, but he really didn't want to be here. The whole situation made him uncomfortable. Spying on coworkers, friends, and family, none of that sat well with him. Especially keeping tabs on his brother. All this was bad news.

The doctor motioned at him. "Sit down. We're not done."

Biting back a retort, London sat. Just then Bruno walked in, pushing a tray with coffee and cookies. London wanted to decline, but, at the same time, good manners kept him where he was.

"I don't quite understand what your role is in all this," London said.

"And you don't need to," the doctor said. "Suffice it to say that the poisons being used in these murders are ones we should know a whole lot more about. My research team is working very closely to develop antidotes. We must have access to who has this kind of information and doing it on a global scale so we can combat it."

London's boss spoke up. "He has clearance at the highest levels."

"People are dying," London said. "One found today, two within the last six months, and four related cases that we know of from before."

"And we could quite possibly put Reginald on that list as of now."

London nodded. "I'm afraid to say that's a possibility,

but it's quite likely true."

"I only met with him once or twice. Reginald was many things, but he was not a people person," Dr. Sartain said. "He's a simple man with simple needs, and one of those was to keep to himself. He should never have been appointed as the head of the conservatory, but he had the most experience."

"And often that's all anybody needs. He was there when needed, and wasn't when unnecessary," London said quietly. Too much mystery shrouded this case. It had gotten very cloak and dagger. He was also concerned why he'd been picked for this assignment. Part of him wondered if they were suspicious of him. Hoping to catch him too while he played their games.

So not London's preferred management style.

London wondered how to get additional information on Sartain without it getting back to him or his boss. Hell, what about his own boss? London needed to know so much more. It boggled the mind that one civilian corporate CEO commanded so much governmental loyalty. Then again, any specialist like Sartain who consulted for the various government agencies at this level, didn't have to pull hard to get the information they needed to stay abreast of current cases. Operating in the blind like this was not London's idea of a good time. It also went against his ethics. But who in the hell could he share his theory with? Who could he trust? Maybe he could play his own game within theirs. Meanwhile, keeping Fern in his sights.

So continuing on with this charade allowed him to do that.

"She said she smelled something."

The doctor froze, his cup midway to his lips. He stared at London. "When?"

London explained. "She never said what, and I certainly couldn't smell anything."

"Did she make it to the back door?"

London shook his head. "I watched her go to the back steps. She made it to the porch and then stopped about three feet from the door, and, instead of turning around, she literally walked backward, down the stairs again. I was there within seconds, but I didn't detect any odor." He studied the doctor, surprised at his reaction. His smug smile meant something London had said just confirmed a belief the doctor held. It didn't make any sense.

"Fern's nose is, as we know, very sensitive. Even in her court case she was forced to prove the extent of her ability— and it turned her case around."

London winced. He'd forgotten what the prosecutor had put her through and how the defense had to prove her ability to smell highly toxic substances from a distance greater than most people's senses allowed. London knew the audience had been captivated. The jurors had certainly not been convinced until the defense got up and ran several tests. At that point, he knew they had been swayed, and the prosecutors were unable to find a way to change that. It'd been downhill from there as far as the prosecution had gone. On the surface, from the start, it had looked like a slam-dunk case, but she'd gotten away with it. As much as anybody ever got "away" from murder charges—considering her life had been destroyed regardless of her not-guilty verdict.

"Dr. Death is an appropriate nickname."

"Lots of people have been acquitted of murder charges," London snapped. "I doubt they all have that nickname."

"No, but she researches poisonous plants. And then, af-ter escaping a murder charge, went to work at those gardens which, of course, are named the Garden of Death. That just added to her notoriety."

London knew all about those gardens. He'd done extensive research once he realized where she'd gone. He'd even spoken to several of the curators to see just what she was doing while there. They'd been delighted to have her. Giving her a place where she was comfortable and welcomed. Hard to imagine anybody could be working in a garden where any plant could kill them. But, as Fern found that humans were against her every time she turned around, she may have felt more at home there than anywhere.

Of course the media had found out and ran several stories on her all over again. All adding to the tourist attraction of the UK garden.

London finished his coffee and replaced it on the tray. "I need to get to the office. It's been a long day, with still a lot of paperwork to deal with."

"Is anybody trailing her?"

London shook his head. "No budget money for that. The hunt right now is for Reginald."

"Makes sense." It looked like the doctor wanted to say something else, but he fell quiet.

London stood. "If there's nothing else, I'll be off."

So far no one had asked about his coworkers. Which was a relief, but also a curiosity as that was his reason for what he was doing—supposedly.

He turned and walked from the room, only relaxing when he exited the house. Nobody really said what the doctor's specialty was or what he did other than be the figurehead of his many corporations. But he was involved in pharmaceuticals, weapons, and the military. And obviously he had an interest in anything to do with the poisons Fern might know about. But, for some reason, Dr. Sartain thought something was special about Fern and her expertise.

The current cop theory was she'd created a lethal combination that was undetectable—contributing to her acquittal—because nobody had been able to determine what poisons had been used on these four deaths.

Outside, London stopped for a long moment, studying the dark gardens surrounding the huge property. Evergreens lent shadows and shade over the large perfectly manicured lawn. All alongside the property, around the base of the trees, were various beds of assorted plants. A part of him wanted to look at the labels atop the long wooden sticks. The other didn't want anything to do with it. He had no idea what grew on this property. He also had no right to check it out. But he suspected they were not roses or anything quite so nice.

He got in his vehicle and drove to FBI headquarters. He had left Steve alone long enough. His partner didn't know anything about London's secret assignment, and Steve wouldn't appreciate being kept out of the loop. For London, working in the dark sucked.

WHAT WAS IT like being home? Did she realize he'd been in her house? Had wandered through her backyard? Had gone through the contents of her car? Did she give a shit? He'd even gotten into her old office at the conservatory so he could know her a little better.

It'd been six months since she'd left the country. He wanted to reacquaint himself with everything she was, so he could take her apart piece by piece.

He prided himself on his achievements. And his next move would see her go down in flames. His greatest joy in life would be to see the cage locked in front of her as he walked away.

CHAPTER 4

S HE ENDED THE call with Stefan. She had so few friends left. And nobody she knew dealt in computers or could handle this email.

Handle what though? According to the email, Reginald had not been able to stop the notification from going through. That did not mean he was dead, but only that he didn't make it to his computer in time to stop it. Nor had he contacted her since then to say he was fine. She stared at her shaking hands. Just the thought of calling the police was enough to make her stomach heave.

She swore she'd never contact them again. Would never do anything to put her in the hot seat a second time. The police considered her guilty, and yet she'd done nothing wrong. She hadn't murdered anyone. She had nothing to do with Derek's decline. She had no idea what the hell was going on in Derek's mind that he'd accused her of killing Ben. Derek used to work at the conservatory—maybe still did. He'd known Ben as well as she had. Hell, he'd had as much opportunity to kill him as she had.

Thankfully, she wasn't even in the country when the other two people died at the conservatory, and even Reginald's disappearance had nothing to do with her. No way the media would say that though. No, they'd print that she'd returned and imply her arrival tied into the newest suspicious deaths. She knew no further details about what was found in Reggie's house. She'd smelled poison and had Stefan's statement about a middle-aged woman. That was it. People didn't understand poisons. They were terrified of them. They didn't see that, in microdoses, some were beneficial.

Her parents had understood that, but they'd had their own sense of loyalty, and it was always to science. As far as Fern was concerned, fast food was a poison. It just took longer to kill people. Hellebore—a Eurasian herb of the buttercup family—was a plant that could both heal and kill. The nightshades were similar. Hundreds of other plants also had an opposing duality of characteristics.

People didn't want to understand how arsenic in small forms was used as a homeopathic remedy all throughout Europe. Or how digitalis helped people with heart conditions, but came from a poisonous plant as well. Mother Nature's checks and balances. It was all about finding the right extractions which the body could utilize versus the amounts that overwhelmed an immune system and killed it.

For every poison she extracted, she worked to find the antidotes. Mother Nature supplied both. But finding the actual plants was a different story. She'd spent her adult life working on it. Dr. Death had been her nickname all through med school. But it had died away until her court case and now stuck as a permanent label. Hardly fair, but nobody cared. Before and after she'd been acquitted, she'd received nasty phone calls and emails; her house had been egged. People had thrown litter all over her place and stuck signs up, calling her a murderer.

She was white. She was pretty. She was young. She was wealthy, and she was educated.

As far as the world was concerned, she was guilty.

They also knew nothing about her life growing up. She could have brought much of that to bear in her court case. But she hadn't wanted anyone to know. Playing the sympathy card wasn't her style. Thankfully, she'd gotten off without divulging that.

If it hadn't been for Stefan and his group of friends, Fern wasn't sure she would have survived after the trial, even though she was living in England. She hadn't been able to sleep until Dr. Maddy had stepped in. Fern hadn't felt secure in her rented house until several of Stefan's men had walked through and put up a security system. She didn't even understand what they'd done, as they hadn't arrived with electronics. But they made sure nobody could intrude in her home while she slept. She slowly put the trial behind her.

It had helped that the Garden of Death had welcomed her with open arms. She'd known that a lot of it was because she brought in the tourists. But, at the same time, the garden could teach her an awful lot. She considered it a win-win situation.

Her thoughts returning to her current problem, she collapsed in her chair and stared at her trembling fingers. What was she supposed to do now? She couldn't understand Stefan wanting her to call London.

She didn't trust him. What she needed was to find a lawyer, a cop, or somebody in Stefan's world who could help. Or, better yet, a psychic FBI agent.

She snorted at that. None were likely to be helpful. At least not in her world.

Her doorbell rang just then, causing her to bolt from her chair. She turned and stared at the front door. It rang again. She crossed to it, glanced outside, but didn't recognize the tall man standing before her.

He called out, "Fern, my name is Grant. Stefan asked me to come by."

She unlocked the bolts and opened the door. She studied him suspiciously. "You have any ID?"

He pulled out a card and handed it to her. "Better yet, call Dr. Maddy."

Her phone was in her hand, Dr. Maddy's icon in Contacts already pressed. When Dr. Maddy answered, Fern said, reading from the card, "Dr. Maddy, this is Fern. Do you know Grant Summers? He says Stefan sent him."

She could hear Dr. Maddy's light laughter. "Absolutely. He's Kali's partner."

Fern glanced at him again and asked Dr. Maddy in a low voice, "Is he safe?"

"He's safe, FBI, and can help."

She let out a sigh of relief. "Thanks."

"No problem. I'll give you a shout later. Sounds like your return to the States wasn't exactly as peaceful as you had hoped."

"The new head of the conservatory is missing, and I smelled poison inside his house as I walked toward the kitchen door. I retreated to find London watching me."

"Definitely talk to Grant. He can help you."

Fern put away her phone and motioned for Grant to come in. With a glance behind him, making sure nobody else was watching, she closed the door and locked it. She turned, her back leaning against it, and said, "Hi, thanks for coming. But why are you here?"

He shoved his fists into his pockets. "I happen to be in town for a few days. I stopped in to say hi to Stefan, and he told me about your situation." He studied her, his gaze quiet yet determined. "I'm sorry about what happened. At least you were acquitted."

She shot him a look. "Yes, it's great that I wasn't convicted, but I should never have been put through that circus in the first place." She led the way to the kitchen. "I'm making coffee. Would you like a cup?"

"Yes, please."

"Dr. Maddy mentioned Kali to me a while back. She works with search and rescue dogs, I believe."

"That she does. She also has some of those lovely paranormal abilities that Stefan and Dr. Maddy have."

Fern froze, then turned and looked at him suspiciously. "Do you?"

He chuckled. "Nope, sure don't."

She snorted, the tension in the back of her shoulders relaxing. She quickly made coffee. "Good. It's a little unnerving talking to those people."

He gave a belly laugh. "Isn't that the truth?"

She motioned toward the kitchen table. "Take a seat. The coffee will be ready soon."

He sat, studying her.

She turned to get two coffee cups, not understanding the look in his eyes. The coffee dripped in front of her as she waited. Finally, she poured coffee for them. She avoided his gaze as she walked to the table.

"What about your own abilities?" he asked. "Are you just finding out that you're as psychic as they are?"

She sat across from him, her heart thumping, the cups in her hands banging on the table as she stared at him in shock. "I don't have any."

He moved one cup closer to him, and the other he pushed from its precariously balanced position on the edge of the table. "Stefan said you were in denial, but I didn't believe it."

"It's not *denial*. I am *not* like them." At least not like Grant might think.

He looked at her and gave her a small smile. "You are a whole lot more like them than you know."

She snorted. "You think I haven't heard that before?" She tried to hide the shakiness within.

But he wasn't fooled. "Why are you so scared?"

She glared at him. "Let's see, I was charged and acquitted for murder, and now somebody is taking advantage of the fact that I just returned to murder somebody else. Doesn't that give me a reason to be?"

He inclined his head. "I can see that. But at the thought of having any kind of psychic ability, you turned to jelly."

"I'm a scientist, a botanist. We deal in facts. Psychic abilities are a completely different realm of thinking and not analytical."

"That does not make them mutually exclusive," he said, his voice calm, controlled. "My wife is a search and rescue specialist. Her work is extremely dangerous and very demanding. But she's also a psychic. She has an innate ability to find people who are lost. Particularly dead people."

Fern stared at him in shock. "I don't think there's anything nice about that ability at all."

His smile was sad when he said, "Many times I think she'd agree with you. Between her and the dogs, they're quite gifted at finding any number of survivors. But the success rate in finding bodies and bringing them home for closure for the families, well, that's phenomenal."

"I imagine it's very hard on the dogs too." Fern stared at her coffee. "Few people consider the effect searching and finding death all the time has on animals."

"Kali is very aware, and her dogs are extremely well-trained. It's a great joy to everyone to find somebody alive after an earthquake. But, at one point, it turns from a rescue operation to recovery, and the animals usually know before the people. So does Kali."

Fern raised her gaze and studied his face. "It must be gratifying to know she's doing some good."

"Indeed. It's nice to know when you're doing what you're meant to and that your gift is helping others." He smiled. "Although I'm sure most people wouldn't see Dr. Death as doing the same thing, I suspect you are. I don't quite understand what it is you do in your research, but I doubt it's murdering people."

She smiled at him, her lips twitching. "I study the effect of poisonous herb and plant substances on the human nervous system. Mostly, I focus on poisonous plants and how long, fast, and in what ways they kill."

He stared at her for a long while, then, in a gentle voice, asked, "And?"

She stared at him in surprise. "And what?"

"I'm not psychic, but I know there is more to it than that."

"Fine. The other half of what I do is find an antidote for each one of those poisons." She stared at him for a long moment. "How did you know?"

"I know people. And though you might be fascinated with plants that kill, you are not a killer."

"It's a broad assessment that could get you in a great deal of trouble," she retorted. "How do you know I didn't poison your coffee?"

"I don't, but I trust Stefan."

She slumped in her chair. "Yeah. Stefan is good for

43

that."

"He believes in you."

"Why would he? I've never given him any reason to."
She looked moodily at her mug. "He says he'll check on a
few things for me. I don't know what that means."

"Probably means me," he said cheerfully. "I understand
you're having a problem with London."

Her back stiffened; she glared at Grant. "Do you know
him?"

"We're both FBI, of course I know him." His voice
maintained a neutral tone.

She shook her head. "Well, if you are here to defend
him, don't bother. I'm not listening."

He gave a short bark of laughter at that. "It never crossed
my mind."

She leaned forward. "His brother is worse. You have any
idea what he did to me? He was more than happy to see me
put away for life."

"London might've been a little too emotional because of
his brother's involvement. Not to mention he'd just lost both
parents in an airplane accident. The concept of losing his
brother too at that time panicked him."

"I didn't know a lot about his parents." Not that it made
any difference now. Still it would have been a difficult time
for London. And it made her realize why he might not have
been there for her.

She had heard Grant's words, but she had no illusion
about the assessment of his gaze. "Look, I don't know what
you're here for or what you think you'll accomplish. I had
nothing to do with killing anybody or poisoning Derek. As
far as I'm concerned, law enforcement and the entire justice
system are not trustworthy. A lot of people expected me to

be found guilty, and, sure, I was acquitted, but I shouldn't have been charged in the first place. What they did to me was wrong."

"People get blind and think they have all the answers. They don't see any point in changing their view because, as far as they're concerned, they *know* the truth."

"As they want to believe it. Nobody was interested in finding *the* truth. If they had looked anywhere other than at me, they might've seen something. But they were so focused on me that they didn't look around for another suspect. And a killer was free to act again."

"That is a problem," he conceded. "Sometimes with law enforcement, when they have a suspect who looks good, they build a case. It goes to trial, and, as far as they're concerned, it's a done deal. The fact that you were acquitted doesn't mean you're any less guilty to them. It just showed they failed to prove your guilt. The case isn't closed, because nobody was convicted. So, if anything happens again, those with a forgone opinion will be that much more determined to make sure you pay the price because, in their minds, knowing that you killed once, you will again."

She stared at him. "And because that woman at Reggie's house just died, they'll think I'm responsible."

"Of course they will." He gave her a lopsided smile. "And, if you were on their side of this equation, you would think you were guilty too."

"You know I just returned to the country, right? It would be absolutely foolish to kill somebody as soon as I came home."

"Not too many people are concerned about whether you're a smart killer or not."

"And the other two deaths at the conservatory... Will

they lay those on me too?"

"If they can blame you for one, they will say they're all connected." He picked up his coffee and took a sip. He smiled and said, "So, let's get this out of the way first. Tell me where you've been for the last couple days. Reginald's been missing since yesterday noon."

"I can't believe I have to do this again." She pulled a notepad toward her and picked up her pen. "So from when?"

"How about 9:00 a.m. yesterday?"

She took a deep breath and let it out slowly. Then she scratched down as much as she could remember of her timeline for the last twenty-four hours. When done, she turned the notepad in his direction. "Is this close enough?

With each jotted note, he questioned her about every detail. "You went to your British bank before leaving for the States?"

She nodded.

"How long were you at the bank approximately?"

"Twenty minutes," she said, "And, yes, I did meet with the manager."

"His name?"

She gave it to him and he wrote it down on the side. They went through everything she'd listed. Even how her eleven-hour transatlantic flight had been delayed at departure.

"Last night, after cruising by Reggie's house, did you immediately drive here to your house?"

"Yes. My GPS will confirm the date, time, and mileage involved."

"Did you sleep alone here at the house?"

"Yes."

"Did you talk to anybody on the phone? Did you send

any emails from your laptop? Was anybody here? Did you see the neighbors? Were you outside?"

"No phone calls. I might've sent some emails, but that doesn't prove I was actually at the house. No neighbors saw me nor was I outside." By the time they were done, she was exhausted. "Are you trying to help Stefan or me?"

"Both." He ripped off the top page. "And Stefan said one other thing."

She stared at him. "What?"

"You got an email from Reggie?"

The color drained from her skin. She closed her eyes for a moment, then said, "Damn, I was hoping to forget all about that."

"I need to see it."

She nodded mutely, stood and walked to the side counter, where she grabbed her laptop, took it to the table and brought up the home page. She quickly clicked on the keys to get to her email program and opened the message from Reginald. When it was onscreen, she turned it around so he saw it.

He pulled it closer, then asked, "May I?"

She nodded.

He read it through and checked the time and date when it came in. "I need to forward this to my own. May I?"

"Whatever you need to do." By now fatigue had set in. She was so done with all this. She wanted to go right back to England and stay there. She got up and went to refill their cups. She was almost out of coffee. She had only bought a little bag of beans, not sure how long she'd be in town. She could pick up another package tomorrow. She sat back down and asked, "Does it tell you anything?"

"Not yet, outside of the obvious." He pulled out his

phone, checked to make sure the email had arrived and showed it to her briefly. "You know this could get you off the hook."

"Or they can assume I worked on my computer skills to *get* me off the hook."

He laughed. "You really don't trust anyone, do you?"

She glared at him. "Do you blame me?"

BACK AT THE office, London dropped into his chair and stared across the room. He wished he could get to the bottom of what Dr. Sartain had to do with any of this. London understood the doctor's various companies were looking for intel on the poisons. But would anything he found in this way be admissible in court? Surely none of it was.

Steve walked in with several others to all find their seats in the bullpen. Steve held two coffee cups in his hand. He nodded at London, placing them on his desk. "The coroner says poison, but he has to run tox screens to find out exactly what type."

London nodded. "Of course it would be poison."

"Too obvious?"

"Way too obvious. She wouldn't make that mistake."

Steve dropped in a nearby chair and leaned forward. "Do you think someone's trying to pin this on her?"

"Well, it's suspicious that she just got back, and some-body else drops dead of poison."

"And how does any of this relate to the other two deaths at the conservatory?" Steve asked.

"Not sure it does." London tossed his pen on his desk and took a sip of the coffee. He winced, stared at it. He loved his brew but couldn't drink this cop version. "I need to see those files again. We can't know for certain they are connected, but, since we have a new victim, we need to look at all the cases from the beginning again."

"I can help with that." Steve walked to his desk and picked up a large stack of files, then dropped them on London's desk. "These are the conservatory deaths since the beginning."

London bolted forward. "Why did you have them? Let me see those."

"I figured we'd go back to the beginning." Steve passed a file over, then took the next one for himself.

Just as London settled in to go through them all, his phone rang. It was his brother. "Hey, what's up?"

"Is she really back in town? What's this about the current head of the department being missing? Is she crazy?" Derek's voice rose to almost a choirboy pitch at the end. "Why hasn't she been picked up yet?"

London pinched the bridge of his nose. "She's back, yes. The head of the department is missing, and, no, we don't know anything about it. And, again no, there is no proof she had anything to do with it."

"Well, we already know having that doesn't do any good because she got off last time. There was plenty of proof then," Derek snapped accusingly. "I still think you did something to get her off."

"So you told me in the past," London said quietly. "Did you have a reason for calling other than to start another fight?"

"Right. Typical London. Always being critical. Has no time for his brother." He half snorted. "Unless it's to spend time with my fiancée."

"Ex-fiancée. Remember you'd already broken up with her."

"But you knew I was trying to get back with her."

"So you say. That's not what she said."

"She's a liar," Derek snapped. "That little bitch. She's nothing but cancer—a disease."

"Whatever. I've got to get back to work. I'll talk to you later." London ended the call and tossed his phone on his desk.

Steve asked, "That was Derek?"

London raised his gaze to his partner and nodded. "Yeah, you could say that. Not the Derek I grew up with, nor the one you knew in college. This is an angry, vitriolic, depressed, even suicidal Derek—probably off his meds again—who blames Fern for damn near everything in his life." He shook his head. "And me. Let's not forget that he blames me for what's going on in his life too."

"Sorry, dude. Once he headed down that path, it was hard to get him to see straight anymore."

London nodded, but didn't answer. There wasn't anything else to say.

He opened a folder. The first of the recent deaths at the conservatory was a heart attack. Everybody was fine with that diagnosis until poison was brought up when the second man died. It turned out the heart attack patient had an extremely high level of an odd form of digitalis in his system. His wife had been on a walk with him at the time. They'd gone on a morning tour, and, halfway through it, he'd looked sick. Forty-five minutes later, he was shaking and sitting down. They called 9-1-1, but, by the time the EMTs had arrived, the man had died from heart failure.

The wife never blamed the conservatory. But the question remained, could his wife attribute it to her husband's absentmindedness? He could have overdosed on purpose. Or had he been given the amount in some other way, shape, or form by a third party?

It remained an open case. Complicating the matter was the fact the wife was a good twenty years the man's junior, and had inherited a sizable sum. But the police had no forensic evidence, so they couldn't prove wrongdoing.

London opened the second folder. This man had been poisoned. A younger man in his early thirties had collapsed at the conservatory and was pronounced DOA at the hospital. He'd been a maintenance worker and was found with an odd form of cyanide in his system.

Ben Kimball, the former head of the conservatory, had died less than two years ago, sparking the media frenzy and subsequent trial of what eventually became four victims. These two had died in the last six months. Reginald was missing, and the most recently murdered, identified as Reggie's long-term girlfriend, was Pam Akers. If they could find Reginald, they'd have more than a few questions answered.

"London?"

He looked up to see Grant Summer walking toward him. "Long time no see."

"I just came from speaking with Fern Geller. She has quite a story to tell."

London snorted. "Of course she does. And?"

Steve laughed from the other side of London's desk. "London has a bit of history with Dr. Death. No doubt she has a sad story. She believes she's been badly treated. At least by him."

London hated the heat rising on his neck, knowing the

growing color there would give away his thoughts. He shrugged off the snickers and studied Grant. "What's your relationship to her?"

Grant's smile had an edge to it. "Let's just say a friend asked me to step in and speak with her, see if everything was okay."

A friend? London nodded. "As it is, we've hardly spoken."

"She doesn't feel she can trust you. In fact, according to her, she might as well murder a dozen people as you'll find her guilty anyway."

"We're not that bad," London said carefully. He didn't know Grant well, but he had the respect of everyone in the FBI. He could make a lot of trouble for London.

"Yet enough that she's too scared to tell you that she got an email from Reginald today." Grant pulled out his phone and clicked a few buttons.

London's email program popped up with the notification. He leaned forward and brought up the new email and read it with dread sinking to his stomach. "Why did she give it to you?"

"Because I'm not you," Grant said with a hard smile. "And she trusts our mutual friend."

"I don't suppose you'd mind telling me who that is?" London asked, studying Grant's face carefully. *Not Sartain.* London would stake his, and Grant's, reputations on that.

"Not now," he said smoothly. "Maybe later, if necessary."

"And if we do need it?" Steve asked in a low ugly tone.

Grant barely glanced at London's partner before focusing on London again. "Obviously I'll be happy to produce it." He leaned forward so only London could hear. "At the same time, I'll ask why you went to 345 Royalton Avenue and stayed for an hour today." He straightened and walked away.

London glared at Grant's back. What the hell was going on, and how had Grant found out about London's visit to Dr. Sartain?

That was supposed to be top secret. No one should know.

CHAPTER 5

A LONE ONCE AGAIN, Fern wandered around her small place and tried to work out her next step. She grabbed a notepad and started jotting down what she knew so far.

The big issue was finding Reggie. She didn't know what Grant was going to do with the email. She hoped there'd be a way to track Reggie through it. She hadn't seen his laptop anywhere in his office or any of the other many places he would normally hide it.

If she had gone into his house that would just give London more ammunition against her. Knowing he had and they found somebody was a little disconcerting. She'd smelled death as well as the poison. Hard not to. She wondered if she should call her lawyer, Jerry Solange. They'd kept in touch with brief phone calls and emails, more because he'd been concerned about her.

Realizing she owed it to him to let him know what was going on, she quickly brought up his email address. In the subject, she typed *it's happening all over again*. Then she took the time to give as much information as she could get down before she hit send. At that point, feeling a little on the shaky side, she got up and opened the fridge.

Not having been home for very long and not sure if she would even be staying, she hadn't done much shopping. She had bread, peanut butter, and tuna, but no mayonnaise.

Nothing that appealed. She could walk to one of the corner shops and get something, or she could drive to the market and pick up fresh food, including coffee.

Still contemplating food, she sat with a thud. Returning to England appealed more and more every day. But she couldn't do anything until she knew for sure where Reginald was. For a lot of reasons, he might not have been able to stop that alert. Him being dead was only one.

She'd tried calling, but hadn't been able to connect, so she sent him a warning email instead. Now she worried that she hadn't done enough. After all he was missing now, and she couldn't help but feel guilty.

Originally she had even hoped to talk to Reggie about setting up a death garden within the US conservatory. They had discussed it before, and that starting one here would be no big deal. She was qualified for such a project. She certainly had a great response from the visitors in England. Nobody there mentioned the court case, murders, or her acquittal as she'd feared. And, as her name and presence had brought in notoriety and, therefore, tourists there, it would do the same here.

As time went on, she had enjoyed her interaction with the UK public. She got to work with her plants, but it was limited to the gardening level as she didn't have research money or the funding to do more.

Here in the States she could do so much more. She'd had funding before, until it had all been yanked when she'd been charged with murder. So many new plants she would like to work on, but she needed money and a lab to do so. Previously, when she'd worked full time at the conservatory, she had spent her evenings and weekends on her personal research at her rented lab space. It had been her name and position that had helped secure the lab space she'd used for years.

If she could get a research grant, then the same lab might give her space in their facilities again. She pondered the options of contacting them. She had been acquitted of all charges, but she didn't know if that was enough to make them open their doors to her once more. They'd been inundated with bad press during the trial too. That couldn't have been good for their business.

Even without taking a huge hit with lawyer fees leading up to her trial, as well as being mostly unemployed, she really needed big money backing her. A ton of it was available for research, but getting it wasn't the easiest. She'd been doing quite well in that department up until the murder charge. She had no idea what response she'd get now.

She did want to continue her work, and that required funding. She had money of her own, and had invested a lot of it to complete her projects at the time, but couldn't afford to keep that up.

She looked forward to getting more into that part of her life again, once this nightmare was over.

As far as she was concerned, especially since reading Reggie's email, there was only one killer. Likely somebody close to her or at least professionally jealous of her. He had to have a lot of motivation to set up these scenarios—or hate.

Who would have either a personal or professional problem with her? At the top of her list was Derek. Second would be London. How sad that her ex-fiancé and his brother were the only ones she could think of. She had had problems with a few people at the conservatory. She'd had to fire one because he'd been stealing plants for his own garden. She didn't remember his name.

There had to be a complete file on the theft as well as on all the employees somewhere in the conservatory's office.

Which brought up the issue with her security card not giving her access to the buildings anymore. She grabbed her phone and contacted Reggie's admin. Rebecca still had no word from Reggie. Fern didn't share Reggie's latest email with Rebecca. She would only worry more. With Rebecca on the line, Fern asked, "Any chance I can get a new access card for the conservatory? I'm still on the board of directors." Rebecca agreed to take care of it. "And, before you go, is it possible to email me all the employee records?" When Rebecca paused, Fern added, "I know this must be a strange request, but I am on the board. And, in Reggie's absence, I think it warrants a closer look at all the employees."

"I agree," Rebecca said.

"I'll put my request in writing and email it right over. That way you are covered. I'll take any blame."

"Give me a few hours."

Who else might hold a grudge against her? She didn't have much in the way of friends, back then or even now. And she eliminated them as suspects quickly anyway.

Some had been fascinated with her profession. Of course her nickname hadn't helped either. When the murder charges had been filed, everybody had completely disappeared from her life. She'd never felt lonelier than when she had walked into the courtroom that morning at the start of the trial, realizing the audience wasn't there to support her, but to watch her, with avid fascination, get crucified. And yet why should she have been surprised? She was used to being alone, unfortunately.

Without her lawyer, she would have been lost. Stefan had been around, but he couldn't handle the type of energy that a court case would bring in. He did testify often in lawsuits as an expert, but had said something was wrong about this one. It was very hard for his energies to be balanced. He also hadn't been able to come in as a defense witness for her because there had been no reason to call him. He knew she was not a liar because he saw the truth in her energy. She snorted at that. The jury would have had a field day with that statement. They'd crucify him *and* her.

She dredged through her memories, looking for more people who might have a problem with her. It was hard to remember anymore as she'd been so vilified by the media that she had no one left now from her former life. Hopefully Reggie was still alive. Then with the court case, she had met Stefan. Eventually Dr. Maddy. Brent. Otherwise she'd been alone for most of her life. Deliberately isolated.

After being charged, she'd received death threats and nasty emails. Her house and property had been damaged. Her gardens at home destroyed, and her life had collapsed. But, after the acquittal, it had gotten much worse for the couple weeks she'd stayed here. She'd received horrible letters in the mail. Initially, she'd turned everything over to the police, but they didn't seem to really care, almost like they wanted somebody to attack her because their hands were tied. Still they'd been forced to go to several people who had made death threats to warn them to stop their actions before they were charged themselves. Which meant the cops should have a list of everyone who hated her enough to do something like this. She certainly didn't.

Besides, few of the letter-writers had identified themselves.

Stefan had kept telling her everything had to happen for a reason, and in its own time, that she needed to have patience and tolerance to get through this.

She had asked why the trial was happening. He just looked at her with a sad smile and said the whys were not part of the human experience. She had pondered that statement for many months. It still didn't make a lot of sense to her. She reminded herself that the letters were just vicious words on a page. Maybe someone should check into them. Grant?

She copied his email from his card and quickly sent him a message, asking him to consider her hate mail folder that the local police should have. She added:

> Many nasty letters came before I was acquitted, so somebody at the police department should have a file. Did anybody look at the list to see if the killer was potentially one of them? I haven't even picked up my mail since I returned, so likely more is waiting for me.

She didn't expect to hear back anytime soon. But, when her phone rang, in her mind she assumed it was Grant.

Instead it was London. Her face twisted as he reamed her out for not letting him know about the email from Reginald. When he was finally done, she just hung up. She never said a word, just simply ended the call. She didn't need any more of that in her life.

There was something very empowering about hanging up on somebody. With a smile on her face, she rose to pour yet another cup of coffee. He called again. She knew he would. If she ignored his calls, he'd come by, which made her next decision that much easier.

She grabbed her keys, phone—which she set on vibrate—and her purse, and headed to her car. She needed groceries and a chance to get away for a little bit.

She drove to the big market, always teeming with tourists. She found a place to park off to one side and several blocks away. With her purse and a straw shopping bag, she headed to the market.

As soon as she felt herself mingling and hiding within the crowd, she relaxed. This was much better. Nobody knew or recognized her.

She quickly finished her shopping, then grabbed a coffee and ordered a sandwich in one of the delicatessens. She took her meal to the patio where she could sit and enjoy the sunshine in peace. She'd gotten accustomed to being by herself, having always done so in one way or another. In the last year she'd made new friends. True ones. Slowly. Hopefully, friends who wouldn't desert her if she ended up in court again. What a terrible thought. Her gut knotted up at the idea.

When she finished eating, she picked up her shopping bag and slowly made her way to her car. With all that was going on in her life, she had some big decisions to make. If she returned to England, should she keep her house and vehicle or just put everything up for sale and start fresh? Or she could work at any facility across the country. She had to check out her network connections first to see if anybody stateside was interested. She had thought her reputation was in tatters. Particularly when it came to raising money. Money was king. And, if that network had dried up, nothing was left for her here. But maybe it wasn't as bad as she'd assumed. A few phone calls would let her know.

After she walked in her front door, she pulled her phone from her purse, debating whether to make an initial network call, then remembered it was set to vibrate. She was also anxious to get the conservatory employee records. Checking her phone, she had missed three calls. Two from London, the third from Grant.

She dialed Grant. When he answered, she said, "Sorry. I turned off my ringer to avoid London."

He chuckled. "He wasn't too impressed about seeing the email."

"That is to be expected. I certainly don't trust him." She groaned. "I also didn't tell you about the reason I returned." She quickly filled Grant in on the threat to Reggie. There was a shocked silence on his end.

"Sorry should have sent it earlier. I'll email it to you." And she hung up.

The phone rang again. Grant. "You don't want to know how I feel about you not contacting the police over the letter, although I understand why you didn't. But that you didn't show it to me when I was there – yeah, I'm not happy about that."

"I'm sorry. I didn't know you. But I'm not hiding anything else."

She went to hang up a second time.

"Whoa. Do you know a Dr. Sartain?"

"Yes, I do, well, at least of him."

"You have a relationship with him?"

Cautiously she asked, "What do you mean by *a relationship*?"

"Have you met him? Have you spoken with him on the phone? Has he had anything to do with your research?"

"A couple times. We discussed some of my work, as well as my parents'. He tried to get me to work for his lab a couple years back. Said he still had some of my parents' old assistants on staff. We had discussed it before the court case, then he pulled the offer when he found out I was being charged with murder," she said. "I haven't contacted him since I returned. Why?"

"London was there speaking with him today."

"Great. Just what I need." At that moment, she decided. "Grant, is there any reason I can't leave the country?"

"No. Although it will make you look guilty, but there's nothing to hold you here." His tone was thoughtful when he said, "Are you in danger?"

"I am from law enforcement. Isn't that enough?" She shook her head. "I'm not trying to take this out on you. But once again, it feels like I'm back in the same boat as before. I would love to see Reginald walk home again and be his normal ditzy self, but after that letter and this morning's email, I'm fairly spooked."

"With good reason. But are you in physical danger?"

She winced. "I haven't gotten that far. But now that you mention it... As I don't know how the victims were chosen, what's to stop them from coming after me?"

"Because you're the patsy. You're their best chance at getting away with murder – again."

"That means someone must hate me – like really hate me – to do something like that," she cried.

In a gentle voice, he asked, "So who do you know who hates you badly enough to see you charged with murder a second time?"

"Other than possibly Derek, or some crazy persons amid all my hate mail, no one. I don't know anyone who'd do that."

"No, you don't know anyone you *think* would, which means you aren't seeing the people around you clearly."

LONDON'S HARD, ANGRY gaze stared at the monitors in front of him. He was caught up in something he didn't like. And yet, he couldn't find a way out. How could he possibly get free of something he didn't understand, knowing that it involved, at minimum, Dr. Sartain, the FBI director and, in another bizarre twist, the woman who had stolen his heart? London's phone rang as he sat there, contemplating this mess. He pulled it out and his mood plummeted even further. "Hello, Derek."

His brother's voice wavered, then climbed higher. "When can I see her?"

London's eyebrows rose. "I doubt she wants to see you." He didn't get his brother anymore. He'd turned from a confident ladies' man into a shell of the person he had once been. His physique had changed as well, from a big strapping muscular jock to this nervous stressed-out-looking geek of a man.

"Good. If she asks about me, don't tell her anything."

"She's not likely to." London stared across the room. His brother and Fern had been engaged for a week, maybe ten days; that was it. Derek had broken it off, then acted like it was her fault. Now he went hot and cold, switching his viewpoint with every thought. London wondered when all the shit would die down and his life—and his brother's—could get back to normal. London had known Fern hadn't killed anyone. That wasn't her. But the cops had been so sure. Now there was this feeling of unfinished business. Like waiting for the other shoe to drop, for this next round to happen.

Still maybe this was a good thing. He wanted his life back. He wanted the same for his brother. He also wanted to stop the asshole who was committing all these murders and causing so much mayhem. That was a joke. The local cops had no idea who that was. And the FBI wasn't getting any further either. As soon as London could, he hung up from his brother's phone call. Then he dialed Fern.

"Don't hang up on me again," he snapped, his temper getting the best of him.

"I will if I want to," she said coolly. "It's my right not to talk to assholes bothering me."

He winced. "I didn't mean to come across so strong the last time."

"You never mean to. It's so naturally you."

He hated how light and detached her tone was. She'd known from the beginning she was his, at least he'd thought she had. The attraction had been instant and, he thought, forever. Then she'd been charged, and he'd been caught up in the nightmare he couldn't get clear of. "I'm sorry."

He didn't know who was more surprised at his apology. In truth, he hadn't expected to do so at all. When she gave a heavy sigh, he realized it had worked.

She asked, "What did you call about?"

"I want to know if you've had any other communication with Reginald or anyone connected to this."

"Not yet. But you need to talk to Grant. I gave him a copy of the initial threatening letter. It's the reason I came here."

He closed his eyes shut. "Damn. I'll get one. What did it say?"

"I want my life back," she murmured, unintentionally echoing his own earlier thoughts. "I want to find Reggie safe and sound."

For the first time in a long time he caught a glimpse of what her life had been like. How having this hanging over her head, and once again flaring back up, must feel. Like her head was on the chopping block, just waiting for the executioner to come along. He never intended for his part in this whole mess. His boss had pulled him from the initial case when London's relationship with Fern came up. At the time, it was a budding one, but his brother had made it seem like it was long-term.

"He's made a mistake this time." A threatening letter to bring her back in time for her to be on the spot while another murder was committed? Brazen. And impatient.

"Oh? Why's that?" she asked bitterly. "I'm being set up all over again. Don't forget how earlier today I was at Reggie's house, with Pam dead inside."

"How did you know who had died?" he asked sharply. Then in a quieter voice he added, "You didn't go inside."

"No, but you can bet I was informed quickly," she said bitterly.

"Right." He winced, realizing several law enforcement people could have told her, then said, "Yes, but she'd been dead a few hours already. She died while you were still at the conservatory, after we talked to you."

A daunting silence filled the phone. Then she whispered in a torn voice, "Oh, thank God for small favors."

He heard her broken tears in the background. He closed his eyes tight and leaned forward. "I'm so sorry," he whispered.

Again, other than her weeping, there was silence. And for a second time he got a little deeper insight into how traumatized her life must've been. She'd walked away from him, moving to England, believing he was part of the madness that had put her in that courtroom. He wasn't, but he had been unable to get her out of the madness. He'd tried desperately to change the course of events. But it had been too little, too late.

With Derek slipping in between them causing trouble, her own stress levels off the wall, his frustration trying to figure out exactly what the hell was going on after his boss pulled him off the case, plus, his own doubts about his brother's word, losing both his parents just one month earlier, and the circumstantial evidence against Fern, he'd had no choice but to let justice take its course.

He knew that, in her position, he'd feel just as she did. Being acquitted was not the same as being innocent in the eyes of the world which had already mentally convicted her. He knew she had suffered. Everyone close to her had backed off. Including him.

He got up and walked through the office, keeping his head down to avoid anybody seeing the turmoil on his face. He stepped out in the hallway, across to the small balcony and took in some fresh air. It was more commonly used as a smoking spot, but thankfully, it was empty now. However, the smell of smoke still lingered. He took several deep cleansing breaths, coughing as he inhaled what was left over from the smokers.

"Thank you," she whispered. "I really needed to hear that today."

"Are you booking your flight back to England?" he asked, half-jokingly.

"I already asked Grant if it was okay to leave the country," she said. "I've no intention of ever living here again. I don't have anyone here anymore. My reputation is in tatters. Maybe, if you catch the real killer, I can rebuild my life, but, in the meantime, the chance of a decent one here is looking pretty crappy."

"Would you go back to the same garden?"

"They've offered to extend my contract by another six months. I told them I had to clean up a few things here first, but I'd consider their offer."

He winced at the thought of her leaving again. "I'd hate to see you spend another six months over there."

"I could spend six years over there, and still people here would not forget. In the eyes of the world, I got away with murder."

He nodded and stared at the overcast sky. "Then help me find the killer," he urged. "Don't fight me on this. Work with me. Let's figure out together who the hell could have done this, who could've dumped this on you and then walked away scot-free."

Again an awkward silence followed as she digested the information. "I tried," she said. "As I look back on it, I'm sure I could have done something else, but I don't know what it was."

"I kept thinking that something would happen at the last minute," he admitted. "Something that would stop this miscarriage of justice."

"The only thing that happened at the last minute was the common sense of the jury to not convict me for something I didn't do."

"We need to find the answers for your sake, mine, and Derek's."

"Don't do it for mine," she said quietly. "There is no *my sake* anymore. Do it for the victims who never got justice. Do it for Reginald, who may end up as dead as the rest of them." And she hung up.

"Shit." London stared at the gray sky, wondering how to

break through the barrier she was determined to keep between them. Could he go that route again?

The door opened. "You okay?" Steve asked.

London slipped his phone in his pocket, turned around and gave his partner a half smile and a small lie. "Yeah, I'm okay. Just my brother, giving me hell as usual."

Steve winced. "Man, I'm so sorry. That really sucks. Derek used to be such a vital guy. I don't know what the hell happened to him."

"Neither do I, but, if I could solve one mystery, that would be it. The other would be who the hell is murdering all these damn people."

"That's why I'm here. The initial autopsy report on the woman we found this morning said poison wasn't the cause of death. She took a severe blow to the chest, causing cardiac arrest, which is what killed her." In a grim voice Steve added, "He's thinking the poison was added to her mouth postmortem."

"And the only reason to do that would be to throw suspicion on someone else."

The two men stared at each other.

"The same person that's trying to nail Fern's ass, once again, to the cross, hoping this time she goes down for good."

Steve nodded. "It won't be easy to get her to open up, but we really need to find out who knows her so well they could pull this off."

"I've asked her, and I'm pretty damn sure she has no freaking idea."

"Then we need to stop asking the wrong questions and start asking the right ones. It may not be somebody who hates her, and just one who finds her convenient. The perfect fall guy for this. So we need to suspect everybody in her circle. Not only those with a grudge against her."

London nodded. "She still won't let us in."

"We can make it official."

"Let's ask for her cooperation first. If she doesn't accept that, then we'll go a little more hardline."

The two men walked back inside and headed to their desks. "You want to go to her place now?" Steve asked.

London thought about it and then nodded. "The sooner, the better."

"What the hell was that about with Grant this morning?"

London glanced at his partner and said, "I have no idea. But I need to see him about something else now. Fern didn't just happen to return. She was forced to."

HE'D DONE A lot to set certain little plays in motion. Who knew it would be so much fun to scramble up the chessboard and watch all the players react? That was why he loved poison so much. It was true and honest, while causing panic, fear, sickness, and death.

The conservatory would likely never recover. Maybe that was a good thing. It was only average anyway. They could've done so much more. If they had had somebody else take it over, then maybe they could develop it into something wonderful. He hated to see potential like that go to waste. Just like Fern had it to be somebody, to be something. Instead, she did everything halfway and never quite achieved anything. It was joked that she might've taken Ben's job, killed him for the opportunity. Not likely. She didn't think big enough.

Besides, she needed to focus on staying out of jail. Not that she'd keep her freedom. He'd make sure of it.

CHAPTER 6

F ERN DIDN'T KNOW what had just happened. But there had been a breakthrough between her and London. One she hadn't expected or asked for. But now that the wall had started to crumble with his apology, memories came flooding in. Memories she couldn't deal with. Memories of the future she'd hoped for and lost.

She grabbed her coffee cup and walked to her rear patio. She was only out here seconds when she realized that same creepy feeling of being watched hovered over her shoulder again. She looked around carefully for a sign of anyone. Perhaps she was just paranoid and, yes, she had reasons for concern. She took several long moments to study the surrounding gardens in the neighbors' backyards.

She had a large piece of property here. It had been her parents', and, upon their deaths, she'd inherited it. That had been a good twelve years ago, and now it felt like a stranger's. And it had been a long way from a warm and loving home before then. But, like any kid, she had mixed feelings about her childhood home. She didn't know if she should keep it or sell it. She wasn't sure she'd ever stay here again after all she'd been through.

She'd hoped the animosity against her had died down over the last six months. And, true, she hadn't had a resurgence of the same nastiness, but few people knew she was back. The abuse would likely start up soon.

She wandered around the side of the house, then stepped onto the front porch that ran the full length of it to sit in the rocking chair. Slowly, gently she rocked for several long minutes, just letting the stress and pressure inside ease back.

She needed to get her emotions under control. Get her life back to normal. Did anyone have news on Reggie? For a brief second, she contemplated that maybe he had been the one to murder his partner, then dismissed it instantly. Reggie was the opposite of confrontational. There was nothing aggressive about him. He'd been with Pam for decades.

Fern's mind switched to food. She had had coffee for breakfast, then a late lunch/early dinner of a sandwich and more coffee. She needed to eat more food, drink less coffee. She was slender naturally, but this last year had been rough. She had lost some muscle which had kept her from being gaunt. Now underweight, she found it hard to keep any on. Something she never expected to face in her life. She loved food. She'd always been a healthy eater. Like so much of her life, she'd just lost interest.

When an animal was hurt, it curled up in a ball and didn't eat. It had taken her several months at the Alnwick Garden before she ate normally again. But, as soon as she'd come back here, she'd fallen into the same pattern of pain. Worry for Reggie ate away at her insides. She racked her mind, thinking where he could be. If his partner was still alive, she'd be the one to ask. Fern briefly considered that. Had somebody killed Pam so she wouldn't talk? Or so she couldn't say who'd been there to visit? So many theories and no proof, nothing to even make one supposition more logical than the other.

As she sipped her coffee, enjoying her moment of silence, a vehicle drove up. It was black, smoky-windowed. An FBI vehicle. But was it Grant? Or London? When London hopped out, her stomach sank. Did he have news? If so, then why not call? Just because they'd had a minor breakthrough did not mean they had a truce. When his partner emerged from the other side and they walked toward her, she could feel all her earlier stress rushing into her bloodstream again.

She sipped her coffee and watched as they continued up the steps to the long veranda.

London stopped, studied her and said, "Good afternoon."

She inclined her head and waited.

Steve said, "Pam was killed by a blow to her chest, which caused a heart attack. She had a weak one already. The coroner believes her lips and the inside of her gums were laced with poison after the fact. Most had dissolved into the membranes."

Fern froze. Her mind laid out the scenario, and she shook her head. "What poison was used?"

"We're waiting for the toxicology results to come back on that. We also should consider somebody added it to throw suspicion on you again."

She nodded. "Of course. The police are all too willing to look in my direction," she said simply. She'd been to the edge of disaster and back. She wasn't sure these FBI guys could do a whole lot else to her that the police hadn't already. She tilted her head back and looked at Steve, then London. "Why are you here?"

"Because we need to know every person in your circle who could have possibly wanted to do this."

"If you're back to looking at who hated me or held a grudge, there's been a few complaints at the conservatory. A couple people were in trouble and overzealous. But all those letters are on file there. I never received any personally at my home until the case started. And then there was no end to them. I received hundreds."

"How many?" London asked in shock. "As part of the investigation, a background check was done on all the conservatory employees but nothing showed up."

"Easily one hundred, if not two." She shrugged. "I took a bunch to the cops just before I left the country—like they cared. I tossed them all into a box and didn't even open them."

"What about the mail since you were gone?"

"I have a PO box. Honestly, I haven't been there to check it. There could be hundreds more by now." She gave a broken laugh. "If you think I have any plans to read them, you're wrong."

"We need to see them."

She shook her head. "That's one nasty well I have no intention of drinking from again." She could feel the men staring at her, but didn't care. They hadn't experienced seeing so much hate directed at her. It had made her feel dirty, but the letters also terrified her.

"We'll go through them. You won't have to at all."

"Just knowing that PO box is likely to be stuffed full again …"

"It has to be done. Somebody is trying to frame you for murder. Don't you want to fight it?"

"I fought it last time. Look what happened."

"You can't give up," London said quietly.

"I'm not. As far as I'm concerned, I can catch the first plane to England tonight. You guys do whatever the hell you want. You always do."

Steve said, "Give us the key, we'll check out what's there."

She glared at both men. As much as she knew this had to be done, she just didn't want to deal with it. But what about her other mail? She had no idea what could possibly be there.

She glanced at her watch. "The post office just closed five minutes ago."

London's phone rang, and he held up one finger. Stepping away from Fern, he took a short call. When he rejoined Steve and Fern, he said, "That was Grant. He got the hate mail from the local cops and is bringing it to headquarters." London faced Steve. "He expects us to meet him there to go through it all."

"Now?" Steve asked.

"Now," London said. Turning to Fern, he added, "We'll stop by in the morning to get you and head to your PO box." He waited for her to nod, then the two FBI agents left.

Fern's phone chimed. Rebecca had sent the employee files as requested. Well, Fern knew what she would be doing tonight.

THE GUYS WERE delayed today since Grant had them stay late at headquarters, reading the older hate mail. When they showed up around 10:30 a.m., she was waiting outside once again. London and Steve approached her on the porch.

She stood and finished her cup of coffee and said, "You drive."

Steve immediately nodded. "Grab the mail key and let's go."

She walked inside, put down her coffee cup, grabbed her purse and jacket, checked that she had the keys to the post office and returned outside. She got in the back of the big SUV.

The location was only a few miles away. They walked into the post office and went to the back where the mailboxes were. Hers was a large one on the bottom. She took a grocery bag from her pocket, put on plastic gloves—also from her pocket—bent down and opened the cover and pulled out the letters. A post office notice was on top. She scooped up the rest of the mail, took her key back, her face expressionless as she held up the notice and said, "They're holding more for us at the counter."

Silently the three walked over, Fern pulling off her gloves, and she handed the card to the woman at the front desk.

The woman took the card and said, "There you are. We were trying to figure out what to do with all this mail."

"I'll take it now, thanks."

The woman returned with a very large USPS canvas bag which she hoisted atop the counter. She nodded. "Glad you came to get this. I'll need a deposit for the bag."

Fern stepped back and motioned to London. "I'm not carrying that."

He walked over to get it and raised his eyebrows at the size and sheer weight of the bag.

Fern turned back to the woman at the counter and asked, "Is the mail still coming in at the same rate?"

The woman shook her head and said, "No, it's slowed down."

"Then we should be good for the next six months." She paid the deposit, then turned and left, the two men following her.

Back at the vehicle, London turned to Fern. "We'll sort

through this mess at your house, so you can retrieve any mail important to you. We'll open the rest in front of you, but you won't have to read them. Maybe you can tell if any smell wrong."

She considered that, then shrugged. "That's fine, but you're buying pizza. I'm not."

He gave a half bark of laughter.

Steve turned to look at her. "You weren't even surprised by the amount of mail, were you?"

She stared at him steadily. "No. When people hate, they do so with a vengeance."

LONDON HELPED FERN into the vehicle. He motioned Steve a couple feet away from the SUV. London wasn't comfortable with the various layers of awareness opening before him. It had been easier to accept his life if he blocked her out. He didn't understand everything she'd gone through—but he was starting to. He'd been too busy dealing with his brother's decline, his parents' death, his brother's accusations against Fern and the realization that the woman he'd fallen in love with was quite possibly a killer. Yet he'd been unable to believe it inside; only he still had to face the evidence that all his coworkers and the police had laid out before him. He'd been so conflicted, and, despite it all, he'd loved her fiercely but had never told her. As he looked back to that time, he realized just how much the killer had to know about her.

"What's up?" Steve asked, joining London.

"Just thinking," London said, but he and his partner had their backs to Fern in the SUV.

The killer had stalked her. Left evidence almost every step of the way. Too much. All circumstantial. All too convenient.

But London's complaints at the time, his protests that she was innocent, had fallen on deaf ears. Nobody wanted to listen to him. He went against the current beliefs held by both the FBI and local police. All were ready and geared up, swinging forward, delighted to have somebody who looked good for the crimes.

"About what?" Steve asked.

"Both sets of murders."

It didn't matter if she was innocent or not. There'd been a lot of cussing and swearing as the court case had taken a sudden turn. She'd stood defiant in front of them all and had stated quite clearly that she'd had nothing to do with any murders. And, when her defense attorney had picked apart the case, built upon layers of hope rather than evidence, the jury had been swift in deciding she wasn't guilty.

But, of course, the fallout for her had been horrific. London had been shocked at the incredible bagful of mail that had awaited her return, thinking about how people had put so much energy into spewing their hate, putting their anger from their own lives into a target they could reach. He was both ashamed and frustrated. He had been caught in a maelstrom the last time. Not convinced, but overrun by the establishment.

"You got anything?" Steve asked, his expression worried.

London shook his head. "Not yet. But it's got to be here somewhere."

He hadn't known quite what to think. His heart wanted to believe in her. But his brother had said she'd been guilty. In the back of London's mind was an inkling of fear that his brother may have had something to do with planting some of that trial evidence. Derek had certainly been eager to turn the cops in her direction.

As London considered that, a memory whispered through his mind. One that made his gut knot.

Derek. At the desk, writing a letter.

At the time, London hadn't thought anything of it. Just his brother being his brother—an oddball, but unique and good in so many ways.

But Derek had quickly hidden the papers. Shoving them in a drawer before London could read them.

"I see you thought of something. What is it?" Steve asked.

"My brother ..."

Now as he thought about the huge stack of Fern's most recent mail, he knew in his heart there would be one letter—likely so many more—from his brother.

And what the hell would he do about that?

Had Derek also manufactured evidence to make Fern look guilty? London's brother wasn't a cop and didn't have anything to do with law enforcement. He was certainly a cop-show fanatic, but that wasn't the same thing. His brother had worked at the conservatory, then left to try his hand at a manufacturing company. He'd lost his job there after falling apart just before the court case, shortly following their parents' deaths.

Derek's decline afterward had been swift. He stayed at home and did basically nothing. But when Fern had been in the courthouse, he'd been one of her loudest accusers. And, with a sinking feeling, London knew he needed to talk to his brother and open the subject they'd both avoided. He would break that silent truce between them right now. If his brother had done something wrong, he needed to confess. Derek had been very angry back then. Maybe getting his revenge on her was enough now. Derek had certainly helped ruin her life.

But Derek's own had fallen in such a way that it was hard to believe she was the only one who had lost that round.

In a low voice, Steve muttered beside him, "You okay?"

London nodded. "I just realized I need to have a serious talk with my brother."

"You're going alone then. I'd do a lot to avoid him."

On that cryptic note, Steve hopped into the driver's side. London got in on his a lot slower. He wanted to ask Steve what he meant by that. But then, as London considered how other people viewed his brother, he realized most thought Derek was a mess. Somebody on his way down, determined to drag others with him.

Although London had only met Steve when his boss introduced them, Steve had known Derek off and on for years, and had seen the decline and wanted nothing to do with him.

London would like to believe his brother had isolated himself so he didn't take anybody else down with him, but Derek had always been weak. Easily influenced by others. As kids, London had used that against him. But, as adults, he'd watched his brother in despair. He didn't know what it would take to make Derek stand up and face the world. London hoped their relationship would survive the upcoming discussion. But he knew it would spark the nastiness he'd been avoiding.

If there was ever a time to stand up for the truth before it became buried in yet another nightmare of accusations, this was it. Somebody had to be close enough to Fern to know her actions, her daily movements. Close enough to understand what she'd done and how she failed or succeeded, and to watch the pain and suffering she'd gone through at the trial.

His brother fit that description before—but not now—at least London hoped not.

London had been numb at the time. And yet inside he knew it was no excuse. He should've stood up for her more. He had, but not enough. Guilt riddled him inside.

He pulled out his phone and sent his brother a text.

I need to talk to you. When's a good time?

His brother's response was quick.

If it's a conversation I'll enjoy—anytime. If you're opening a subject I have no intention of discussing—never.

London winced, then sat back and thought about it. But there was no alternative. Derek must face the facts. He typed a response,

We need to talk. It's a discussion that'll happen whether you like it or not. When do you want to do it?

He waited, checking his phone several times. But there was no response.

I'll stop by at the end of the day.

Steve had noticed London on the phone and said, "Bet he won't see you. That guy is in denial mode."

"You're right there." Unfortunately, they were past the point of that being an option.

In the back of the SUV, Fern sat quietly beside the huge bag of mail. London glanced at her, gave her a reassuring smile and got a cold look in return. He shook his head. Under his breath, he whispered, "What a mess."

Steve gave him a sharp look. From the back seat came a snort.

"Now that it's involving you, it's a mess," she said in a mocking voice. "It's been affecting me since forever." She settled in the back of the car and didn't say another word until they got to her house.

IT WAS HARD not to laugh. If the FBI intended to help her, that would be a complete recipe for disaster. They'd been such a great help last time—not. He chuckled quietly. The FBI was going around in circles. That was because the main dog in the alpha pack was sniffing the bitch's backend. You should always keep personal shit away from business.

Man, he'd done something right when the world turned against her like that. It was a weapon he wanted to utilize more. Some avenues here were completely unexplored. It fascinated him to see the group consciousness rise and attack with the mentality of a pack of wolves.

It didn't matter if they thought she was guilty or not; they were prepared to believe she was just so they could lash out. They were insignificant and angry little people who needed something to release the irate poison from their souls. They were fools, but they were comical ones. He quite enjoyed watching it all happen. He'd even gone in and checked her laptop at one point. She'd left her email open, and, seeing all the nastiness coming in, had been amazed.

She was never on social media—which was too bad. He

could have learned more about her that way. So he'd hunted the Internet for any reference to her. But eventually the news stopped writing about Dr. Death. He'd been happy with that, thinking her professional life was over and done. Until she had showed up at the Garden of Death. Her anonymity gone, her notoriety bringing in thousands of dollars for the UK garden. What a joke.

Even then she showed up, smelling of roses.

Bitch.

CHAPTER 7

BACK AT THE house, the men unloaded both bags of mail—her plastic one with mail directly from her box and the USPS canvas bag with all the overflow. She walked into the kitchen without even looking at them. She knew what the letters would say. This trip into the poisonous past was not one she wanted to take. After putting on coffee, she turned to find Steve ordering pizza. She laughed. "Good, you took me seriously." Then she spun and snapped, "You'll have to pick it up. No one gets to know I'm here."

He stared at her to see if she was serious, then nodded.

She was still hesitant about having the two of them here with her bags of hate mail. But, if ever she needed to accept an olive branch, it would be this one. She stared at the huge canvas bag like it was a deadly snake, ready to strike out and bite her.

London studied her face and said, "This has to be difficult."

"It *was* very difficult," she replied calmly. "I don't want anything in there. I have seen it a hundred times over."

But she had to make sure. She snapped on plastic gloves again, stepped forward and pulled out the mail that had been in her box and casually sorted through it on her kitchen table. A couple things were from banks, but even they were mostly junk. She got a garbage bag and designated it as such.

She sorted through the top of the heap.

A handful she figured belonged to the hate file. She tossed them at London and said, "You can start with these."

When it came to the postal bag, Fern upended it on the floor. Just as she turned to toss the bag aside, she caught sight of pale green tendrils, and froze.

London reached for an envelope as it slid closer to him. The envelope was thicker than the others.

She raised her hand. Studying the shade of green, she saw the energy around it. She moved it off to the side and said, "You don't want to touch that one."

He stared at her, studied the letter, focused back on her again and asked, "Why?"

"Because it's been tainted with belladonna berries. Four of them are enough to kill a child."

She studied the pile of envelopes and said, "Don't touch anything."

London and Steve watched her very carefully.

She sorted through the heap, but saw the green tendrils reaching for her at the bottom of the pile. She carefully pulled out another suspicious envelope. "This one's been dosed with aconite—monkshood." She studied the two envelopes and said, "They're both from the same person."

The two men neared her, and London asked, "And how do you know there's something in them?"

"Outside of the obvious?" She shrugged. "One has a rare form of belladonna. In a homeopathic tincture, it's not harmful, but too much of it in its raw form, and it is. There's any number of herbs he could have used rather easily. It was somebody who had access to the plants, and chose ones I'd have access to as well. The belladonna and monkshood each grow at the Garden of Death in England." She paused, then added, "Of course neither are hard to grow and both are easily available over the Internet."

"You need to give us more details on the plants. And how would anyone know what plants were used?"

She shrugged. "In many cases the poisonous ones are classic cottage plants. They're often found in backyards and empty lots. People don't know the dangers. A laurel plant variety will give you blisters on your skin for up to six or seven years."

She glanced around at the envelopes and said, "Thankfully, none of that is here."

"Blisters for seven years?"

She nodded. "At the Garden of Death, we must wear full protective suits when working around the plants. Just skin contact is enough to cause horrific rashes, itching, and blisters." She shrugged. "And many are found in everyday gardens."

Both men looked at each other and then back at her and the two envelopes. "We need to take those in for analysis."

"Go for it. I already know what's in them."

"What about the letters inside?"

"Poison versus poisonous words." She shrugged. "The same damn thing to me."

She grabbed two plastic bags, stuffed each poisoned envelope into its own, wrapped a twist tie on the top, and handed them to the men. "Do tell the lab to be careful." She pulled off her gloves, dumped them in the garbage can and walked back to the coffeepot. She stared for a long moment, contemplating cutting back on her coffee drinking. She snorted. "Too bad." She poured another cupful.

By now Steve was opening letters and reading them. The silence grew heavy as the men realized the enormity of their job.

"If you want to know if anybody hated me, read these. There's enough hate here for the entire world." She delivered the coffee to the men, brought out some cream and sugar, and put it on the table beside them. Then she stepped back. She didn't want to deal with the letters but neither did she feel comfortable walking away, leaving them in her kitchen all alone.

She stared aimlessly at her backyard. She opened the door and stepped outside in the fresh air. Anything to help her think of something else.

She heard the front door close and a vehicle start up. Likely Steve getting lunch—hopefully enough for her too.

With her coffee, she stood on the deck and took several deep cleansing breaths. How did she find somebody who hated her? She knew what the worst-case scenario was—wait until they acted again. But this guy was leaving a pathway full of dead bodies. She didn't want him to kill anyone else. She took the steps to the rear patio and wandered the gardens. She hadn't taken any time with them in a long while, although she had paid a maintenance company to care for the place while she was gone.

Sipping her coffee, she continued, studying the plants, happy to see everything looked to be growing nicely despite her absence.

A huge six-foot-tall fence went all the way around her property. Hers was a large lot with the house in the center. All the other residences in the district were similar. Her backyard had no access except on the side of the house. This had always been one of her places to gain solace from the craziness in the world around her.

As she slowly walked back to the house, she glanced up

to find London standing in the doorway, watching her. She stiffened and walked closer. "Did you find anything?"

"I found out a lot about humanity I'd like to forget." His voice was dark, deep. Concerned. "The mail is nasty."

"I remember." She snorted. "I tried hard to forget these disgusting pieces of humanity."

He shoved his hands into his jean pockets and said, "Did you keep any?"

"I told you how I gave them to the cops."

He nodded. "All of them?"

She frowned. Then shrugged. "I don't know if the last ones went or not. At that point, I was ready to just leave. They are probably still in the front closet."

He nodded and turned away as if to check, but she called out, "Did you get through all the mail yet?"

He shook his head. "We'll be on it all day."

She heard the doorbell just then.

London checked his watch. "I'll get the door. Probably Steve. Only ten minutes round trip." London returned to the kitchen door and said, "Come on in, it's Steve."

She slowly made her way inside to see two large pizzas on the counter. With a plate each guy had scrounged up from her cupboards, they returned to the table, opening mail and eating pizza. She went to the cupboard, got a third plate, took a slice of pizza and headed for the front closet.

As she opened the door, she found the box she'd packed away. She brought it out, and, using her foot, gently kicked it toward the kitchen. The men looked up as she arrived, still eating her pizza and nudging the box forward. London looked at it and then at her.

She said, "This is what I packed away before I left."

He nodded. "We'll make sure we get through that one

too then."

She stared at it and said, "I'll go through it first. It would've been from six months ago. If I needed to see anything, it should be in this one."

She pulled over a kitchen chair, put down her pizza plate, donned yet another pair of gloves and then proceeded to open the box. Sure enough it was stuffed full of mail. Anything of interest she stacked on another empty chair. By the time she got to the bottom, two letters were of interest. One had her aunt's return address in Maine. She opened the letter and pulled it out, then winced. With a heavy sigh, she set it off to one side.

"That didn't make you happy." London stated.

"From my aunt, telling me how I've destroyed the family name, should be ashamed of myself, and, as far as they're concerned, I'm dead." She tossed the letter in his direction and said, "It's always nice to have the support of family."

He picked it up, glanced through it, then handed it to Steve.

She opened the second one. Its return address was the conservatory. Maybe that letter would explain why her ID card didn't work anymore. Instead, a piece of paper was inside with newspaper words cut out and taped on top like a childish attempt to imitate a cop show. But nothing about the message was childish.

You got away easy. I'll make sure you don't get off again.

Silently, she handed that and the envelope to London.

He read it and then passed it to Steve while he checked the envelope. "This is from the conservatory?"

She nodded. "The envelope is part of their stationary,

but not the letterhead the message was created on."

He nodded. "And it was mailed after your court case, just before you left?"

She shrugged. "As far as I can tell, it was at the bottom of the box."

"You weren't tempted to open these?" Steve asked curiously.

"All I cared about was getting the hell out of the country." She groaned. "Which is how I feel right now all over again."

It was a grim business, opening each envelope. London and Steve made stacks of letters they would check into later. Some had full addresses and names of people with nothing to hide who were quite open to expressing their opinions. Others gave no indication of the sender. A few were handwritten, others printed, some in marker, and even one in crayon. London sorted and clipped the envelopes to the letters.

Fern busied herself with a book—or jumped on her computer at times, struggling to get through reading all the records of the various employees at the conservatory over the last few years—but kept an eye on the guys' progress. She just wanted all that hate mail out of her house.

AS THE HOURS went on, the business of reading her hate mail got gloomier, nastier, and darker. It became an onerous chore to continue, seeing the words of hate on the pages.

London opened the hand-addressed envelope he was holding and pulled out the letter. His heart froze. He knew that writing. His brother might've made it look like someone else's, but London had been reading it since he was a child.

He read it through, wincing at the wording. Derek had called her a liar, a cheat, and a killing machine. London shook his head and set that letter to the side, then kept going.

Steve asked, "What's with that one?"

Without a word, he handed it to his partner and said, "I want to keep that in a separate pile."

Steve studied it, then flipped through a stack near him and pulled out two more. In a low voice, he said, "And you better keep these with it."

With a hard glance at his partner, London grabbed the other two, reading them through and realizing they were the work of the same man. He sank back and closed his eyes for a long moment. "There's a lot of hate here."

"I can see why she didn't want to go through this."

"Why would anyone?" London motioned to the table completely heaped with letters. "Why would someone think sending a letter like this would help?"

"*That* I can help with," Fern said quietly. "They want a target to direct their own anger, anguish, and pain at. It makes them feel good to know it's not them being slowly dissected by the world." She got up, refilled her cup with coffee and walked away.

He watched her enter the nearby room, pick up a book from the shelf and sit down. He glanced at Steve and said, "We still have hours here."

"Then we better pick up the pace and get through this faster."

And that's what they did. In an efficient move, they opened the letters, read the contents without hesitation or a second read out of disbelief, segregated them into piles and kept on going. By the time they came to the last one,

London had seven letters in his brother's handwriting. He unclipped them, took a photo of each, then clipped them together again. "Keep these with all the rest."

Steve looked at him. "You sure?"

"I'm sure. I think enough damage has been done by my family already. Let's not go hiding evidence."

Steve nodded. They stacked as many of the letters as they could in the box and several others Fern had found. It was dark outside. London checked his watch.

"Are you going to catch up with Derek?"

"I'll try. I just don't know what I'll find."

"I expect him to run away," Steve said quietly. "Your brother hasn't got very much sense of responsibility left in his body."

"Makes you wonder if he ever did." London nodded in the general direction of his brother's hate letters and said, "I should've expected this, but was still blindsided."

"I wouldn't worry about it. We can never know anyone 100 percent."

"I thought I knew him though."

"You do, but something is eating away at him. Something major. I don't know if it's mental, physical, or emotional, but your brother is on a downward slide."

"I had hoped he wouldn't hit bottom and would wise up again." He motioned at the letters. "I just can't imagine."

He walked to the doorway of the adjoining room where Fern sat under a lamp, reading a book. It was a huge tome, not light reading at all. "What are you reading?"

"*Preparations for Medicinal Herbs from the 1800s*," she said without looking up.

He wasn't sure what to say to that. "We've gone through the letters. We'll take them if that's all right with you."

She snorted, nodding at the kitchen sink. "The mailbag has to go back to the post office. Please do not leave anything behind. I don't want any more of that garbage here."

He and Steve took another hour to cleanup, pack everything in boxes, and then load up the SUV. As the two FBI agents walked out her front door, they said good-bye, but she didn't even raise her head. London wanted to apologize, but he wasn't sure what he could say. Just as he was about to close the front door, her phone rang.

"Hello," he heard her answer. "What?"

He stepped back inside, looking at her.

She turned to stare at him, shock in her eyes. "What do you mean the conservatory has been broken into? And why are you calling me?"

He listened to her say a few more things, and then she hung up. "Why did they call you?"

"Because I'm still on the stupid staff list. Although my passcode didn't work in the offices earlier." She grabbed her purse and keys. "Can you call the cops for me? I don't really feel like going in there alone right now."

He shook his head. "I'll take you."

She snorted. "You mean, come with me? You're with him. You don't have your own wheel, and I'm heading straight there."

Steve was busy loading the last of the letters into the SUV. London walked outside and explained what had happened. Fern headed to her car.

Steve turned to Fern and said, "We'll all go. This could be related to Reginald. We'll call the cops as well."

She nodded. "I'll meet you there."

London turned to Steve. "I'll go with her."

Steve nodded. "Hurry up. This doesn't feel very good."

London said in a low voice, "Nothing has since she returned."

"That's a guilty conscience speaking." Steve got into the SUV and backed out of the driveway.

London got into the passenger side of Fern's BMW, wondering at Steve's words. Was that why this was all twisting up his insides? A guilty conscience? He certainly felt like he'd not done right by her; at the same time he wasn't sure what else he could've done.

"You don't have to come with me, you know."

"I'm coming." London buckled up as if to emphasize his words.

Fern turned on the engine and reversed the car from the garage.

"Any idea what's going on?" he asked.

She shook her head. "No. Neither do I know if this is related to the murders. But the only way to have this come to a head is to have the killer make another move. We don't know who he is, or anything about him. So, until he does something else, we're stuck waiting."

"But we do know something about him. He tracked your movements. He knew where you went, what you did, and who you did it with. He's very close to you."

"The only person close to me back then was you. So, unless you're the asshole who did this to me, you need to look elsewhere."

There wasn't a whole lot he could say to that.

HIS LIFE WAS in limbo. He had to move carefully. Lay out the tests in a way he could control the outcome and see the results. There was big money involved. As well as his reputation.

It wasn't so easy to do though when no one else was watching, and he couldn't afford to let anyone understand.

But he needed answers. He'd gone down this path a long time ago, although to no usable end. He wasn't prepared to go there again unless this was truly viable.

Which meant he needed proof.

And that was something he would have to get himself.

He didn't trust anyone else.

Not now. Too much was riding on the results.

CHAPTER 8

T HE TRIP TO the conservatory was fast and furious as she ripped through the 5 mile trip in what seemed like two minutes. As she parked outside, she saw several police cars, but no sign of anyone. She got out, staying until London stepped beside her. Together they walked through the main office to find the police waiting for her. She said, "I don't understand why I was called."

"You're second on the list so once the night watchman came on and found the security system down he called us. Then you."

Of course, Reggie was first. She shook her head. *Why wouldn't they have changed that?*

The police let her enter the conservatory. One large plate glass window on the outside wall had been cracked, as if somebody had thrown rocks at it. But she knew it was particularly strong and would have taken decent force to break it. If it was just vandals, it was distressing, but a problem easily fixed. She walked through carefully, looking for damage to any of the plants, walkways, or internal parts of the conservatory. It was a huge area, and she took her time. With London at her side, she didn't say anything, but carried on throughout the entire place.

She returned to where the police waited and said, "I don't see anything missing or damaged in here, other than the plate glass window."

One of the cops took notes. "Let's take you to the office to make sure nothing there has been disturbed."

"I can look, but can't tell you for sure. I haven't been through this area recently." She backtracked. "I was here the day before yesterday, but I'm not sure I could tell you exactly what could be missing as I haven't been working here for the last six months. I've been in England on a special project."

"Can you contact somebody to check this out tomorrow morning?"

"I can do that," she said. "The security cameras don't cover this area, only the parking lot and entrances.

She walked through the offices, relieved the security was still in place on the other portions of the building. This section contained the main reception room for ticket sales and the gift shop. None of the other windows were broken. As such, she couldn't quite understand why anybody would care to damage the conservatory's glass walls.

She quickly walked through, finding that nothing looked disturbed nor damaged. If any inventory was missing, that would have to be checked tomorrow morning by someone who knew more than she did.

When she walked back outside, she stopped in the parking lot, addressing the police. "Has anybody searched the outside grounds?"

They looked at her, and one said, "Not yet."

"I want to take a quick look around here. Some special plants are outside as well. The gardens are full of very particular species." She led the way around to the side where the glass window was broken. A large series of flowering shrubs were here. She quickly walked through, but the dirt didn't seem to be disturbed; the plants weren't flattened, and no damage was visible. London and the police walked along the pathways, everyone taking a quick look. As she got to the far side and turned to look back, she froze. One of those pale olive clouds slowly approached London. She recognized what it was, even as her mind cataloged it was impossible.

"London, stop," she shouted.

He froze and looked at her. "What's the matter?"

She shook her head, her feet already picking up, racing toward him. "Back up slowly."

With his arms folded and the other cops watching, he carefully did as she said. "What are you smelling?"

"Poison," she said, her voice grim.

She approached from the other side, motioning for London to continue to back up. The cops all stayed where they were. She went around the side of the pathway where she'd seen the olive cloud and stopped. Crumpled on the ground was one of the security men. She saw the green floating, dissipating around him, and realized, once again, somebody had used poison for their own agenda.

She glanced at the nearest cop. "We have a body." She bent down, her fingers going to the man's neck. Not only was he not moving and she felt no pulse, but rigor had set in. She stood. "He's been dead for a while, more than a couple hours at least."

The cop asked, "Is it safe to approach?"

She assessed the green wave and realized though it told her poison was here, there wasn't any danger. She called out, "Yes, it's safe to advance."

All the men, including London, arrived at her side. The security guard had crumpled on the side of the path. There were no obvious signs of an injury, just the fact that the body was rigid, stiff.

She stepped back and glanced around the pathways. "Check for footsteps." She pointed out the rows of gardens beside them. "Do you have a flashlight?"

One of the cops turned his on and searched the gardens.

"Are you assuming this man was murdered? Maybe he died from a heart attack?" one of the cops asked. He stared at the body. "There is no bullet wound, knife wound, blood, nor obvious damage to the body. How can you be sure he didn't just keel over and die naturally?"

She glanced at him and said, "I can smell the poison."

He stared at her for a long moment. "You're Dr. Death, aren't you?"

She nodded. "That's what they call me."

"Can you identify the poison?"

She nodded. "I can. Actually this time you probably can too. Smell the almond?"

The cop looked at the dead man. "But he doesn't look like he's been poisoned. There's no foam in his mouth and no blue to indicate any kind of toxic reaction."

She nodded. "I'm not sure how or why, I can only tell you the presence of arsenic is here."

Another cop said, "That's good enough for me. The ambulance is coming, and we called in forensics. The body count is rapidly increasing here. We need to get this solved fast."

London glanced at her. "Are you staying here?"

She shrugged. "I don't need to. Once the forensic team comes, they will go over this place anyway," she said. "I just don't understand. Why kill a security guard, break the glass window, and not do anything else?" She eyed the glass and frowned. She walked directly toward it and studied it with more scrutiny. "This isn't an easy glass to break either. So why? Why bother?"

She stood outside the conservatory, studying the part of the garden that had been affected. She turned back and asked the police in general, "Does the security guard have a weapon?"

"He does," one of the cops said. "He's an off-duty cop, moonlighting. Not sure he's carrying the weapon for his job here though."

"Doesn't matter. Has it been fired? A bullet quite possibly damaged the glass."

London walked over to her. "Why would the security guard shoot an intruder?"

Another cop had joined them. "Maybe the intruder had a weapon as well."

Moving carefully, she walked back to where the security guard lay, studying the angle of his body.

London stepped up behind her. "He's not sporting any other injuries that we can see."

She nodded, her face grim. "The coroner may find something when he moves the body." She turned her gaze down the path, wondering at the green she had seen originally. Poison was one thing she was well acquainted with. That she saw the clouds of green wherever poison had been administered or such plants grew naturally in the wild was one thing. But she hadn't recognized that dark green edge to the clouds she'd seen earlier. As if this toxin had layers to it. Or more than one poison had overlapped. Was the person who'd killed the guard working with poisons? Ingesting them? Why? None of this made any sense.

Stefan whispered in her mind, *And that's probably exactly what it was. Accept your intuition. It's gold in our world.*

She glanced around as if to make sure nobody else could

hear Stefan. She couldn't speak telepathically easily yet and definitely not in a way others wouldn't notice. She pulled out her phone and called him. When he answered, she asked, "What does that mean?"

"Can you see where the source of that green is coming from?"

She turned around in a circle, observing the crime scene. "It's like a bubble. It's just sitting there."

"Can you see a much fainter green energy drifting off to a specific side?" Stefan asked.

"Not really, no. I just see the green because it tells me it was poison, but not where it came from."

"Not yet. You're not looking deep enough."

"I can't tell anything. I swear to God, it's my nose that sees the green cloud."

He gave a short laugh. "A nose that sees?"

She made a jerky hand motion. "You know what I mean," she said in irritation.

"Oh, I do, indeed, because you're involving two senses and refusing to use them both effectively. But you will in time. You will." Cryptic as always, Stefan ended the call.

LONDON WATCHED FERN, trying not to be obvious about it. Who the hell was she talking to? He heard the name Stefan, and that was enough to make his heart freeze. Everybody knew Stefan—if it was the psychic, Stefan Kronos, who worked with the police, and had for decades. But he was controversial. Did she know that Stefan? If so, how? He'd heard a lot of stories about her poisons that seemed over-the-top, too much to be disbelieved or believed. In fact, they bordered on fantasy. He wasn't exactly sure what he was supposed to do with the little bit of conversation he'd overheard.

He tried to hear more, but he got the nuances of her side of the telephone call more from the look of outrage on her face than from her actual words.

He turned his head to watch the cops, but didn't feel he could leave her alone. Something odd was going on. That she smelled the poison from what, thirty feet away, was incredibly suspicious. But he'd been with her when they had received the call about the break-in. He turned back to the cops. "Any idea when this happened?"

The cop shook his head. "We took your call an hour and twenty minutes ago." Coming up behind him, Fern said, "The conservatory is open until seven normally. Today's Monday, so it closes about nine. It's almost midnight now. Not a big window of opportunity."

The cop nodded and made a note, walking away to talk with his buddies.

London turned and glanced at her. "Can you tell?" he asked abruptly.

She looked at him with a raised eyebrow. "Can I tell what?"

"Either how long he's been dead or the poison has been here?"

She turned her gaze to the dead man lying on the ground. He saw her nostrils flaring as if she sniffed the air. She bent her head to the left, but didn't step forward. He calculated the distance from where they stood to the location of the dead body, and mimicked her movements. He lifted his head and sniffed the air, but couldn't smell anything. "How can you smell a poison like that?"

She shrugged. "I've been doing it all my life." She turned

and walked toward her car.

"Must have been tough," he said, running to catch up to her. "Even when you were little, I'm sure your parents were astonished."

She turned to look at him. "They were. So?"

"I'm just wondering how you're not dead. How did you survive all those years until you knew what you were doing?"

She gave him a flat stare that he'd come to recognize as telling him to mind his own business. Then she turned and walked off again. He watched her go, her shoulders and spine straight and stiff.

"I didn't mean to upset you," he called out.

She raised her hand and waved as if to say, "It's nothing." But she didn't say the words, so it might've been an "F-you, I'm leaving" type of wave.

He shook his head, glanced around and realized he should leave too. Absolutely no point in staying here any longer. He'd have to catch a ride back with Steve and glanced at Fern. She sat inside her vehicle, staring at the conservatory. She hadn't turned on the engine and wasn't on her cell phone. She just sat there, staring at nothing. Her face blank. He rapped on the window.

She rolled it down and asked, "What?"

"You okay?" He motioned at her just sitting there. "I hope I didn't say anything to upset you."

"Finding dead bodies always upsets me," she snapped. She turned on the car engine, then rolled up the window as she said, "I'm fine." The window sealed shut.

She put her car in reverse and backed out in front of him. He watched as she disappeared from the parking lot into the night. Instinct had him run to the SUV, hop inside and follow her, leaving Steve behind. London couldn't understand if it was to make certain she got safely home or he just wanted to ensure she didn't run off anywhere else. Stefan's name still rang in his mind. If she headed off to visit him, London wanted to know.

That he was following her for no good reason was something he needed to look at closely. Except instinct said not to let her out of his sight. She pulled into her driveway and turned off the engine. He drove past, gave a friendly honk so she'd know it was him and headed back to the conservatory to collect his partner.

CHAPTER 9

A S SOON AS she walked in the door, she threw the bolts and checked the rest of the house to make sure all was secure, then dropped in a graceful sitting position in the middle of the living room and contacted Stefan.

Instantly, he flicked through her mind. *What's the matter?*

I'm home again. Alone. What I couldn't say earlier is ... I got two letters from him.

Who is him? Stefan asked cautiously.

London came, and we picked up all the mail since I'd left the country. A huge bagful, plus, what was inside my PO Box. Among all the hate mail were two envelopes, one full of poisonous aconite— monkshood is the more common name— which can cause a severe reaction, even death through physical contact of open skin. Dried belladonna root—more commonly known as deadly nightshade—was inside the other. I didn't open the envelopes. I could smell and see the different shades of green all around them. The whole bag was full of it, but I didn't say anything to them.

Did you tell London the letters were full of poison? Stefan asked in alarm.

Of course. I told them to warn the lab to be careful.

Good, Stefan said in a brisk tone. *Now we must find out where he is, who he is, and what the hell his problem is. Because he'll apparently do anything he can to take you down.*

There was silence for a long moment, and then she asked in a small voice, *Do you really think so? I've been gone for six months. All this mail was just sitting here. I'm not sure he's doing anything right now at all.*

And yet you got that threatening letter, Stefan reminded her. *One telling you Reginald would die if you didn't get back to the country in twenty-four hours.* Stefan waited a moment and then said, *Now that he's missing, how do you feel?*

She winced. *Better now that I think he may be alive somewhere. As you remember, I did follow the letter's instructions. I came running back. And yet there was no sign of Reginald when I got here.*

Did you tell anybody about the letter?

Stefan could hear her speak, but he couldn't see her unless he focused at a much higher level. She was nowhere near as good at the telepathic stuff as he was, but she'd joined a group in England and had worked hard on her own to get to this level. *I warned Reggie. I tried to tell the CIA and FBI before I left England. Grant. I told him, no one else.* She hesitated, then said, *You know they won't believe me.*

Was it just London with you and the mail or was somebody else with him?

His partner, Steve.

Was Steve involved the last time the murders occurred?

He wasn't. I'm not sure what happened to London's previous partner. He just kind of up and disappeared—probably reassigned. I think the FBI wasn't terribly impressed with his performance or something. She snorted. *Which I'll take to mean he didn't believe I was guilty.*

Not all FBI agents are bad, Stefan cautioned her.

Not all are good either, she came back instantly. She

groaned. *I don't know what I'm supposed to do now.*

You need to find out where the energy is coming from. I presume the only reason the toxin cloud set so heavily still on the envelope is because it was tied up in the back of the post office.

Yes, and jammed in with hundreds of other letters in my box too.

He nodded. *Of course, if he's psychic, he also could've set a trap,* Stefan said. *And you may have just tripped it.*

She glanced around the room. *How the hell did I do that?*

You disturbed the energy of the poisons. That would have triggered the trap.

She rubbed her temple. *Will he know?* She shook her head. *What does that mean? Is he likely to come here? Does he know I'm home?*

He won't know if it was triggered at the post office, police station, your car, or house. Unless he can track the signature of who triggered the trap.

Right. So, if the post office gets broken into … she said on a note of sour humor.

I do have people not too far away who could set up an alarm for you. You need a security system to make sure nobody can get in.

What kind?

One that works. Like we did for you in England. In other words, not electronic. Wires can be cut. Video feeds can be shut down. This one rarely fails.

And just like that he disappeared from her mind. She opened her eyes to find she still sat in the center of her living room.

After one of these sessions with Stefan, it was always the same. A moment of disorientation, then a sense of being confined. Going from a world with no lines, levels, or limits, back to a room with walls, a floor, ceiling, and doors was always a hard adjustment.

She slowly got to her feet, did a couple stretches and walked into the kitchen. The faint odor of the poisons still wafted atop the table and floor where the letters had been. It would dissipate with time. According to Stefan, she must follow it before that happened. She had had no real success with that the first time she did it.

She considered the problem, remembered some things she had heard from her special UK friends and got a candle, then lit it. She held the candle right in the middle of where the poisons lingered. Instantly the smell intensified, making it harder to discern the two poisons, but together they blended into one much stronger. She sat in a chair at the table and gently laid her fingers on the tabletop amid the mist. She closed her eyes, reached out a hand and touched the ivy plant on the sideboard. To ground her. To connect her with nature. She could barely reach it, but, once her fingers touched it, the dirt inside the pot and the energy around her fingers tingled.

"Show me the way," she whispered to the empty room, her eyes still shut. "Show me the pathway."

And, with a method she hadn't used since she was a child, she slowly let her body dissipate, the same as the gases would. She could feel parts of her becoming one with the gas, with those tiny toxic particles in the air. In her mind's eye, she saw it drift out the back door. She followed, urging it ever onward. Pouring energy, light, and bright intense feelings of will into the green fumes, as if she could force it to do what she wanted it to. With a piece of her consciousness firmly attached to the vapor, the aroma, that tiny essence of the poisons, the rest of her body relaxed in the kitchen chair as she followed the gentle pathway, trying to see it in the bigger cosmos. The trail was so very faint as she made it outside her house and past the back fence. And there she lost it. It dissipated into the houses around her. It told her nothing.

She opened her eyes, noting how dark it was outside except for the moon and stars, then waited a moment to regroup and reached out to Stefan. *It didn't work.*

You didn't try hard enough.

She shook her head, stood. *I've been trying since forever.*

Don't force it. When you want to do it, it will happen. You should be letting it do its will and taking you along with it.

How did any of that make sense?

Standing to shake off the intensity of the last few moments, she looked out the front window to see a small black car drive slowly past her house. Instinctively she stepped behind the corner of the wall. The car didn't pick up speed, and it didn't slow down. It was almost at a crawl. She hated to think that people were once more doing drive-bys—probably getting ready to egg her house again. She hadn't done anything wrong the first time. She sure as hell didn't need to be slammed a second for not murdering people.

She couldn't see the license plate from where she stood, and that was frustrating. Slowly it drove on.

She walked through her house, locking the rear kitchen door. Shaking her head, still thinking of how she could possibly "try harder" as Stefan had said, she wandered into the living room, hitting the light switch, and turned, letting out a shriek. Stefan—in ethereal form—stood before her. She glared at him. "Would you stop scaring me like that?"

He raised an eyebrow. "You know perfectly well it's much easier for me to travel like this."

"Well, how about bringing a bell with you and ringing it before you suddenly arrive at somebody's house?" Then she realized he hadn't come alone. She turned her gaze on the faint form of a man beside him and frowned. "I don't know you." She hated that her voice was stiff, hard. But she'd met way too many men and law enforcement officers who weren't on her side. The last thing she wanted was somebody who was against her in her own home.

Even if he was in ghost form.

Stefan said, "This is Detective Drew Sutherland. He has a couple very beneficial talents he's been working on. One of them is the ability to travel, like I am now. And he's very good at security. He'll spend twenty minutes making sure your house is set up for the rest of the night—early morning now really—okay?"

She nodded. The two men went to work, and she stood back. "I wish I could see what you are doing."

Sutherland turned toward her. "Shift your third eye to the left slightly and peel back a layer. Every time you do that, you will see more and more. If you're good, you can just blink hard and tell your mind you want to see the colors."

"Colors?" She reached up with her hand and mimicked peeling a layer off her third eye. Instantly the room glowed a soft yellow. She frowned as Detective Sutherland turned away and continued to work. She did it several more times, then got frustrated and blinked hard, ordering her mind to do what he'd said. When she opened her eyes again, it was to see blues, greens, oranges, and reds all around the surfaces in the living room.

She gasped in awe. "How beautiful."

The windows were surrounded by a vibrating bright yellow color. The front door too. As she checked every window and door, she realized Detective Sutherland and Stefan were both securing these frameworks with some sort of energy.

"What happens to someone who tries to cross that?"

"The bad guys get burned, possibly fall or a blast could send him backward," Detective Sutherland said cheerfully. "I'm always happy to see what happens."

She shook her head at him. "And if I need to get out?"

He reached out a hand and touched her shoulder. Of course he wasn't physical. He was here at zero-body, almost ghostlike, but, as soon as he touched her, a jolt shot through her system. But it wasn't an electric shock; it was more like a warm heating blanket suddenly wrapped around her.

"Now the energy is of the same frequency as you."

"So I can come and go anytime I need to?" she asked, making sure she understood.

"Exactly." And just like that, the men were done.

They convened back in the living room, and she saw Detective Sutherland's form fade quickly. She said in a rush, "Thank you very much."

He sent her a bright smile. "You're welcome. Stay safe." And he was gone, just like that.

She turned to look for Stefan, but he had already left too. She was alone again in the massive family home.

LONDON PULLED UP to his brother's house. It was dark outside, past 1:00 a.m. after all, and, of course, not a light was on inside. His brother had likely run, like he always did. When had this behavior started? Probably in childhood. Never outgrowing it as an adult.

He remembered Fern saying something to that effect as well. At the time, London had been angry. It felt like she was dissing his brother undeservedly. But now, as he looked at Derek's behavior, he realized she'd been right all along.

"Damn."

He walked up to the front door and knocked. No answer. On an off chance Derek might've gone to bed, he pulled out his keys, unlocked the door and walked inside.

"Derek, you home?"

Silence.

The house had that empty-nest feel to the atmosphere, signifying that his brother had, indeed, left. The question was, had he gone away for only a few hours and, if so, where?

He didn't have a new girlfriend, and he wasn't leaving the condo to sit in a movie theater all alone. But he had become the kind of guy who would sit in the pub solo. London wandered through the bottom floor of the house, realizing more than just an emptiness was here. There was a cold feeling.

With his suspicions thoroughly aroused, he walked into the kitchen and looked around. It was super clean, as if nobody had been here for days. He opened the fridge and found it empty. In fact, his brother hadn't been here recently.

He pulled out his phone and dialed Derek's number. It went to voicemail. He left a message. "Derek, I'm at the house. Where the hell are you?"

He put away his phone and walked through the downstairs, then headed upstairs. He found his brother's room with the bed slightly tossed, but half the clothes in the closet were missing, and a lot from the dresser. His brother wasn't just not home; he'd gone. London pulled out his phone and called again. "Where the hell did you run to? Why aren't you here? And when did you leave?"

116

But, of course, voicemail had no answers. He pocketed his phone again, feeling the frustration building inside. Goddammit, his brother should be where he was supposed to. Especially now that they'd found the hate letters he'd written to Fern. His brother had to tell London what that was all about and if Derek had done anything else. They were past the point of needing answers. They needed *honest* answers.

He walked back downstairs and into the kitchen, standing in the quiet, dark room for a long moment, as if the space would give him the information he needed. His intuition had always been strong, and now it buzzed. But not in the sense that there was danger. More that something damn sneaky had gone on. He hated that. And it always happened around his brother.

He had been communicating with him for days. London grabbed his phone and stared at it. Even though Derek had been responding, he wasn't calling from home. And why hide? If he had run, why? Was it because his hate mail had been found?

Frustrated and irate, London walked onto the rear deck and stared at the backyard, slapping his phone against his leg. The small yard was fenced-in with plants all up and down the sides. Hearing an odd sound, he pivoted about, finding the next door neighbor standing on his porch, staring at London. He pushed the button to start the video on his phone then waved it as if to say 'hi.' "Have you seen Derek lately?"

The man shrugged. "I haven't seen him for a while."

That wasn't good. London asked, "Any idea when you last saw someone here? And who it was?"

"A woman was here recently. Small, long blond hair,

kind of a crimp wave to it, as if she'd just taken it out of a braid."

London pinned him with a hard stare. "How old?"

He shrugged. "Late twenties or early thirties. Slim. Used to see her a lot before, but it's been a long time."

Again London nodded. "Any idea when you last saw my brother?"

The neighbor shook his head. "Not for a while. Not for a long while."

London turned and headed back inside the house. Once in the kitchen, he closed the door. He could certainly get the owner's name for the house next door from the property records. But that didn't mean the man who stood there was the owner. Just to be sure, London sent the image to Steve and texted,

Can you confirm this is the neighbor on 627 Laurel Road? My brother's neighbor. No sign of Derek, and, according to the neighbor, the last person here was Dr. Fern Geller.

His information sent, he wanted to face Fern and ask her why the hell she hadn't said anything about having gone to his brother's house. Why the hell had she been here in the first place?

He sat in his car for a long moment, then said to himself, "I'll find out now." He made a U-turn in the middle of the block and headed to Fern's house.

He walked up to the front door and pounded on the wood with a heavy hand. He waited a long moment, then she opened the door. The look on her face said she was unimpressed at having him back again.

He pushed open the door and stepped inside. "To bad if

you don't want to see me, because I want to see you."

"Now what?" she snapped.

He sent her a look, turned on the lights so he saw the expression on her face as he asked, "Why did you go to my brother's house once you returned?" If he hadn't been watching carefully, he wouldn't have seen the surprise and dismay before she masked it. His heart sank. He reached out and shook her hard. "What the hell game are you playing at, Fern? Don't you realize if you're convicted this time, chances are you will not escape a life sentence?"

She shrugged off his hands and glared at him. "Who the hell are you to talk to me about that? You're the one who sat in the court proceedings as everyone accused me of killing my boss. I didn't, and you know that. Nor did I have anything to do with Reginald's disappearance either. For all I know, your brother is involved." She glared at London and said, "I went to Derek's place after I landed because I wanted to ask why he lied. Why he hates me so much. But he didn't answer the door. I walked around for a few minutes and left." She swung open her front door. "You can leave now. Maybe you should just forget my address too."

He stared at her in frustration for a long moment, and then something snapped inside. He reached out, grabbed both her shoulders and hauled her into his arms. "Goddammit, I wish I could," he growled just before he closed her mouth with his.

THINGS WERE HEATING up. Just not enough. Good thing the asshole Derek had disappeared. He hadn't wanted to take him out—at least not yet.

That would always be the end game.

But Derek was only *one* of the threads to be cleaned up.

Although, depending on where he'd run to, there could be a problem finding him. He might have been useful, but he was also weak. A coward.

Still, for now, if he stayed out of sight, that was a perfect plan. Made him look guilty.

He'd find Derek eventually.

He would take care of him then.

Besides, right now, it was more fun to watch London suffer a little more every day.

CHAPTER 10

A T THE FIRST touch of his lips, Fern's body melted, but her mind screamed, *No*. This can't be happening. Not again. This man was dangerous, lethal. She shouldn't have anything to do with him. But it was so damn hard. The touch of his lips ... so familiar, yet not. Something about him evoked passion all the way through her. Something was so solid, dominant, and powerful about him, that, in the past, she'd come completely under his spell, knowing he would take care of her. Then she wouldn't have to worry. He'd be there no matter what.

And having found that truth to be one of the biggest lies of her life, she knew she didn't dare go back there again. She wouldn't recover a second time. She did her damnedest not to respond—to hold back the passion coursing through her.

His lips had always been like that. His touch. A magnet, drawing her into his will. He pulled back, wrapped her closer in his arms and whispered, "Lord, I've missed you. So damn much."

And he kissed her again. This time she had no re-sistance—his words thawing her frozen heart. She wanted to cry out against the injustice that had her still wanting the man who had hurt her so badly. How could she be so weak? So lost? She knew better. Her brain knew better. Yet her body succumbed without protest. And her heart? ... Well, it was ... rejoicing. She had no willpower where he was concerned.

By the time he lifted his head, she was a warm pile of jelly. He gave a harsh exclamation, picked her up in his arms and carried her to the couch. "I'm so sorry," he whispered.

She didn't have any way to respond. How did one deal with a shock like that? She'd been doing fine, keeping him at a distance, ignoring his presence in her life, knowing too much of her pain was caused by him. She was almost numb to the torment he'd already caused her. She sat on the couch in his arms as he held her. Just that little bit of understanding brought tears to her eyes. How long she'd waited and how much she had longed to hear those words from him and yet never expected to. Like so many men, he wasn't long on talking, more on action.

They never had a chance to be anything and certainly not *one*. His brother had found them, not sharing their first kiss, but, in that initial moment when it seemed they'd suddenly become aware how much more there was to them than they'd realized. And, of course, Derek was nothing if not cutting and mocking. He jeered at them, called her cold, icy, and frigid in bed, and that was why he had broken up with her. She listened, shocked at his vitriol, unable to defend herself. They'd broken it off all right. But she'd been the one to dump him, months earlier. And they'd never had sex.

Still, that had been a poor reason for tossing her name into the ring as being the one responsible for the deaths of those four people from a couple years ago. He'd had the gall to say she'd confessed to him that she'd killed them. Of course she hadn't, but, at that point, nobody listened to her.

Because the cops had a witness, somebody who'd heard

her confession. To them, Derek was a vital nail in her coffin. From that moment on, they'd done nothing but focus on her as the killer.

London stared at her, waiting for some response. Only she was still in shock, horrified by the events in her world. She shook her head. "I shouldn't have come back."

"You mean, you *should* have," he said harshly. "We have to solve this mess and get it behind us once and for all."

She turned and looked at him. "Why?"

He tilted her chin up to look in her eyes and whispered, "I care." He stroked his thumb across her chin. "I have a lot to atone for. I'm still not sure how everything rollercoastered as fast and as far as it did, but I couldn't stop the legal machine. I couldn't find anything that proved your innocence. The cops didn't have any forensic proof you were guilty. But it was so damn hard to get anybody to believe you. I tried. I almost got fired for trying. I told them you were being railroaded, but they didn't care."

Was he telling the truth? She shook her head. "It doesn't matter anymore. It's too late. Too much has happened."

He turned her face toward him again. "Do you think I don't know that? It doesn't matter if you forgive me or not. I still have to find the killer and solve this so I can sleep at night. You should never have been charged. For all I know, somebody in the FBI is after you. I don't have any way to know."

She shot him a look and said, "Maybe. But you'll protect whoever it is when you realize how close to home this is." She watched as he settled back.

In a gritty voice he asked, "Do you really think Derek did this?"

"I know Derek started it. But how far has he gone? I

have no idea." She gave a broken laugh, her voice climbing in hysteria. "Of course he was all about being a good witness, somebody they could count on. Nobody would suspect him. I listened as the lies tripped so easily off his lips. The defense psychologist said Derek was a liar and quite possibly a sadistic killer, all in his own right."

London closed his eyes and leaned back. "Damn."

"You believed your brother over me, and not just when it came to the trial, but also when it came to our relationship." She shook her head. "He told you that he'd broken up with me, that I was no good. Even though I told you that our relationship was done and over months before."

London winced. "He still says that."

She nodded. "Of course he does," she said sadly. "Because, if he fesses up, what would happen to him? He'd be charged with perjury. Just think, then you can nail *his* ass to the wall." She struggled off London's lap and stood, glaring at him. "And, when you don't, then I'll nail yours." She took two steps toward the front door. "Now get the hell out of my house and don't come back without a warrant."

LONDON OPENED HER front door, sat down on the stoop. "Go to bed. I'll stand watch."

"Knock yourself out." She slammed the door.

He rubbed his face. What the hell just happened? Then this was his life these days. He didn't have any proof or a way to find out if his brother had been involved in all this. If he did, then at least maybe some of this would make sense. As it was, none of it did.

He leaned back against the door. A weird buzz went through him. He shifted and got another. He turned to look around. He couldn't see anything, but out of the corner of his eye was a kind of shimmer. He glared at it. "Where the hell is that shock coming from?"

He got no answer, not that he really expected one. He studied the door and window frames, but saw nothing definite except a blurring around the edges. He'd heard about something like this but had no idea she could do it—or maybe she knew somebody who could. It made his standing watch out front a joke.

Surely he had something more productive to do.

He pulled out his phone and called Steve. "Hey, did you get those poisonous letters to the lab?"

"Yeah. I also dropped off the others in Conference Room 12 for this case. The experts are analyzing them to see if there's anything there."

"Sounds good." He hesitated, hating to ask his next question. "What's the general atmosphere regarding Fern right now?"

When he got no response from Steve, London stared across the dark street in front of him as he sat outside Fern's house. "Derek's neighbor hasn't seen him in a long time either. The house is cold. No food is in the fridge, and a lot of his clothing's gone."

"He bolted?" Steve's voice rose. "Where the hell would he go, or, maybe the bigger question is, why?"

"As soon as I can find that out, I'll let you know. In the meantime, I don't have a freaking clue."

Hell, there wasn't much he did know.

"The picture you sent has been confirmed as the legal owner of the property next door to your brother. And," Steve said, "the security guard's time of death clears Fern. She was with us then."

"Good to know. What was the COD?"

"Let me find the autopsy report." London could hear papers shuffling around. "Okay. Here it is. Abnormally large amounts of arsenic."

London asked Steve, "What the hell does that mean? That we all can have small amounts of arsenic in our systems on a regular basis? Isn't even a little a problem?"

"I've heard low levels of arsenic aren't. When it's continuous in small amounts over a long period, it becomes deadly. A series of cases from way back when had several women feeding their husbands small doses in their thermoses every day. When stopped, the men recovered. But, as it continued over time, their symptoms grew worse, and eventually, they died."

London shook his head. "So, he was found to have an abnormally large amount of arsenic. Does that mean it was done over a long time? To the point it became lethal? Or had he had a large dose that day?"

Steve checked the autopsy report again. "It doesn't say."

"Send the report to my phone, but, in the meantime, give me the coroner's name and number." London jotted down it, then hung up to call the coroner.

The coroner said, "It appeared to be a large amount all at once. His stomach contained food and arsenic at the same time. Yet no food was found anywhere in his office. No thermos, no cup, nothing to have contained any kind of poison."

"Could he have inhaled that?"

"It was in his stomach contents. He may have inhaled a small amount as well. But chances are it wouldn't have been anywhere near enough to kill him. The amount in his stomach was lethal, however."

London thanked him, sent a reminder text to himself to affix a note to the autopsy document and initial the note so people would know he'd added the additional information. He also referenced the phone call to the coroner. He'd learned a long time ago that, anytime he needed to add something to the record, he made damn sure he could back it up with a name, exact date, and source.

He put away his phone. Luckily, they had proof she didn't kill the security guard, so it was a little hard to imagine she had anything to do with murdering the others. All four deaths were related to the conservatory and were poison-related. He had to go back to the recent case files. There had to be another connection between the victims. Then he'd compare what he found to the previous four murders.

London walked to his car and pulled out his laptop. He still had a good three hours of battery life. He sat on the front step and pulled up the case files, then slowly went through them.

He checked out the names, their addresses, places of employment, and criminal records for each of the second set of four victims and still found no connection, other than the conservatory. Three died on the grounds; Pam Akers in the house of the head of the conservatory. They were all over thirty. As far as he saw, their lives didn't intersect, other than through the conservatory. One female, three males. He researched Pam first, but couldn't find a connection between her and the conservatory, other than dating Reggie. He searched further to see if she had ties to the three dead men. Nothing. He checked out the three men. Again, no connections among them. Frustrated, he sat back. Unable to help himself, he pulled out his phone and called his brother yet again. The phone rang and rang. When voicemail kicked in, he said, "It's London. Call me."

Of course, Derek wouldn't. He'd disappeared into the wind. With all the people dropping dead around London, he didn't want to think his brother was involved too. Yet...he was connected to the conservatory.

London straightened. Could his brother be another victim? Why hadn't he considered that before? Maybe his brother wasn't in the wind, but had been kidnapped?

Or worse—murdered.

CHAPTER 11

S HE STOOD INSIDE by the front window and stared out into the night. London's truck was in her driveway. All the neighbors would think he was staying overnight at her house. Not what she wanted them to see. Or think.

Then again, she hadn't given a damn about what the neighbors thought for a long time. But obviously she hadn't given up caring about London.

Even now anger thrummed through her. She was so enraged and so frustrated that he'd believed his lying, scheming snake of a brother. She wanted to believe Derek wasn't involved any deeper in this mess. But, if he was, it would be justice when she saw him locked up for life. Yet he was such a weakling. She couldn't see him killing anyone.

On the other hand, he was easily manipulated. Somebody behind him, yanking his chain and forcing him to get involved, now *that* she saw.

She felt her ire rolling through, building higher. She crossed her arms over her chest, like holding in her anger. No way she could sleep tonight. Not with this going on.

She spun on her heels and stormed back into the kitchen. There was still leftover pizza. She emptied the boxes, putting the few remaining pieces on a plate, off to the side. She took the boxes out to the recycling bin and tossed them in. Back inside again, she cleaned up the few plates. She grabbed a broom, turning on the light on both sides of the kitchen as she swept up pizza crumbs and little bits of lint and dust from the post office bag. As she bent with the dustpan to collect the pile, she caught sight of an envelope half under the kitchen cabinet that held her towels. She cleaned up the dirt, dumped it into the garbage can and replaced the broom and dustpan, then walked back to the envelope.

No green was around it, for which she was grateful, but there was an odd look to it. One she couldn't define. She glanced around at the windows and back at the envelope. There was almost a shimmer around it. Was it a bleed-through from whatever Detective Sutherland had done to the windows and doors? Or was it something else entirely?

She reached out a hand and then pulled back. She went to the pantry, put on plastic gloves, returned to pick up the envelope. Her first name and box number were written on the front. Yet no stamp, no return address, nothing to identify who the sender was. She stared at it with misgivings.

And then she realized London might still be on the front step. Should she take this to him? Or open it herself? If she did open it, and it was suspicious, she was sure the cops would say she had created it herself.

She walked to the front door, unlocked the bolts and pulled open the door. London sat to the side, leaning against one of the big support posts on the front porch. He turned toward her. She held up the envelope and said, "You guys missed one. It slid underneath the cabinet off to the side." She held it out so he could read it, and she turned it over. "There's no identification, nothing to say who the sender was. But it looks and feels odd." Yet she couldn't decide in what way. It wasn't full of poison, but there was almost a hint of it. But so faint … so old as to not be.

He motioned at her gloved hands and said, "Does it also smell like poison?"

No mockery was in his voice so she answered honestly. "No, there's no poison, but I don't like it."

He studied her face for a long moment and then glanced at the envelope. "Let's figure out what it is." He carefully pulled on gloves he had in one pocket and then withdrew a pocketknife from his other pants pocket to slit open the top of the envelope and to withdraw the letter. He unfolded it, and his eyebrows shot up. He turned slowly so she saw it was another letter made from cut-out newspaper lettering. This time the message was very clear.

I won't be happy until everyone around you is dead. Just like everyone around me is dead—because of you.

She stared at it and shook her head. "That makes no sense."

"We really need to talk about this," he said quietly. "The sender of this letter seems to think you have something to do with killing his family or friends."

"Why? I didn't kill anyone," she cried out. So fed up with it all, she just wanted to slam the door on him again. "So what if there's another crazy person looking to blame me for the injustices in his life? For all you know, this wacko went off his meds, killed his own family, all because, in his head, I wouldn't go to the prom with him."

Silence followed her outburst as he stared at her. "Who didn't you go to prom with?"

She raised her hands in frustration, then popped off her gloves. "None of your goddamned business." She stormed back into her house and went to slam the door. But he stuck his boot in the way. She glared at him and waited.

In a gentle voice he said, "It is *my* business. When people around you are dying, we have to know everything there is to know about you. If you have an unhappy suitor after you, maybe it's because you *did* turn him down for the prom."

"I never went to prom so not an issue." She continued to glare at him, not willing to give an inch. "I didn't do anything to anyone. My research was never used on humans. As far as I know, I had no enemies before being charged. Now the world hates me." She pointed toward the envelope he still held. "I can't be held responsible for every wacko who uses me as a target."

"Calling yourself Dr. Death doesn't help," he urged. "It's like asking to be a target."

She stared at him and gave a bitter laugh. "You have no idea. I've been dealing with death since I was two years old."

She tried again to slam the door, but he held out a hand and asked urgently, "What do you mean?"

She gave him a flat stare. "Figure it out yourself."

When he wouldn't move, she reached back and kicked the door. The force of it popped his foot off the threshold, and the door slammed shut. She threw the bolts and returned to the kitchen. She dropped the gloves into the garbage can, then took a careful look around the floor to make sure no other letters had been dropped. It appeared to be clear. She shut off the lights and walked upstairs.

She had intended to take the leftover pizza to him while he sat in his lonely vigil. But now she was too mad to be bothered.

Upstairs she grabbed her laptop, set it on her bed and quickly took a shower before getting into her pajamas.

After climbing back into bed, she contacted several of her friends in England. What she really wanted to know was whether the extension for a contract at the gardens was open. She was so done with all this. And she wanted out before things got any uglier, and everyone here turned against her again. She fired off several emails.

When everybody had first spewed their poison and hate to such an extent that it made her violently ill just seeing one more comment, she'd closed all her social media accounts, swearing she'd never open another one. Not able to help herself, she typed her name into the Google search bar to see if anything new came up.

Of course she found an article about her having found the body tonight—late last night—at the conservatory. And how the hell the media had found that out so soon, she didn't know. Her name was in the article about the death of Pam Akers as well.

And thus a resurgence of interest was spawned as to the two previous deaths of the maintenance man and the visitor at the conservatory. Of course they somehow got her nickname—Dr. Death—into that new rewrite of that older news. Her nickname brought sensationalism, making it almost mandatory to work into the articles. Nobody gave a damn that it ruined her life. That she was an innocent victim in all this.

Finally, when she could read no more, she turned off her laptop, put it on the far side of her bed, snuggled under the blanket and grabbed a book. Of all the things she missed about being relocated, it was her pets. She'd had two beautiful cats, but she had been forced to give them away when it looked like she was headed to jail. No way would she leave them in a shelter.

Reggie and Pam had taken them. Now Fern worried about who was taking care of her cats now. She was also afraid, when she woke up the next morning, that she would be the headline news—all over again.

LONDON STUDIED THE latest cut-and-paste letter, realizing it needed to be with the others. Was he really doing anything of value sitting here like some lost Romeo, waiting outside her house? Not really. He suspected the killer was more interested in hurting her than killing her. Although the end game would be her death for sure. Particularly if she got off through the court system again. And that would imply he expected her to be charged once more.

London grabbed his stuff, walked to his truck and hopped in. He had to get back to the office to see about those letters.

He drove to FBI headquarters, pulling around to the back. A couple people were still here but not many. Using his keys, he let himself into the office and headed to his desk. Steve said he had put all the mail in Conference Room 12.

Setting down his laptop, London walked into the designated room and to the table with the piles of the various letters. There was the first one done with newspaper. He laid the two of them side by side. Then he walked over to the scanner, scanned each in and brought the pictures up on the big screen. In his mind, he had no doubt they were from the same hand. Were there others? Earlier ones? He got his laptop and brought up the case files.

None put into forensic evidence as far as he saw, and no notes said someone had written letters like this back then. He sent off an email to the lead detectives on both sets of the murder cases, asking if they had seen anything like this. He attached the two images and hit Send.

He glanced at the amount of mail sitting here for them to process and shook his head. So much hate. How was it possible for the world to lock on to one target? He walked out of the conference room, shut off the light and closed the door. When he got back to his laptop, he found an email message flashing. From one of the police detectives. So it wasn't just him working late. Then some cases were like that. London sat and read it.

> She brought in two similar to this. We never did find out who sent them. They weren't deemed a high priority.

"How about now?" London asked the empty room. He continued to read.

> Where did you get these two letters?

His reply was short and sweet. He thought about whether to add anything else to the email and then typed:

> I'm concerned. She was acquitted once, but it seems like someone wants to make sure she doesn't get off a second time.

He hit Send.

The response was almost instant.

> I never believed she was guilty to begin with. When she was acquitted, several were furious. Now that time has gone by, there is a little more distance. People are less likely to jump on her as a possible suspect. Nobody wants that circus we went through before.

London finished typing his response and sent it.

Neither does she.

London sat back and wondered if somebody had walked into her house and left that envelope there. An unnerving thought. He picked up his phone and called her. When she answered, her voice sounded sleepy. "What's the chance that the letter under your cabinet wasn't in the mailbag?"

"What are you talking about?"

He could hear her, like she was shaking the sleep from her eyes. He bolted to his feet and said, "What's the chance somebody put that letter in your house?"

There was silence first, then she asked cautiously, "Like an intruder?"

"Yes." He grabbed his keys. "I'm coming to your place."

"Why would you think of that suddenly? Do you think I'm in danger?" she asked in alarm.

"It's always been in the back of my mind. You continue to be his target."

"I have security on all the windows and doors."

"You might have, but what good is that security if you set it up *after* the intruder got into your house?"

"What are you saying?" Her voice rose in a short gasp.

"I mean, what if someone's in your house right now."

He heard her gasp of shock. And her heavy swallow.

She whispered, "Get your ass over here *now*." It was followed by a *click* as her phone shut down.

Damn it. He needed her to stay on the line.

HE TILTED HIS head back and contemplated life. He was at an interesting stage right now. Something he had wanted for a long time, and here it was—within his grasp. That elusive second chance.

But he had to play the game like a pro. He needed her. But he doubted she'd come willingly. He'd given her the chance. Once.

After that, well, she'd had a taste of freedom. He had no compunction about taking it away from her again. If she'd been jailed like she should have been, he'd have gotten to her there.

But she'd been acquitted. Something he still didn't understand.

But he was nothing if not adaptable.

Maybe another test or two. She'd passed everything he'd flung at her so far.

He could wait. For a day or so. Not more.

He was too eager to get back to the results he'd watched roll in for years. He was desperate to see them again.

CHAPTER 12

F ERN STARED AT the phone in her hand in shock. And
then in fear. She pulled the covers to her chest slowly
and set the phone on her night table as she digested London's shocking statement. She understood only two things.
One, London was on his way to her house, and, two, he felt
there was a damn good reason. And that just terrified her.
She sat in her bed, just waiting—asking—to be attacked.

She slipped out from under the covers, shoved her feet
into her slippers, grabbed her robe, and, with her cell phone
tucked in her pocket, walked to the bedroom closet and
studied it. She took a deep breath, pulled the closet door
wide. Rows of clothes stared back at her. That wasn't good
enough. She dove into the back to make sure nobody hid in
the shadows. Not that she knew what she would do if
somebody were here. Feeling slightly better to find it empty,
she turned to stare at her bedroom door.

Another two bedrooms and a bathroom were upstairs.
This house was huge. An intruder could be anywhere. She
crept to her bedroom door. Turning the knob, she opened it
soundlessly. She tilted her head to hear any sound. But all
was silent. Except the hairs on the back of her neck stood up,
and her heart pounded against her ribs. The atmosphere
might appear calm, but, in that moment, she understood
something else. London was right.

Something was *wrong* in the house.

She didn't know what; she didn't know who; she didn't know how, but she was no longer safe. Her options were limited. She had little place to hide, and she didn't know where the sense of wrongness came from. It could be just London's panicking. But it felt like something else altogether. There was no way to know. She closed her eyes, trying to slow her heart rate. She'd had private lessons on meditation to control the stress after she'd been charged with murder. She'd practiced a lot while leading up to and through the trial. She even continued her practice in England.

She never wanted to endure such a horrible nightmare again. With her eyes closed, all the sounds in her house were amplified. She focused on her breathing. One slow, careful breath at a time. Then a second one. Now the third. Anything to keep her nerves from making her race downstairs in a blind panic. She should have asked London how long before he would be here.

Then she heard it.

A squeak on the riser.

She froze, then stepped backward, closed her bedroom door and threw the bolt home.

This was her parents' master bedroom. They had always worried about her escaping her prison in the night. Signs of a guilty conscience. They had locks on the door. But no way in hell that would keep out anybody who was seriously after her. She raced to the windows and looked out. There was no fire escape. She did have a small balcony, and she was only on the second floor. Jumping would be rough. Although, given her options, she would risk a broken leg. But she gained no benefit by escaping her house to be on the grounds with a broken leg and still have the intruder coming after her. The letter she'd received had said she would suffer. She figured this asshole wanted to see her locked up in jail. Not killed.

Then again, who said the same person was after her now?

She raced into the bathroom, looking for a weapon. She found a can of hairspray and several towels.

Wrapping a towel around her arm, she grabbed the hair spray. She opened the doors to the balcony. Then an inspired thought hit. She turned to her bed, tore off the top sheet and tied it to the bottom railing of her balcony. She would slide down. She stared at the ground and swallowed. Behind her the doorknob jiggled, as if someone was trying to come in.

She put the hair spray in her pocket, climbed out over the railing and grabbed the sheet. She jumped, hanging on to the sheet, her weight sending her sliding down the silky material until she hit the ground. As soon as her feet touched the grass, she bolted around the side of her house, heading for the neighbor's home.

She had no way to know it the intruder was alone or if more than one asshole was after her. She climbed up the rocks of the side grounds and over the fence into the neighbor's property, heading for the main street. She was still dressed in pajamas, a bathrobe and slippers. It wouldn't be too hard to follow a trail of tiny white threads ripped off her clothing. As she raced into the street, at the far corner of her yard, headlights came from the end of the road. Was it London? Or was that a cohort of the asshole in her house?

She pulled out her phone and called London. When he answered, she said, "He's inside the house. He was trying to get in my bedroom. I went over the railing of my balcony.

I'm two houses past mine, standing close to the street corner."

With relief, she heard him say, "I see you. I'll be there in a second."

The truck at the far end raced toward her. Nervous, she crouched behind some bushes. When he slowed to a stop, she saw London's face. She ran toward him.

"Get in the car," he ordered, leaning across to open the passenger door.

She hopped in and slammed the door shut.

"Did you see him?"

She shook her head frantically. "No, he was trying to open the bedroom door, but I had it locked."

He glanced at her. "Those locks are generally easy to pop."

She nodded. "My parents had a dead bolt put in."

His eyebrows shot straight up. "Interesting."

She shrugged. "They liked their privacy," was all she said by way of explanation.

He pulled a U-turn at the intersection and slowly went past her house again.

She stared at her property, the shadows long and eerie. But found no sign of anyone. She hated to think she was jumpy and had let her imagination get away with her. She shook her head. "Please tell me that I didn't imagine it."

"I doubt it. But, if he got into your bedroom, he'd see the sheet you tied off the balcony. Then he'd know you escaped."

She turned to look at him. "Then what? He could still be in there? Or has he bolted?"

A second vehicle pulled up on the far side of the street. She watched a man come toward the SUV. "That's Detective

Sutherland."

"Who's he?"

She shot London a hard look. "One of the men who helped set up the security on the house."

London pulled the SUV over in front of her driveway and snorted. "Well, he did a piss-poor job of it." He rolled down his window.

Detective Sutherland came over, looking at Fern. "Are you okay?"

She wrapped her arms around her middle and nodded. "He made it to my bedroom."

"None of the alarms were triggered except for the one on the stairs."

She stared at him in surprise. "You put an alarm on the stairs?

He nodded. "Yes."

"What the hell did you put on her stairs, and who the hell are you?"

Detective Southerland looked at him. "A friend of hers. Somebody who would like to keep her safe and not railroaded into taking a murder charge for someone else."

Oops. Served him right. "Any relationship to Grant Summers?" London asked.

LONDON CAUGHT THE hard look on Detective Sutherland's face.

"Grant Summers, who works for the FBI? I've heard his name. Don't believe we're related."

London wondered about the resemblance of their features. Not to mention their hard-ass attitudes. He might bring it up with Grant the next time he was hassling him.

Throw him off his stride too.

They walked toward the house. At the front step, he turned and looked at Fern. "Do you have a way to get in or did you unlock it?"

"I didn't bring my keys if that's what you're asking."

Detective Sutherland reached forward to find the door unlocked. He pushed it wide and waited.

London watched as the detective did an internal check but from the front porch. London didn't understand what was going on. In fact, as he turned toward Fern, he realized she had a faraway gaze as if she were lost in thought. "What are you doing?"

She glanced at him and flushed. "You wouldn't believe me if I told you."

When Sutherland walked in, she stepped in behind him.

Frustrated and angry at being left out of the loop, London snapped, "You can try me."

"What good would that do? You didn't believe me before. You won't believe me now."

Yes, he probably deserved that. But, at some point, she had to let this go. "I made a mistake once. A mistake I've tried hard to fix, and I couldn't. Injustices happen. That doesn't mean it's my fault."

Her shoulders sagged ever-so-slightly. She nodded and said, "No, it isn't. But you're the only target I have."

He could say little regarding that. He didn't want her to blame him. He blamed himself enough.

As they walked through her house, he stayed close enough to hear her conversation with Sutherland. Something was going on here that London didn't quite understand.

"Any idea how he got in?" she asked Sutherland.

"No, not yet." Sutherland did a quick pass through the

living room and the rest of the main floor.

London watched, not understanding what Sutherland was looking for. He didn't approach any of the windows. He seemed to visually check the latches and the locks on the door.

"Nothing's been disturbed," Sutherland said. When he headed to the stairs to go up, he stopped and smiled. "There's the trigger I felt."

As he pointed halfway up the stairs, she nodded. "I heard a squeak when he came up. My parents were quite paranoid. They often had discussions about getting the stairs fixed, but my father said it was a hell of an early warning system, so they never did."

Sutherland nodded and headed up. She followed. London, still quiet and watchful, brought up the rear. They went through the bedrooms; again Sutherland looked at all the windows and the doors, but he didn't touch anything. At the master bedroom, he stopped. "It looks like he went down the sheet, the same as you."

"Shit." London walked around them and headed to the balcony. His blood ran cold when he saw the sheet she'd tied to the bottom railing. To think she'd been forced to escape her own house like this was just mind-blowing.

She laughed and said, "I guess I don't need these anymore."

London turned in time to see her unravel the towel from her arm and pull the hair spray from her pocket. She returned both to the bathroom. His jaw tensed. No woman should fear for her life, especially in her own damn home. He turned to Sutherland. "How can you tell he went out the window?"

Sutherland, a mocking smile playing at the corner of his

mouth, said, "I can see his energy." He spun on his heels, turned and walked out.

London glared at the empty doorway.

Fern exited the bathroom and smiled. "Stefan sent him, and I trust Stefan."

"Kronos?" He stared at her in frustration, his hands in fists he couldn't quite unlock. He hated feeling helpless. He hated feeling like he was on the outside. It was as if these two had a bond. A knowledge and a connection he couldn't access. It really bugged him. He wanted to be part of her inner circle but didn't even know what the hell her inner circle was. And that bothered him even more.

He was prepared to do anything to get back into her good graces again. Last time she'd shut him out, and he'd been forced to watch her day by day fade a little more in front of him. And he had been helpless to stop the circus. He still didn't understand how she'd gotten off. But she had, and, for that, he was incredibly grateful.

Arriving downstairs, he heard her last words to Sutherland.

"Stefan says the energy trail ran cold quickly."

Sutherland nodded. "I'd suspect he may have had a vehicle close by. Might've been a block away. He likely went over the back fence. I haven't checked that out yet. I want to know where he was staying and why."

"What do you mean, *staying?*"

Sutherland turned to study her. "He was inside when I set up the security."

She stared at him in shock. "How is it you didn't know he was here?"

London snorted. "That's exactly what I'd like to know."

"Remember you said no other windows or doors were

downstairs?"

"Did I say that?" She frowned. "There are two windows in the basement though."

He nodded. "I was only setting up security at all the points of entry."

She nodded. "So he gained access, in and out, via those two basement windows."

In a tired voice, he said, "And I didn't pick up his energy inside the house."

She winced. "I suppose if he'd been here long enough, there wouldn't have been much residual energy?"

"No. Like an air freshener that diminishes over time, energy dissipates fairly quickly. Or he isn't leaving much of the trail. Maybe he has a way to hide it."

She stared at him in confusion. "Is something like that possible?"

"As far as energy learning goes, anything is possible. It seems like the more you can dream up, the more people can do."

She nodded and pulled open the door to the basement. "He came from down here then."

London stepped forward, pulling his weapon. "Stay back. I'll go first." With his weapon ready, he headed down the stairs, doing a quick search. He called back up, "It's all clear."

The other two came down, and they all looked at a stack of furniture and boxes. Fern said, "Those chairs were on top of the couch before."

"How long ago?" London asked her.

She shrugged. "I haven't been down here since before the trial. After the trial, I left for England right away. That was more than six months ago."

"So it could have happened anytime."

"My vote is he was here in the last twenty-four hours," Detective Sutherland said. "This area's still full of his energy."

"You're saying he was here, hiding in my basement while I was upstairs?"

Sutherland nodded. "Predators are predators for a damn good reason. They are good at it. They stay hidden and undetected for a long time. But they do make mistakes."

London turned in a slow circle. "But if he was here for a long enough time, he would have used the washroom."

She pointed toward the far end. "There's the bathroom."

London opened the door. It was, indeed, a bathroom. Shower, toilet and sink. Water droplets were in the sink and water on the toilet as if it had been wiped. A large closed door had been long painted over. The more he studied it, the more uneasy he was. He turned to the other two. "Empty but recently used. I think he wiped it down afterward."

Sutherland swore softly.

Fern turned to look at both men. "What does that mean?"

"It usually means a pro."

She stared at him, the color completely washing out of her skin. "A pro what?"

Gently he said, "A professional killer—at least one who's done this before." He paused, then added, "Or at least someone who understands police procedures."

CHAPTER 13

ERN WANDERED AIMLESSLY around. Sutherland had
reset the trap, added a second one to her bedroom door
and walked out. He told her that she'd be safe for the night
and that he'd know when anyone triggered the traps and that
he'd come. She appreciated the thought, but it was terrifying. London, on the other hand, reached down, tugged her
into his arms and gave her a hard kiss on her lips, then he
walked out as well. Without saying a word. The front door
closed, leaving her all alone inside the house.

No way would she go to sleep again. Although she might
be safe, she wasn't feeling safe. She was still angry and getting
more so by the minute—to think London just turned and
walked out. He left her alone. Where the hell was that
protective instinct of his? This was way worse than she
thought it would be. She shouldn't have to deal with this one
time. She didn't want to again. She didn't want anything to
do with this. And it made her all that more anxious to leave
the country and return to England.

It was only past three now. It'd be another four hours or
so before the sun rose. How could she possibly sleep?

You'd be better off going to bed, Stefan said in her head.

Stefan, stop jumping in like that. It's terrifying.

*What would you have me do now? Knock and wait to be
invited in?* he asked in exasperation. *You know what it's like to*

have so many people I can talk to but who don't hear me approach? When I do show up, like you, they are irritated.

I'm sorry, she said, rubbing her temple. *I just feel lost for the moment.*

Why is that?

She stared moodily at the front door. *I didn't expect London to get up and leave.*

Then you're not thinking clearly. Look out the front window.

In the living room she pulled back the curtain ever-so-slightly. Parked in her driveway was London's SUV. He appeared to be sitting in the front seat with his laptop open as the glow lit his face. Maybe even a phone on his shoulder. *So he didn't leave?* she asked in relief.

Nor will he be leaving. The two of you are entwined in a way only you two can understand.

No, we aren't.

Stefan laughed.

He let me down, Stefan. How the hell can I ever trust him again?

You might want to take a chance to see it from his side too. The court case was well underway before he ever entered the courtroom. He didn't know what had happened to you because he was up north. When he did hear, he came immediately, only to have you treat him the same as you did everybody else.

She shoved her hands deep into her bathrobe pockets and stared at the man in the SUV. *But he didn't fix anything.*

Wouldn't it be nice to think he could be a white knight and come rushing in and save the damsel in distress? Stefan said drily. *You forget the court case was already going on. It was all he could do to help the defense as it was.* Stefan's voice deepened. *You know he got thrown out of court once by the judge.*

Also reprimanded by his boss that, if he didn't stay out of the case, he would lose his job too.

I heard something about him almost getting fired, she said slowly.

And, if he was fired, how the hell would he help you then?

Yeah, but he hasn't done anything since I was gone. She shook her head. *Of course not.*

What would you have him do? Stefan asked in a soft voice. *He's been doing what he could since you came back. He's been here ever since. But you keep pushing him away.*

She shivered. *Trust once broken …* She left the rest of the words unspoken.

Absolutely. But that does not mean you can't learn to trust again.

She shook her head. *I'm too tired to work my way through all this. Did you have a specific reason for stopping by?*

I'm just checking to make certain you're safe, to ensure the pathway to you is open. So, if I need to jump in and wake you up or let you know something dangerous is happening, I can do that.

Her eyebrows rose as she contemplated the thought. *That would be a hell of a decent warning system,* she admitted. *If it works.*

It does. But I do have my antennas turned on as well.

Sutherland came because his trap on the stairs was tripped. So he knew instinctively when somebody who shouldn't have been here crossed it.

He's very good. Particularly with security systems.

She nodded, staring at London. *London asked him if he was related to Grant Summers. They look so much alike.*

A short and odd silence followed. Then Stefan chuckled. *I know both very well. They don't know each other.*

She frowned, interested at the tone and voice shift. *So does that mean they are related or they are not related?*

Not my story to tell, but what is secret will always come to the surface. In this case not for a while yet.

Always so cryptic.

Maybe, maybe not. But fate has a way of making things happen. If it must happen, it will in its own time. Not just because we want it to.

From that I'll take it to mean they are related but they don't know, and, somewhere along the line soon, they'll find out.

He chuckled.

Yeah, I'm not quite a fool, Stefan.

You're not a fool at all, my dear. You're incredibly intuitive and very smart.

She shook her head. *So smart I'm all alone. So smart I forgot about the windows in the basement because I can't stand to remember anything about that time of my life. Thus Sutherland didn't set any traps down there, and, if he had, you probably would've found the intruder before tonight.*

I'm sorry your childhood was rough. I didn't know about you then, so I couldn't do anything to help you. But if I had known …

She bowed her head and looked at her hands. *It doesn't matter. It was a long time ago.*

Events from yesterday affect the future.

I have a dead bolt on the bedroom door. How many people have those?

At some point you must clear your childhood and make room for a much better future.

Right now my current life exceeds the conditions of my childhood, she said quietly. *And that was poisonous.*

Very astute if you consider the type of work you do. Did you happen to see any green clouds down there?

She started. *I didn't even think to look.*

After a short laugh, Stefan said, *How is it you can't see it naturally?*

Because I don't try? She shook her head. *It's not intuitive for me. I must focus.*

When you focus, how is it you don't see it all the time?

She shrugged. *I have no idea.*

I bet, if you tried, you would.

Maybe. She rubbed her temple again. *I need to talk to London.*

Good luck with that.

Stefan disappeared from her head. Tired and over-whelmed, hating the memories brought back from her childhood, she slowly walked out the front door.

He was on the phone, staring at something on the screen in front of him. She waited for him to see her. When he didn't, she rapped on the window, hard.

Startled, he turned and glanced at her. Said something on the phone and put it on the seat beside him. He rolled down the window. "What are you doing out here?"

"Isn't that my line?" she asked.

He shrugged. "Just catching up with stuff. The fact that you had an intruder changes things."

She shook her head. "It doesn't change anything. It's still the same thing. Somebody is after me. They want to make my life nasty and miserable." She frowned at him, hating to see his fatigue and worry. Most of all, the guilt every time she looked deep into his eyes. It lurked in the background. "Come on inside the house."

"Who said I was staying here the whole night?" he joked.

She shot him a hard look. "Come inside where you'll be

comfortable. I'll put coffee on." She turned and walked up to the front steps. Her slippers were soaked from the evening dew when she had run out in the neighbor's yard. Inside she slipped them off so they could dry on the mat and pulled out another pair from the front closet. She put those on and walked into the kitchen.

She had closed the door so he couldn't get in without her. She walked back to open the door and saw him getting out of the truck. She waited until he entered.

HE TURNED TO look at the bolt. "Why did the intruder unlock the front door if you went out the bedroom window?"

"I think he unlocked the front door so he could get out the fastest, most direct way he needed to. Then, once I escaped from my balcony, he went after me to see if he could find me."

"That makes sense." He studied her. "You're awfully calm."

"I'm not. I'm just tired."

"Then why are you making coffee?"

"The coffee is for you," she snapped. She led the way back to the kitchen and went to the cabinet to put on the coffee. When he didn't say anything about not bothering, she realized he probably did want it. She glanced at his laptop. "Did you find anything interesting?"

"Not yet. We must be missing something."

"I said that a long time ago, but nobody cared." She shook her head, hit the button on the coffee machine, turned around and leaned against the counter. "That's not fair. I don't blame you, you know."

He froze and slowly turned, looking at her, his eyes gone dark. "Why wouldn't you? I do."

She shook her head. "I wondered if you were part of the legal mechanism that made my case appear to be a slam-dunk. Everybody knew you and I had a new relationship, and you could be difficult," she said. "Removing you from the picture made it a whole lot easier for everything else to slide into place."

His eyebrows shot up. He frowned. "I never considered that." *Before.*

"I didn't either, until Stefan just reminded me that it wasn't your fault."

"Stefan again?"

She nodded. "Love or hate him, he is very good at what he does."

"How did you hook up with him?"

She pulled out a chair and sat. "I have special skills. He seems to think they're psychic skills. I don't."

"And how did he find out about your skills?"

"You really won't believe that. He contacted me one day after I met him in the police station, after being charged with the earlier murders. He said the work I was doing was helping to strengthen the world around us. A third barrier. It's a divide between this dimension and multiple others according to him. And it's got several tears he's working to repair."

London's eyes grew wide, and his lips twitched.

She nodded. "Yeah, that was my reaction too. The thing is, he really believes it, and the more you talk to him, the more logical he appears to be. Sutherland really does have the ability to use energy as a security system. And there's a whole lot of other people who can do a whole lot of other things."

"Have you met these other people?" he asked cautiously.

"Some of them. Do you know of Dr. Maddy?"

He sat back in his chair and crossed his arms over his chest. "Doesn't everyone?"

"I never did until I met her in England."

"What was she doing in England? She has Maddy's Floor here that she looks after."

Fern nodded. "She was helping to set up another center in England. I was lucky enough to meet her there. I have yet to see her here, although the invitation stands."

"You are moving in high circles."

She shook her head. "I'm not moving in any circles. I'm ground to a stand-still. Completely paralyzed with fear I could end up back in court, and this time I'd go to jail. I don't sleep. I barely eat. According to Stefan, I'm letting this asshole control me. And I know he understands what I'm going through, but, at the same time, I don't have the power to stop it."

"What is it he told you to do?"

"I haven't really discussed it with him. But he told me that I need to draw on my history."

"And that means?" London stared at her and shook his head. "That's hardly helpful."

She nodded. "I have a good idea what he means, but I haven't tried it yet." She settled back into her chair. "When I get a chance, I will try it because Stefan hasn't steered me wrong yet. And I have nothing but good things to say about Dr. Maddy. Of course her healing ..." She closed her eyes and leaned forward a little with a smile. "Her healing is magical."

"Magical, meaning psychic?"

"At what point does your body's self-healing process and

magic and psychic abilities blend to become one thing versus being three separate things that nobody can really define?"

"I do know somebody who was a patient at Maddy's Floor for a time," he admitted. "A boy."

Her eyes popped open as she stared at him. "Did he survive?"

London nodded. "He not only survived but he had this miraculous recovery. Nobody understood how or why. The parents, who were already religious, said it was an act of God, and they were content with that answer. He's doing fine, has been ever since."

"Are you content with that answer?"

He stared at her. "Dr. Maddy worked on the child."

A grin slid out. "She is magical. She can get the body to kick in its healing, kick out all kinds of diseases and maladies, heal mental and physical and emotional conditions. What Dr. Maddy is, is not containable by the physical definition of a human being."

"Have you seen her work?"

She nodded. "When I was in England, I spent some time with her. She did things I couldn't imagine."

London leaned forward. "Things, like what?"

She smiled. "Like inserting her hand into a woman's stomach to remove a tumor without a scalpel, no blood, nothing but her hand, and the tumor slipped free of the body, was removed and placed in a dish. And when she slid her hand back out, the skin closed behind her." She shook her head. "Every time I think about it, it just gives me the shivers and makes me believe in the impossible."

"You know it's not possible, right?"

"And yet you asked for some reason." She studied him. And she knew. "You've heard something like that before, haven't you?"

He nodded. "The boy had a tumor on the side of his heart. The heart was struggling and slowed to the point he couldn't have surgery because he wouldn't have survived. He could have had a heart transplant, but there was no time. According to the boy, Dr. Maddy placed her hand inside, touched his heart and removed the tumor because it was bothering him."

Fern laughed. "I love children. They are so innocent and yet so damn honest."

He stretched his arms over his head. "Is it really possible?"

"It really is possible," she confirmed. "I've seen it happen. ... It's made me open to an awful lot of other things I didn't think possible. And I now realize a whole world of possibilities is out there that I'd never allowed myself to understand before. As a child and the way I grew up, ... I was told it was wrong when I saw things. But once I watched Stefan and Maddy, I saw the potential of life, the way they saw life. Well"—she shook her head again and smiled—"it seems so inadequate to say I finally believe."

"What if you're wrong?"

Her smile fell away. "And, if I'm wrong, so what? I've been wrong before. At least believing in their ability to do what they do gives me hope that my situation might come out all right at some point. Even if it doesn't take magic or psychic abilities or healing like Dr. Maddy can conjure up."

"I won't let you go away again," he said. "You won't spend another night in jail if I can do anything to help it."

She leaned forward and cupped his hands, which he'd turned into hard locked-down fists, and whispered, "There isn't anything you can do about it if it comes to that."

He shook his head. "We can run. I can fly you to another country with no extradition rules."

She stared at him for a long moment. "Would you do that for me?"

He nodded. "I would do everything I could to avoid it, but, if that's the only option left, I promise you that I will not let you go to jail for a murder you did not commit."

HE WALKED ALONG the fence perimeter until he approached the correct row. His footsteps clicked on the cement, a quiet rhythm that echoed in the evening air.

The place should be empty at this time of night. Still he was hoping his quarry was here.

They needed to talk. He wanted to see where this man was mentally. He'd been so passionate for so long. But, at one point, the fatigue and disillusionment had stepped in.

That wasn't good. He didn't know how much more this guy could help him. Except for passing over information. And one important piece was where Derek had hidden out.

Only his quarry couldn't know why he needed that.

He stepped up to the corner and peered around the edge of the last unit.

And saw the faint glow of a light coming from under the door.

Good, he was here.

CHAPTER 14

D ID SHE BELIEVE him? She studied his expression, but all she saw was honesty. That made her suspicious. She lowered her gaze to the table and shook her head. "If you feel that way now, why the hell didn't you feel that way before?"

"I had just come back into town. I hadn't seen you since that lovely fight with my brother. And, throughout our association, I felt like you were holding things back—hiding things from me." He lifted his coffee cup and took a sip. Then smiled. "Now this is real coffee."

She gave him a sharp look but stayed quiet.

After another sip, he continued. "I wasn't sure how much of that was because of your relationship with my brother or something else entirely. If you recall, you're the one who shut me out." He shrugged. "My boss sent me back east, assigned to a case. I thought at the time it was awfully convenient timing to be sent away. But maybe my bosses knew my personal life was a bit of a mess. I had deliberately not kept up with the news while I was gone. I was angry. I didn't realize what the hell had happened. And, by then, the court case had been mounted against you. I didn't add to it, but I found myself struggling to find something that would clear your name. There were always more rumors and lies." He leaned forward. "Then you were acquitted, and you ran away. But the lies and rumors persisted." His gaze locked on hers. "If you'd just told me the truth, all this wouldn't have happened."

She gave him a sad smile and said, "Of course it would have happened."

He raised his hands in the air. "Really? What's that supposed to mean? More of Stefan's words about fate needing to happen in its own time?"

"I don't have a clue what fate will do. It's not that easy to open yourself up and become a public media circus. Some of those details are very difficult." She turned her head and stared out somewhere behind his shoulder. "I didn't want to go back to my childhood. My history. I hated my life. I spent all my adult years building a new life. Why the hell would I ruin that? Why would I want to go back and dissect my old life?"

"Do you mean my brother?"

She snorted. "Derek was an experiment."

He stared at her. Shocked, but not for the first time.

"I was trying to have a normal life. A normal relationship. But I failed at that too." She waved her hand in dismissal. "I should never have bothered."

"And with me? What was I? A second experiment?"

"You? We didn't have a relationship, remember? I hadn't expected to find myself attracted to you. You rolled into my life, stole my heart." She glared at him. "Then you were suddenly gone while I was being crucified. Your brother was leading the attack."

He nodded. "And I'm really sorry for that."

Once again, she was tired of it all. With a grunt, she said, "It doesn't matter anymore. It's all over with. All of it is part of my history. I have no intention of going back there."

"And yet maybe this is all related to your history. The

history you won't talk about. The childhood you never mention. The parents who died, but you don't talk about. Do you have any other close family?"

She shook her head. "No. Remember the letter from my aunt? That's as close as my family gets."

"Everybody has somebody."

She stuck out her chin and glared at him. "Why the hell do you think I tried to have a relationship? Because I was tired of being alone. I was tired of not having anybody. I thought I could make it work. I thought, if I worked hard enough, cared enough, I could make it happen. Walking away was the best thing for me as it showed me that I didn't need anybody. Why does anybody want a relationship? How do people ever trust one another? I don't get it."

He tried to answer.

She snorted. "Don't bother. You can't answer it because nobody can." She got up, took her coffee cup to the sink and filled it with water. Then she turned around. "Get on with what you plan on doing here. I'm going to bed. One of us needs to get some sleep."

She turned and headed up the stairs. Inside her mind was tumultuous, her heart churning. But there was also sadness. The world was not a nice place to live. Why had her parents tried so hard to keep her alive? Now for the first time she realized it was too bad they did that. Maybe she shouldn't have survived.

She walked into the bathroom, sat on the side of the bathtub and turned on the tap. She couldn't go to bed without washing her feet from her earlier escape. With just a little water in the tub, she quickly swished her feet around and grabbed a washcloth and soap. When done, she dried her feet with a towel and stood up, hating the aches and pains and soreness. It wasn't just fatigue but the adrenaline panic from running across her yard, over her neighbor's fence and across their lawn. She probably should have a hot bath, but it was now almost four o'clock in the morning. The last thing she wanted was to delay sleep. Looking in the mirror, she saw her bathrobe was no longer white. With a grimace, she hung it up on the back of the bathroom door and headed to bed. It just felt so strange. The French doors to the balcony were still open.

Realizing nobody had retrieved the sheet, she struggled to untie it. After she pulled it up, she dropped it in the laundry hamper and closed the French doors. She turned around, brushed her hair back off her face and froze.

A faint pale-mint haze was all over her bed. She turned, looked at the balcony doors, realizing they had been open even when Sutherland had been here the second time.

Had he reset the windows and the door security? Did that work if the door was open? They should've pulled up the sheet because otherwise her stalker might have climbed back into the house. Swallowing hard, her hands trembled, even knowing London was downstairs. She studied the green cloud, hating what it meant.

The trouble was, right now she couldn't tell exactly what toxin was involved because it was so faint. Was there poison all over the bed? Did the intruder have poison in his system and lay on the bed? It should be her own energy here, but she hadn't been on the bed in a couple hours. She'd bolted out of here when London had telephoned her. So why was that gray-green essence here now? She approached cautiously, turning on all the lights in the bedroom. A faint energy trail from the poison was at the window and the double doors that she had just closed.

She turned and opened the double doors leading to the balcony and stepped outside. In the darkness, the trail was much easier to see. Her intruder had gone from the back of the garden, over the neighbor's fence and through the backyards. There were yards upon yards; it was easy enough to hop a fence and disappear into the neighborhood with a few jumps.

Hating to disturb him, but knowing she had to, she pulled out her phone and called Sutherland. "Did you reset the alert on the double French doors?

"Yes, I did."

"But we left the sheet outside, correct?"

"Yes," he answered slowly. "Was it inside when you went back to the room?"

"No, it was still hanging outside close to the ground, where anybody could've used it to climb back up, and the double glass doors were still open."

"But he still would have had to cross the barrier to enter," Sutherland said quietly.

She could hear his mental processes buzz as if trying to figure this out. "And yet there's a cloud of poison over my bed," she murmured. "As if he lay down or spread something over the top."

"You're the poison expert. Can you see anything?" he asked, his voice rising in alarm.

"No, that's why I'm asking. It looks like he went through my backyard and over the neighbors' fences."

"Can you see his energy?"

"I don't know that it's his energy, but I can see the faint trail of poison."

"Can you see if anything else is toxic? Damaged? Anything stolen? Do you trust there isn't any poison on the bed?"

She shook her head. "I don't trust anything or anyone. I'll sleep in another room. I'll remake my bed in the morning."

"Maybe you shouldn't even be in there. You're tired and not thinking straight. It could be any number of poisons. I don't want to think of you dying in the night while sleeping."

She hesitated, then shrugged. "I'll be fine. I just wanted to check if he could've crossed the open door if you reset the alarm."

"If he was inside at the time I reset it, it's possible his energy was accepted."

"But he left, and then you reset it." She struggled to figure out how this worked. "Does that mean he'd always be welcome in my house now?" God help her if that was the case.

"I can change the vibration on that energy. He shouldn't be allowed back in any more than anybody who you may have let in already."

"You mean, like London?"

"Correct. Of course there's a possibility this person has psychic abilities. In which case, he can be way harder to catch."

"But, even if he does have psychic abilities, how does he cross an energy barrier like that?"

"Dammit, I don't know. I'll come back out and spend the night at your place. And then we'll redo it from scratch. I'll do a full cleansing and then reset it to my energy."

"And what does that mean? Only you can then come back and forth?" she asked cautiously.

"It means nobody but who you allow in can come

through without you opening the door."

"Except when you reset it, I walked in and out several times as did you."

"Yes, but he didn't. He'd already left the house."

They both froze.

"Or did he?"

"We saw his energy leave, but ..." Sutherland swore deeply and fluently. "Look, you don't need to be alone tonight. I don't know what the hell's going on. I'll come and stand guard."

She shook her head. "No, you don't need to. London's downstairs. He's standing guard. He was at the front door, and I brought him inside."

"Are you sure?"

"Yes, I'm sure. Get some sleep. I really could use your help tomorrow to figure this out. I don't understand how he could've gotten back in or out after the second security fix."

"Neither do I." His voice was resigned. "The problem is the system will work with 99 percent of the people. And then you find one asshole who has a trick never seen before, and there is nothing you can do about it. It's up to us to learn from it and move on."

"When you get here tomorrow—which is today actually if you can still make it—you can learn from it," she said drily.

"I can make some adjustments from here. I might not need to make a physical trip."

She hung up and turned to stare at her bed. Folding up all the bedding in the center of the bed, she quickly bundled it up into one big package and carried it into the hallway to her washer and dryer. She dumped everything into the machine and set it for extralarge, extralong. When that cycle was done, she would redo it again in the morning.

As she returned to her bedroom, London called up the stairs, "You okay?"

"Yes." Sure she was. She was always fine. Even if she was unnerved at the idea of someone being in her room.

"You need any help?"

She shook her head. "No. I'll be fine."

She walked back into the bedroom, closed the door and leaned against it. How could she possibly explain to any of them that no poison known to man could hurt her? But, if she had the wrong poison clinging to her, any man who came and gave her a hug could die. She dragged a blanket from the top shelf of her closet, lay it on the bed, then rolled up in it. As she closed her eyes, her last thought was, *How the hell did my life get so messed up?*

LONDON REALIZED HE should have helped her make her bed earlier. They hadn't even taken the sheet off the balcony. What did that say about him? The asshole could've just come right back into her room again.

And who's to say he hadn't?

Shit.

The asshole could easily be hiding inside again. And why not in the basement once more, where he'd successfully stayed the first time? London did a quick walk-through the main floor, then entered the basement.

As he turned on the lights and studied the room downstairs, he remembered something he'd seen earlier. A wall with a door inset but painted over so it was hardly visible.

He walked to the bathroom and checked it out. A small door was on the far side. Determined to get to the bottom of at least one mystery, he walked through the bathroom with the lights on to open the other door. It was stuck. He gave a hard shove. Cracks appeared in the painted-over corners. Something was distinctly off about this place. And his intuition was killing him. He needed to open this door to find out what the hell was going on. Find out what Fern was hiding ... and why.

He pushed it open slightly, then stepped back as old stale air came wafting through. He stood in place for a long moment, wondering what the hell he had just found. Using his phone's flashlight, he held it to the small opening. The door was only open a few inches.

As he pushed it farther open, he saw a massive piece of furniture, but it was hard to decipher what it was. He tried to push the door open even wider. That's when a weird set of bells rang through the house. Not a nice sound. Not like wind chimes. More like an alarm. As if pushing this door had set off something.

He could hear footsteps as Fern raced down to the main floor and on to the basement. She bolted into the bathroom, shock and horror on her face, and came to a skidding stop.

"What are you doing?" she cried out. "That door can never be opened."

He turned to study her, seeing the panic on her face. She clenched and unclenched her hands. Then, as if realizing what she was doing, wrapped them around herself, holding herself tight.

He stepped back ever-so-slightly. "I'm sorry, but it occurred to me, since we had left that sheet hanging, then the intruder could come back into the house, and I wanted to make sure he wasn't here hiding still. I saw this door and thought I should check it out, just in case he'd returned."

She gulped for air, and he realized this was no regular fear. He gently grabbed her arms, softly stroking up and down. "Take it easy. I don't know what's in there. I haven't opened it very much."

"Close the door. Close the door, please!"

As she wouldn't stop pleading with him, nor would she calm down, he reached over and pulled the door shut tight. Even then her eyes were huge as saucers; horror still written all over her face. He saw the shaking take over her body.

Barefoot, barely enough clothing to cover her, she shivered with cold. He picked her up and carried her upstairs to the living room. There he sat on the couch and held her close.

When her shaking had stopped enough, he asked, "What's in that room?"

She shook her head, not moving off his chest. Once again her voice was hysterical. "Nothing. I'm not telling you."

And he realized this was the crux of the mystery behind who Fern was. He gently and slowly stroked her back. "This is one of the reasons why you can't trust people. You must let go of whatever is inside that room. You need to let me in on that secret. I can help you deal with it."

Her laughter was freakishly loud.

He winced, realizing just how badly injured she was inside. Whatever that room represented terrified her. "Easy. Just take it easy."

She lay on his chest until her shakes and sobs slowed. When she finally calmed, she sat up. "Don't ask me."

He opened his mouth to do just that and snapped it shut. He searched her gaze. "How is it that room can cause such terror?"

She shuddered and wrapped her arms around her chest. "Please don't ask me about that room."

The investigator in him wouldn't let it lie, he knew that. But obviously now wasn't the time. "I'll let you off the hook," he said. "It's obviously extremely traumatic. However, we have to know what's in that room."

She stared, the tears welling up. "No. There's nothing in that room now or ever."

"Whatever it *is*," he challenged, "hurt you in the deepest and most fundamental way possible."

Tears, great big fat ones, dripped down her cheeks. His heart broke as he realized just how much this meant to her. How damaging this was to her psyche. How absolutely tormenting it was for her. He shook his head. "You need to face it."

And that seemed to snap her from tears to anger. "You think I haven't tried? Do you think I haven't lived with that for all my life? You have no idea what I went through down there." Soft tendrils of hair clung to the tears on her face. "You have no idea how terrifying that space is for me."

"I don't understand," he said. "Were you locked in there? Was it a punishment room?"

She stared at him and pinched her lips firmly together. And he realized she wouldn't talk. Not now and, if she had her way, not ever.

In as gentle a voice as possible, he said, "To move forward, you have to let this go."

Mute, she shook her head and then said, "You don't know anything." She got up off his lap and headed back upstairs.

When he heard her bedroom door slam and lock behind her, he sat back down again. "I might not know anything yet, but I will get to the bottom of this."

CHAPTER 15

S HE CURLED UP in her bed, her teeth chattering. She thought she had dealt with her past. She'd hoped she'd dealt with it. Instead all it took was London opening that door to bring the nightmares to the surface. Why had he opened it? When the workmen had painted over it, she thought for sure nobody would consider opening it. But the outline of the door remained. So, of course, he had to open it. Only it wasn't any of his goddamned business. Tears burned hot in her eyes. They poured down her cheeks as the pain of her childhood once again ate into her consciousness.

She'd hoped this day would never come. But she knew it would. Only it wasn't supposed to be for another fifty to sixty years—hell, maybe not until she was long past dead. The house was old, but some curious person would go down there. Like London had.

How the hell could she possibly live with this now?

No way London would walk away from that subject. It didn't matter what she said; he wouldn't. The FBI agent in him would keep pushing. The only recourse she had was to leave the country. Immediately. She would never show him that room.

She lay here so cold inside and out. So lost, so alone and so unloved, she didn't know if she would last much longer. How could any one person suffer so much pain?

It wasn't fair. Other people had normal childhoods, normal families and normal lives. She knew that most people would have a definition of what *normal* meant, but, in her case, it was anything but what she'd lived. Still she was a survivor. She wouldn't go back to that time again—there had to be another way. But, as she went through the options, she knew none were viable. Unless she left him, London wouldn't walk out of her life again. Because he felt guilty he hadn't stopped the circus from happening the last time.

But she meant it when she said she didn't blame him. Law enforcement was a machine. Once they ganged up on you, it was hard for any one person to stop it. Her lawyer had been the most help. Even he had wanted to bring up her childhood and her family. She'd been adamant against it. No way in hell would her childhood take any kind of role in her defense. And her lawyer didn't know the half of it.

Now here London was, trying to dig it up all over again. And she couldn't let that happen. As she lay here, the solution came down to just one. She had to leave.

She got up, turned on all the lights in her bedroom, pulled out her large suitcase that she had barely unpacked only to pack it up again. She had several suitcases to fill.

As far as she was concerned, this time she wasn't coming back. She'd sell the house from a distance—or maybe not. She could hold on to the property just to keep her personal history buried. She had enough money that retaining the house—paying property taxes and maintenance—was possible. With the death of her parents, she'd inherited a sizable trust. None of it could make up for what she'd been through. Her eyes dry now and her body warmer, she moved around. She carefully emptied her dresser and walked to the closet.

A lot of clothes were here but not necessarily any she wanted or needed. She'd always been cold in England. Something about the wet weather over there, even though it was warm outside this time of year. She packed up several more sweaters. By the time she got halfway through her closet, piles of clothes were on the floor. Some she would keep, and some she would toss. She hung some she was not sure about back in the closet. She could always have somebody collect them if she really cared. Hell, she might be forced to come back for a court case. It wouldn't hurt to leave clothes for that instance.

The first suitcase was so full that she had to sit on it to get the snaps closed. Just as she closed the second one, a knock came at her door. She froze. Of course London had heard her. She'd made enough trips back and forth that he was probably wondering what the hell she was up to. It was none of his business. None of it. She refused to answer the door.

His voice came through the door loud and clear. "Fern, open the door."

"No."

"Look, I'm sorry. I didn't mean to upset you."

"Too bad. You did."

"Let me talk to you."

"You are talking." She rolled her eyes at his idiocy, but she understood exactly what he trying to do. "I'm not opening the door. The dead bolt is in place. If you force it open, I'll call the cops."

An odd sound came from the other side, and then she realized he was banging his head against the door, figuring out what to do to make her open up. But there was nothing anybody could do.

She'd hit the wall. That lovely proverbial wall that had so many dents and bumps in it from all the times she had hit it. But she'd always found a way to climb up, to get around it. She never found a way to get through it, and she'd already heard Stefan's lesson on just let it dissolve in front of you with a cynical attitude.

Fern didn't know what his childhood was like, but, if he had any idea what hers had been, he wouldn't say that.

My childhood was no better.

Was it any worse?

I don't know. We're not in a competition to see who suffered the most. The thing is, you are who you are because you survived. Will you really let them do this to you? Chase you away from your home? Send you running yet again? If you do this, will you ever stop?

His voice rippled through her mind; her heart set, her muscles once again shivering in shock. She sat on the bed and cried out, *You don't understand. I don't have a choice. London's not giving me a choice.*

I understand more than you think. I know more than you expect me to know. I don't want this either. But, as those cards were dealt, and he is part of those cards, you must deal with him.

I don't have to deal with him. I can walk away.

What will that do? Stefan asked curiously. *Would it solve what you're trying to ignore in your history? In your basement?*

She sagged in place and said, *Of course not.*

So then open the door and deal with this. Don't walk away. Face it.

I can't. This time no anger was in her words. Just the traumatized child she'd always been, crying out in pain. *Do you really understand? I want to scream and run away. It's all I can do to control myself.*

I know, he whispered.

His voice was so gentle, so soft, it brought tears to her eyes. She gave her face a good scrubbing with the palms of her hands and said, *It will be easier for me in England.*

He chuckled. *But, if it was easy, you wouldn't be doing it. You're not known for taking the easy path. In the past, you've taken the stuff you have learned and the things that you can do and put it with what you have. It's purely amazing.*

Her back stiffened. Cautiously she asked, *What do you know about what I can do?*

He smiled. *I know a hell of a lot.*

And just like that, he disappeared from her mind.

She stared at her hands, hating that she was trembling. She murmured to the empty room, "Who are you, Stefan, that you can step into my mind and talk to me like that? Who knows so much about me that I probably don't even want to acknowledge myself?"

She thought he was gone, but his voice drifted through her mind, almost through her soul, when he said, *I'm part of you, as you are part of me.*

And just like that, she burst into tears. *It can't be. Nobody knows me that well. Nobody understands me.*

Because you keep yourself hidden. You give life a shot, but you only let out 10 percent of yourself, so they all know that you're hiding something. It's hard to trust you when they know you're hiding something so very elemental to your personality. You're asking a lot of anybody.

Is there anybody out there who can trust and love me without knowing all of me? she asked.

London. But you won't give him a chance. He needs to know. He could live with not knowing, but it's better for him if he does. Stefan gave a quiet sigh. *Would you rather someone take you on face value but never really care to know who you are inside? Would you rather know somebody is out there who knows you, even all the scars, the festering poisons that are inside your soul? Who sees into the heart of you and loves you anyway?*

She fell backward on the bed. The suitcase racking her spine from top to bottom. *It's not possible. There is nobody out there who would do that.*

Because you've never opened yourself. It takes two. You have only tried the other way—a surface relationship, where your partner doesn't know anything about you.

She realized Stefan was talking about Derek. *That was a mistake.*

Of course it was. You were strangers. You tried to be what he wanted you to be. And, in the end, you gave him a false impression of who you are. Of course he felt betrayed by you, and so he betrayed you.

Her eyes flew open as she contemplated his words. *Is it that simple? Is that why he did what he did?*

People who are hurt, some of them feel the need to hit back at others as badly as they were hurt themselves. You don't need Derek. At some point he will no longer exist in your life.

That's not possible if London is in my life. Derek will always be there.

No, Derek is on his way out. His energy is thin, his cord faint. I don't know where, what, how or why, but Derek is dying right now.

She froze. *Are you sure?*

Positive. I see dead people all the time. But I can't control who or when. And rarely those that have recently crossed over. I have to have a personal connection to those people. Which I don't have in Derek's case. And he's barely holding on.

Shouldn't we help him?

I doubt there's anything anyone can do for him at this stage.

I've never been able to connect with him so I can't check on him.

WHEN THE BEDROOM door opened while he leaned against it, London almost fell through. He pulled himself together, mentally and physically. He stared at her with hope. Then he saw the look in her eyes, one of complete dread. He lifted his gaze to the room behind her, and everything inside him locked down. "You're leaving?"

She took a deep breath and nodded. "I can't do this anymore." She headed toward the double glass doors she'd escaped from earlier. As he stared at the suitcases, he knew this time she wouldn't come back. If he couldn't make her stay, then it would be all over for them.

And another fundamental truth hit him. He couldn't let her go. "Give me a chance to fix this," he said. "Or I'll move with you."

She spun and stared at him in shock.

He gave her a crooked smile. "Yeah, nobody's more surprised than I am that I said that."

She snorted. "Then take it back, so I won't believe it."

He shook his head. "I am very much the person you see. And when I say something, I stand by it."

She glared at him. "Versus the person you see standing in front of you right now, one lie after another?"

"What I do know is that the person who you are is somebody I don't really understand. I don't know much about you because you won't share any details."

"I built this life very carefully," she cried out. "It's the kind of life everybody would believe and everybody would want. No questions asked."

He froze, his attention on her face. Such interesting words. She crafted this image? She created her history? That explained why the police were so damn sure they had something on her because she was hiding so much. But right now, he was damn close to getting to the heart of this. "Tell me who you are inside. Show me who you are inside. Not this facade you've created. The real you."

"You can't handle the real me." She sneered. "You think life is all black and white, good and bad, right and wrong." She shook her head. "What about those of us caught in the middle of it all? The ones never given a choice to be either but stuck in-between."

He opened his mouth to say something, but he didn't know that it would matter because she rode right through him.

"Do you think it's easy to be me? You have no idea. Why is it you can't accept what you see at face value?"

"Because what I see at face value isn't real. It's a mask. It's fake. But I really want to know what's behind that."

"Why?" She spun to face the window, yet again her hands clenching into fists.

"Because inside is something good. There's something special for you. For us. I don't know what it is. I don't know how it got there. But I want to nurture it. I want to keep it alive. I don't want to crush you or your soul. I think the police and the circumstances of your life have done enough of that. But there's so much else out there. And I can feel it. I can see it inside you."

He reached up and clasped her shoulders, intent on drawing her back to lean against his chest, but she was stiff as a board. She lowered her head and stared at the floor for a long moment. When she raised her gaze and turned to face him, he knew he'd lost.

"I know if I open the door and let you in, you'll be horrified, and you'll turn and walk away. Anybody would. Any sane, normal male would run as fast as he could."

"Is that why you've never been in relationships for very long?"

"Derek was the only long-term one. I tried hard to make that work."

"He was afraid of you," London whispered.

She nodded. "Smart man."

London shook his head. "No, not smart. Weak."

Her green eyes flew open, and she stared at him, a mocking glint to her lips. "You think you're strong enough? Do you think you really can handle what you see before you?"

He could feel everything tense inside him. He knew how important his answer was. How whatever he said here would matter. Then he nodded. "Will I react in a negative way? At first I might. Because we can do very little about a shock that hits our system. Does that mean I can't rationalize my way through to the inside of it? Of course I can. But if you don't give me a chance, I can never prove it."

"And, if I give you a chance, you'll know, and you'll tell everyone else." She shook her head. "What's in this for me?"

"I won't tell anyone. I promise."

Her eyes were huge fathomless orbs. "I don't trust anyone."

He nodded. "And I haven't given you any reason to trust me. But you must trust someone. Trust Stefan then."

She tilted her head to the side as she studied London. "I do trust Stefan. I don't understand why or how, but I do."

London felt jealousy drive through him. "Then tell him.

Let him see your childhood. Let him see who you really are on the inside."

"He already knows who I am. And he still talks to me."

London grabbed on to that. "Good. You have one person. One person who knows who you are inside. He hasn't betrayed you. He won't betray you. Why can't you let me in?"

"I didn't tell him. He already knew. He can see into my soul, into my history, like so very few can. But, to let you in, I must open myself up. I must speak the words. And that's much harder."

"It's all about that room downstairs, isn't it?"

She nodded. "A lot of it is."

"Then take me there and show me." She stared at him, and he saw her panic and fear but, at the same time, he thought he saw some hope, her hope that maybe he'd be the one who would stand by her side. His heart melted. He gently rubbed her arms. "I know those aren't the words you need. You need action. But I can't give you the action you need if I don't know what's behind that need."

She gave a clipped nod. "I'll show you downstairs."

When she faced him fully, her chin held high, he saw such a sense of finality, as if she were already saying good-bye. She glanced at her suitcases, then at him, and said, "Afterward, you can drive me to the airport."

And his heart sank, this time right to the bottom. What the hell was in that goddamned room, and who the hell had done this to her? He'd do a lot right now to have that person where he could tear him apart limb by limb. If only so he had a chance to put her back together, so she wasn't so scarred and so damn terrified. All he could do was hope he was man enough to deal with whatever was there.

With a fatalistic attitude, she slowly walked in front of him to the main floor. She stopped in front of the basement door, closed her eyes. In a sudden movement, she pulled open the door and walked into the basement. She turned on the light at the bottom of the stairs. Instantly a yellow halo filled the large, mostly empty space.

From behind her, London asked in a quiet voice, "Why did you never get rid of any of this stuff?"

She shrugged. "I never did much with my parents' stuff."

She walked in a straight line to the bathroom. The bathroom that had been neatly remodeled. She opened the door and turned on the light. It was a good-size room with a bathtub, shower and double sink vanity—an unusually large bathroom for a basement. At the same time, maybe not so unusual, in that the basement was spacious enough to turn into a suite or at least a media room.

London stepped into the bathroom as she moved forward to the wall, her fingers touching the cracked paint.

"How is it that you thought you could open this?" she asked.

"It appeared to be a door. I just reached out and pushed," he said, his tone apologetic.

She nodded, hit a button on the top of the door he hadn't seen and placing both palms on the door. And then pushed. Silently the door opened completely. London stayed quiet beside her—afraid to say the wrong thing and have her stop. She reached her hand inside, flicked on the light switch, and then, taking a deep breath, she walked across the threshold into her history.

London had no idea what was behind the door. He doubted it could be as bad as she made it out to be, but no doubt it was bad for her. If he could help her make peace with this, he knew it would be important to who she was ever after.

He stepped into the room, his gaze telling him why the basement had seemed smaller than the upper floors. The rest of it was walled off here. This space was huge. At least twenty by thirty. No windows and no exits. It was an odd space. As he stepped in, he realized she had taken ten steps forward and stopped. As if waiting.

He didn't understand. But he needed to. In front of them appeared to be tables and horticultural equipment, all of it old and in disarray. There were large planting boxes. As her parents had been botanists, that made sense.

He walked closer, seeing the hydroponics setup, understanding where the moistness came from, because no ventilation was built into this room. He wandered up and down long multiple rows. Six waist-high planting boxes. As far as he could tell, this looked like where a gardener planted seedlings early in winter before they were ready to be set outside. But he knew there had to be so much more.

At the end of the rows were various apparatuses confirming his initial beliefs. Fertilizers and nitrogen supplements, watering cans and gardening tools. The full-on protective suits made him stare in wonder. But his mind just couldn't come up with a logical explanation for her deep-seated horror.

He walked across to the far side of the room to see yet more. More boxes, more planters, but also a drying area, a large long counter with a grate hanging above it, complete with hooks. Maybe where herbs had been hung and dried. Also a table that looked like experiments had been done there, with a lab tester, small petri dishes and various little single burners. Almost a chemistry lab set down here. But again, no ventilation.

What about this space terrified her?

He kept walking down the far side, looking at Fern once or twice, but she never moved. She watched, her eyes haunted. And still he didn't get it. He was about to open his mouth and ask what was so fearful about this space, when he came to the end of the tables and stopped.

In front of him was a single bed, a child's coverlet crumpled on top and a teddy bear in the center. To the side was a pile of stuffed animals. A small shelf held folded clothes and a stack of books. And from where he stood, the books made no sense either.

Dobson's Poisons of Choice. Encyclopedia of Natural Herbs. The third title got him too. *Healing for the Unhealed.* He shook his head. "Interesting book selection."

He wandered around this small bedroom set up in a corner and asked, "Did someone crash in here?"

There was no answer.

His gaze went from one book to another book, then back to her. "Were you down here all the time?"

He spun around to look at her, but she said nothing. She just waited in the middle of the room, as if to see if he'd figure it out. He wanted to, but this disjointed set of facts made no sense. There was still one more corner to the room.

He turned to take a closer look. Found a blanket thrown atop something. He reached down and pulled it back, and his heart froze. A chair—like a dentist's chair—but with straps for the legs and one for across the chest. He stared at it. In his mind he realized something was very wrong in all of this, but he just didn't understand what fully.

Behind the chair were shelves. As he walked forward, he

saw the bottles on the shelves, the little tiny labels on each. He read off a series of names and only a few made any sense, because they were poisons, like arsenic. Digitalis. Belladonna. And some were plant names, like oleander, foxglove, cherry laurel. But they were small samples, as if the parents had been running tests.

His gaze ran from the long rows of planter boxes to the child's bed to the chair, and the truth smacked him inside his body—inside his heart, where the facts wrapped around and squeezed so tight he couldn't breathe. He almost collapsed, his hand reaching for the chair for support. Then realizing what he touched, he stepped back, his hands up, warding off the truth. He spun in a circle, his mind cataloging and finally accepting, and slowly, ever-so-slowly, he turned to look at her. And saw the truth in her eyes.

"This was your room?"

She gave a tiny, almost imperceptible nod.

"They strapped you in this chair?" He hoped against hope she would shake her head and say, no, this was just a big joke. Instead her eyes darted away from his.

She gave another tiny nod.

He glanced at all the plants. "That makes no sense. They were famous botanists. They studied plants to heal."

Her eyes stared at him, willing him to make the connection and not force her to say it.

"Did they give you diseases, then heal them?" He shrugged. "That doesn't make any sense and doesn't seem likely."

She said nothing. She just waited.

And then he read the labels on the bottles once more. His mind went *click, click, click.* "Did they grow poisonous plants and test them on you?"

She closed her eyes. They filled with tears, and she nod-ded.

BRAVE MAN. OR stupid man. A man in love was always foolish, but London's actions now went way beyond that. Still he would get what he deserved. She'd kill him and many more if she wasn't stopped.

Maybe that was the way it was supposed to be.

Still he thought when they'd broken up months ago that London would have seen the light. That he was smart enough to stay away from the murderous bitch.

Apparently not.

CHAPTER 16

S HE'D WONDERED HOW long it would take him to realize what she'd been through. Not that he knew everything, but at least he knew something now. He'd get up and walk away. And he'd never come back.

She watched him take the first few steps, sorrow clearly delineated on his features. His hands fisted, his arms and back rigid. She knew how he felt. But she always had anger for her family. When he grabbed her by the shoulders and pulled her into his arms, damn near crushing her against him, she was slow to react. She wasn't sure why he was even still in the room. She felt his chest shake, his shoulders sagging, his chin dropping on top of her head. She knew she was feeling something she didn't understand and couldn't really expect to understand. It was so foreign to her. She slowly raised her arms and wrapped them around him. That's when she realized his chest, his whole body shook. She squeezed her arms tight around him and held him close. "It's okay. It's all right."

He stepped back ever-so-slightly so he could look at her.

She saw the moistness in his eyes, which astonished, shocked and deeply touched her. She reached up to touch a tear just sitting and ready to drop. "It's okay. It was a long time ago."

He shook his head. "This will never be a long time ago.

This is something you live and breathe every day."

She gave him a lopsided grin. "Yeah, precisely. This was my torture. This was my world. It was my shame."

Her voice fell, and she cast her eyes to the floor. The child in her knew she was to blame for this. Her parents had told her often enough. As an adult, she tried to rationalize it away, but she'd thought that, if she'd done better, they wouldn't have done this. If she'd just given them the answers they wanted, the various times they'd asked, they would have let her go.

They said they would. It had taken their deaths for her to realize they never planned to let her go—ever.

London grabbed her chin, tilting it up. "This is not your fault. You were not to blame for this. You are not to be ashamed of this. The people who did this to you are the ones to blame. They are the ones who didn't deserve to have you. They should be ashamed for having done this to a child. To their child." He twisted his head to look at the corner where her bed was. "How long were you here?"

"Years."

He stared at her in shock. "Did you go to school?"

She nodded. "College. I went to college."

"Primary school, secondary school or high school?"

She shook her head. "I was homeschooled here in this room. I finished all my schooling before I was twelve. I did my first degree online. I started my second degree and finished it in person."

"Did they let you out? Did they take you to restaurants or parks or to attend plays or anything?"

She gave a half smile. "Yes, occasionally. When I needed new clothes, new books or schooling supplies, I would travel with them once or twice a year. But here, this was my room.

As I grew bigger, I was allowed in the rest of the basement some of the time. And when I was bad, I was locked in here. That bathroom has a two-way lock. It was mine to use, but I could never leave."

She no longer saw sadness or grief in his voice, no longer saw moistness in his eyes. His hard chin said retribution was at hand. She wished. Because there was nothing anybody could do now.

"How long were you locked in here?"

"Sometimes a week, a month, six months, sometimes longer." She gave him a half smile. "It all depended on how good I was apparently."

"How did you get out? When did this stop?"

She gave a twisted smile and said, "I'm not even sure how I got out. I remember talking to somebody. I was probably delirious when they found me. The police told me that my parents were dead. I was taken to the hospital and checked out. Malnourished and dehydrated but aware. I was sixteen—smart enough to know my life would change forever. And that I needed to keep my mouth shut." She shook her head, wishing she could shake off her memories.

"I needed a family member to take me in, or I'd end up in foster care. I contacted my uncle and told him that I was perfectly capable of taking care of myself, that I already had one college degree and was finishing my second one. All I needed him to do was sign off on the paperwork."

"And he did?" London asked incredulously.

"He asked for one hundred thousand dollars. I gave it to him, and he signed." Her voice was clear. "I paid gladly. I understood the value of money back then, but more so I really understood the value of freedom."

"So, you have been here alone in this house since you

were sixteen?"

"Yes. Slowly but surely trying to integrate into society, trying not to be the weird one. The Internet was a fascinating place for me. I always had computers because I needed schooling. I probably could've contacted somebody for help and asked them to save me. But the fear of retribution stopped me. My father was also a computer geek. He monitored my Internet use." She shook her head. "If they hadn't died, I don't know where I would have ended up. Because, if they had let me out, I'd tell the world what they'd done. They were eminent experts in their field. They had respect. They had good jobs at that point. They had reputations to consider. Very few people even knew I existed."

"I'm glad they're dead," he snapped. "Otherwise I'd commit murder now myself."

She stared, then dropped her gaze.

Silence hung in the air.

He took a step toward her, his hands out. "How did your parents die?" he asked, his tone soft, gentle. But a thread of steel ran through it.

She took a half step backward and came up against the wall. He took a full step forward, his breath warming her face. She tried to ignore the memories of the last time she'd been this close to him. He was so overwhelming, and all she wanted to do was curl up in his arms and believe a normal life with him was possible.

"Fern, how did your parents die?"

"In a car accident." She shrugged. "It's a matter of public record."

He turned her to face him, stooping to see her expression.

She gave him a lopsided smile. "What did you think?

That I poisoned them?"

He shook his head. "No, I don't think you killed anyone."

"But you can't be sure, can you?" She stepped to the side and backed away from the proximity of the memories closing in around her. "After all, I am Dr. Death. That's what I specialize in."

"And the police made good use of your services before you were charged," he acknowledged.

She snorted. "Yeah, they did. For a couple years, I consulted on poison cases. But they turned on me as soon as they had a chance."

"Why is that?"

She shrugged. "I'm not sure. But, once they turned, they turned in a big way."

She walked to the child's bed where she'd spent many a year and stood at the end, staring at it. "They didn't always treat me this way. It started because I was bad."

She heard his breath, his footsteps so soft as he came up behind her; she should've realized he had followed her.

"Bad? A child so bad they should be poisoned?"

"I snuck in here one day without their permission." She shook her head. "What they didn't understand was I had this affinity for the plants. This urge to be near them. I didn't understand that. They didn't understand that. The first time it happened I was only two."

His voice dropped to a deadly tone as he asked, "First time what happened?"

"The first time I helped myself to the pretty flowers down here."

He closed his eyes, and sweat broke out on his forehead. "Are you saying you ate some of the toxic plants?"

She nodded. "My parents freaked. I don't know the full story as they wouldn't talk about it." Her smile turned sad. "I think honestly the scientist in them was triggered. Not only did they want to see what happened to me but they didn't understand why I wasn't hurt by the poison."

"What did you take?"

She chuckled. "I was fascinated with the flowers. They said, when they found me, I was completely covered in the belladonna spore. I had been sitting, nibbling on the flowers, my skin covered in the petals."

He stepped around her slightly so he could look at her. "And are those poisonous?"

She nodded. "But I wasn't terribly discerning. I had leaves in my pockets. I was eating the berries, which are deadly." She shook her head. "There's no rhyme or reason to it. I should've died. But that's when it started."

Walking over to the long counter, she added, "When they found me, I was sound asleep under this counter. I had half a dozen plants all around me. They thought I was dead, I lay so still."

"Of course they rushed you to the hospital and had your stomach pumped." But his tone said he didn't believe it; it would be the truth that he so did not want to hear.

She walked toward the empty tables. "Not at all. Because then, of course, they'd have to explain how their daughter got loose in a roomful of poisonous plants."

Half under his breath but loud enough for her to hear, he said, "Right, of course not. That would be way too simple for proper parents. And they blamed you for that?"

"They both did. But, like I said, they were scientists. I should've been dead a dozen times over. Not only did I survive, I flourished." She held out her hands. "Essentially I haven't found a plant yet that hurts me. My body has an affinity for poisonous plants. I don't know why. I don't know how. I know Stefan is certainly intrigued by the concept but for a whole different reason. But whatever this affinity is, when people give me poison, my body accepts it with joy instead."

She turned and walked out the door, leaving him standing in shock. She walked upstairs to the kitchen. When she turned around, she watched him standing in the doorway, his hand on the frame as if for support. She walked closer and asked, "You okay?"

She reached out a hand for him, but he grabbed it, making sure she stayed right here. "Did you just say, when *people* give you poison?"

"Yes." She frowned. "My parents fed me poisons all the time. All different kinds. And they documented every symptom—every itch, rash, sniffle. They took samples of blood, skin, mucus, tissue, hair and checked it under the microscopes."

"Was it *just* your parents giving you poison?" he snapped. "Or has somebody else tried to kill you?"

She stared at him for a long moment. "There have been other attempts."

His hands went immediately to cover his eyes. When he pulled them away, he asked, "How many attempts?"

She nodded slowly. "Once at the beginning of the court case and once at the end."

"And you didn't tell anyone?"

"Who was I to tell? Who gave a shit? If I was dead, the whole trial, everything would just go away. It would have saved our taxpayers thousands of dollars. So who cared?" she added.

"Do you know who did it?"

She lifted her face with a shuttered look, wondering what could be achieved by telling him the truth. Could he handle it? She shrugged. "I have a good idea of at least one person."

"How could you know who poisoned you and do nothing about it?"

"Because he poisoned himself at the same time," she said.

His eyes grew wide; then he glared at her. But in the back of his mind was that *click* of knowledge. As if he suddenly understood whom and what she was talking about. He held out a hand toward her as if reaching for support. She grasped his hand. He asked in a low voice, "Was it Derek?"

She gave a decisive nod. "Of course it was. I thought you knew."

He stared at her. "You thought I knew he tried to kill you?"

She shrugged. "Sure. He said he would tell you. It was his answer when I questioned him about trying to poison me. I knew he would tell you that I poisoned him instead. But in truth he poisoned my coffee. I told him how I saw the poison in it, and he said that was a lie and dared me to have some." She shrugged. "I didn't care one way or another. I picked it up and drank it. Then I held it out to him and told him I would survive, but I didn't know about him." She paused. "That's when he said it didn't matter if he survived or not because the police would find his dead body and that would lead them back to me as the killer. And he drank his too."

She could tell from London's face that he knew an exchange like that was all too possible.

"Why would you drink the poisoned coffee?"

"Because, like I said, I have an affinity for it. My body likes the stuff. It's like getting a shot of nectar from the flower. His body, on the other hand—of course, as you well know—has been in a decline since."

"Weren't you terrified he'd die and you'd be blamed?"

She pulled out her phone, went back to some videos she had kept and hit Play. Derek's voice filled the air. London listened to the conversation she'd recorded. Derek shouted at the end, saying she'd be charged for his murder.

"That's my proof. If I was ever charged or asked about his death, I would've just played this."

He stared at her phone as if it was poisonous itself.

She turned and walked to the coffeemaker. She had considered Derek might be the one after her now, but she doubted he had the strength. Had he searched for a treatment? Or was he suffering on his own? Had he even connected his current condition to his attempt to poison her?

"Why didn't you tell me?"

She hit the coffee button to start the brew dripping and turned, leaning against the counter. She stared at him. "Why would I? You lived in your perfect little world. You love your brother, thought the world of him, and you'd never believe he'd kill me."

"You hit Stop on the video. What else happened after that?"

She gave him a flat stare. "I'm not telling you."

He took two strident steps forward. "Why not?"

"Because it's personal."

"I'd like to hear it." He shoved his hands in his pockets, and she had to admit he was handling everything decently.

When someone finds out their brother was an attempted murderer and suicidal, it did tend to rock the boat. She'd had months to deal with Derek's betrayal, whereas London was just now hearing about it. She wondered if she should tell him the rest, then decided *what the hell.* She pulled up the video and hit Play, letting it resume.

"Why are you doing this?" she asked Derek on the video.

"Because that's what you deserve."

"I didn't kill anyone."

"Maybe you haven't, until now. Maybe I'll be your first. But, if I can keep London away from you, I don't care."

"You don't want London to be happy?"

"He can go find his own girlfriend."

"But you didn't want me anymore. When I broke up with you, you were relieved."

"Because there's something off about you. We never got to bed. Who does that? Currently everybody has sex first."

"We didn't go to bed because you never had a sex drive that would get us there," she said softly. "You kept coming up with excuses."

London watched the two of them in the video as Derek shoved his face closer to hers and said, "Because I can't sleep with a freak."

Fern winced, watching her reflection take the emotional hit in a stony manner. "Then why did you ask me to marry you?"

"I wanted to be engaged to you. I thought the thrill would add to the excitement. But instead it terrified me. I was afraid I wouldn't survive the night."

In the video, she shook her head. "So then you tried to kill me and even yourself."

"I hate myself. I wanted to take you to bed. I wanted to

show all the guys I was strong enough, brave enough to sleep with Dr. Death. They all thought I was. But I knew I wasn't. I was a fraud. So, as much as I hate you, I hate myself even more."

"And yet you won't let London have a relationship with me."

"No. Because London *is* strong enough. He won't give a shit about what anybody else says. If he wants to take Dr. Death to bed, he'll take her to bed and handle the consequences."

Fern hit the button on the video. Then she pocketed her phone.

London stared at her and then at the pocket where the phone was. "You never slept with him?"

She shook her head. "I'm not sure he could perform at all."

"So why were you engaged?" His voice dropped, his gaze deepened, heat warmed the deep dark depths.

"Because I was tired of being alone."

LONDON CLOSED HIS eyes. The shock waves kept slamming into him. They hurt on so many levels. When he opened his eyes again, he studied her bent head, wondering what the last admission had cost her. He couldn't believe his brother had tried to murder her, and she accepted that as if it were a just punishment. To be so lonely that she would get engaged to somebody she didn't love and who didn't love her in return? What the hell was wrong with his goddamned brother? He shook his head. "My brother is a fool."

She snorted and turned her back on him. She reached for the coffeepot and poured two cups. He watched her go through the motions, seeing the tremor running through her fingers. She wasn't unaffected, but she'd spent so long trying to appear as if nothing mattered that she was doing a damn decent job of it. He had to admit he was ecstatic she had never gone to bed with his brother. That part had always bothered him. He'd have gotten over it, but there would always be that little bit of jealousy. That his brother had gotten to spend special time with her, when London wanted every single minute of her day, every single moment of her time. To hear the videotape she had … "Is he dying?"

"Most likely."

He took a deep breath at that. His brother had been in a steady decline. But to think he'd brought it on himself … "You said someone tried to poison you after the court case. Was it him too?"

"I can't be sure about that. But it's possible."

"Tell me what happened."

"I was alone in a room, waiting for the lawyer to return. I'd been acquitted and would be released from the courthouse, but we were waiting for the crowds to die down. The media circus was outside, and my attorney wanted to go over the media statement we would give. He carried a tray with coffee and a couple doughnuts from one of the rooms. He was excited, talking a mile a minute. He took the coffee cups off the tray and put them on the table. I looked at him. I knew that one of the coffees had poison in it. I saw a hint of green around it. I studied it and then asked, "Where did you get the coffee?"

"At the courtroom cafeteria," he said. "The guys were handing them out."

"Did you see who handed them to you?" I asked him.

"Yes." He shook his head and said, "I didn't recognize

the man who gave it to me. But I got one with double cream for me, and yours is black."

I nodded and asked, "Did you tell him it was for me?"

He grinned and said, "I did, indeed." The smile fell off his face as he studied mine. "Why? What's wrong?"

I gave him a half smile and said, "It doesn't matter."

She turned back to London, her expression cleared of the long-ago memory and said, "I drank the entire cupful. Like I said, my body likes it."

For London, it was like the world had fallen out from under him. He just couldn't comprehend her body could handle so much poison or that she could be so nonchalant about people trying to kill her. What if they used a gun next time?

"Was my brother there at the time?"

"He certainly was. Where he went afterward, I didn't see. Why would I give a shit about that?"

"Did you tell the lawyer?"

"No," she said in a soft voice. "I kept that to myself."

He stepped to the side so he saw her face. "Please tell me you still have the cup."

She glanced at him in surprise and then nodded at the closet. She walked to the front hallway and pulled out a box. He hadn't seen this one before. She took it to the kitchen table and dropped it there. "This is everything I have from the trial. The cup is in here."

He opened the lid. Inside were files and court documents. Several disposable cups in plastic bags. He turned to study her and asked, "Are all these poisoned?"

"No, not at all. I didn't think about it. I threw it all in the box just in case and walked away."

He glanced at the contents and asked, "Is it safe for me

to touch?"

"Don't open any of the bags."

He reached forward hesitantly and lifted a bag with a small take-out cup inside of it. "Is this the poisoned one?"

Her face hardened. "Yes. For all the good it will do."

"We might find fingerprints on it."

"You might," she said cheerfully. "If you can, thank you."

She grabbed her coffee cup, pushed open the kitchen door and stepped into the backyard.

He came behind her and said, "How can you be so calm about the whole thing?"

"Because I've had a long time to deal with this," she snapped. "Look at all those stupid threatening letters you took to the police. I lived with that. Day in, day out, it was shoved down my throat, filled my dreams. Every waking moment was filled with hatred from people I didn't know, directed at me." She shook her head. "When I went to England, I walked away from it all. Over there I could start fresh. And they welcomed me. They didn't treat me like I was dirt or something to be taken out back to put in the trash. My knowledge was respected, not violated, and I made new friends. But it was always there in the background."

He couldn't imagine. He bent his head, pinched the bridge of his nose and whispered, "Jesus Christ, how did you survive?"

"I survived the way I always have. By pulling inside and existing alone. I've been alone one way or another most of my life. Do you think being in that basement was fun while my parents plied me with poisons, knowing I wouldn't die, but I would possibly show reactions they could document and further research? But I did it. I went through it. I loved them anyway. Even in spite of my hate for them. When they died, it freed me from a life in their prison."

"Do you wish they were still alive?" he murmured. "If they were, I would kill them myself."

"I think someone beat you to it." Her voice dropped as she added, "Honestly the official verdict is that they died in a car crash, but I'm pretty sure they were murdered."

CHAPTER 17

THE LOOK ON his face was something else. She stared at him in surprise; then a warm feeling swelled within. "You really care, don't you?"

He stared at her and gave an abrupt nod. "Always have. But I struggled knowing you were keeping big secrets. It made it feel like I was only connecting to half of you."

"Secrets were the norm in my world," she said quietly. "My parents did warn me constantly that I couldn't tell people I was living in the basement or about the chair with the straps or about the poisons." She shrugged. "Not that I had much chance to talk to anyone. Silence had become the norm. Life came every damn day, yet it didn't give me a chance to figure out how to fix it. When my stomach was retching from the headaches, the cold sweats or from the hallucinogenic dreams and I wanted it all to stop, morning always came."

Her mind returned to all the faraway memories she thought she'd looked away from. The days of waking up and hating how she was once again alive. Determined to find another way out of this existence, hoping that overdosing the next time would work. And yet none of them were viable options because what was she but a child? Nobody called the authorities and stopped her parents. Something else he wouldn't understand either.

"Unbelievable." He leaned against the porch railing. She joined him.

"You must remember this was the only life I knew. I thought every other child in the world lived in their basement with parents doing similar things to them. That every doctor and nurse and teacher went home and did this to their kids. On the surface I was normal. Just like they all were. So I assumed, because I wasn't normal on the inside, they weren't either. There isn't anything easy about growing up like that. But it was natural. When something is so natural it doesn't matter how bad it is, you still prefer it over the unknown options. Where was I to go? Foster care? No, it was better for me to succeed. To thrive, become better than they expected. And that I could do. My parents did change some over the years." She frowned, trying to remember how. "Changed experiments in some cases."

He pounced. "How? Why?"

She gave him a quizzical look and asked, "What about me is different from other women?" She held his gaze as he studied her eyes, trying to see if she was serious.

She was serious. He shrugged. "Well, your skin for one. There's something very otherworldly about it. It's creamy and smooth and soft, with an odd glow to it."

She nodded. "What else?" She realized he was uncomfortable. That wasn't what she wanted. "Honestly, what else is different?"

"Your hair. Your hair has this look to it. The whole package almost gives you an odd fey look. It's incredibly attractive. Like you're some kind of fairy creature." He looked foolish, embarrassed. "I don't know how to describe it. Your eyes, everything about you, just give you something slightly different than other women I know."

She chuckled. "And now you know it's from a lifetime of eating poison. You are right. All three of those things are very different, as are my nails. She held out her long nails in front of him, bending the nails forward and backward. She heard his gasp, saw him wince in pain. She chuckled. "I can't feel any of it. These probably aren't the only things that are different." She shrugged. "There's nothing I can do about it. They are what they are." She stared out at the backyard and added, "I considered suicide at one time."

He turned her to face him. "Don't talk like that."

She gave him a sad smile. "Why? I don't have anyone to discuss it with. When I said I'm alone, I meant I have been alone *most* of the time."

"But you're not alone anymore. So stop saying that. Stop trying to distance yourself, putting up a barrier between the two of us. It won't work."

She jutted out her chin. "You can't stop me."

He shook his head, and his mood dropped the atmosphere around them, instantly changing from heated and dark to hot and electrified. "Maybe I won't stop you. Maybe life with you is the only way I can live. Maybe if you kill yourself, I'll kill myself."

She snorted. "What good will that do anybody?"

"Exactly." He lowered his head, sliding his hands to cup her face, his palms holding her jaws, his thumbs gently stroking across her cheeks. Just before his lips touched hers, he whispered, "You might have been alone then, but you're not anymore. If you take yourself out of the equation, you'd leave me to live alone for the rest of my life. Don't do that, please." Then he kissed her.

The touch of his lips sent myriad emotions into her so fast she didn't know what was coming at her. From rage and passion to loss and regret to hope, all of it wrapped up, pleading and grasping for love. Her body was buffeted by his energy that slammed into her. He held her close, his hands holding her head locked against him. She couldn't have moved if she'd wanted to. Her hands gripped his forearms hard as he deepened the kiss as if stealing into the very soul of her. As if to make sure she couldn't walk away and leave him alone. As if, by pouring himself deeper, harder, and more passionately into her body, she would realize she couldn't do anything without him.

And, for once, she realized she really didn't want to. But how could she trust he'd be there for her when he hadn't been before? How could she trust he wouldn't walk away, or worse, throw her under the bus like his brother had? If she did trust him this one time, would he look at her as a freak? The closer they got to making love, she wondered if he wouldn't consider the same thing. She wanted to fight against it. She wanted to tell her body to behave. But there was no controlling, no tempering this.

She pressed against him, her body pinned against the railing along the back porch, her legs between his thighs as he held her firm in his embrace. She could feel his erection surging between them. She marveled at it. She'd treated her virginity like the group of girls she'd known at the time. They got rid of it as fast as they could. She'd done the same thing, trying to figure what all the fuss was about. She hadn't enjoyed sex. She'd loved being held afterward, but the actual process was messy, uncomfortable, slightly painful and embarrassing as hell. Being held in her lover's arms afterward had been the best of everything. Just some things in life one did to get to the payoff, she presumed.

Not this time.

She could feel the dampness between her thighs. Her breath came in small gasps as he traced his lips along her cheek to her ear, where he gently circled it with his tongue. His warm breath shuddered through her, feeding her warmth, adding comfort and peace, in contrast to the cold she'd held for so long. She let out a shaky breath, her hand clutching at his shirt. Her body trembling with new awareness.

He wrapped her up close and held her against his chest, his head resting on top of hers. "Easy. Take it easy."

That's when she realized she was trembling so badly her body didn't know if she should jump his bones or collapse to the floor and burst into tears.

"How do I deal with this?" she whispered. "With these feelings?"

He tilted her head back and considered her eyes. "You don't deal with them. You just let it happen. Let the gates open. Let the flood flow." He lowered his head again, and, just above her lips, he whispered, "Do it now. Feel your body's need."

She stared at him, not sure she understood what she was supposed to do.

"Let go of the control. Let go of the restraint you used in your life until now. Release who you really are inside. Just. Let. Go."

And he took her lips with a passion she'd never felt before. It drove in spikes through her spine to pool in her belly. Her breasts swelled, tension twisting deep inside her. She got one leg outside his and wrapped around his hips as she rubbed against the ridge at her groin. He reached down and cupped her rear, pulling her to him, hard. He slid his tongue into her mouth, gently rubbed against her, coaxing, teasing, demanding a response.

She whimpered. Her arms wrapped around his head as she cried out for something, she knew not what.

"Let go," he whispered.

His lips trailed her throat to the open neck of her shirt, his tongue leaving fiery pathways on her sensitized skin. She groped his chest; he pinned her against the railing. His body was exactly where she needed him—only they were both fully clothed. She cried out in frustration.

He cupped her breasts and squeezed gently, his tongue sliding inside her mouth, in, out, in, out.

She shuddered.

"Let go."

"I can't."

"You can. I'll be here. I'll catch you."

She shook her head, crying out, "I can't. Don't you understand? I can't."

But he wasn't listening. He looked into her eyes. She could barely see—blind with passion, knowing they could go anywhere; yet frustrated, torn, her body thrust against his with a need she'd never felt before.

He whispered, "I love you." He whispered, "Not just for now—forever."

Her gaze locked on his. She heard the words with wonder. She studied him. He smiled one of the gentlest, softest, most caring smiles she'd ever seen before.

"Yes, it's true," he whispered.

She was so desperate to believe him. She didn't want to be alone anymore. Her life was so cold, so lonely, so lost.

"Believe," he whispered, his lips at her temple. "Trust." He dropped kisses on her eyelids, her nose, her chin.

"Let go." And then he repeated, "I love you," before he

took her mouth in a mind-searing kiss.

Her body exploded into a million shards of experience—fired by his passion, completed by his words. And knowing that, … for the first time in her life, she was no longer alone.

When it was over, he'd picked her up, twisted her around and held her close while he sat perched against the veranda railing and just cradled her in his arms.

When she could, she lifted her head and said more than a little shyly, "Why would you do that?"

"Because you needed it. Because we needed it. Because I promise I will always do what's best for you from now on."

She laid her head against his chest. She so wanted to believe in him. She wanted to trust him. But how did she do that after all they'd been through? She should be embarrassed. She should be mortified. Instead she felt so damn good, and none of it mattered.

THAT WASN'T WHAT he intended to do. But she was so tense, so wired, so completely unaware of how close to the edge she was living.

When he first touched her, passion erupted inside her.

The same as it always had been. He never had a chance to drink fully from the well. Her sweetness and light touched him so much at the time that he'd been shocked, overwhelmed and enticed, but he'd been slow to make his move. More concerned about making sure she was all right that it was him, not his brother, who held her.

The last thing he wanted was to have her imagine Derek holding her and not London.

She slipped out of his arms. He reached for her, figuring out how to take her from where they'd been to where they currently were, without making her uncomfortable. Hell, his own need screamed at him.

She spun out of his arms and turned to stare at him. "What did I just hear?"

He froze, tilted his head and said, "I didn't hear anything."

She shook her head, bolted into the house. He raced behind her. Glass shattered, followed by sounds of something rolling. He'd heard similar sounds too many times in his life. He picked up speed, tried to grab her. Only to find her spinning and pushing him back out again.

She screamed, "Run. Run."

"Not without you." He grabbed her hand and hauled her back toward the back of the yard. "Come on."

She pulled free and yelled, "Get out before it kills you. Find the man who did this."

He gave her a startled look and saw the fog, a white cloud coming behind her. He shook his head. "It'll kill you."

She gave him a sad smile. "I'm not sure anything can kill me."

She pushed him once more out onto the deck and slammed the door. Through the door she yelled, "Keep going. You need to be well away from the house."

He bolted to the far side of the yard, feeling like a coward. He spun around and grabbed his phone, punching in Steve's number. "I don't know what the hell just happened, but it's like a smoke canister shot into her house. She said it was poison and screamed for me to get out."

"Is she with you?" Steve asked in alarm.

"She locked the door behind me. She's still inside."

Silence was on the other end, then Steve said, "Why would she do that?"

London shook his head. "I have no idea. I'm heading to the front of the house now." His feet were already on the move as he raced around the side of the house. In front of him he heard an engine turn on, power up and race past him.

He didn't get a look at the driver, but it was a private car with no logo on the side of the vehicle. Nothing to discern who and what owned it. The license plate was covered. He had no way to track it.

"You're still there? What the hell's going on?" Steve yelled into his ear.

"I don't know, but another attempt was just made on her life."

"What do you mean by another attempt?"

"She told me some things today. Someone tried to poison her in the courthouse after she was acquitted. Apparently my own asshole of a brother tried to poison her before the trial started."

Steve's voice faded in and out. "I'm in a vehicle heading toward you."

London raced up the front steps, putting his phone away. The front window had been broken as the smoke bomb, or whatever the hell was, had been thrown in. He was at the front door but had no way to get in. It was locked. He took his jacket off, and, using it as a protection, he widened the hole in the living room window.

He raised his nose, sniffing for the gas. He didn't smell anything. He stepped inside, his boots crunching on the glass underfoot. He raced to the kitchen where he last saw her. She lay on the kitchen floor, her hand wrapped around the canister. Her skin was white, waxy. She looked more fairy dust than human.

He reached out a hand, placing it on her neck and felt no pulse. "No," he roared.

He punched in the number for emergency. Just as the call connected to dispatch, the front door burst open. He spun, expecting to face a new threat, but the doorway was empty. London had this weird feeling, as if a conversation was going on around him. As if somebody was here, but he couldn't see who. He straightened and yelled out, "Who's there?"

Gun out, he spun around, searching the front of the house. And the same thing happened again. He felt the presence of someone. "What the hell's going on?"

The room filled with weird colors, weird energy and weird everything. He reached out a hand as if to touch something and almost had a heart attack when it looked like a hand reached back. He jumped backward and said, "Who are you? What the hell's going on?"

Then a burst of air hit him. But he couldn't quite figure out what he saw or what he heard. He stepped forward only to come up against a barrier he couldn't cross. He tried to force his way through, but he appeared to be up against a glass wall that he couldn't see—with Fern on the other side. The colors on the other side built and glowed. He stopped and stared, his jaw falling open as he realized, for the first time, that maybe something was alien about Fern. Maybe she wasn't even of this world. He didn't understand. Questions pounded through him. And whoever it was, whatever *this* was, it was trying to help her.

The voice whispered through his head. *Step back. We're burning too much energy keeping you out.*

Instinctively he took a step back. His hands came up defensively. "I only want to help her."

That's what we're doing.

"She said there wasn't a poison that could kill her."

When people mix cocktails and add unnatural stuff to them, they might not kill her, but it could put her in a coma for the rest of her life.

His hands dropped, and he stared in shock. "Please help her."

We are.

With that Fern rolled to her back and opened her eyes. She glanced around and smiled. "Stefan, Dr. Maddy. Both to the rescue again."

London heard the words but struggled to make sense of it. Had that been Stefan's voice? How the hell did that work?

He'd heard the rumors. In law enforcement, Stefan's name was legendary. But London had always tossed it off as being something blown out of proportion.

Of course Dr. Maddy was an icon. All was very hush-hush, but the stories about her were incredible and had grown over time. To the extent that they opened a new wing in the hospital where children of all ages and nationalities with different illnesses came and were miraculously healed. The hospital did their best to keep the news quiet. The media had some agreement to keep it all quiet also. Apparently negativity affected the healing of those within. And he realized that, if anybody could help Fern, it was Dr. Maddy.

"Will she be okay?"

A male voice slid through his mind again. *She'll be fine now.*

"I don't understand." London pointed at the canister Fern held in her palm. "That was poison in the canister?"

Yes, it was.

"So someone is trying to kill her?"

Maybe. Stefan's voice was harder to hear and getting fainter.

"Wait," London called. "Don't leave without giving me some answers."

The answers are for you to find. You've broken through some of her barriers. But now you need to keep her safe. Those poisons from that canister should never have made it into her house. She would've seen and heard that well before.

London felt a shock, the guilt like a blow to his heart. "I didn't know."

Neither did she, Stefan said softly. *She's opened herself up to another, and that's weakened her shield. She lowered her defenses and let you in, so now you must keep her safe.*

He shook his head. "What could I do to keep her safe when she can neutralize poisons?"

She doesn't neutralize them. She absorbs them. Her act here wasn't to save her own life. She did what she did, knowing a foreign substance was in this cocktail, to keep you safe. She didn't think about it. She just instinctively sucked it all into her energy, into her lungs and her body, in the hope her act would save your life.

London spun and said, "No way the poison has been contained. It should be everywhere. It should be all around us. I should be dead."

And you would've been if she hadn't taken it all inside her energy field. She has an affinity to poison, that's true. Like a drug addict.

And, with that, the male voice left his mind, leaving London standing in shock. Lost. Guilty.

A woman's gentle voice whispered through his mind and said, *Don't feel guilty. She let you in. It is a bond you had before this nightmare began. So it was much easier for you to break through her defenses now. She's always had a weakness for you. And that weakness still exists. She forged the wall closed again with no hope of a future with you. But it was never as strong. Now it's open. She hasn't had time to put a barrier around both of you to enclose you within her inner circle.*

London didn't know what to say. This was such a foreign concept he didn't know how to make it work.

There's nothing to make work, the woman said, obviously capable of reading his mind. *What you must understand is what she did was a selfish act. One of love.*

And the voice faded. Along with the fading came a snap and crackle, as if energy around him changed. He did a slow circle, figuring out what just happened. When he turned to stare at Fern, she was sitting up, her gaze deep, fathomless. The green in her eyes was like bejeweled emeralds. Her skin was even more translucent.

She shook her head. "I'm sorry you had to see that."

He fell to his knees beside her, clasping her hand. As soon as he touched her, there was an odd zing. She pulled her hand back and smiled, scooting along the floor to put distance between them.

"Oh, no, you don't. You're not backing away from me now." Her wary look made his heart break. "You're not alone anymore. Especially not after Stefan and Dr. Maddy were just here."

Her eyebrows rose. "Did you see them?"

He shook his head. "I don't know what the hell I saw. I saw colors. I reached out a hand, and it looked like a hand reached back."

A small smile played at the corner of her lips. "It can be pretty traumatic the first time."

"And they spoke to me," London said in a low voice. "Or I'm losing my mind."

Her voice was soft as a whisper. "No, you're not losing it. They're telepathic. Even if you don't want to, they can communicate with you. Both are so damn strong in what they can do. And every year, every day that they're out there doing what they're doing, they get stronger and stronger."

"Are you like them?"

She shook her head. "No, I'm not like them at all."

He hated that he was relieved to hear that. There must have been a flicker in his face because she nodded as if confirming something to herself.

Using the counter, she pulled herself to her feet and said, "I might be weird, but I'm not completely nuts."

DID THEY LIKE his gift? As a test subject, she was fascinating to work on. Of course she had no idea she was being tested. He'd seen her walk past the windows so knew she'd survived. How?

There'd been enough poison in there to kill several full-size men.

And she was just a slip of a woman.

So, what skills or adaptations did she have to survive something like that? There was a slim chance the canister hadn't opened as expected—mechanical failures were something he had to deal with on occasion. As irritating as it was, he couldn't quite get away from it.

Still, that wasn't likely in this case. He'd seen the cloud. He knew she'd been exposed.

So how had she survived?

He wanted to knock her out and throw her into his lab so he could find out.

Soon. Very soon.

CHAPTER 18

H E LOOKED LIKE he'd been shell-shocked. Then she felt that way too. She slowly stood up, feeling her body less solid than ever. That was something she had yet to share with anyone. Every time she ingested poison, she became more one with it. One with the plant world around her and a whole lot less than who she was before. It was an odd feeling and hard, if not impossible, to describe. She walked a few steps to the couch and collapsed.

Instantly London was at her side. "How are you feeling?"

She gave him a wan smile. "I'll be fine. It just takes a few minutes to regroup."

"Regroup?" he asked in disbelief. "Is that what you call this?"

She studied him carefully. "What would you call it?"

"Recover. Heal." His voice held confusion and bewilderment. "Although I'm still not close to adjusting to the shock."

At a heavy pounding on the front door, London jumped to his feet. But she didn't move. It took energy to move. Not much was left. She watched as Steve blasted into the room as if expecting major trouble. He came to a stumbling stop when he saw her sitting calmly on the couch.

He bent in front of her and asked, "Are you okay?" His gaze zipped to London. "What the hell happened here? You were talking about poison and canisters and all kinds of shit. I came as fast as I could, and yet I see you both, looking like nothing's wrong."

London pointed to the canister on the floor, in the other room. Steve straightened so he could look. He froze and stared at it. "What the hell is that?"

"Some kind of special gas canister." London shook his head. "I don't know if it's army issue or made special for today, but I'd sure like to know who sent it."

Steve looked at Fern. "Is it safe to approach it?"

She shrugged. "I think so."

He turned to London. "Let's get it to the lab."

London walked into the kitchen. An empty grocery bag sat on the counter. London grabbed it and went back to the canister. He held it for them to study. No logo, no serial numbers. Nothing to identify where it was made or by whom. He turned it upside down, and she tapped the AMAX logo on the bottom. London took a deep breath. "Well, that's not good. That's Dr. Sartain's pharmaceutical company."

Steve asked, "How did somebody get hold of a weapon like this?"

London looked at him. "Have you seen one of those before?"

Steve nodded thoughtfully. "Yes, only I'm not exactly sure where. This one is bigger than those I've seen though. I thought the top was supposed to come completely off, but this just separated, allowing the gas to escape."

"It could be a new model." London put it on the coffee table gently.

She watched as London took pictures of the canister. When he was done, she picked it up, making sure no one would get hurt. It appeared empty. London could take it to the lab, though she doubted they'd find anything. As she replaced it on the coffee table, her arms trembled with the effort. Not sick, not injured, but the blast had shaken her. Dr. Maddy had done her best, but Fern would need time.

She moved toward the stairway. "You two can discuss the merits of that canister some other place. I'm heading to bed. Let yourselves out please."

London rushed up behind her. "I'm not leaving."

She gave him a hard glance. "Yes. You are." She needed to make sure he understood it wasn't safe for him here. She glanced at Steve. "Take him and the canister." With that she motioned toward the front door.

There was a hard silence. London shook his head. "No way in hell am I leaving you here alone. Somebody just tried to kill you."

"And they didn't succeed. I'm going to bed before anybody makes another attempt. I doubt anyone is stupid enough to come back again tonight." She grew weaker. And then she decided she didn't give a shit if either of them left or not. She continued upstairs and headed for her bedroom. At the doorway, she stopped to stare at her bed.

It was still unmade, still full of suitcases. She bowed her head. Her legs barely held her up. She briefly contemplated going to one of the two spare bedrooms at the opposite end of the long hallway and lying down there. But even that would be too much effort. She walked to her bed and dragged one of the suitcases off the surface and onto the floor. Then dumped the second one beside it.

The blanket was crumpled underneath. She tossed it straight across the bed and lay down on top, grabbing the corner, and rolled herself up. When Dr. Maddy had said it would be like a blast had hit her, she wasn't kidding.

Just healing energy ran through her system right now, so she didn't know where she started and where she stopped. She figured, if she could have a few minutes alone to sort through the images, the energy and the poisons, maybe she could learn something. But she was so exhausted she doubted it would be possible. As soon as her head hit the pillow, she zoned out.

She wasn't asleep, but she wasn't awake.

She was caught in-between.

After a few minutes of lying in a fog, she got up to lock her bedroom door, intent on keeping London out. She didn't know why it was so important. Except she wanted him to be safe.

She leaned against the door and suddenly found herself on the other side of it. She froze and glanced back, but the door was solid behind her. She stared at her hands. She was glowing green as if her whole body was infused with a poisonous air. Which of course it was.

Most of the time she looked normal. Acted normal. Not many knew she needed a diet of poisons to keep her system functioning. The doctors would lock her up in a mental hospital if they had any idea.

At least half of them would. The other half would put her in a lab and run as many tests on her as they could, like her parents had.

She walked to the top of the landing, not exactly sure what was happening to her body. She stared out the front windows and watched as Steve got into his vehicle. He had the canister with him. But he was alone. He reversed down the driveway and headed along the street out of sight. She bowed her head, so not ready to deal with London. But he wouldn't give her any choice as she heard his footsteps coming up the stairs. She turned to face him and realized he didn't see her. He walked right past her and headed to her bedroom. He pushed the door open wide and stepped inside.

She raced behind him, calling out, "Why didn't you leave?"

He faltered, turning to look down the hall and then back into the bedroom. She watched the frown flicker across his face. She stepped into the bedroom behind him and gasped. He jumped several footsteps to the side and stared at her.

"Can you see me?" she asked.

He shook his head.

"But you can hear me, can't you?"

Wordless, he nodded, his gaze going from her to the bed and then back again, shocked.

Of course he was.

She was too.

Her body lay on the bed. Exhaustion having claimed every part of her, except her soul. Her soul buzzed with the energy of the poison circulating through her system, visible as a green floating gaseous mass separate from the physical form that lay still, waxen like death, on the bed.

She'd heard about this phenomena from Stefan but hadn't expected to experience it herself. She walked over to the bed and lay a hand on her arm. Her skin was cool. She studied her complexion, seeing the eerie look that London had tried to describe.

She sat on the side of the bed. "I'm not even sure I want to go back inside."

Behind her a strangled sound escaped London. "Can you get back inside or are you dead?"

EVER SINCE HE had first met her, his belief system had been pulled from one direction to the other. Was she a murderer? Was she innocent? For a while he worried about this, then he believed the other, only to have his brother drag him back to the opposite side.

Now he sat, facing it all over again.

And so much more.

He stared at Fern's glowing green vision in front of him and the pale white solid body on the bed and realized he had no idea what to believe. The only thought he could latch on to was: he believed in *her*.

"Would you believe you've been right all these years, and everything else you've seen and felt and heard were wrong?" She smiled, but it was sad. "You can get out. You can walk away. You don't ever have to come back."

He stared at her green form. "It's not easy to walk away from a lifetime of knowledge."

"No, but it wasn't a lifetime of knowledge. It was a lifetime of limitation. You don't have to stay in that close safe little box anymore. You can open yourself up to seeing and believing and experiencing so much more. But I'd understand if you can't do this. I understand if this is more than you can take on."

"Too late." His smile was crooked. "I went through a lot during the trial, trying to figure it out. Then you were gone, and I was lost. There were no answers. No closure. Just more questions. Since your return, I've done nothing but make one crazy jump to another." He spread his hand and motioned at her two figures, one ethereal and one physical. "Part of me wants to ignore what I see in front of me right now."

She smiled. "At least if you are seeing what's in front of

you, that's halfway to believing."

She turned toward her body and, in a weird transposition, lay down on top. As he watched, she slowly sank deeper and deeper and deeper into her physical form. He stared, his jaw falling open. How was any of this possible? And then she opened her eyes and stared at him. He jumped back. She gave a gentle sniff. "So, you are afraid of me?"

"You startled me," he protested. "That doesn't mean I'm afraid of you."

"Maybe you should be. I just absorbed all the poison from that gas."

He sank on the side of the bed, close, but not touching her. "I understand that's what you did, but I don't know how."

"That's where your belief will get stretched one more time because I can't really tell you how. I can just tell you that I absorbed it, that my body was happy to take it in."

"Then why did Dr. Maddy step in and help?" he asked sharply. "If it was something you should be doing, something that was good for you, you shouldn't need their help."

"Good point." She shuffled under the blanket and propped up against the headboard. "It's because this time other elements were in that poisonous combination. They are harder for me to deal with."

"Other elements?"

"Synthetics. Chemicals. The poisons I have an affinity for are natural poisons. Poisons which Mother Nature creates on her own. But when man gets involved, they create nasty, horrible concoctions so my system has a much harder time with them. They could probably kill me," she admitted. "But I can't know for sure."

"So, if somebody knows you can't be killed with natural

poisons, have they added the other poisons on purpose?"

She took a deep breath. "That's quite possible. It's also quite possible somebody's testing me. Trying to see exactly what I can do, how much I can absorb, what I will react to."

He sat back and studied her. "Like you're some kind of lab rat?"

She nodded, her gaze solemn. "That occurred to me. Every poison has been a little different. The delivery has been a little different. It's almost as if they can't run legal tests on me, so they're running illegal tests."

"By trying to kill you?"

"And yet is it really trying to kill me? Or are they just seeing what I'm capable of?"

He swallowed hard. How the hell was he to keep her safe from him?

CHAPTER 19

S HE FELT SORRY for London. She'd had time to get used to the strangeness of her reality. But, for him, it was almost impossible to make the leap in understanding. This wasn't logical. This wasn't factual. This wasn't scientific. This was so far to the left it didn't make any sense. By the time she'd come to accept that, she realized there had to be some answer somehow.

But right now, her suspicion was running hot. Was someone using her as a lab rat, as London had so blatantly put it, slowly testing to see what would eventually kill her? She figured they would rather not have her dead but confined to a space where they could do what they wanted for a much longer time. She understood that mentality. After all she had grown up under it. As far as she knew, her parents never said anything to anyone. But how did she know? She'd been a child then. Sworn to silence, punished for any infraction.

Lost in her memories, she stared in surprise as London turned and walked downstairs. She closed her eyes, feeling the hot tears behind them. She didn't want to lose him. The loss of her parents had been devastating in so many ways. But to lose London …

That would cripple her. She bolted to her feet and raced behind him. She didn't say a word. She stared at her hands, happy to see the veins on the backs. Was he hungry? Pizza was a distant memory, but she didn't know how long ago that had been. She walked into the kitchen, not sure if he would stay or if he planned to leave. Such an odd air ran around him that she realized he needed his own space.

Only she couldn't give him much.

She opened the fridge and pulled out the fixings for sandwiches while he sat at the kitchen table, silent, withdrawn, clicking away furiously on his laptop. She made two sandwiches. She carried them to the table and, for some reason, poured a glass of milk for each of them. The childish touch made her smile. That made it worthwhile.

She sat and said, "Eat."

He raised his gaze over the laptop, saw the sandwich with surprise.

"You need to keep your strength up," she added.

"And your strength?"

"I'm working on it," she admitted. She nodded toward the laptop. "What are you researching?"

"Stefan's psychic abilities and astral body projection." He shook his head. "There is so much more to learn ..."

"It'll take a lot of time. The Internet is stuffed full of lots of information and misinformation."

That blue gaze of his pinned her in place. "You've done the research?"

"Ever since I was old enough to ask questions, I've been looking for answers. Once I met Stefan, I had a whole lot more questions. After meeting Dr. Maddy, I had that many more." She gave London a small smile. "Once you travel down that path, it's like this great big black hole sucking you in."

He nodded. "You want to tell me more about what happened to your parents?" London closed the laptop, setting it off to one side and pulling the sandwich closer. "You said you thought they were murdered. But you never said by whom or why."

"I believe it was the pharmaceutical company they worked for."

He froze, his sandwich midair, and stared at her. "What pharmaceutical company?"

"AMAX." She lifted her sandwich and took a big bite.

In contrast, he slowly lowered his to his plate. *Sartain.*

She studied him, glanced at the sandwich, then at him. "Is there something wrong with yours?"

He shook his head. "Why do you think AMAX?"

"My parents were doing research for them. They never really told me too much about it. I remember they signed paperwork here. After they were gone, phone calls came, and the odd person passed by, a lab tech came looking for their research of something in progress but it was presumed burned in the fire. I don't remember who else." She continued to chew. "At one point, he seemed to be very interested in me. I was afraid my parents were doing the research on me for him."

"What do you think now?"

"Pretty damn sure that's exactly what they were doing. After their deaths, several attempts were made to take over my guardianship."

"And what happened?"

"My uncle Jamie knew signing my custody agreement was on the shady side of legal, so it was in his best interests to keep our agreement private. In fact, my attorney kept Jamie's name out of everything and received all correspondence as my agent of record. On the surface, everything had to look normal—I was nobody's fool. I knew somebody was trying to get hold of me. When I turned eighteen, all the documents changed. My lawyer set up my estate to protect me before and after that turning point." She felt London's surprise. "I had time to think about this. A lot of time to think about it."

"Not many kids grow up thinking about how to regain control of their life and keep it their own."

"No? My father talked about it occasionally, saying, if anything happened to them, I would have to be smart and might need a lawyer. I'd already done a lot of research on the law, given my situation. It wasn't something I ever mentioned to him though."

"You have any idea how long before he died when he said this to you?"

"Less than six months."

"Do you think they knew they would die?"

She put down her sandwich, wiped her hands on the paper towel and leaned back. "I think they suspected something was wrong. They changed. They were more nervous, like forever looking over their shoulders. My father went through the house every night to check the bolts on the doors. I don't know if they'd received any threats or just had that intuitive feeling, but they seemed to be much more cautious."

"And yet they didn't do anything to protect you?" He shook his head. "Who was this uncle who you paid?"

She snorted. "Uncle Jamie, my mother's brother. Never met him in person. My lawyer drew up the paperwork."

"Was that ethical on the lawyer's part?

"It wasn't illegal. We needed a contract with Jamie. If he was prepared to be a guardian in name only, nothing else was required. When I turned eighteen, he got an extra bonus to sign off."

London shook his head. "Jesus." But he bit into the sandwich and chewed with obvious enthusiasm.

She watched him for a few moments, slowly picked up her sandwich and continued to eat. She thought about it and knew it probably sounded like something out of a horror flick. A cold, calculating serial killer setting about her goals. "I never touched my parents."

"I wouldn't have blamed you if you had."

"I loved them. Yet hated them. They were all I knew. I was absolutely lost afterward. Angry, confused, defiant, and yet so very lost without the structure my life had been built around before."

"I can imagine. You must have had a hard time making friends."

"I don't think I did. I wasn't a prisoner anymore. I acted like I just moved into town. I changed schools, from online to a physical one, so it would look like I was a new arrival. I'd already researched how I would enter society. It was awkward, confusing and hard. It took a while to adapt, to fit in."

"Why would AMAX have killed them?"

"I think my parents realized they had put me through enough, and, as an up-and-coming adult, how would they keep me locked up forever?"

"You think AMAX wanted them to continue? And, if so, why didn't AMAX kidnap you after your parents were killed?"

"I don't have an answer for that. I wondered about it. But nobody made any attempt that I'm aware of, so I'm not sure." Silence fell on the room. She finished her sandwich while she thought, then said, "I could eat a second one."

"I'm sure you burned a lot of energy doing whatever it was you were doing," he commented. "Go ahead and make a second one."

She smiled, settling back to watch him. "Maybe later. Can you check out my parents' file? See if there's anything of interest there?"

He gave her a slow, thoughtful look. "I already have. I couldn't see anything out of the ordinary in it. AMAX's name didn't come up in it."

"No reason it would," she said calmly. "It wasn't advertised. You'd have to contact the lab where they rented space. Maybe you'd find something there."

"They rented lab space?"

She laughed. "Yes. For their private research they couldn't do elsewhere. And for the longest time I used the same lab but a different room."

"For your research?"

She nodded. "Until I was charged with murder. Then I wasn't deemed the type of customer they wanted creating poisons onsite."

"What type of work did you do?"

"I was looking for plants that were poisonous but, in different formulations, also healed."

"Did you get far?"

"I did for the longest time, but the research still isn't complete."

"Can you start it again? Pick up where you left off?"

She shook her head. "I doubt it. When I was arrested, the media found out about the connection. Protesters were outside the lab space I rented, talking about AMAX helping killers create terrorist weapons." She snorted. "The lab got rid of me very quickly."

She stood up and collected their empty plates. "I don't want to sit here and wait for another attack. Surely we can do something to track down whoever is doing this."

"Let me call Steve, see if he's found anything." He got up, kissed her forehead. "Shouldn't you get some sleep? You've been up all night."

"So have you," she said.

He nodded. "I've caught my second wind. Why don't you try to lay down again while I head back to the office?" He waited for her answer.

She gave him a slight smile and a quick nod.

Then he walked out the door to the back of the deck, his phone in his hand. She washed the few dishes, hating the feeling that she was once again at the whim of other people's actions. She was under attack again—and no one seemed to know by whom or how. And that was unacceptable.

There had to be a way to stop this asshole. And, if the normal cops couldn't help, maybe the other cops could—if there were any psychic cops. Not that Stefan would like that "other" label.

LATER THAT DAY, London walked around the conference room table. The team had gone through the letters, further separating them into piles. They were already doing follow-up phone calls to people who had left names, addresses and contact information. As for the other letters, they could only guess who they were from.

They had separated some letters as per style and type. The ones they took seriously were placed on the side. Unfortunately he saw many more still to go through.

He walked to the end of the table and looked at the pile of his brother's letters. Another stack was off to the far end. He stopped and studied the top one, then picked up the stack and slowly read through them. They were more of the same nasty viciousness, words he'd read earlier. He hadn't seen these, as Steve had looked at some of them himself. But enough were here to make his skin crawl. How she must've felt reading these, realizing how much hatred was directed at her, and for what? Particularly as she was innocent. How fair was that?

"There you are."

He lifted his gaze from the letters to find Steve walking into the room. "Yeah. Sorry. Seems like I've been everywhere but here these past few days."

Steve shrugged. "Can't say it's much of a problem. We're hurrying up and getting nowhere fast. So far the people we contacted about their letters have admitted they sent them and now feel a little on the stupid side. A couple were belligerent, but nothing there to raise a red flag. Nobody had any cause to go any further than writing."

"And this stack?" London asked, shaking the pile in his hands.

"It's the worst of the lot. Those people we are more concerned about. Just too obvious. Chances are something horrific was going on. Whether they went past the letter-writing stage, it's too early to tell. The handwriting expert, Alice, has been all over them."

"Right. But, unless we have something to compare it to, it doesn't make one bit of a difference."

"Yet it could lead us to the killer."

Steve's voice was so cheerful and positive, London was hard-pressed to rain on his parade. Plus, from Steve's tone, he was obviously looking at people, not just at Fern. "I'm glad they are searching for other options. Fern isn't involved."

"She's in the clear," Steve agreed. "She wasn't there when the security guard was killed. She wasn't in town when Reggie was first noted as missing."

Relief washed through London. "Now that is good to know."

"It is. Still a lot of people will find it hard to let go of Fern as their favorite suspect. This softening is not to say she's innocent, only an acknowledgment we could have a second killer."

"I never thought she had anything to do with it," London said.

"Why is that?" Grant Summers walked in and stared at him.

Steve raised an eyebrow but stayed quiet.

London didn't know what Grant's connection was to Fern, but London knew he'd better watch what he said because it would make its way back to her. "I never really believed in the circumstantial evidence or my brother's statement. My brother lied on many issues. So I question whether he said anything truthful on the stand."

Grant froze. "Are you sure he lied?"

London held up his phone. "I need to confirm it. I've been trying to contact him. But he's gone, missing or on the run. Or"—he took a deep breath—"he's dead. I'm afraid he's become another victim."

Grant walked to the far end of the conference room table, picking up the letters London's brother wrote. "What about these? Steve suggested they were your brother's."

London wanted to shoot Steve a questioning glance but

barely restrained himself. "That's part of what I want to talk to Derek about. But, after speaking with Fern today, she disputed pretty much every bit of my brother's statement, from the reason they broke up to his statement to the cops."

Grant studied him with a hard tone. "You know it won't be easy on you if your brother is involved?"

London nodded. "Nothing I can do about his mistakes. He's been making them for a long time."

"Good that you understand that. We need to find him. If he perjured himself, we have to start at the beginning." Grant raised his hand. "Where could he be?"

London shrugged. "He used to have friends, but these last couple months he's been mostly a hermit. His physical health has so greatly declined he's been staying at home most of the time, but he's not there now, and he doesn't own another property, so I have no idea where he has gone. Of course he has some money from our inheritance so could be anywhere." He winced, then decided to share another truth. There'd been enough lies. "According to Fern, my brother tried to poison her."

"Explain," Grant snapped. He pulled out a chair, motioning at the one beside it for London to sit. "When did you hear this, and exactly what did she say?"

London sat, took a moment to collect his thoughts and then tried to encapsulate everything he'd learned so far.

"And the cup that the lawyer gave her? You have it?"

He shook his head. "I saw it. It's at her house in a box. But it's a little hard to prove where that cup came from."

"Unless it still has the lawyer's prints on it." Grant nodded. "That's something we can take care of. At least it would allow us to confirm something she said as being truthful."

London winced. "I think everything she said is truthful.

We've done her a huge disservice. I'm really afraid of what my brother might've done," he added in low tones.

"He's not been himself lately," Steve added quietly.

Grant got to his feet and strode toward the door. "Go find your brother, London. I'll talk to Fern and collect that cup and get a copy of that video. Plus I want you to write down everything you just said, so we have something to refer back to." Grant walked from the room.

London groaned. "Why the hell didn't I tape it when she was telling me?"

"No idea. It would've been good to have. We need a copy of that video she has too." Steve stood. "I'll get you a notepad. Stay put."

London pulled out his phone and sent his brother yet another message.

Where the hell are you?

As usual there was nothing but silence.

HE HADN'T EXPECTED to enjoy watching London agonize over his asshole of a brother. It did give him a spot of pleasure in this dark mission. London was also agonizing over Fern.

London was a fool. And getting to be a bigger one every day. Double the fun.

Still Derek was a loose connection that had to be snipped. No ends left to catch him up.

Still this Derek crap was pissing him off. Even though he'd found him he was being very uncooperative. Yet asked him for a safe place to stay until this blew over. He glanced at his phone, wondering at the sense of meeting with Derek again. He was damn sure he'd get the same answer as before. *Fuck off.*

Talk about unappreciative. Still Derek was just an asshole. And soon he'd be a dead asshole.

CHAPTER 20

S HE WALKED TO the window and placed her hand on the barrier Detective Sutherland had put up. She closed her eyes and called out his name. She felt his jolt of surprise. She opened her eyes, and the connection broke. She closed her eyes, realizing she'd pulled her hand away from the window. Once again back in position, she reached out a second time. *It's Fern.*

I know who you are. I wasn't aware you could reach out and contact me.

His voice was light, amused; apparently he was okay with it all.

What can I do for you?

She took a deep breath. *I know you're a cop in physical form. I just haven't had very much luck with cops myself.* She took another deep, stuttering breath. *So I was wondering if ones—on the other side—if I'd have better luck getting help from other psychic cops.*

She heard his low chuckle.

Damn. She shook her head. *I'm sorry. That was probably a stupid question. I was just so hoping somebody would be capable of tracking this energy on my bed. Or could help me find the person who had been in my house. Or, I don't know, maybe find London's brother so we can get answers from him before he dies.* She released her hand from the window, shaking her head, as if to say, "What the hell." *I'm sorry. I shouldn't have bothered you.*

She walked quickly into the kitchen and poured herself a glass of water. What was going on in her world that she'd even consider contacting them about something like that? The last time she checked, she wasn't completely crazy.

And you're not now.

She froze. *Detective Sutherland?*

Yes. When you contacted me, you opened a pathway between us that makes it easier for me to contact you. And how did you manage to contact me, by the way?

I remembered you touched me to make the energy around the doors and windows tuned to my energy or something like that. And I wondered if I could contact you by touching the same energy tuned to you.

Smart, he said in admiration. *You go to the top of the class.*

Why the hell would that happen? she asked in a mocking voice. *I failed in every other aspect of life.*

No. His voice was hard. *That you have not. What you have done is survive. Sometimes in life that's all any of us can do.*

She leaned on the counter and stared out the window. *That's a terrible way to view life. Is that the only thing I have to look forward to?*

I didn't say that. You only have a little idea of what's available on the other side of life. I must admit there isn't a psychic police force, but that would be a hell of a decent idea. I must run that past Stefan.

And this time there was much less humor from him. *If we can do all this shit, why the hell can't we talk to the dead at will? It would be so much easier to reach out, tap them on the shoulder and ask, Hey, who did this to you?*

He chuckled again. *You realize some people can talk to the dead, right?*

She froze. *People can talk to the dead?*

Within reason. Yes. But, of course, like everything else, it isn't cut and dry.

She spun around, rubbing her forehead. *So not all dead people are in the same place?* She winced as she said that. *Just listen to me. I'm sounding like a crazy person again.*

He hesitated.

She waited, wondering what was bothering him.

My wife, Alex, she's been known to speak with the dead.

Fern froze. *Isn't that like your sister-in-law's ability? Kali? How does your wife find the dead to talk with them?*

A startled silence came from the other side. *I don't have a brother, so I'm not sure who you're talking about. I do have a distant cousin Drew, but I doubt you've met him. Although I do know Kali. She's a search and rescue specialist. My wife has in the past seen and spoken with dead people, but her affinity is toward children. And it's not something she can control. She doesn't call to them, they call to her.*

Oh, my God, that must be terrible.

It is terrible. His voice was low, thoughtful. *Who do you think is my brother?*

She frowned. *Grant Summers, the FBI guy. You could be twins. I assumed you were brothers. Maybe you're cousins instead?*

We aren't related. At least as far as I know. But this time Drew's voice was hesitant, less positive.

She could feel his thoughts turning, like on a big wheel. *Sorry. I just assumed the relation, when I heard you were both involved with Stefan and had such similar features, and I imagined a family relationship.* She shook her head. *But none of that has anything to do with finding the killer of the people who are involved in my case.*

No. My wife is extremely talented, and she does have the ability to help spirits cross over. She often works with Stefan to do just that. Speaking of which, Stefan could possibly find out for you as well.

I got the impression Stefan is very busy.

He is, indeed, Detective Sutherland said. *It's more than that. Thousands of people die every day. They can't all communicate. And even of those that can people like Alex or Stefan can't talk to them. It's a small percentage of dead people that they can talk to. Rarely are they recent deaths.*

Right. And tracking my intruder, that's not so easy either, I presume.

His laughter was back. *And yet look at what you've done already.*

And just like that, he was gone. She reached out mentally for him, but the connection wasn't there. She looked around her kitchen. "So he can access me whenever he wants, but I can't access him whenever I want to? How fair is that?"

"If you don't like it, fix it."

Stefan's voice drifted through the kitchen. Not through her mind but through the kitchen. She walked into the center of the room, looking. "How is it you can do that?"

"The same way you can do it. The same way *you* can follow the killer's energy. The same way you can track the poisons. You must lock on to what you're hearing, what you're seeing and what you're smelling. Forget about the physical limitations of the body you are in and just follow it."

"It's not that easy," she cried out in frustration. "Not all of us can do what you do."

After her outburst, there was dead silence. She raised her hands in frustration. "I'm sorry."

Then a quiet chuckle came.

She glared at the empty space in her kitchen. "You guys are making me crazy."

"What guys?"

"I just talked to Detective Sutherland," she muttered. "He'll probably tell you anyway, but I asked him if there was some kind of a police force on the psychic side of life." She waited for Stefan's laughter. When there wasn't any, she said, "Well, he laughed at me."

"I doubt he laughed *at* you," Stefan said calmly. "I'm sure he was more than startled at the concept, but it's a good one."

"Right, like you can interview people to see how they can police criminals from the other side." She shook her head. "Then I mentioned I thought he and Grant Summers were brothers or at least family in some way they have such similar facial features. I think, by the time he got away from me—which he did rather abruptly, by the way—he was a bit peeved." She was tired, fed up. "I doubt he'll be talking to me very much after this."

Once again silence filled the kitchen.

She spun around in a circle. "You know, when you're in person, it's easy to read cues from your face or your body language. But, when you aren't here, how the hell am I supposed to know what the silence means?"

"What did he say about a family relationship between Grant and himself?" Stefan asked.

"He didn't say a whole lot, just that he didn't have a brother and didn't think they were related in any way. Then

I thought maybe they were cousins, but he said no."

The room warmed up several notches.

She frowned. "How is it that I can feel you smiling?"

He chuckled. "And, if you can *feel* me smiling, you can *see* what your nose is smelling."

"That's confusing," she admitted. "I never tried to explain any of this stuff before."

"You need to find something constructive to do to solve this problem. The cops are doing what they can. They're trying to connect the victims, delving into Pam Akers and the security guard, looking for a motive. They're all over the eight deaths connected with the conservatory."

"Nine, if Reggie is dead."

"When you think of those nine people, is anyone closely connected to you?"

"Reggie. And Ben second."

"Then I want you to drop to the floor right now, so, when you jump out of your body, you won't collapse, and I want you to think about Reggie and Ben."

She froze. "Jump out of my body?"

She heard his sigh.

"Okay, forget about it. Sorry I asked."

She dropped to the floor and sat cross-legged. "If anybody saw me now, they'd know I'm ready for a loony bin."

"Some of us have been there," he admitted. "We won't let anyone think that about you."

She snorted. "You couldn't even save me from the trial, so I highly doubt you could do anything to stop people from thinking I'm crazy."

"How do you know I didn't have anything to do with the trial?" he asked, his voice low, quiet.

Her eyes flew open. "Did you?"

"Who do you think told your defense team to set up the smelling test?"

She stared, a smile breaking free. "Really? You barely knew me."

"There's a lot I know. First, you need to put that nose of yours to work, see the green in your mind, or see Reggie the last time you saw him. Smell the odor you detected at his house, or from your house, whichever is strongest. Go follow it, and don't tell me you can't. When you're done, call me, and we'll discuss what you found."

For the second time that day, another person disconnected from her.

She closed her eyes, thought about the trail she'd seen heading over the fence. Following Stefan's instructions, she sent out her mental thoughts, looking for the way it had gone. Feeling the pathway, she tracked it to the fence line. Once there, she looked over the fence. She could hear his voice in the background, saying, *Don't question everything. Just let it all go.* She needed to do that. So that's what she did. She accepted something was here. Something to learn was available to her.

Learning had always been easy for her. She didn't understand why this was so much trouble. Intuitively she realized it was because her mind was analyzing. Before with her studies, she would always ask questions and look for answers. This time the answers had to be felt. The answers were here, but she had to step out of the way of the analytical part of her brain. In her mind, she could then see where the energy went over the fence. But it was so faint, so distant. Yet she should see more. Do more—at least according to Stefan.

She mentally followed the poisonous trail to the base of the fence where the ivy meandered underneath the wood slats to the far side. Zipping to the other side, she could see where the faint trail continued.

Excited, feeling more positive, another bit of the same green showed up. Not fast, not easy, but as she got to the end of that piece, another piece became visible. And she realized it was like the headlights of a car. She only saw so much at one time. She had to trust as she came to the end that more would show up.

When she made it to the far side of the block, a good dozen houses away from her home, it dissipated into something so thin, so faint it was hard to understand where he'd gone. He came to a stop at the edge of the curb. Excited she opened her eyes and smiled.

She called out gaily to the empty room, "Hey, Stefan. I got to the end."

And what did you find?

"The energy came to a spot alongside the road. I think the person got into a vehicle and drove away."

Good. How far away did you go to see that?

She thought about the distance she had traveled and said, *About a dozen houses.*

Much better. What about the canister downstairs? That energy is newer. But the energy contained in the blast should be still here.

She winced. *Not really. When I absorbed it, I took every-thing inside. I think that means I also took in the energy you would like me to track.*

There was a startled silence beside her. *Very interesting.*

Why's that?

That you can absorb the percussion blast.

It wasn't very much, she exclaimed. *It was just a gas canis-ter.*

True. But his tone was pensive. Contemplative.

She had to wonder for a moment what he was considering. *I don't think I can do something like that with a grenade,* she said.

No, but it would be interesting if somebody could.

Hey, I'm already happy I got out of the backyard to the end of the trail. Let's not go too far, too fast, she joked.

Is there any other incident you can track?

I saw poison around the security guard at the conservatory. But it was mostly contained to him. I saw a little bit of a green trace around him, but there were so many people, I didn't really get enough time to inspect where the green wisp went. Plenty of poison was around the guard though.

Why would somebody do that?

And then came the answer. *So I would be under suspicion? Possibly.*

She shook her head. *That's just bizarre.* She put that tidbit away. *I know that somehow all this fits together, but now it's looking like random chess pieces.*

In this case, when you find the right missing piece, it will all come together.

London's trying to find his brother. Derek has a lot to answer for.

Can you track him? Stefan asked. *You feel strongly enough about it, so you should catch his trail and follow it.*

And with that he disappeared. Into the empty room she called out, "Would you stop disappearing like that? It's really unnerving."

His chuckles were faint as they disappeared.

She shook her head but then obediently closed her eyes. Into the empty room she called out loud, "Derek, where the hell are you?"

She thought about the poison he had used to try to kill her. The poison he had drunk himself. The poison he'd been taking all this time. Poison was her forte. Yet she didn't know about all poisons, and lots of combinations she'd never explored.

Yet when singular natural poisons had been used—like on the recent victims—she could usually isolate them. She stretched out her senses, mentally separating one poison from the other. The killer used arsenic where the security guard had been killed. A visitor had been killed with digitalis, mimicking a heart attack. The maintenance man with some kind of cyanide. She didn't know what poison had been used on Reggie's partner, Pam. Fern wasn't sure the FBI had told her that.

But this poison usage in itself was a connection.

She pulled out her phone and called London. When he answered, she said, "There is one connection between the victims."

"What's that?"

"I think every one of them was killed with a different poison."

WHEN HE ENDED the call, he looked at Steve and said, "Fern brought up the fact that every one of the victims was killed by a different poison. She's making a list of anyone she knows with this kind of skill."

Steve nodded. "Then it's a specialist."

"Maybe a hobbyist who has the time and knowledge and understanding of how to use each of these without affecting themselves."

Grant spoke up from where he sat, studying Derek's

letters. "Did your brother know about poisons?"

London shook his head. "I don't think so."

"You two used to be close."

London sighed. "We were, but our parents were killed just before Fern's trial. It's partly why everything was such a mess. My brother was falling to pieces. I was trying to hold him together, deal with the loss of both parents and handle all the details of the funerals."

Grant's features slightly softened, as if he finally understood how London could've made such a mistake.

"Don't worry. I blame myself," London said in a harsh tone. "Even though she forgives me, I still must forgive myself."

"Sometimes life happens. Nothing we can do except pick ourselves up and carry on."

London nodded, but he knew it wasn't that easy. "She said she'd write a list of everyone she knows in her professional circle who may have some knowledge of these poisons. It's likely to be a big list. But if we cross-reference the locations as to where everybody was at the time these murders occurred," London said, "we should find some answers."

Grant spoke up again. "What was that about her parents?"

London quickly explained. "She believes they were murdered."

Grant studied London's face again.

"Her parents," London said, "if they were alive, would be at the top of the list. Are we sure they are dead?"

"I read the accident report," Grant said. "Nothing suggested murder. That doesn't mean it wasn't. As to whether they are truly dead ..." He shrugged. "We'll take another look at the case to see." Everyone frowned and went back to their work, but their minds were spinning. He could almost hear the collective brain pool searching for answers.

His phone rang. While he answered it, London impulsively pulled up her parents' accident report, found the pathologist's number, then dialed him. The man was respected in his field, and London had spoken with him several times on various cases. Not wanting to disturb the others in the bull pen, he walked to the end of the hallway. "Dr. Horton, this is London. I'm looking into a closed case from twelve years ago."

"Nice of you to make it easy." Dr. Horton snorted. "Why not ask about one of the dozen cases on my desk right now?"

"Sorry about that. This would be a car accident with two prominent botanists burned beyond recognition."

"Dr. Geller's parents."

"You remember?"

"Not too many cases like that. Usually something identifies them. In this case, there was nothing. You have to understand that not much was left. That, in itself, was a warning, but I couldn't find anything to confirm foul play. According to their credit card statement, they had just fueled up prior to the accident. The gas tank exploded. They also had a lot of paperwork in their vehicle, adding to the fire."

"Dental records?"

"None we could find—in that they never went to the dentist for us to match. They lived and worked but were very private, secretive."

After hearing a few more details, London got off the phone, walked back into the conference room and said to Grant, "The bodies were burned beyond recognition. No dental records were available and no positive proof of identification. However, it was their vehicle, and the bodies were the right height and sex."

Grant nodded his head. "Sometimes it works out that way. And by the way, no useable forensic evidence on the box Fern kept from her trial."

"Of course not." London shook his head. "Sometimes I wonder why we bother."

"Are we considering maybe the parents are not dead?" Steve asked.

London said, "It's not likely but we should consider the possibility just so we can dismiss it. They could have completely disappeared. We are not sure how caring the relationship was between them and Fern." He almost choked on that. "It couldn't have been that easy to have left behind a sixteen-year-old daughter, their house, their work—everything. However, their credit cards and bank accounts were untouched after their deaths."

"But then nobody ever searched for them afterward." Grant leaned back. "We've seen it happen time and time again where somebody has 'died' only to reappear years later."

"Motive?" Steve asked. "What possible motive could there be to walk away from everything you have?"

"Fear," London said. He couldn't share their particular fear of being caught for their mistreatment of their daughter. "Fear for their own lives. Could be any number of motives. They were well-off, although not superwealthy."

"They were well-respected in their field. I keep returning to having a daughter and a life. If they were to take off because they were afraid for their lives," Grant said, "why didn't they'd take their daughter with them?"

"To save her?" Steve asked.

"It's possible. Maybe they didn't think she was in danger but could only have a life without them, or she'd be better off without them ..." Grant frowned. "Maybe we need to look further into that aspect. Find out more about what her parents' and the family situation was like. Then check to see if they've surfaced anywhere."

London winced. That was not a good idea.

"We're making the assumption they would've done this themselves," Steve said. "Any chance somebody kidnapped them? Made it look like they died but took them away to some secret lab underground?" He gave a half chuckle. "I know it sounds pretty stupid, but again it's not like we haven't seen things like that in our world."

"I'll talk to her about the family scenario," London said. "See if there is any basis for this line of questioning."

Grant picked up a notepad and jotted down a few things. "I'll check if their names or IDs have resurfaced."

Steve shook his head. "I still think it's a stupid idea but whatever."

"Sounds good to me." London sat back down. He sent Fern a quick text.

How about I pick up some Chinese and bring it for dinner?

The response came right away.

Only if you bring a bottle of red wine with it.

He chuckled.

Done.

CHAPTER 21

CHINESE FOOD PROBABLY shouldn't be paired with bottled red wine, but she didn't really care about etiquette at this point. Fern was all about comfort, anything to get through this nightmare. She had tried to sleep once London left but couldn't stop her mind from racing. She had been up for over thirty hours straight now.

The latest update from Grant had said Reggie's latest email wasn't suspicious other than the fact that Reggie couldn't stop it.

Fern called his admin at the conservatory. "Rebecca, still no word from Reggie?"

The other woman sniffled. "No, not one word. Did you hear about Pam Akers?"

Fern winced. "Yes, I did. I'm so worried about Reggie."

"Me too. They were planning a holiday soon. It's so sad. I know Pam was hoping Reggie would ask her to marry him after all these years."

"Oh, dear, that just adds to the sadness."

"I know."

"Where were they planning on going?"

"A cabin on an island just off the Oregon coast. Reggie said it's been in his family for a long time."

"Any idea of its whereabouts?" She tried to keep her voice calm, casual, but inside she wanted to scream. Maybe

that's where Reggie had gone. "I keep thinking that, if his world was just too darn crazy, he might've gone into hiding, like he always does."

"I know," Rebecca murmured. "I was thinking the same thing."

Fern hung up and immediately phoned London, passing along the cabin information. "Can you get it checked out?"

"Will do." London hung up.

She stared at the phone. His tone was testy. But he had been up over thirty hours straight too, plus was back at work, something she'd lost her perspective about. She'd pushed back going to England for now with London being in her life again, and Brent had confirmed the Alnwick Garden job remained open for her with no time frame limit. That was one less thing to worry about.

She picked up her tea and walked into her basement. She couldn't stop thinking about the room she'd spent so many years in. Deciding to go in again without London here to hold her hand, she opened the door and stepped into her prison. It was really strange that, after all the years she'd been in here, she didn't blame her parents—as if she'd bought into their propaganda. They had just left her with a really twisted childhood. Still, she was different now. The scientist in her, although fascinated, wouldn't have done that to any child.

Whenever they had strapped her in the chair to watch for symptoms, she'd been terrified. She cried to be released many a time. And always her parents told her it wasn't safe. She had wondered about that. Was she not safe in the world or it wasn't safe from her? She remembered her mother getting very sick at one point and her father blaming Fern for it. For the longest time, she'd been trying to figure that out but never found a decent answer. Her memories were hazy. She didn't know if the experiments caused that or if her mind willingly forgot.

Lab notes. She really needed all her parents' research. That would explain some of the early memories Fern had, as well as the progress her parents may have made with the poisons and the antidotes. Even though she'd searched after their deaths, she had never found anything. Which wasn't surprising when the police had said how her parents' vehicle, involved in the fiery crash, was full of paperwork. She'd wondered if her parents had been transferring their lab notes to a storage unit when they'd had the accident.

She'd never found a storage unit, and, according to the cops, the papers in the car had helped turn the fire into an inferno.

Maybe they were taking the boxes to their rented lab space? Storage lockers were there. She'd not been given access to her parents' lab after their deaths so had no idea. She'd understood why at the time but hadn't liked it. She'd been only sixteen at the time and up against many powers, and all of them had vetoed her.

AMAX must have had access as her parents had been under contract with them. How could she get that information? How could she find out if AMAX had anything to do with her parents' death? This was what she really wanted to know.

She stood inside the basement, wrinkling her nose at the smell—wet earth in dark places. She walked through the room, looking for anything that would tell her about her parents' research. They'd used computers and storage devices, but she'd never found anything with their work on it. The place was empty outside of the hydroponics equipment and the bedroom. Out of the dungeon again, she closed the door and walked back upstairs.

Inside her home office, which had been her father's, she sat and surveyed the space. A large walnut desk dominated most the room. She opened the desk drawers and went through papers she'd already seen many times. It was all hers now. Papers to do with the property and more having to do with her guardianship.

She didn't have her own research work here. She kept that all in cloud storage. But her parents' deaths were before that technology, although disks were reasonable. Full bookshelves were on the far side of the office, including her parents' music collection. She remembered hearing music through the house when her parents had been alive.

Not remembering much about the kind of music it was, she walked over to the stack of CDs, slowly going through them. The first one was classical music.

Unable to help herself, she opened and closed every disk cover, checking nothing was hidden inside. When she got toward the end of the CD cases, she found one unmarked disk. She pulled it out and checked the last three cases in the row. All were unlabeled. She grabbed an external CD drive and plugged it into her computer and popped in the first CD. It was empty.

She popped in the second one—also blank. The third one opened to say it was full. She clicked on its contents to find dozens and dozens of folders. Her excitement built as she read the names on the folders, finding some with her name thereon, and realized each of her folders represented one year of her life. She'd been sixteen when they died. She had been two when she had found her parents' basement lab and all the pretty flowers. There were fourteen files. That tracked perfectly.

She opened the most recent file and found her parents' research. At least as far as she could tell. Charts, data and images. She quickly sorted through the information. It covered a calendar year. It started on her birthday and went through until the day they died. Finally proof of them running tests on her ...

Did she really want to know all the things they had done? Yet something useful could be here. How could she not look?

She clicked on the last month to see what they had been working on. She frowned as she read the entry.

> That was a brutal plant. It can create blisters that would form for years and years. I haven't had a chance to do much testing on her yet. She stares at me, huge tears in her eyes, begging for her freedom. For the first time in a long time I'm staring at my own consciousness and wondering how I could even consider this. To do this to another person— my own daughter. I might not be emotionally stable enough to go through all the testing ...
>
> For my wife, Fern ceased to be a person. For me, well, I'd hoped my deception hid my love for her. But I'm afraid, in the search for scientific knowledge, I've lost even that little bit of humanity.

For that Fern was grateful because she couldn't imagine having to deal with the blisters. Particularly if she was locked up downstairs. Although she remembered some similar symptoms. So maybe they'd tried it on her after all.

She scanned through the information and closed that folder, opening the first one. She'd been through it physically. She already knew the general accounting of what had happened when she was two. She read the first entry, like hearing her mother's voice from when Fern had been sixteen.

Today was the first day of the rest of our lives. Life will never be the same after this.

Fern was missing for most of the afternoon. We panicked, called in friends and neighbors, but nobody could find her. The police were the next step. I was about to call them when Joseph wondered if there was any chance she was in our hydroponic room.

When we found her, she was lying cold on the floor surrounded by belladonna flowers clutched in her hands. Berries and petals in her mouth, which she had eaten when she'd gotten hungry. Just like any toddler, she'd picked and put in her mouth everything she could possibly grasp. We thought for sure she was dead. She was cold, still, lifeless. We knew we'd be in trouble because we had left the poisons accessible. We didn't know if any laws stopped us from growing these plants, but we'd not safeguarded our daughter.

How could we have been so irresponsible, so lacking in parental instincts that we allowed our little girl to make it into the room full of toxic plants? I picked her up and carried her upstairs to the bed, screaming for Joseph. He wanted me to call the police, but I told him that we would be charged with manslaughter at the very least. No way this could be covered up.

Of course what we did was wrong. But never in our wildest dreams could we have considered our toddler finding her way into our lab. For that very reason a tall step precedes the actual footing before the door, so that she couldn't get over it and inside. The door was also higher up, so she could not reach the doorknob. And the door was heavy and latched, so then she couldn't open it. We have no idea how she got in.

We told everyone she was safe, that we found her sleeping in the basement and called off the search. A small lie. But not very small because it had been the basement. But we didn't tell them how she had just eaten enough poison to kill several healthy adult males. We knew we were in trouble. We didn't know how to get out of it. Fern was upstairs in my bed, while I lay crying, weighted down by my foolishness and irresponsibility for allowing something to happen to our beautiful little girl.

Distraught, we just held her limp form in our arms. Joseph had been devastated and had fallen into an exhausted sleep beside us.

Her body was so cold. There weren't enough tears to wash away our mistakes. Nothing could cleanse our souls. This was just something too big, too horrific to ever recover from.

Until ...

Fern rolled over and opened her eyes. I screamed, but it wasn't in joy. Fern had had no heartbeat. Fern had had no pulse. Her skin was beyond cool; it was cold. But she rolled over, opened her eyes and looked at me. She just looked at me; she knew me. She opened her mouth and said, "Hello, Mommy."

Bolting off the bed, terrified and screaming, I pointed at Fern. By now she sat up, her own fear triggered by my screams, and she blundered off the bed, her arms out, wanting to be picked up. I couldn't touch her.

I couldn't get anywhere close to her. Joseph rushed over and picked her up and held her in his arms. He turned to me and said, "She must've just gone into a coma. There's no other explanation."

I shook my head. "She was dead. I know she was dead."

"But there was no rigor."

"That must've been delayed by the poisons. But she was not alive. No breath came from her chest."

I stared at the child who was now alive, looking back at me as if nothing had happened, but I knew nothing would ever be the same again. I wanted nothing to do with her. I hated her. I wanted to have my little chubby toddler back again. But I did not want this unnatural replacement in my house. Joseph tried hard to talk some sense into me. But I couldn't accept his explanation. Finally he said we needed to learn from this. We needed to understand how she'd done what she had done, and it could be the answer to so much more. My scientific mind agreed. It was the only answer to dealing with this nightmare.

I'd never have done anything to my beloved Fern. But this wasn't my baby. Not any longer.

As I grieved and tried to comprehend the enormity of what happened, my mind couldn't let go of Joseph's words. He was right. Something miraculous had happened.

We needed to find out what that was.

We ran the tests on her. We checked her saliva,

gathered urine and blood samples, even took tissue samples. Everything we could possibly do to figure out how she'd survived this. And that was just the start.

She would never be my daughter again. I tried to feel something for her. I tried hard. But I couldn't. Because she wasn't my little Fern. She was this poisonous little baby, and, as she grew older and older, I knew I would have trouble with her. We kept her locked up most of the time— taking her out enough so the neighbors would not be suspicious. But we never took her to the doctor, and I knew she could never go to school.

Fern raised a shaking hand to her temple and thought about what her life was like back then. Images were in the next file. She clicked on them, and there she was at two years old, nude, skin pale, her eyes light-green in color. She glanced through the pictures. She was obviously alive, but, for all intents and purposes, she looked completely dead. "Did I know back then what my life would be like?" she asked bitterly. She shook her head and kept looking.

She skimmed through every year, checking the notes, looking to see little personal tidbits. When she got to her fourteenth and fifteenth years, things changed. Her parents had become more fearful of getting caught. She fought through the homeschooling to advance to online college courses, which was the only way they would allow her to learn.

Her appetite for new learning was unheeded by any other distractions. She didn't need anything else. And then, when she insisted on having a computer, she had leverage of her own to use.

Her father's notes at this time were more terrifying.

Fern is growing in leaps and bounds as a person. We're heading into a difficult time, Bethany and I; we've created a monster. We have no idea how to stop this roller coaster.

We've added more locks to the doors. And now I'm forced to add another one to her basement. To keep her in. To keep ourselves safe. She's threatening to leave us, to expose us. We're not sure how to handle it. The one thing we do know is we can't poison her. Poison doesn't kill her. And we've tried. How is that a thing to even write down here? Bethany's never been the same since Fern's death and rebirth. She's been distant, incapable of giving Fern a hug. Bethany will hold Fern's hand in public but hates to be around her the rest of the time. I've spent my life bringing food up and down the stairs, spending time teaching Fern, helping her to feed her scientific mind. But I know I have failed her in a way that's so monumental I can never be forgiven. I don't know how to step off this path. It's not what I dreamed of and cried for when we first found out that Bethany was pregnant.

We had had such high hopes. And intellectually Fern is so fast and so far beyond what we have accomplished. Her brain so superior to what we have that we must wonder if the poison or maybe her limited lifestyle didn't enhance it. Either way it's fascinating—and I hate to say it—but my mind is intrigued. Would the result be the same with another subject? Or the combination of the poisons and the lifestyle? Or is it because she came with the best genes possible from the two of us?

After Fern read the notes, a terrible cold descended on her. Cold to the touch, cold inside. Her parents had completely morphed into paranoid scientists, wondering how to preserve their own lives against her and how to stop her from telling the world, destroying their reputations and all the work they'd done.

Her father's last entry was the worst.

We must do something. We must do something about it soon. She needs to die. God help me. I need to kill my daughter. I can't see any other choice.

"HOW LONG WILL you be?"

London stared at the phone in his hand. "Another hour maybe?"

Nothing but silence was her response.

"Unless I need to be there sooner?" He frowned, recognizing the stress in her voice. "Is something wrong?"

"No, nothing that can't wait until you get here."

"I need to tie up a few things. Then I'll pick up dinner."

"Okay," she said, her voice forceful. "That works."

"You sure?"

"Yeah, I'm sure." And she hung up.

As he put down his phone, another text came in. Dr. Sartain.

Any news?

Frowning, hating the duplicity of this aspect, he quickly texted back.

No. Nothing.

"Hey, you okay?" Steve asked. He lifted a to-go coffee

and said, "Picked you up one. Looked like you were working hard here."

London snorted as he checked his phone, but no response came from Dr. Sartain. Good. He turned back to Steve. "Thanks. So much here just makes no sense. I've been going over the court transcripts, looking for anything, but I keep getting hung up on Derek's testimony."

"Sorry. I was friends with him for a long time, but I don't recognize the man Derek is today."

"Neither do I. Neither do I." He lifted the coffee, took a sip and shuddered. "Why the hell is the coffee so bad lately?" He shut down his computer and hopped to his feet. "I also can't get anywhere with the threatening email that brought Fern running from England. The email address is no longer valid."

"Figures. Where are you going?" Steve asked, stepping out of London's way.

London froze. "Damn. I need to send someone to check out a possible location for Reggie."

"I can do it. Give me the deets and I'll send someone. You obviously have other things on your mind."

"Thanks. Appreciate it." London quickly passed over the information. "I'm off to dump this coffee then to pick up dinner." He flashed his partner a grin and walked out of the station. As soon as he was outside, he checked his watch. He should be staying longer at work, but his intuition's insistent prodding said he should get to Fern's side. He didn't like leaving her in the first place—Stefan's warning always in the back of his mind.

But Fern had already proven adept at looking after herself—only it wouldn't do to become complacent. And given a choice, he would stay by her side forever.

It wasn't up to him.

Unfortunately.

But hopefully he'd convince her to let him take up that role soon enough.

HE NEEDED PROGRESS. He was chafing at the bit—wanting so much more. It was bad enough he had waited a dozen years to take this step, but now that he understood *what* Fern was, who she was, he had no compunction about moving forward. In fact, he was damn pissed at having waited this long.

Enough now. Progress. And fast. Or he would have to take drastic steps. Yet look at what he'd already found out about her.

The girl could withstand lethal doses of poisonous gas. And possibly save others around her. How?

He needed to know. He was desperate to know. Unimaginable applications needed her skills, her knowledge.

She couldn't be allowed to keep this to herself.

Not any longer.

CHAPTER 22

WHEN LONDON ARRIVED with dinner, she told him what was in her parents' research notes she had found today. She felt sorry for him again; she'd had a little bit of warning. He had none.

He stared at her in shock and then exploded. "You're serious? To make this go away, he would kill you?"

She nodded. "He doesn't give any details, doesn't say how or why or when, just that it needed to be done."

"My God, they were sentencing you to death." His anger made him snap at her, his voice vibrating.

She reached across and covered his hand with hers. "They also struggled with the problem of getting rid of my body."

He shook his head. "Honestly I saw them locking you up, sealing you in by cementing the doorway and painting it over. Nobody would have ever known. Like no one knew about your life up until that point. After a week or two, you would've died as quietly as you'd lived. And they wouldn't have had to face their actions yet again."

Her face blanched. "Here I thought maybe they would have hit me over the head or given me an overdose of a chemical or narcotic. Hell, there are a lot of ways to kill people but to consider sealing me up alive ..." She shuddered, her stomach ready to throw up, and she hadn't eaten the Chinese food yet. It sat, waiting on the table. "That's so wrong." She didn't want to believe they'd be so cruel, … but, from what she knew of them and how they'd treated her, it was all too possible.

"That's wrong?" he asked. "Are you kidding me? The whole thing is wrong. When you were missing, they should have contacted the police. When you were located and dying, they should have taken you to the hospital and had your stomach pumped."

She snorted. "They did that themselves later—out of curiosity. Everything they did was for science. My mother figured I was dead, and the child who woke up wasn't hers. She was something not human—less than human. It would only cause *them* more harm. And what they did ever afterward?" She shrugged. "That wasn't acceptable by anyone's standards."

"Your parents were murderers. Negligent in the beginning for not doing what they could have to save you and later planning your murder to save themselves …" He shook his head, words completely failing him. He frowned and looked at her. "It also puts a question mark on their deaths."

She nodded. "Were they murdered? Or did they commit suicide?" She grabbed a couple plates and two wineglasses and added them to the table.

"I didn't even consider suicide." London distributed the Chinese food, setting it all out on the table. "They were inherently cowards. If you'd been in the vehicle, then maybe I saw suicide to take you all out at the same time. Or finding a way to send the vehicle off a cliff, where they could escape, but you didn't."

She shook her head. "I'm not considering that possibility. They'd have a lot of questions to answer in that case."

"Unless he made sure they disappeared." London dished up a couple selections on his plate, offering her some too.

She shook her head. Not sure she could eat now. "That's possible. But they needed a cover story, explaining my disappearance forever. I was old enough for them to say I had gone to boarding school. In a few years, maybe sell the house."

"It's possible." He shrugged. "We need to look at AMAX further. If they knew your parents were doing all these tests on you, maybe AMAX wanted you in the lab?"

"No law in the world would have allowed that." Fern opened the wine and poured some for both of them.

"Blackmail is a wondrous thing," he murmured. "And one thing your parents couldn't allow was for anybody to know what they had been doing to you. So, what if someone—one of the scientists at AMAX or one of the CEOs—found out? Blackmail would be easy."

"I have to read more of the notes to see if that's mentioned at all." She stared at him. "But what would be the logic of AMAX killing them?"

"So the company could have you to itself."

She shook her head. "I don't see how."

London grunted. "You're thinking within the law. These people aren't. And you were a minor, only sixteen. Your parents basically hid your existence from nearly everyone. Who would notice your absence?"

She frowned. "I don't want to consider that either. But, regardless, why wait until now?"

"I don't know," he exclaimed in frustration. "But this could be a valid reason, regardless of the timing."

"If someone wanted me in their lab, no point in getting me charged with murder or having me incarcerated for twenty years."

"No, you're right. That part doesn't make a lot of sense." He grabbed the dish of noodles and served himself some more.

"I need to write this down on paper. I don't think so well in my head when confused." She got up, pulled open one of the sideboard drawers, grabbed a notepad and pen, and went back to the table. And stopped. "I need to see how soon after he wrote that last note that they died." She headed to her office. The entry was still up on her monitor. The date was seven days before the accident.

Seeing nothing more of interest she walked back to the kitchen.

"He couldn't see any other choice in his notes just one week before they died in a car accident. Maybe something in there changed. Or he hadn't come to terms with how my situation would end." She shook her head. "And, as much as I would like to think they committed suicide instead of killing me, I just don't see them as self-sacrificing at that point in time."

"Except with all their documents in the vehicle, maybe they were also intent on hiding all their research data so their reputation could never be impinged."

She considered it for a moment and then shook her head. "You don't understand my parents. Everything was about the work. They wouldn't have destroyed anything. They might've been taking copies to storage, but no way they would've permanently destroyed everything."

"And did you find all the data?"

She shook her head. "I have no idea if that's all of it. I seriously doubt it."

"So there could be another disk?"

"Maybe. I have to keep searching."

He popped his last bite of noodles into his mouth and stood up. "Let's go look."

She led the way to her office and sat down at the laptop. She'd put the folder with all their annual files on one monitor and kept her father's notes up on the other. She pointed to the bookshelf on the far wall. "I found the disk in with the music CDs over there."

He walked to the same set of CDs she had checked. Confirmed they were all music recordings. Then he carefully took all the books off the shelf, opened each one, before replacing it in the same place it had been.

She watched him with a smile on her face. "Looks like you have a little bit of training doing that."

He laughed. "Just a little."

She returned to her father's notes and scrolled to the day before their death. It was more preamble, more confusion and more complete paranoia that they would get found out. She scrolled up days and then weeks, finding one of her mother's notations. And gasped.

> I told Joseph today. AMAX wants to purchase the experiment. In exchange, we'll get all the lab facilities and the money that we want to continue our work.

Fern leaned in, her heart pounding. The note continued.

> Joseph was horrified that I had said anything. He didn't understand that, to me, she's too valuable not to utilize fully. She has untold secrets we need. I don't understand how she came to be here, and for a long time I hated that she existed, but now she holds the key to everything for us.

Fern kept scrolling through the pages. Reading the notes, arguments, fights, discussions. One drew a chilling blank in her mind as she contemplated the words in front of her.

AMAX said we must do this, or they'll tell the world that we've done illegal human testing.

Even without the experiment's name, they could cause us to lose our funding. Our reputations would be worthless once these charges are made public. Our research would be confiscated.

To avoid jail, I will give AMAX the experiment's name. But they demand our joint cooperation.

Joseph is against it. He says we never should have come to this point. I can't say that I care. We're on the cusp of something big. Something miraculous. To consider that people could no longer die from poison—that's worth so much more than the life of this experiment. He tells me that I can't call her *the experiment* anymore in front of him. That this is my daughter, Fern. But he's wrong. Fern died a long time ago. I have no problem exploiting what we have in its place. In fact, I'm glad for it. It's allowed me to do so much more than any protocol would have allowed, without the FDA hovering over me, without all the regulations restricting me. Now, with more access to AMAX funding, there will be no end to what we can learn. We may have to leave the country, but I don't have a problem with that. It's Joseph who's the problem, with his attack of consciousness.

Such a waste. So stupid. So completely useless at this point. For fourteen years, we've been administering poisons and taking blood samples, tissue samples and urine samples. Everything we could possibly find out, we did. And now he cares. I think he only cares because AMAX knows. Of course AMAX is now trying to get what they want, a taste of what's available, and they want it all. I don't know how to convince Joseph this is what we need to do.

I'm wondering if I should just do it without him.

Fern trembled at her mother's words.

London turned. "What's the matter?"

"AMAX found out about me, in theory at last. They offered my parents a deal or else ... My mother really wanted to take it and go to work for them, giving me to them, and was considering that she might do this without my father."

London walked closer. "She could have left him behind?"

Fern shrugged as she scrolled down, looking for more personal notes. "She doesn't say. It's possible, if she arranged for me to be kidnapped and separated from him at the same time. What was to stop her? She was the heartless one."

"Would your father kill you over something like that?"

"Was he trying to kill me or to save me? She stared at London. "Jesus, what a mess."

"Do you want to switch up? Let me read and you can search the bookcase further?"

"No." She still shook her head seconds later. "I should do this. If only because it might bring up additional memories that could help as well." She scrolled to the next set of notes, which were more of the same fights between her parents. Her mother really wanting to move forward, her father blocking her mother at every step.

Joseph has become unstable. Completely irration-
al. Not sure what the answer is. We are running out
of time.

That was four days before her father's final entry.

I don't know what to do about Bethany. She wants
to sign Fern over for a permanent life as a lab rat.
The only saving grace at this point is that at least
Bethany hasn't divulged Fern's name. I understand
why Bethany's disappointed in me. I understand
how to her this is a betrayal. But why is it she can't
understand that, to me, it's betraying our daughter
at the same time? Who knew I would hit this wall?
In my mind, there would be an end to this. Fern
would be free one day. Build a career, get married,
have children, have a life. A normal life. And somewhere along the line, I forgot to put that into our
end game.
    What kind of a father am I?

The desolate entries were scary. She had been living in
the basement, trying to figure out just what kind of a life her
parents had planned for her and how to escape it and them.
Wondering what it would take to have her parents let her go.
She never found an answer. She was always locked in, and
her father always came to deliver food. Sometimes late,
sometimes several meals at once. She was always in the
basement, mostly locked in that horrible windowless space.
Being in the whole basement had been so much better. She
could look out the windows, the windows she'd forgotten to
mention to Sutherland. She could run and jump and dance.
But, when she was difficult or emotional or in the middle of
an experiment, she was locked up in the windowless base-

ment section. And that was, of course, the part she remembered the strongest. That's when she realized London was correct. Her father was concerned as to what would be the easiest way to end this—to end her. But, to do that, he would have to deal with his wife. She would never let go of anything so precious, so important as a lab rat. The only way he could seal Fern up in the basement permanently was if her mother ...

A scream caught in her throat, her thoughts continuing to their inevitable conclusion. *If her mother was no longer there to protest*—not out of any undying maternal loss, but, because as a scientist, her mother demanded more time with Fern, *the experiment.*

She looked up at London. "We were both right."

He turned, a book in his hand, and looked at her. "Both? What was I right about?"

"Murder and suicide. I think my father murdered my mother and killed himself."

LONDON STARED AT her, his mind processing bits and pieces that he knew. "Can you see him doing that?"

She nodded. "My mother wanted to turn me over to AMAX to have unlimited funding for her experiments. My father was against it. They couldn't agree. The AMAX blackmail threat kept her pushing at my father. But he would rather kill me than consign me to a lifetime as a lab rat. Yet he needed me to die in such a way that their reputations weren't ruined or their work wasn't wiped out. That's all they lived for. But, at the same time, no way would my mother go for it. She didn't want me to die. She wanted to sell me. So I think he loaded the vehicle with the documentation that didn't matter, maybe as an excuse to get her in the vehicle with him—saving the real research somewhere else—then took my mother for a drive, stopped to get gas, rigged up the vehicle for an explosion and made sure to drive off the road in a location where there was no room for second thoughts. Where there would be no saving her or him."

London shook his head and stared at her. "And you? What did he plan to do with you?"

She gave him a sad smile. "I think you were right. I think, with their deaths, he thought nobody would've known about the basement. Nobody would have searched the house. I would've died a very slow, painful death in that little room."

He stopped and looked at her for a long moment, wondering at her unnatural calm as she discussed her parents— her father killing her mother and himself in one tragic event, leaving Fern to die of starvation. "How did you get out?"

She shrugged. "The door opened. Nobody came in. I waited a few seconds, but that was all, and I bolted out to find the police. That's all I can remember."

"You never found out who opened the door?"

She shrugged. "I assumed somebody upstairs had banged on the floor, and it popped loose." She stared at the monitor, then closed her eyes. "And, given the circumstances, I think I'll hold on to that possibility." A sob escaped. She reached up to cover her face with her hands, but the tears couldn't be held in.

He rushed to her side, pushed her chair back, pulled her to her feet and wrapped her in his arms. "Take it easy. It was a long time ago. Take it easy."

"And some wounds never heal." She stared at him.

"How could he have possibly thought of killing me when I hadn't even had a chance to live yet?"

"They had to bury their mistakes," he said simply. "Killers only think about their needs and wants and the impact of their actions on themselves. They don't give a shit about anybody else." He sat in her chair, pulling her into his lap. "And I'm so sorry."

She sat quietly in his arms—calm, too calm.

How could she process such a betrayal? He winced. Easy. She'd had a lifetime of practice.

Over her head, he saw the monitor. The words so damning.

"What we have to do now is find out who in AMAX was blackmailing them," she muttered.

He took a deep breath. "I hate to ask, but did your menses start on time?"

She sniffled and stared at him. "No. I was late, somewhere around fourteen, fifteen. Probably due to all the stress and toxins in my body."

He nodded thoughtfully. "Your menstrual cycle could have been another reason they realized things had changed. You were a young woman then. Maybe that was just the shock your father needed. Up until then, you hadn't been anything but a female child. But, when your cycle started, you turned the tide from childhood to womanhood, and the enormity of what he'd done and the passage of time both stared him in the face."

"My mother didn't care. She was disgusted. She didn't want me to have periods because it would interfere with her ability to get the results she wanted. She was forever testing my blood pressure and pulse rate and temperatures. All things she could count on, giving her a baseline as a standard. Ovulation and the menstrual cycle shifted everything. She was really angry."

"She was a fool. She was psychotic after the loss of her child. A completely unhinged woman who was already unstable," he said. "Who was given an avenue to continue her decline into madness."

"She needed something to believe in."

"People do all kinds of crazy things, but they also react in all kinds of crazy ways to emotional trauma."

She nodded, pulled out of his arms, grabbed a tissue and blew her nose. "I guess we'll go with that for the moment."

"Exactly."

CHAPTER 23

S HE DIDN'T REMEMBER much about London picking her up and carrying her upstairs. But he took her straight to her bedroom, saw the filled suitcases and unmade bed and headed toward the nearest spare bedroom. There he drew back the covers and laid her gently on the double bed. "Do you need anything from the other room for the night?"

She shook her head. "No."

He nodded, walked to the bedroom door and closed it. Then he returned to the bed and helped her take off her jeans. "You want your shirt and bra off for the night?"

She sat up like a child and reached her arms over her head. Within seconds her shirt hit the floor, and her bra followed. She lay back down and curled up in a fetal position. He pulled the covers to her shoulders and dropped a kiss on her cheek.

She smiled.

She didn't remember when she'd hit the wall. When the bed behind her sagged, she realized he intended to lie down with her—fully dressed and atop the bedding. She twisted and said, "We both need sleep. We've been up for two whole days. Strip off and get under the covers with me."

He hesitated, then stood, shrugged off his clothing until he stood only in his boxers and crawled under the covers with her. He wrapped his arms around her, pulling her to him and whispered against her ear, "Go to sleep."

She closed her eyes and drifted off.

She awoke with her bladder insisting she move. She sat up and looked around, disoriented. She wasn't in her bedroom, and that meant no bathroom was attached. She walked to the hall bath to use the facilities and stopped as she exited, staring in the mirror, wincing at the deep, dark circles under her eyes. Even the look in her eyes had a bruised appearance. She ran her fingers through her hair before returning to slip under the covers. She wondered if she'd woken him, but he was still sound asleep. This time she wrapped herself around him, her arms sliding across his chest, her head against his shoulder. She was too tired to do anything other than sink in and enjoy the novelty of sleeping beside someone.

Heat woke her the next time. Waves scorched through her body as hands stroked down her slim form, exploring and caressing her skin. London laid a trail of hot kisses from her chin to the swell of her breasts. She groaned, her body arching.

London shifted higher, looking down on her, hot skin meeting hot skin. Fire meeting fire. He slipped his hands under her head, tilting her face so she looked at him. But she kept her eyes closed. His voice deep and dark, he said, "Look at me."

Slowly she raised her heavy eyelids. Her body trembled in his grasp. A mind of its own, a will of its own and a need of its own. She gazed into the heat and saw so much more. Tenderness. Caring. Passion. But most of all there was love. Tears came to her eyes.

He made a sound of distress and gathered her close. Rolling to the side, taking her with him, he asked, "Why the tears?"

She shook her head, overcome.

"It'll be okay. I promise I'll never leave you again. You're my heart. You're my soul. I could never hurt you." He whispered gentle things she'd always longed to hear but never thought the day would come.

She also understood so much more. To think she'd come to this point with him made her heart break, and yet her soul rejoiced. It seemed her heart had been in so much pain for so long that it was in a state of disbelief. She wanted this. Wanted him. Not just the union of their bodies but also the union of heart and mind that she'd learned was possible from Stefan.

She took a deep gasping breath, trying to control the sobs, and said, "I'm not upset. Just overwhelmed."

Gently he stroked her back, her shoulders, leaving tender kisses on her temple, her forehead. "You have the right to be. It's been a brutal year."

She gave a half-snort, half-laugh. "It's all just too much."

He settled back on the bed and relaxed.

She realized he was withdrawing physically from her. "No, don't." She struggled to push herself up on an elbow and looked at him. "It's not that I don't want this right now, because I do. My emotions are just finally ..." Her voice trailed off, and she didn't know how to explain it.

With a gentle hand, he stroked her cheek. "I'm not a teenage boy. Is this the right time or isn't it the right time?"

She smiled at him and said, "If I have learned one thing through all this, even from my childhood, it's to take the moment when the moment comes, because you don't know if or when it'll happen a second time." She leaned forward, her lips barely above his, and whispered, "So right now is the right time."

He tilted her chin toward him so he could look deep into her eyes, as if to make sure she meant what she said.

She nodded. "Yes, I'm serious." And she kissed him. It was a gentle kiss, an exploratory kiss. She kissed the tip of his nose and said, "Honest." A kiss landed on his cheekbone. "Truly."

Another kiss landed on his chin, and she smiled as her tongue licked his bottom lip. She gently tugged it into her mouth and suckled. Then released it to whisper, "Believe me."

He wrapped his arms around her and hugged her, holding her tight against his chest, as if he would never let her go. And she realized how insecure she'd made him feel. All this time that she had been worried about her reaction, she'd never given thought to his, how much he'd gone through. To the loss he'd experienced. Not only his brother's mental and physical mess but he'd lost his parents at the same time too. No wonder he'd struggled with his own emotions.

Their relationship had never been easy. He had cared. He had done everything he could to help her get out of that court case, searching for evidence, anything that would release her from the nightmare she was in, but she couldn't see past it. Walking away for six months, without a good-bye and without even a glance in his direction, that had to have been brutal.

She felt so ashamed. "I never even considered what you might have been going through. I was so caught up in the nightmare I was in. I was so selfish not seeing the effect of that trial on everyone around me."

He gave a half-broken laugh. "It doesn't matter. What you were going through was bad. Don't feel guilty over something you couldn't control. We both needed to move on. We needed to learn from all that pain, to know that wasn't the time. It is, however, time for us right now."

She looked at him and asked, "And Derek?" She watched as the sadness whispered through his eyes.

"Derek's been making his own mistakes for a long time. He is who he is, and he must live with the consequences of his own actions. I wish I knew where he was. I wish I knew how to contact him. But I don't, and so, once again, I'm left cleaning up whatever mess he leaves me."

She smiled. "At least he led us to each other again."

London slid his hand into her hair, against her scalp. "This is where you've always belonged." Then he kissed her.

She didn't want to rush the process. She wanted to savor it to make the most of the time they had, time she'd thought would never come.

He slowly resumed his exploration of her body, easing her into this transition to share a deeper relationship with him, his soft kisses and gentle words working in conjunction with his curious hands.

She writhed in his arms, her body supersensitized, craving his touch, craving the fulfillment she knew he promised. Once the restraints were freed, she couldn't get enough. Her hands tugged, twisted, stroked, pinched and still he didn't move fast enough. She dug her nails into his shoulders. He gasped, his back arching, and pinned her in place with his hips.

He lowered his head and whispered, "What do you want? Tell me."

She wrapped her legs around his hips and cried, "Come to me. Now."

But the words weren't even out of her mouth before he

surged deep inside and froze. The sensation was so new, so complete, so damn perfect, she could barely breathe. A shudder ran the full length of her body.

"You okay?"

She nodded.

Then gently she scratched his back. He crushed her against him, his tongue hot, deep, thrusting, to match his body's tempo. Driving them both harder, higher, faster. She twisted and clung, her arms holding him tightly to her. Her body searching for release, and yet it was just out of grasp.

Sweat slicked their bodies as he pounded into her. He arched his back and a guttural sound slid from deep inside his throat. As the climax rippled through him, he whispered, "You're mine. Always have been, always will be. I love you."

His words were a final magical touch, and her own release stuttered through her. Joy permeated her soul.

But not so much from the physical release. It was from his words, knowing that she was no longer alone.

And maybe, just maybe if she was lucky, she'd never be alone again.

LONDON WOKE WITH a sense of completeness. He opened his eyes, found Fern's arms wrapped around him. She still slept. But, from the height of the sun, it was easy to see it was late morning. They'd slept well past his normal wake-up time. Then again, they'd been up for forty-eight hours straight, then were up half of last night too.

As he lay here, memories of the basement and all the stories she'd shared filtered through his mind. They needed to make sure all that research was safe. The story of what she went through needed to be recorded for the years ahead. He knew she'd do a lot not to share this, but it was also important data, evidence if somebody else was framing her.

He glanced at her as she slept. He didn't want to wake her, didn't want to stir up more horrible memories with his questions. But the questions needed to be asked. More specific ones too. And it would be hard on her. He had to get her to go through her disks of information to see if other lab techs were involved. Or even other people her parents might've done this to or spoken to about it. Given that they had an absolute lack of conscience, there was an all-too-great possibility that Fern was not their only human lab rat.

He had to track down somebody in AMAX who knew what happened to her parents. Maybe even had a hand in it. His phone buzzed. He gently disentangled his arms, sat up and reached for his pants on the floor, pulling his phone from a pocket to find a text from Steve. **Call me**. London walked out to the hallway and dialed his partner. "What's up?"

"Where are you?"

"At Fern's."

"Anything wrong?" Steve voice was sharp, hard with questioning.

"A lot is wrong," London said. He rubbed his face. "But nothing I can really share. Anything new relating to the case?"

"The botanists at the conservatory say potentially snippets of a couple plants are missing. But nothing major and won't cause any damage to the plants."

"Potentially? Snippets? Couple plants? Does anybody know anything for certain?"

"Not really. They've been doing a lot of work cultivating the plants. Trimming had already been done. But none of the plants were dangerous or rare. So they said they weren't worried about it. It's happened before by overzealous gardening fans. No damage was done to the plants, and, outside of the conservatory, nothing else here would appeal to anybody."

"Gardening fans?" He shook his head. "Do people really break into a conservatory to steal plants?"

"We see people steal a lot less," Steve said. "Grant has been searching the background of the security guard, but so far I haven't heard back from him. He did say he found nothing to show Fern's parents are still alive."

"Well that's something at least." London wandered over to the master bedroom and stared out at the backyard. "So much is going on. We must track down AMAX. I think her father probably committed suicide, killing his wife deliberately in the process. A murder-suicide."

"Really? Why?"

"I'll tell you when I see you, but we found some of her parents' data and personal notes that show a troubled mind looking for a way out."

"Makes sense but why the paperwork in the back seat?"

"I think he was concerned about somebody finding their data and using it for ill." London stared at the gray skies. "Or he hid the real data, and this was a diversion so people would think his research was gone."

Steve snorted. "Mad scientists. I love it."

"Also somebody in AMAX was blackmailing her parents."

Steve sucked in his breath. "Now that's interesting. We need the proof to get a warrant for AMAX."

"And, before we can get that warrant, we need a whole lot more than data from twelve years ago."

"Shit."

London contemplated the difficulty of getting something on the AMAX staff from so long ago. "Let's start with an employee list, including all who may have left in the last fifteen years."

"Why fifteen? How does this relate to Reggie's partner or the security guard?" Steve asked. "And, by the way, anything new on your brother?"

London's stomach cramped at the thought. "No," he said softly. "I have no idea where he is."

"Sorry, man. It's got to be tough." Steve's voice turned brisk. "I'll get the AMAX staff list."

"Send it to me when you've got it. I want to see if any names are mentioned in the data here."

"Sounds like interesting data," Steve said. "Talk to you later." And he hung up.

Interesting data, yes. But how would it help Fern get through this if all that data had to be made public?

He turned and headed back to their shared bedroom, not wanting to leave her alone any longer than he had to. Thankfully she still slept. He dressed quickly to go downstairs, to start some coffee and to bring it to her. As he left the bedroom again, he heard her voice.

"I'm awake," she murmured.

He wandered over, reached down and kissed her gently on the cheek. "Hold that thought. I'll make us some coffee."

She smiled and gave him a three-finger wave.

He raced downstairs and started the pot, opened the fridge and winced. Minimal food was here, with little left to even make sandwiches. But leftover Chinese could be breakfast. He did a quick check through the main floor of the house, wandered into her office, realizing they'd left the monitors and computers turned on. He quickly hit the keyboard to make sure the data was still there. Thankfully it was.

He had no reason for his doubts, but, as he glanced at the monitors, he saw her father's last words. Rather than admit his own shortcomings and his own wrongdoings, her father had decided to let her die. Asshole. London walked back into the kitchen, quickly poured two cups and went upstairs.

She hadn't moved a muscle.

"Are you sure you're awake?"

"I am."

He set the coffee cup on her night table and then walked over and placed his cup on the other side. He crawled atop the bed beside her. "How are you doing?"

She rolled over and faced him, then stared at the ceiling. "I'm fine. Better than I expected. I still feel like somebody beat me up, shoved me under the bed and stomped on me a few times, then just walked away."

He gave her startled laugh. "Well, it's not quite the answer I expected …"

She grinned. "No, I don't imagine it was. For your ego's sake, last night was … perfect. Helped me to get over the pain of my parents' last words. Still, it's all good. I do feel better for having told you."

"And how do you feel about me using some of that information to get a warrant to check AMAX?"

A shudder ran down her body. "Shit."

He winced. "I know. I'd like to filter the information, copy over your mom's notes on the blackmail. Use part of the email as leverage to get a warrant."

"What good will that do?"

"It seems the only other people who had any idea what

you could do, or what your situation was, would be some-body at AMAX. I don't know how it relates to what's currently going on in your world, but I can't see any other direction to look." He shrugged. "Unless you can tell me if anybody else had access to your finances or to your parents' data. Did they have an assistant? Did they have lab techs working for them who we can look at? As their deaths were ruled an accident an indepth examination into their lives never happened. But we should go deeper into their finances and other employees now."

She frowned and slowly worked herself into a sitting position, leaning against the headboard, pulling the covers across her chest. "Over the years, I heard about various lab techs, but I don't think anybody knew about me."

"Did you ever see anybody else? Was there ever a doctor who came to the house because you were ill? Did your parents have friends over? Did any of them see you?"

"A couple throughout the years, but I don't remember who. I don't remember why they would've been here, and they wouldn't have been here for me. They would've been here for my parents."

"It would be helpful if you could think of any names. A lab technician who may have dropped off work to your parents at home. Someone from AMAX who may have come over with a contract or somebody from the labs that you've used. AMAX had access to the lab data, so could somebody from the lab itself have shown up here?"

"I wouldn't be mentioned by name in their formal re-search documentation. Plus those materials should've been confidential. Everything was stored away. When I rented my lab space, we had lockers or storage units."

"What lab did you use?"

"I used my parents' lab, which was an off-site AMAX

lab. The company had expanded, and, when financial difficulty hit, they contracted out the facilities. We did sign a contract releasing them from any liability for any of the work we did and promising all the work was legal."

"As we well know, what your parents were doing was certainly not legal. I need to get in contact with somebody who was there back then and may have had access or known about you."

"Almost two years ago, when the murder rumor about me started, AMAX canceled my contract a few months later when I was formally charged. Of course the trial was many months later. I had used their facility for about four years."

"So, we need to go back six years to see who worked there and check them out, see if there's any cross-reference with AMAX or your parents."

She looked at him. "Is that even possible?"

He downed the rest of his coffee, got to his feet and said, "Not only is a possible, it's very likely." His intuition was telling him to get at it. And to get at it now. "I'll go downstairs and get to work." He turned and looked at her. "Are you gonna be okay here?"

She nodded. "I'll be just fine. I'll have a shower, then come down. I'm fairly hungry."

"How about leftover Chinese? That's about all we have available unless you want a bare-bones sandwich."

She winced. "I'd rather go out."

He nodded. "Get your butt downstairs. I'll see what kind of information I can dig up. I just need permission to knock on doors. Then we'll go from there." He raced downstairs, for the first time feeling positive about the couple lines he had to tug.

His intuition told him that he was finally getting to the right lines.

CHAPTER 24

S HE WAS GLAD London had something to work on. For herself, she felt like another six hours' sleep was the answer. Only she wouldn't get it, and she couldn't do a whole lot about that. But a shower would help. She got out of bed, straightened up the bedding and walked back to her bedroom. She frowned at all the suitcases. She certainly had made a mess of her space. Then again, her space had made a mess of her too. Shaking her head, she walked into the bathroom to undress and stepped in the shower once the hot water appeared. Instantly she felt better.

By the time she'd shampooed her hair and was wrapped in a towel, standing in her bedroom, she felt a whole lot more human. But her stomach still didn't want Chinese food for breakfast. Dressed now in a sweater and jeans, she headed downstairs, hearing London talking excitedly on his phone in her living room. She refilled her coffee cup, sat at the kitchen table and pulled the notepad toward her.

She'd looked at her notes from the night before, but nothing triggered anything of any value. Names were at the bottom. Obviously London had done some research already, adding a couple names of people at the AMAX lab for her list. She frowned at one, her finger tapping on the name. *John Zanders.*

It had a familiar ring to it.

Realizing London would probably be a few more minutes on the phone, she picked up her coffee and walked into her office. She frowned. She'd left all the material open on the monitor. Fern quickly copied the entire contents of the CD and stored it in her off-site cloud storage.

She printed the pages that talked about the blackmail, using AMAX's name. London might need it for a warrant. She didn't really want everybody to know her entire history, but, if it had to be, then it had to be. A sense of fatalism washed through her. So much had happened, so much had gone under the wire already, that just knowing she had no ability to do anything about it now had her caught up in the current, with little control over events. And maybe that was okay too. It was different this time. She wasn't the target. And she wasn't alone.

With the research documents open, she did a search for the company name. She found quite a few references she had skipped over the previous night.

She stopped at a couple that referenced work her parents had been doing. She quickly printed off those selections and kept going.

Then she did a search for Zanders. And, sure enough, the name came up. She leaned forward to read those notes. Apparently he worked at the lab and had done some work for her parents. Her mother had notes about him being extremely eager, fascinated by the plants, and she thought he would be a perfect protégé. Her father, however, had notes that said Zanders was slightly unstable, and it concerned her father. And she realized her parents' views had diverged on a lot of these tests.

Her mother was willing to do anything and to try everything. To her, no limits, no boundaries, no layers or no levels were too far. For her father, every level had to be considered; every boundary that her mother pushed against, he balked at. Fern wondered about their marriage. How could they have survived so long?

As she kept reading, her mother's notes got shorter and less personal. Fern didn't understand that initially, until she realized her mother must have had a hidden place to store her "real" notes. As her mother's path had diverged from her father's, she'd minimized her notes.

Fern got up from the computer, walked back to the kitchen, grabbed her notepad, then returned to her computer. She quickly searched for the other names.

But the only name she came up with in her parents' research notes was Zanders. Good, now she had somebody to focus on. She quickly jotted down any notes and pages that referenced him and/or his work. She copied those references to a separate document. But now she was concerned.

What was the chance her mother had research projects totally separate from her father's work? Was it even possible to have hidden something like that? Fern decided that her mother's attempts at hiding her research notes on her parents' *shared* studies would have been easier than hiding the actual testing of her mother's "other" *experiments*. And, if her mother had done so, had her father ever found out about it? Could that be what had finally sent him around the bend? Sent him to commit murder and to take his own life?

He had to have known that things would blow up one day. No way this would end well. And, if he botched the job of killing his daughter and/or his wife, and couldn't go through with his own suicide, he'd face life in jail. Now that the idea had entered Fern's mind that her mother may have had other documentation, notes, lab projects, Fern couldn't let it go.

She went through all the files from the CD. And then did a search for Zanders on the entire disk. When she found over four hundred different references, she knew somewhere in all this mess was what she was looking for. Searching by the location, she found one that had a list of charities. She brought up the document, realized it had been created three years before her parents' death. And had nothing to do with charities.

She sat back and began to read.

When London walked in a half hour later, he stood in the doorway and asked, "What did you find?"

She lifted her gaze. "She was doing experiments on somebody else."

He stared at her in complete horror. "Who?"

"Zanders. My mother wasn't satisfied with just one subject. She had to have a second. But there's too much material here to read in five minutes. We must find him. Make sure he's okay."

"And how does he relate to the hate letters you were receiving? Or the court case? Or the letter threatening Reggie?" London asked.

"It might not have anything to do with all that, but I can't ignore the fact that my mother poisoned someone else."

"Agreed. Can you spend an hour and read through all the material or are there days' worth of it?"

"Likely weeks." She pushed her hair off her face with a shaky hand. "He worked at the labs where I had my contract as well. Only I don't remember his face."

"Would you recognize him if you saw him?" He turned toward the kitchen. "And we need to eat and go."

She glanced at her watch and realized how late it was.

"Let's check out the lab first and then stop for lunch."

"The sooner we solve this, the better."

She reached for her sweater and purse and followed him out the door.

Her rented lab space was a fifteen-minute drive from her house. She walked in the front office of the building with a weird sense of déjà vu. "I might even have been here as a child," she whispered to London. "But the memory is so old I can't really tell."

"It's within the realm of possibility. Just think about it. If your parents took you out, they would have often combined business with pleasure, so they could've run by to check on something or spoken with somebody. Who knows?"

She nodded.

At the front reception area, she waited for somebody to come to the counter. When nobody came, London reached across and hit the bell. Less than a minute later, the door opened and out came a young woman in a lab coat. Fern didn't recognize her. Then again, the woman wasn't looking at Fern either. She stared at London with an overly bright smile on her face. Until London pulled out his ID.

Then her friendly face disappeared behind a pinched mask. "I hope this isn't about Dr. Geller's work."

Hearing the odd inflection, Fern tilted her head. "Why is that?"

"Because we've had people asking all day." The woman shook her head. "Hard to get any work done having to deal with questions all the time."

London asked, "What kinds of questions? Were they about the young Dr. Geller or the older two?"

The woman looked puzzled briefly, then her face

cleared. "Oh, my God! I forgot about them. They've been dead for a long time now. No, all the questions we're currently getting are about the younger one. *Have I seen her? Is she back in town? Is she doing more of her work at our lab?* Things like that." She shrugged. "Honestly I haven't heard from her, and, if she's back in town, I wouldn't have a clue."

"But you did know her from before, correct?"

The woman shook her head. "I started working here just after she escaped her murder charges."

Fern stiffened at the woman's choice of wording, *escaped her murder charges*, but stayed silent.

"It was tough enough dealing with all the calls then. And I hadn't known anything about it."

"People were still calling after the trial?"

"The media mostly. They wanted to know if she would work here again. What she might be doing. Questions like that."

"We're looking for a Zanders who works here."

"John Zanders?" She shook her head. "He's been let go, I believe."

London raised an eyebrow.

Fern happened to catch the motion as she glanced at him.

"Any idea why?" he asked her.

"He was unstable, not showing up for work. He worked here full-time for quite a while years ago, then left and came back. He was fine until maybe a year ago. But, in the last six months, we thought he was very ill. He said he was fine physically, just a lot on his mind. So the lab gave him several chances to shape up, but he became more and more erratic. Then a couple days ago, he just went AWOL. His behavior was deemed unfit, not what the lab wanted to represent them. So he was let go permanently."

"Is anyone here right now who I could speak with about that?"

She walked to her computer and checked. "Dr. Dan Royce is here. Let me see if he can speak with you." She disappeared into the back.

Fern turned to London. "I remember Dr. Royce. He's one of the managers."

"And Zanders was let go just since you returned to the States."

She nodded. "The significance is not lost on me. Neither was the fact they assumed he had some kind of major illness."

"You are thinking poison?"

She shrugged.

The woman returned, a portly gentleman, also in a white lab coat, behind her. He looked at London, then Fern and back to London. Dr. Royce's gaze zinged back to her, and recognition flashed. "Dr. Geller?"

She reached out a hand and said, "Hello, Dan."

He beamed. "It's so good to see you. I'm glad to find you doing well."

"You mean, not in jail as everyone thought I would be," she said drily.

The other woman made an odd gasping sound.

Fern refused to look at her. After all, the woman hadn't said anything more than the rest of the world had said.

Dr. Royce smiled and said, "I always knew you couldn't have killed anybody. You spent your life working with poisons and antidotes to save people, and it was senseless that you would make a reversal like that."

She chuckled. "Well, you are one of the few who believed in me. So thank you for saying that."

He turned to London and asked, "Now what's this? What is it you need to know?"

London repeated his questions about Zanders. Essentially they were given the same information. But a little more clear-cut.

"He'd been written up several times for oddball behavior in the last six months, but he had an absolute public meltdown two days ago. He'd been reading something on the monitor, and started yelling and screaming. Unfortunately that was the last straw. I had to let him go. He'd been a great employee up until then."

"When did this start? Was it about a year ago?"

"Maybe not quite as long." Dr. Royce tapped his hand on the counter as if casting back to that period. "It could be around that time as he seemed to be horribly fascinated with Dr. Geller's court case unfortunately. When she was acquitted, he seemed fine for a while. And then he just slowly went off. Every time we gave him a write-up, he would appear to be much better for a week or two, only to completely fall back into the same pattern again."

"What kind of pattern? What kind of behavior?"

Dr. Royce winced. "I don't have any proof, so I can't really say with any kind of certainty, but it was almost like he was doing drugs, coming in to work still high. His speech would slur sometimes. He had an unfocused look, and his eyes were dilated. I questioned him about it several times. He said he was on medications and having trouble getting the dosage regulated." Dr. Royce glanced at Fern and added, "At the time it seemed a reasonable answer."

"I don't remember him myself, but his name is familiar."

Dr. Royce nodded. "No surprise there. A long time ago

he worked closely with your parents. But then he was gone for maybe about ten years. He was doing some private work with AMAX. He only came back around a year ago."

"Any reason why he returned?" London asked.

Dr. Royce nodded. "He was doing more personal research and wanted private lab space. One of the advantages of being an employee here is you can request your own lab. Otherwise it's fairly expensive."

"So he came back full-time or part-time?"

"Part-time. Then he had money troubles and asked for full-time, and, when we noticed his erratic behavior, his hours were reduced to part-time, and now he's gone."

"What about his lab space? Is he still renting it?" London asked.

"Not sure what he'll do yet about that. This just happened a few days ago. I don't think he's even had time to clean out his space."

Fern straightened. She saw awareness hitting London at the same time. "Can you confirm that?"

Dr. Royce walked over to the monitors and quickly punched in something on the screen. "His key code hasn't been used in the last forty-eight hours. I can't confirm what he may have left or taken prior to that."

"I am trying to get a warrant. I don't want you to let him back into his lab space today."

Alarm lit up Dr. Royce's face. "Has he done something wrong?"

"Potentially very wrong." London took a few steps away and made a phone call.

Dr. Royce turned to Fern. "I'm not even sure what to say about all this."

She gave him a gentle smile. "Let the FBI do their thing.

If London can get a warrant, we may find answers in Zanders's lab."

The woman at the front desk said, "He brought in boxes of paperwork the last time I saw him."

"When was that?" Fern asked.

Happy to be helping, as if to make up for her previous gaffe, she said, "Maybe three days ago. He made several trips to get it all in."

"Does he have a storage locker here?"

"It's shared lab space, but he does have his own locker."

Fern walked over to London and held up her finger. He pressed a hand over his phone. "What?"

She explained that the warrant needed to cover the personal locker and how Zanders had made several trips bringing in documentation.

He nodded.

She walked back to Dr. Royce. "Were you here when my parents used this lab?"

"Oh, yes. I was indeed. Your parents were lovely people," he said warmly. "I was so sad to hear about their accident."

"Yes, it was a difficult time. Do you know what happened to their research? Do you still have any material or data from their work here?"

"The lab handed everything over to the estate," he said with a frown. "Maybe talk to the executor at the time. It was a lawyer, I think." His face cleared. "Give me a minute, and I might be able find something." He disappeared into the back room, leaving London on his phone and the young woman behind the desk.

As soon as Dr. Royce left, the woman leaned forward. "I'm so sorry for what I said."

Fern gave her a lopsided smile. "You just said what the rest of the world thought. But I can tell you this, I never killed anyone. I was charged, tried and acquitted. And even though I was acquitted, the world still found me guilty. It's not a good place to be."

"I can't imagine."

"I'm still trying to find out who killed my former boss."

"It was four people in total, wasn't it?"

Fern nodded. "One was my boss." She frowned. "Two were a couple who worked in the conservatory part-time, and I thought the other was a friend."

The young woman shook her head. "One of the media outlets said they were cousins."

"I don't remember that," Fern said. "Interesting." Her mind flashed to the letters that said she had killed the letter-writer's entire family. She spun around, looking for London. He was just putting away his phone.

He walked toward her and said, "Warrant in process."

"Good." She relayed the information the other woman had given. "Can we confirm that?" She lowered her voice and said, "I'm thinking about the letter that said I had killed his entire family."

London stared at her in surprise for a long moment, pulled out his phone again and said, "Steve, I need you to check on something."

She couldn't believe how much information had come to light. She had three separate cases—everything that went wrong with her parents, the murders she'd been acquitted of and everything that was going wrong now. That any one person could have so much bad luck was more of a coincidence than she was ready to take on. She'd often wondered if it was all related, but there had been no proof, no way to even begin to connect the dots. Dr. Royce returned a moment later. He held up a piece of paper for her. "Here is the name of the person who we gave everything to."

She reached for the note, looked down and smiled. "He's still my lawyer. I'll give him a quick call and see what he's got." She glanced at Dr. Royce. "Thanks for your help."

LONDON STAYED ON the line as Steve searched through the records to find the relationship between the previous four victims. "According to the receptionist here, she said she'd read it in one of the media outlet. But I don't remember seeing anything about it," London said. "I was a little distracted."

London waited for Steve to check. London saw Fern and the other woman talking beside Dr. Royce. Fern held a sheet of paper in her hand. He wasn't sure what was going on and hated to miss the conversation, but, at the same time, this was important.

"They are cousins. The couple who was killed were cousins of the head of the department. The fourth victim was the niece of both." Steve added, "So they were related, although not closely. I'm searching for headlines right now, but I'm not seeing much," Steve said. "Weird."

"I think Dr. Death made for bigger headlines." Unfortunately that was all too true. "Let me know when the warrant comes in." He hung up and walked over to Fern, motioned at the paper in her hand. "What's that?"

She smiled. "Dr. Royce found out who was given all my parents' lab material after their deaths. It was my lawyer."

He nodded. "That makes sense. Time to ask him about that." With a wave good-bye, they left.

"You know it's funny, because I don't remember the lawyers ever mentioning anything about my parents' research."

"More than one lawyer?"

"Two brothers owned the law firm. One has since died. Then my current lawyer took over my estate, even though he was more into criminal law. He said he looked after families. Whatever was required."

"I think, if I was dealing with an estate, I would like an estate lawyer," London said. "Anything less is shortchanging yourself."

"And yet this lawyer got me the acquittal."

London stopped. He turned and looked at her. "The lawyer who you had in court is the same one who handled your parents' estate?" he asked incredulously.

"He only took over handling the estate after his brother died." She shrugged. "That's one of the reasons why I went with him. He knew the family situation. And I liked him."

"When did the brother die?"

She frowned. "I've no idea."

"Anything to do with your life is suspicious."

"Okay, I'll give you that." She chuckled. "Are you going to feed me now?"

He snorted. "Absolutely. And then we'll talk to that lawyer of yours."

"Great. I need to find out about my parents' research. And I'd like to get some answers to a few questions."

GOOD, HE'D FINALLY got Derek set up. Now he could relax a little. It was damn hard to keep the pieces rolling in the right direction when all the players had it in their heads to do their own thing.

There was more to do. Lots more. But a few odd things were happening that worried him. The cops and the letters were one. The damn canister was another. Like, who sent that gas canister into her house?

She had enemies, but he doubted she'd pissed off anyone with a military background.

Not to the point of killing her.

That wasn't part of his plan.

He wanted her to suffer like he had. But, if that wasn't an option, then he wanted her dead. But he would do the job—no one else.

He hated to think someone else was after her.

This was his gig. And only his.

The other asshole could fuck off.

CHAPTER 25

H ER LAWYER, JERRY Solange, greeted her with a big smile and a handshake. When he remembered London was an FBI agent, he turned his gaze back to Fern. "Have there been more developments?"

She laughed, took a seat. "Not now, although who knows about tomorrow. But there have been new deaths."

The lawyer sank into his chair, his face paling. "I think you better tell me what's going on."

London filled in the lawyer as much as he could with Fern interjecting bits and pieces. "So, you see, I wasn't even in the country when these murders were committed."

"Thank heavens for that. I don't mind telling you how part of me thinks we got very lucky last time. I'd hate to have to defend you again for similar charges."

She shook her head. "I wouldn't like that much either."

"And why did you come back to the States?" the lawyer asked.

"I got a letter threatening Reggie if I didn't return in twenty-four hours."

"You what?" London asked, glaring at Fern.

She turned to look at London and frowned at him but faced her attorney to finish her story. "So I booked my flight. But the airline had a problem and delayed my schedule. Even though my flight was changed, I still got here within the warning period. Yet Reggie was already missing."

London cleared his throat. Loudly. "You do realize that, if somebody has killed Reggie and wanted to make it look like you were the guilty party, they would have checked the airlines and saw the day you were returning, but maybe they didn't realize you were delayed ..."

"And they went ahead with their plans, not knowing I now had an alibi?" With a shudder, she added, "Good for me. Bad for them."

"Are you withholding any other information from me?" London asked, none too happy.

"That's it," she said, watching his expression.

He shook his head. "You got lucky." Nudging her, he asked, "What about your parents' research material?"

When she asked her lawyer, he glanced at her in surprise. "I have no idea. My brother handled all that."

She nodded. "I never thought to ask about it before, but it's certainly something I could use now."

He pulled the keyboard toward him and quickly typed. "If there is a storage locker, I would imagine the material is all there. I don't remember seeing the specifics." He glanced at the monitor, then at her. "Your parents rented a storage space only months before they passed on. My brother noted the research materials were placed in the locker. The estate pays for it."

"I didn't even know there was a storage locker."

"Back then you were too traumatized to deal with it, so I can understand my brother not bringing it up to you." He tapped the desk. "I haven't done more than take a cursory look at the estate details. Now that you're an expert botanist in your own right, potentially this is the right time to review your parents' work. Besides storage lockers are cheap. You'd be surprised how many people use them for all kinds of reasons."

"Where is it? What unit number? And how do I get inside?"

He checked his monitor. "It's on Rutland Road, Morgan Storage, locker number 247. Apparently the key is in your file." He got up and walked over to a big set of wall cabinets, pulled out a drawer, slid hanging folders to the side and pulled out a large file. Inside he lifted a key on a long key ring. "This is it." He handed it to her.

She stared at it as if she'd been handed the key to the world. "Oh my."

"I'm sorry. I didn't even realize this was here. I could've told you about it the last time we met."

She shook her head. "Last time we met, you were trying to keep me out of jail for the rest of my life. I'm very grateful you focused on that problem, not this."

He nodded and smiled at them. "If I can do anything else for you, let me know."

As they took their leave, she said to London, "I want to go to the locker now."

"I already looked it up on the GPS."

Fifteen minutes later they walked between rows of storage lockers. Up ahead they found the one they were looking for. She unlocked it. London bent, grabbed the huge garage door and raised it.

They both stopped and stared.

Boxes upon boxes were stacked on the right-hand side. On the opposite side was a desk, tables, office chairs, a filing cabinet and lab equipment, any number of which might've come from a lab. Yet it had been arranged into a usable space within the locker, as if it hadn't just been stored here but was in recent use.

Considering open files were on the desk, that just confirmed her belief. "Somebody else has a key to this place."

"And we need to know exactly who that is."

She walked to the desk and the open file. "This is Zanders's file. And it's recent. As in last week." She flipped
through to the beginning. "Experiments that had been done
on him. It's a record of the last year."

She shuffled the pages, seeing just what was happening
here. Some of the handwriting was hard to read, which was
typical in some cases. But the lab tests, they weren't hard to
read it all.

"He was testing different poisons and their antidotes on
rats with some success but hadn't enough to move to
humans. If it did work, he planned to inject himself with the
antidote."

"So he's either been poisoned or has poisoned himself."
London wandered among the large boxes, opening a box
here and there, looking for anything that would give them an
idea of who else may have been in here.

She opened a drawer in the desk. Business cards, nap-
kins, gum and pens. "Somebody's been using this space for a
long time." She turned to gaze around at the rest of the
space. "It'll take forever to go through this."

"We don't have to go through it all. Although I imagine
at some point you may want to. Right now we're looking for
names. Anyone involved in your parents' research."

She nodded. Opening the top drawer of the nearby filing
cabinet, she flipped through the files. The second-to-last
folder was a name she recognized. "Susan Miller was the
niece of the two cousins who were killed, right?"

"Yes."

She picked up the folder and said, "I have a file on a Su-san Miller here." She read the details. "Thirty-eight years old."

She continued to read through it. "The woman came to my parents somehow, but I can't tell exactly what they were doing with her. Or why." At the end of the file she said, "I found the last entry."

"What is it?"

"She became quite ill, and they had to stop working on her."

"Poisoned?"

"Not that I can tell. I believe it was cancer. She left the study approximately six months before my parents' death."

"Anything else in the files on the cousins? One was Tere-sa. Her maiden name was Miller."

Fern checked the drawer. "There's a file here on her, but it's very thin." She read through the notes. "She was tested to see if she'd fit the program but didn't. So they didn't bring her into it. But it was somewhere around the same time they brought in her niece."

"And yet Teresa was murdered as well."

She nodded. "Zanders tested her." Fern opened Susan Miller's folder. "Zanders is named as the tester on Susan as well. He was attached to the program, working for my mother. I don't even know for sure if my mother met either of these people. It would've been Zanders doing the work directly."

"So why kill them a decade after your parents died?"

"No idea. Unless he was hiding their participation in this earlier program." She turned to stare at the filing cabinet, hating what she would likely find. "We also don't know if this is my mother's work or if this was Zanders's work on the side."

"Is that likely?"

"It's possible." She shook her head. "All kinds of scenarios come into play here. The bottom line is, they weren't allowed to do human testing yet, and they might have been found out. Maybe Zanders decided to kill them off because they were the only ones who knew what he was involved with."

"Or maybe he gave them something he wasn't supposed to give them."

"Or he tapped the patients my mother dealt with and offered them a new treatment, a sure result." On a hunch, she opened the middle drawer of the filing cabinet. Two fat files rested inside. She pulled out both, set them on the desk and opened them.

"He was working with the Millers himself," she announced. "After my parents' death, he either contacted the patients, or they contacted him, but he started working with them directly then. And, according to the date here, it was less than thirty days after my parents' death."

"So your parents died. He takes over their work, starts doing experiments. Something goes wrong, and he's forced to kill them to hide his tracks?"

An exhausted voice from behind them said, "I was forced to kill them to hide somebody else's tracks. Your mother's in fact."

Fern spun around to see a man leaning against the edge of the doorjamb. Sweat poured off his forehead, and his body shook so badly he could barely stand.

London strode over to him. "Zanders, I presume?"

The man nodded. "I was carrying on Dr. Bethany Geller's research. She was worried about your father but didn't realize he would be as dangerous as he turned out to be. We would've done something about it earlier if we'd known."

Fern stayed silent. The last thing she wanted now was confirmation that her father had killed her mother, killing himself too.

"Her work was important," Zanders whispered. "She was so damn close to finding antidotes for some of these major poisons. Poisons affecting people from common uses. Arsenic on treated lumber. It's an antifungal, but some people reacted more severely than others. Just a simple example. Another is pesticides. Some of those were incredibly powerful, having long-term effects. But, in her case, she worked on the more common medicinal ones."

"Where did she find her patients?"

"Hospitals and clinics. She had several doctors who she met with on a regular basis."

"Did they know her experiments were without approval from the regulatory bodies?"

He shrugged. "Of course she didn't tell anyone exactly what she was doing. Only that she was searching for subjects with certain parameters. And, if there were any, to send them her way. I don't think the doctors knew what she was doing, but also I don't think they cared."

"Why the Millers?"

"I don't know who or what Dr. Geller did her original testing on. She was very secretive about all that. I've spent the last dozen years trying to duplicate her results, only I didn't see the same effects. I gave up the research until somebody at AMAX contacted me. They said they knew exactly how your mother got her results. They wanted me to continue her work, but they wouldn't tell me who the original lab subject was."

London asked derisively, "How did that help?"

"They wanted to know if I could duplicate the results." He smiled. "I was so excited for a while. I really thought I could do it. But I had no success. Finally they told me how she'd been using the same subject for years. And that person had the ability to produce the proper antibodies. When I realized that, I started testing myself." He held out his hands. "As you can see, my results were less-than-positive. And, as my patients started dying, I realized only three of Dr. Geller's patients were alive from before. If I wanted to wipe the slate clean, I needed to take them out too. Chances where they would die somewhere in the next ten years, but I couldn't wait."

"What do you mean, you couldn't wait?"

"AMAX. They wanted me to bring them in for testing, like lab rats. I couldn't do that to them. It seems like all we've done was give these poor people hope and then take it away again. AMAX was insistent—threatening to pick them up on their own if I didn't cooperate. I told them how I had been testing on myself, but none of the research was working. That's when they promised they knew somebody who could give me the type of results they wanted. And they wanted to know if I could develop it from there." He shook his head. "But I didn't trust them. Too many years had gone by with too many promises and too much had happened. I was not interested at all."

"So you turned around and killed your last three patients?" Fern stared at him in shock. "That makes no sense."

"AMAX would pick them up and take them to their labs anyway."

"That's kidnapping," London said. "Holding them against their will. While drugging them, keeping them as test subjects, is illegal as hell."

He nodded. "Yes. Exactly. So what I did was a service to them. I put them out of their misery," he said. "Ben's death wasn't planned. Susan told him about the treatments. And me. He contacted me a few days after AMAX turned up the pressure. I felt I didn't have a choice, but it made it easier knowing he was a bastard. He'd been harassing women for decades but never was punished for it."

He glanced at Fern apologetically. "I'm sorry that those deaths were laid at your feet." He labored to bring in his next breath. "I need to finish off the nightmare. If your father hadn't killed your mother, Bethany and I would've done wonderful things. But, in the meantime, I became less of a researcher, less of a scientist without her. Who knew?" He held up a syringe, stabbed himself and shoved the plunger home before Fern or London could reach him. He gave her a bitter half smile and said, "It's better this way."

"Who in AMAX was doing this?"

His eyes glazed, and he went into convulsions. She heard London on the phone behind her, calling for help.

"Who?" she whispered. "Please tell me who."

But he died in her arms.

"Who is it?" London asked in a hushed voice at her side.

She lifted her wet gaze to his. "I have no idea."

LONDON CHECKED THE man's pockets, confirming he was Zanders. London made more calls. Before long they had both an ambulance and the coroner on site. At least now there would be no problem getting a warrant for Zanders's official lab. London would meet Steve there as soon as the paperwork went through.

In the meantime, as much as London hated it, Fern's life

would get flipped as Zanders's confession meant the bulk of his material here had to be gone through. And London knew how little of her own personal life would remain private if her name was mentioned anywhere.

As he studied her face, drawn and pale, her arms tight across her chest, he realized she already understood just how intrusive this would be for her. He walked over and stood at her side in silent support.

The local cops were less concerned about all the paperwork on the right-hand side of the storage unit, once they understood it was her parents' research. But they were very interested in knowing what kind of work Zanders had been involved in. As far as anybody could tell, the files on the left-hand side were his. Fern flipped through them and confirmed the bulk were lab tests.

The female cop shook her head. "Mad scientists. They keep popping up everywhere."

Fern then stood off to one side, flicking through the folders in her hands, looking for anything that would give her answers.

London also watched the cops as they avoided any interaction with Fern, other than several guarded looks. A huge divide still existed between law enforcement and her. That wouldn't be an easy bridge to cross.

Some of the cops took most of the boxes, leaving the rest of the officers to handpick items of interest out of what was left.

Fern curled up on the office chair, completely disassociated from what was going on around her.

"Are you ready to go?" London asked.

She lifted her gaze to his. "I was ready to go a long time ago."

He nodded. "The police are moving Zanders's files to

the station."

"Technically this should all belong to me because it's in my locker. I don't have a problem with the cops looking at the stuff, but I do want it all back."

"Do you think it's of any value to you in research terms?"

She shrugged. "I don't even know what my parents were working on. But, if they made progress, I would like to know what the data supported. That Zanders carried on some of the same research and quite possibly crossed ethical lines at every turn doesn't mean the experience and the knowledge he gained should be lost."

"That makes sense." He made a mental note to talk to the cops about returning all paperwork to Fern.

She stood. "It's late. I need food soon. Did the warrant come through for the lab?"

He nodded. "I'm meeting Steve there. The local police will be with us."

She stiffened slightly. "Of course. It's a law enforcement issue. I don't belong there." She glanced around. "Maybe I'll pick up some food and return here to go through some of my parents' material."

He hesitated.

She shot him a look. "You can't stay here with me, and I can't go with you. Cops should be all around here for quite a while, so I'll be safe."

He glanced toward the men busy taking photographs. He knew they still had a lot of forensic evidence to look at. He nodded. "I'll speak to them about keeping an eye on you."

Her voice dry, her tone hard, she said, "Sure. Keep an eye on me. But not for my safety. For theirs."

He winced. "They don't know you like I do."

She chuckled. "They don't know me at all."

On that note, he walked to a pair of detectives, comparing notes. London explained he was leaving, but Fern was staying. "Keep her safe."

One detective nodded and said, "No problem."

"Any idea how long you will be here?"

The detective looked at the size of the space. "We're stuck here for a few more hours."

"Then I'll head over to the main lab, look at what we find there. I'll be back." He turned toward Fern. "And I'll bring some food."

"I'll pick up something and then come back."

"I don't want you going alone."

"A sandwich shop is around the corner. That's hardly anything to fuss about."

He turned back to the detective, who held up a hand. "We'll make sure somebody goes with her."

With that confirmation, London walked to the car. He'd be as fast as he could.

It was hard not to be excited about the breaks in the case. Maybe they would finally get answers. And possibly Fern could get her life back.

WHY COULDN'T HE get answers? He needed answers. The damn cops were blowing up over the case. He needed to know what they knew.

How could he forward his own agenda if he couldn't get direct and accurate information?

He picked up his phone and sent off a flurry of texts. Normally he'd get someone else to take care of this shit, but right now was touchy. He couldn't afford to have anyone else know....

CHAPTER 26

D ECIDING SHE NEEDED food first, she grabbed her purse, slung it over her shoulder and walked away. She heard voices behind her but didn't slow her steps. No way would she ask anybody to come with her. To hell with that. She'd seen how law enforcement took care of her in the past.

She continued to walk, but two policemen came up on either side of her. They never said a word. Her shoulders sagged. They shouldn't have done that. Now she'd have to be nice to them. In a low voice she muttered, "Thanks."

The man on the left didn't say a word, but the man on the right said, "We're happy to help. We're sorry for what you went through before."

She shot him a look of incredulity. "Really? I know you all think I got away with murder, but you're wrong. And while you were focused on me, somebody continued to kill people."

He nodded, shoved his hands in his pants pockets and said, "Which is why we are renewing our efforts and considering the cases again. Somebody out there is still trying to set you up."

"Do you think Zanders was working for someone?" asked the man on her left. "Could there be more killers involved?"

"Or he's being blackmailed, like my parents were years

ago."

"Blackmailed? Your parents? What's that got to do with any of this?" Lefty asked.

She tried to explain, keeping it superficial, saying she'd handed over the information to London with her mother's notes about being blackmailed by AMAX.

Lefty whistled. "If you want to take on an enemy, it's a big enemy to take on."

She nodded. "Within a few months my parents were both dead. And everything laid low for a long time. Until I grew up. I never had anything to do with AMAX. They just owned the lab I was renting space in."

"Isn't that rather unusual?"

She explained about AMAX. "Maybe I chose that space because it had something to do with my parents," she confessed. Inside she hated even hearing the words come out of her mouth. Was that the reason she'd gone to the same lab? "It's also difficult to get independent space like that."

"You think Zanders took on your mother's research?"

"From what I understand, he carried on my mother's work. Both took a dark path, crossing some ethical lines by getting involved in something they shouldn't have. I don't know all the details. I never worked with Zanders, and I don't remember ever seeing him at my house. But, if he did come to my house, it would have been a long time ago. My parents died when I was sixteen. And I wasn't privy to any of their research at the time."

She didn't know what else she could say without getting into her entire history. And that was the last thing she wanted to do.

The sandwich shop was up ahead. She said, "I'm heading in there. Do you guys want anything?"

"I'll stay outside, stand watch," the man on her right said.

"I'll come inside and get something. I missed breakfast," Lefty said.

Inside the business, she ordered a large chicken breast sandwich with everything. As she paid for the sandwich, the cop placed a similar order. Outside, they met up with Righty and headed to the storage unit.

"I hope you guys get the right person this time," she said, trying to ease the bitterness in her tone.

"We intend to."

She shrugged. "A lot of people right now are either missing or dead."

"Who's missing?"

"Reggie, who you know about, and Derek, the guy who had all that lovely proof that I killed those people."

"The FBI agent's brother?" Lefty asked. "What do you mean, he's missing?"

"Nobody can find him. He's not answering his phone, and he is not at his house. No way to know where he's gone."

"Any idea why he'd run off?"

"Maybe because I'm back, and his whole life has unraveled. He perjured himself on the stand, and, as much as I'd like to see justice for what I went through because of his words, I doubt there will be any."

She considered what Stefan had said about Derek dying. She wondered if anyone would find him before he ended up dead.

"Derek?" Lefty said. "I might have seen something in the files with that name."

She turned to look at him. "What files? Where?"

"In the storage locker."

She frowned, remembering what London had said about his brother's condition. "His health is poor. He might have a major illness that maybe Zanders was helping him with." She shook her head. "But none of this research is deemed safe enough to experiment with poisons on humans at this stage."

"Lots of people try a lot of different things, particularly with herbs," Lefty said. "The industry is largely unregulated."

She nodded. They weren't saying anything she didn't already know. "When we get back to the locker, I want to see where his name is mentioned."

"Those files have gone to the station." The cop pulled out his phone. "I'll call and see if we can do a search."

By the time they made it to the storage locker, the order had been passed along, but so far nobody had called about finding anything. She pulled out her phone and called London. She didn't mean to bother him, but, if Zanders had a home office, maybe something could be found there that would pinpoint to Derek's location.

"London here," he said in a brisk tone.

"Derek may have had something to do with Zanders. It could explain why Derek's condition is fading quickly."

"You think Zanders poisoned him?" London asked in alarm.

"No," she rushed to reassure him. "It's possible Zanders was trying to help him. Unless we find a Zanders's file on Derek, we can't be sure. The detectives think that file went to the police station."

There was a hard silence on the other end of the phone. "We just found Zanders's home address. Or at least we're told it was his home. I'm heading over there in ten." And he hung up.

She told the detective what London and his partner had found. "Let's hope they find a whole lot more to get to the bottom of this."

"We will. The case is breaking open. We should have answers by the end of the day."

She brightened. "That would be nice."

Inside the storage locker, she sat on the chair and polished off her sandwich. Then she headed back to her parents' filing cabinet. She waded systematically through the files, recognizing the protocols her parents had been following but with other subjects. And Zanders was one of them. No wonder he wanted to keep his research here with her parents'. The files with his name on them gave all his history as well. Several other people were mentioned but only their first names, never last names. She could only hope that, if they cross-referenced these files to Zanders's files, they could find more information between the two filing systems and thereafter from the patients themselves. Although Zanders might have killed them too. And what about Derek?

She couldn't get rid of the feeling something was horribly wrong. And this wasn't about Derek. She paced the storage locker, wondering who was in trouble now. Finally she pulled out her phone and texted London.

Are you okay?

When she got no response, she fretted again. Finally, after another ten minutes, she sent the same message. Again no response. If he was busy at Zanders's home, all kinds of things could be happening.

When she couldn't stand the silence any longer, she called London, and it went to voice mail. She walked over to Lefty. "Any idea how to contact the men who went to

Zanders's apartment? I'm trying to contact London, the FBI agent, but so far he's not answering his phone or text messages," she confessed. "I'm getting worried."

The man gave her a sharp look, pulled out his phone and called the station. She only half listened as he asked for assistance getting hold of whoever was at the apartment.

"Four men went," he told her. "London was one of them. They are contacting them now. I should hear back in a few minutes."

She nodded and gave him a smile. "Thank you."

But inside her stomach knotted; her gut churned. Her throat was so damn dry she knew something was definitely wrong now. "Do you have that address?" She tried to keep her voice calm, controlled.

His phone rang. "Right. Okay. I'll tell her." He turned back to Fern. "London and his partner are searching the rest of the building."

She nodded. "Any idea where it is?"

He shrugged. "Willow Crescent. Only a few blocks from here."

She tried to remember where that was and realized it was one of the streets across from the sandwich shop. "So just around the corner." She turned as if she saw the property in the right direction. But, of course, trees and fences were in the way. "I'll walk down and take a look."

"Are you really that worried?"

She gave him a hard stare. "Yes."

"Then I'm coming with you."

With him following behind, she picked up the pace and raced toward the location.

LONDON WALKED DOWN the stairs from Zanders's apartment. "Interesting that nothing was there. It's almost as if he didn't live here. Then given all the research we found in his lab and locker maybe that makes sense too."

Steve nodded. "Maybe he has another place. Like his family has other property he could've gone to. Somewhere in all this mess, we still have to find your brother."

London didn't bother answering. He hated that he hadn't been able to say good-bye to his brother. A part of him knew it was already too late. The thought of his brother dying slowly, alone somewhere, with nobody looking out for him, hurt, cut through his heart in a deep way. He didn't understand who his brother had become, but that didn't mean he wanted such a death for him.

"Three floors to this building. There's still hope," Steve said. "Zanders was on the top floor. I suggest we start at the bottom, check all the apartments, ask if anybody has seen Zanders and ask about your brother."

London nodded. "I want to go to the basement also. See if any storage lockers are down there. The cops can canvass the rest of the hallways. I'm heading to the boiler area first."

He opened the door to the stairs leading down, turned toward Steve, who stood with a frown on his face. London grinned. "Are you are coming with me, or are you going in the field?"

Steve rolled his eyes. "When you put it that way, I'm obviously with you."

They slipped down the stairs to the basement area. London found a set of light switches. He hit them to illuminate the decent-size basement with storage compartments. Most were an open construction of slatted wood to see inside—a collection of bikes and snowboards, old furniture, suitcases and boxes.

As they walked along, he searched for the number that correlated to Zanders's apartment. "Not on this row so it must be around the corner."

They kept going until they came to one that was totally stuffed. London saw through the slatted door that boxes were up against it. A shiny new lock was on the outside. He glanced at Steve.

Steve shrugged and said, "The lock might be new, but the hinges are old."

London reached out, and, with a hard yank, the hinges and lock came right off the frame, popping the wooden door open. He could barely squeeze through the line of boxes.

He froze.

Beyond the boxes, lying off to one side on a cot was a male. London checked for a pulse. The blankets were tucked up tight to the man's chin. He pulled them back and gasped. It was his brother. He dropped to Derek's side, twisting to look back at Steve. "Call an ambulance."

Steve gave him a startled look, then walked out of sight to make the call.

"Derek? Derek, can you hear me?" Derek's body was cool, still. His breath faint, barely audible. London tried to wake him, but his brother appeared to be in a deep coma. Unconscious with death wailing at the door. In that Stefan had been right.

A voice slammed into his head. *I told you.*

London bolted to his feet and spun around in a circle, looking for Stefan.

Stefan's voice rang through his head, strident, loud. *I've been here. The same place I've always been. I've been knocking on the outside of that goddamned thick skull of yours for over a year now.*

Hesitantly London asked, *Stefan?*

Yes. Who the hell do you think goes around talking to people this way?

His voice was so full of exasperation that, in any other circumstance, London would have smiled. He stared at his brother. *Did you know he was here?*

I didn't know he was here. I knew he was dying.

London nodded. He stared at his brother, whose emaciated form was a mere shell of the big boisterous young man he'd been. *What happened to him?*

Jealousy. Insecurity. Complete lack of self-confidence.

London heard the words, but they didn't make any sense.

Finally Stefan said, *He's been poisoned.*

London dropped to his brother's side again at the tone of Stefan's voice. It was sad, sorrowful. *Who did this to him? He didn't deserve this.*

He did it to himself. Check around. You think he's been a prisoner in there?

The door was locked. He couldn't have gotten out.

Stefan snorted. *You snapped off the lock with a hand. Only a visual deterrent to anybody on the outside. If your brother wanted to get out, he could have.*

But why? What was his connection to Zanders?

You know what direction to look. It's up to you to find proof. Only this time make sure Fern stays out of it.

And just like that he was gone. London pulled out his phone and tried to call Fern. The reception was terrible down there. He pocketed his phone and, unable to help his brother, got up, looking at the rest of the room.

Folders and files were all over the floor. One of them

had his brother's name on it. He flipped through it, realizing his brother had willingly been taking poison. Administered by Zanders. London shook his head. "Derek, why?"

But, of course, got no answer.

He stared at his brother, his heart aching for what could have been.

Ten minutes passed, then twenty. And still no sirens. No sign of Steve. He'd probably gone outside the building to make his call. Maybe he went back upstairs to get the men's help? To bring them to the basement? No, that didn't make sense. Shit. No way would London leave his brother. Not right now.

He kept going through the files. He saw the same names repeatedly. The ones Zanders had killed to hide his poisonous actions. Maybe he'd even meant to kill Derek too. Or had it been Derek's willful decision? London would have to read the entire file to know. It would have been nice if his brother had left a suicide note. Kept things tidy. But of course not. He'd never been accommodating.

At the bottom of the heap he found files with notes in Fern's mother's handwriting. He flicked through them, looking for answers. One file caught his eye.

> Elliot Marsh. Condition critical—patient terminal.
>   Initially administering poisons for comfort. Patient is allergic to morphine. He shows a slight improvement. We've switched up the poisons, the drugs, to see if we can help extend his life.

And the notes went on and on. In the end, the patient died six months into her care. But then he'd been terminally ill, so no shock there. Marsh's wife's file was on the floor. She too had been a patient. Terminal. Experimental drugs administered, drugs created from their poisonous plants.

He shook his head. "Why would they try some of these plants?" But then again, as he understood from Fern, many plants were used as medicines. So maybe it wasn't so far off after all. And desperate people did desperate things.

But this family's story was heartbreaking. Both parents had terminal illnesses, and they had two children. The mother's genetics had passed down to the daughter. And she died less than two years after both her parents, leaving the boy the sole survivor.

He wanted to believe Fern's mother had tried to help them. He had no idea where she stopped at the end of the day, whether she just administered too strong a dose to put them out of their misery, or whether she moved on to other patients, cold-heartedly taking notes as to how her patients had passed. It was hard to think any good thoughts about Bethany Geller after hearing of Fern's childhood. But maybe that was doing Bethany a disservice.

In the name of science, many experiments had been done, hurting a patient, but allowing them to save thousands more. He flipped through Mrs. Marsh's file to see if anything else was of importance. The police would have a heyday going through all this. A family photo was included in the file. Two kids, two parents. Happy, smiling, before everything blew apart. He looked over the picture. The only surviving member, a boy, smiled at the camera, not knowing his world would never be the same again. London flipped it over and read the names on the back, confirming it was the family photo.

And then he read the name of the boy, and his heart froze. Slowly standing, the picture in his hand, he turned to face the gate. "No ambulance is coming, is there?"

Silence rang hollowly throughout the storage lockers.

Complete silence.

London turned to look at Derek, still alive, but his life slipping away. And London couldn't save him.

London, grief slowly welling up, realized what a fool he'd been. He'd not seen a viper in his own backyard. It had had to be someone close to Fern. London just hadn't seen that connection because he'd been so busy looking in the forest that he hadn't seen the trees.

"There's no point in hiding anymore, Steve. Not now that I know who you are."

Steve stepped so London could see him at the other end of the small pathway between all the boxes and stared at him. "I wondered when you'd figure that out. I had hoped you never would," he confessed. "For a time I had hoped she'd never come back. But, when I thought it over, I couldn't resist trying again."

"Why? Why do all this? Why kill Derek? Pam? And why Reggie?"

Steve snorted. "Reggie and Pam were my foster family. The guy is as much of a loser as he possibly could be. But I didn't kill him."

"Where the hell is he then?

"No idea. But, I'll be checking out that address you gave me as soon as we're done here. If ever a guy was good at hiding, it's him. The same as he always did when things got tough. Pam was nice to me. She's the only mother I've known—because Fern's mother killed my own."

"That's not true. They were all ill."

"Yes, they were. But they believed in Fern's mother. Her lies. They didn't take any modern medicine, like chemotherapy. They wouldn't do anything except what Bethany Geller told them to do. And she killed them. As surely as I stand here before you today, she took them all from me one by one."

London could just imagine how Steve felt as a boy, watching his family picked off one by one. And there was only one common denominator—Fern's mother.

"I doubt Bethany tried to kill them. For all you know, she was trying to help them."

"She was a quack. But my parents believed in her lies and her string of half-truths," he cried passionately. "She deceived them, and they paid the ultimate price."

London stared at his partner in bewilderment. "Why did you wait so long before you decided to attack Fern?"

"I was going to leave it. I wasn't going to do anything. I thought I'd dealt with it. Until the former head of the conservatory died, along with three of his family members. And something about that just hit home." He shook his head. "I knew I couldn't walk away. I knew that would never be a choice. I had to do something."

"So you didn't kill Ben and those other three people?"

He shook his head. "No, of course not. But I made it look like it had been Fern. After all, she was working in the same damn lab her parents had been in. She was picking up all her mother's work, carrying on the same dastardly deeds of her mother before her. I couldn't let her do that. It was only a matter of time before she went down the same road her mother had."

"But you couldn't find any real evidence to put her away ..."

Steve shrugged. "No. I tried hard though."

"You couldn't because she didn't do it. Zanders did."

Steve stared off in the distance. "I didn't hear what Zanders said today. I'm sorry I missed that. I had questions. I'm hoping the answers I have been looking for will finally show up in his files."

"Zanders admitted to having killed all those people. Why did you pin all this guilt on Fern when she didn't do anything?"

Steve snarled. "Because she did. She and her family. They're responsible for my entire family dying."

London shook his head, not knowing how to get through to his partner. "Her parents may have been indirectly responsible, but not Fern. She didn't do anything. Her mother tortured Fern all her life. Her mother didn't do anything for her out of love. She treated Fern worse than she did her patients."

An odd spark lit the dark depths of Steve's eyes for a long moment. Then he shrugged. "It doesn't matter. I killed Pam. I didn't kill the other two people in the conservatory. Not even sure they were murdered. But, if they were, I'd lay the blame for that at Zanders's door."

"And yet you still killed Pam? And tried to pin it on Fern?"

"I'm sorry about Pam." He shrugged. "I planned to kill Reggie too, but he suspected something before walking in the door, begging me to not hurt Pam before he even saw her body inside. I dusted him with a toxic powder, but he raced away instead and only got a little bit. Still I'd hoped it would be enough. Considering he's still missing, maybe I did kill him after all. And typical of Fern, she changed her flights at the last moment and thus had an alibi. I couldn't believe it when she was acquitted before. But I hadn't killed anyone at that point. I hadn't done anything other than plant evidence and make it look like it was her. That's what I could do. But

I knew she was coming back now. I knew this time there had to be real evidence. Or she'd walk, and the world would never be safe again."

"Did you throw the poison canister into her house?"

Steve shook his head. "No, that wasn't me. It was an odd moment to realize I wasn't the only one after her. I wondered if it was Zanders. I'd reconnected with him years ago. A morbid curiosity to see if he was carrying on Dr. Geller's research."

London was still trying to figure out just how complicit his partner had been all these years. It was bad enough he had killed Pam, the only mother he'd known, but London needed to know if Steve had killed anyone else. "Did you have anything else to do with this mess? Did you kill anyone else?"

Steve smirked. "I had to get rid of your brother."

London's heart seized, his breath caught in his throat. He glanced at his brother, even now dying, and whispered, "Did you do this?"

"Well, he is not dead yet. But, by the time the police find his body, he certainly will be."

London closed his eyes and swayed in place. "What did you do?"

"It didn't take much of anything. Of course all these killings had to be done with poison. It was kind of fascinating reading. My mother took notes, you know. She kept notes of everything that Bethany Geller did. Notes of everything the family did with Fern's mother. Dr. Geller talked a lot. My mom taped Bethany's conversations. Fascinating. Listening to those tapes, I learned a lot about poisons. Poisoning your brother was easy. And then I sent him to Zanders for help." He smiled. "I liked that twist."

"How did you poison him?"

Steve opened his eyes wide. "I put a fine powder in his bed. I put it on his couch so he breathed it in. It takes time to make someone ill. But, once it locks into your systems, you decline. According to the research, very little is known about it." He shrugged. "Not that it matters." Steve angled a look at Derek. "He's dead finally, isn't he?"

London swallowed, didn't want to confirm his brother's death. "You killed Pam and Derek?" It was way worse than he'd first thought. That anyone would hurt his brother. "My brother is a fool, but he didn't deserve to be killed."

"He so deserved to be killed. I should've done it a long time ago, when he let the bitch get acquitted. Do you really think your brother worked for a living? You really think he deserved the money I paid him to lie on the stand? To fabricate that conversation that she'd killed everyone? The little bits and pieces of evidence found, that was all him. I couldn't get close enough. I didn't want to get close enough to that bitch."

Steve smiled. "It took Derek a long time to break down. Partly because I only gave him a little bit of poison at a time. He blamed Fern. And a confrontation they had had. I just helped it along. That was fun. It was also fun to watch you be so upset that he was fading away and becoming such a neurotic mess. Derek was a nuisance. The world's much better off without him. Zanders, ... well, he knew it all had to stop, and, at the very end, he knew he had to go too. So he took himself out. Still, I wish I'd been there to see it."

"That was you who broke into Fern's place?"

Steve nodded. "Absolutely. I stayed in the basement. Listened to some of that mumbo-jumbo. What a joke. But then she went out the back bedroom window," he said. "I had to go out the same way, and then I lost her in the neighborhood. She's got the damnedest luck."

London took a step toward the gate.

Steve shook his head. "You know I can't let you go."

"You can't leave me in here. My brother needs medical help." At least London hoped that Derek could still be saved at this point.

"Your brother needs a coffin. And soon so will you." Steve's voice was gentle.

London stared at his partner in shock. He edged closer to Steve. "You poisoned me too?"

"Every time I made your coffee, picked up a coffee or brought you a coffee," he said. "You really should stop drinking that stuff. It can be deadly." He smirked at that. "Your system won't recover from that poison. You won't get that chance. Because the last couple days I upped the doses. I don't know how it is you haven't been showing the same effects," he said in frustration. "According to Zanders, you should be almost bent over, crippled by now." Again he smiled. "And, of course, I've dusted this place. Your skin absorbed that. You should be having trouble breathing." He glared at London. "You should be on your knees collapsed by now. That's why I'm back here, out of the way."

And that's when London realized that, although Steve was technically here, he'd never stepped into the locker, as if he didn't want to touch—or to breathe—anything. London turned in a slow circle, taking another step closer to Steve, now seeing the dust. The particles in the air moved every time he did. Of course, as soon as he thought about it, he realized just how unhealthy he did feel, how his lungs burned, how his eyes stung. He turned completely around and asked, "Why?"

"Because I can. Because I must. For me to walk away from this free and clear, it's what I have to do."

"Steve," Fern called from the end of the hallway. "Have you seen London?"

London took one more step and opened his mouth to warn her, but Steve smiled, took a step closer to London and shot him with a tranq gun. Pain burned the side of his neck, and such a horrible burn scorched the inside of his jaw, through his throat and down his stomach. He sank to his knees. Fern, who had already seen too much and had so little chance to experience anything new, was in terrible danger.

London watched, helpless as she slowly approached Steve. "So it was you." She shook her head. "I wondered."

"You did *not* wonder," Steve snarled. "No way you could have known."

"Of course I could. I can see the green of the poison you've been experimenting with all around you at this moment. I wondered why you were in my bedroom. Why you'd hidden out in my basement. But I never saw the exact same shade of green twice, so I didn't understand it. But it was the mix of different poisons changing the colors, and the age since you'd last touched them. I didn't understand so it was as if you were someone else." It also explained why he'd been able to cross Sutherland's security system. She'd let him inside several times – making his energy acceptable to the system. "I'm rather new to seeing all these things, you know." She spoke in a conversational tone.

"You can't see any of that shit," Steve retorted. "Even if you could, it just makes you a bigger freak than I first thought."

London could only watch as he slowly sagged to the floor. But Fern wouldn't look at him. He wanted to mouth that he loved her and that she was to live a life past this, not to mourn him. But she refused to look at him. Her hand reached out to the slatted wall as if to casually lean against it.

"You can't save him, you know," Steve said. "The poison has already taken effect."

"Of course it has." She shrugged.

Steve pulled out his gun and pointed it at her. "I'll do one better." And he shot her with the same weapon he'd fired at London.

It hit her, throwing her back just enough that she lost her footing and fell against the wooden slats. Panicked, but failing quickly, London scooted forward, half-out half-in the storage space, reaching for Fern.

Steve chuckled. "There you go. Fern kills London, then takes her own life. How very perfect. And of course, Fern had already killed Derek. A three-way love triangle, all ending up in a murder-suicide. Perfect." He pocketed the weapon and turned to walk away, calling back, "See you in hell."

London barely heard a multitude of voices, yelling, "Stop! Raise your hands. Police! You're surrounded."

And then he slowly lost consciousness.

CHAPTER 27

F ERN, WHEN SHE realized the cops were taking care of Steve, dropped to London's side. "Take it easy, London. I'm here."

As the cops approached, she called out, "Stay back. Poison is in the air."

"An ambulance is on its way."

She nodded. "But I don't have time. He'll die." She placed her hand on an acidlike burn wound on his neck. "This isn't just one poison. Multiple poisons are at work."

"But it's not having the same reaction on you?" one of the cops asked.

She shook her head. "You have no idea how immune I am to poisons. My parents tried to be God and fed me poisons all my life, and I'm still here." There was silence in the room as the four cops stared at her. She gave them a grim smile. "Yes, from the age of two onward, I was a prisoner in my parents' home, dosed repeatedly as a lab rat, for them to run tests on. I was sixteen when they died, and I finally found my first taste of freedom. Until you assholes tried to put me away last year. And all for crimes I didn't commit."

Several of the cops closed their eyes. One of them said, "Can you do anything to save London?"

She looked at him and smiled. "I already am."

When she lifted her hand, they saw the burns on London's neck had improved.

Then he coughed, and blood poured from his mouth.

She gasped in shock. "Don't touch me or him while I work on him. Do you hear me?"

They all nodded.

She threw herself over London's body and closed her eyes.

Then she sealed his mouth with hers and inhaled the poison from his lungs. She took it deep inside her own. She lifted her head and coughed; gaseous fumes floated from her mouth as she exhaled heavily. She waved the cops back, then repeated the motion. Instead of giving him CPR, she sucked out the air, sucked out the blood. In her mind, she screamed, *Dr. Maddy, can you help?*

I'm standing right beside you. But you are doing fine. Keep it up.

Fern shook her head. *I can't do this, not alone.*

You are doing it. Keep pulling out the poison. Use your hands. Feel instinctively where it is. It doesn't matter what goes into your system, because you know to throw it off again. Pull it from him, far away from his solar plexus, out of his chest, out of his muscles.

Listening to Dr. Maddy's instructions, she worked feverishly. Instinctively she already knew what to do. Her body had been doing it for decades. Only London showed no improvement. She cried out to Dr. Maddy, *It's not working.*

Stefan stepped forward, bringing a bright cloud around her, and said, *Because you can't fight this. You must join with it.*

She lifted her head and stared at the apparition she knew no one else saw, and she realized what he meant. She was poison. While his body struggled to take it and was losing that battle, her body accepted it and won. He had to learn to accept the poison, and, to do that, he needed her.

Dr. Maddy whispered, *You can do this.*

And if I can't?

Don't even think it, Stefan commanded. *Get down there and help now.*

She draped completely across London's body. Instead of trying to suck out all the poison from his system, she poured into him every ounce of her.

She stopped sucking the air from his lungs. Instead, she gave him the air from her own lungs. Poisoned air. Air she had learned to tame and to breathe with poisons that she had been able to channel, hung on to and made her who she was. And had the capacity to make him who he was. She gave a great big deep sigh. At the same time, she let her soul, her mind and her heart blend with him.

She could hear shocked gasps from around her, but she didn't dare take her focus off London. She could feel herself sinking deeper and deeper and deeper. She was traveling farther and farther into the green vapor his body was soaked in and surrounded by. She'd seen some of that greenish tinge earlier and had wondered and worried. But hadn't seen the green to this extent.

Stefan's words went through her brain, and she embraced them. *Don't be afraid of it. Open your arms to it, and open your arms to him.*

When she opened her eyes, London was before her with a crooked grin on his face. "There you are," he said. "Took you long enough to find me."

She threw her arms around his neck and kissed him, their souls merging tight—bonded, sealed, fused forever. And she slipped into the same state as he was. Both as one.

LONDON OPENED HIS eyes and stared up at the white ceiling. He'd seen and experienced one of the wildest, craziest dreams of his life. The dream didn't even make sense; it was more a nightmare. A catatonic episode. He didn't know what to call it. But it looked like he'd survived. He turned his head to see Fern snuggled beside him. He was in a hospital gown; she was atop the covers. As he stared, reaching a finger to gently stroke her cheek, her eyes flew open.

She leaned over him. "How do you feel?"

"I feel wonderful. I have no idea what happened, but I feel like I slept forever, and I'm now so rested."

She smiled. "Glad to hear that. You ready to wake up now?"

He looked at her and frowned. "What are you talking about?" Just then a woman and a man approached the bed. "Do I know you?"

The woman smiled. "I'm Dr. Maddy. I believe you've heard of me."

The man stepped forward. "I believe you know me. I am Stefan."

London shook his head in disbelief. "Why do you look so strange?" A beautiful dusting trailed through the space in front of him.

"Look strange, how?"

"As if you're not quite there."

Dr. Maddy smiled and said, "Look at yourself."

He sat up and stared down at what should have been his physical body. Instead he saw things through his body—the sheets, the bed, everything beneath it. Even as he stared at Fern, he saw right through her. "Am I dead?"

"No," Fern said with a big smile. "Maybe for the first time you're fully alive."

He stared at her. "Where are we?"

"In the dimension outside of the physical," she said. "It's where I spent a lot of my childhood. The physical world was cold, dark, unpleasant. Somehow, as a necessity for my sanity, I found my way to this place. Here I was in the light. Here I had friends."

"You are definitely in denial." He grinned at the wry twist on her features. "Friends?"

She nodded. "For the longest time, I thought they were all make-believe. I tried to tell my parents, but they thought my visions were side effects of the poisons. When my parents died, I realized I was really in trouble. I screamed for help. Stefan answered, and he's the one who arranged for me to be released from the basement. I didn't know Stefan back then. But I played with children. He told me they were dead children. I didn't know, and there was no way I could tell anyone that the only friends I ever had were ghosts."

"So, when you said you had friends, you actually meant *imaginary friends.*"

She laughed.

"I'm not dead?" he asked. "I'm just making sure here."

She laughed again. "Exactly. You're not dead. We're all walking in the space that I used to spend a lot of time in. When you went down with the poison, I had to take over your system and feed you from mine. You needed the healing of my body, which was well adapted to poisons, for yours to survive the onslaught. But, at the same time, it's easier psychologically if we walk away while our bodies heal, so I brought you here. So that, when you woke up, you would have a choice."

"What choice?"

"The choice to go back or not."

He stared at her. "So I could stay like this? Is my brother here?"

"No, Derek didn't make it. You aren't as far gone. You could stay here, yes, but then your body would be dead."

He thought of his life, what he did and the things he knew. There was so much pain surrounding his brother's life and death. He would miss the young man he used to be. But he didn't want to go the same pathway. At least not alone. "Are you dead?"

She shook her head. "No, I'm alive."

He gave her a slow grin, stroking her face, and said, "Well then, I want to live a full life with you."

She turned to Stefan and said, "Now."

And was ripped out of his arms.

CHAPTER 28

FERN OPENED HER eyes to see white. All white. Every-where she looked was white. Ceiling. Floor. Walls. Sheet covering her. Bed beneath her. White. Sterile. Empty.

A lab.

She closed her eyes, her mind screaming out at the ethers, hoping someone would hear her.

Easy, Stefan said, *I can hear you.*

So can I, said Dr. Maddy.

I'm here too, Detective Sutherland called. *We're looking for you. Hold on.*

She gasped, then filled with joy as she realized this wasn't the same thing all over again. She was no longer alone.

Not now.

You will no longer be alone. I'm here too, came the low fervent whisper beneath the others. Not as strong. Or as clear, but unmistakable nonetheless. London.

Tears poured from her eyes, and it was all she could do to not bawl.

Until a door opened, and a voice filled the room. "Awake, are you?"

She froze. In her mind, she could hear Stefan warning her to be quiet but to observe and tell them everything she saw and heard.

A face loomed over hers. Silver-haired male face. And a total stranger. She stared at him in bewilderment. "Who are you, and why did you kidnap me?"

He smiled at her. Only the smile was razor-thin, pointed. "You've been a pain in the ass for a long time. But I have high hopes we'll have a long, happy working relationship."

She swallowed hard. Only one reason anyone would do this to her. And that was to run experiments on her.

Easy. It won't happen, Stefan murmured. *Stay calm.*

"What did you do to London?"

He straightened in surprise. "Nothing yet. We left him to heal at the hospital. Of course the staff isn't expecting him to live. He was in rough shape. If he dies, he solves a problem for me, but I didn't have a hand in his condition. Honestly I thought he'd have died when the canister of gas that Zanders made was shot into your house, but you survived the test beautifully. Really amazing as I believe you must have had a hand in saving London at the same time."

So much admiration was in his voice that it made her sick. "What else did you do?"

"Oh, nothing much. I tried a few experiments to see what we could get away with. The two people who died at the conservatory were mine. And the security guard. All attempts to monitor response times. I had someone watching them the whole time. It's amazingly easy to poison someone." He shrugged. "Your parents opened me to a world I'd never believed possible, but, once you take away regulations, and ease up on morality, ethics, so much more becomes possible."

Her mind twisted on the possibilities of who this man was. And only one name came to mind. "AMAX Ltd., I believe."

"Well, I certainly am part of that, yes," he said. "I'm Dr. Sartain. I have fingers in many companies. And lines into the FBI. I've spent a lifetime developing my connections." His grin was sly, ugly. "I've waited since forever to meet you. I only realized who you were at your trial, my dear. I'd followed your career rise with great interest wondering if you were following in your parents' footsteps. I was hoping you were a better candidate than Zanders to carry on your parents work. After your parents died, I thought he would know the secret to their success. But it's only at your trial that I wondered if you were your parents' work – your mother's experiment as she referred to you. Imagine my surprise when I finally figured it. It's too bad your mother never told me. If she had the last decade would have been so very different."

She could hear London's cry in her head. She twisted, lifting her hands, but she'd been strapped down. Straps she already knew she'd never loosen on her own. She couldn't have London worrying about her. He had to fight to stay alive in the hospital.

Like hell, he said, his voice harsh, strident. *I'm not leaving you to face this bastard alone. I had to report to him and my boss privately.*

Find his location, Drew said quietly. *I'm running him now, but he's correct when he said he's involved in a lot of companies. You could be anywhere.*

"Don't bother struggling. You'll only get rewards if you're good, and one of those rewards will be to have the straps loosened."

"Where am I?" she asked quietly. "Still in Portland? Or did you fly me across the country?"

He chuckled. "Oh, you're not very far from your house in fact. You should know this place well. You rented space here from us. Do you remember me? I saw your parents several times. I was at your house on occasion. I met you once. They kept you hidden away, didn't they? Such a fascinating experiment. That you turned out as well as you did is amazing."

I've got the location, Drew said. *Hold on. A team is coming.*

Thank God. She snorted at Dr. Sartain's comment. "How would you know?"

"I've been watching you. Testing you. Such a fabulous opportunity your parents had. And they exploited it beautifully."

"Did you hire London to get close to me too? He met with you privately, I know."

"No, to keep tabs on you. And Steve. He was a bit of a wild card. Zanders warned me about Steve. I'd hoped he'd get killed in all this mess."

"Did you know all he did?"

"No, I still don't. But he's a minor card in this game. You, my dear, are the prize."

A light groan escaped. Hadn't she been through enough shit? Couldn't she just once run out of bad guys?

Dr. Sartain gently stroked the hair off her face. His touch light. Caressing.

Her gut clenched at the thought. But it did give her a solution. She closed her eyes and willed big fat tears to drip from the corner of her eyes.

"Easy now. I know this must be a shock, but it won't be a bad life," he promised.

"Can I have a hand free to wipe my eyes and blow my nose?" she blubbered.

He glanced around and then nodded. "Of course. You'll see. I'm not a monster."

He undid one buckle and lifted her hand to give her arm a little shake, as if to get the blood circulating again. She reached up as if to stretch it, then wrapped it around his neck and jerked him toward her.

She took a deep breath and sealed his mouth with her own.

Then exhaled, filling his lungs with the air from her lungs. He choked and gasped as his delicate tissues opened to accept the poisoned air, only to shrivel and die in her arms.

She could sense the others in her mind. Their shock and wonder ...

Shame filled her. She was an animal.

No, London said firmly. *You are a survivor. That's what's important right now. You need to stay alive, survive until we get to you.*

I'm okay, she whispered. *He can't hurt me anymore.*

She released her arm and watched sadly as Dr. Sartain slid to his knees before crumpling to the floor—dead.

The door burst open, and several cops raced inside. Cops she recognized. The ones from Zanders's apartment. The ones who'd watched her help London.

Only to now conclude she could kill too.

She dropped her gaze, not wanting to see the revulsion in their eyes. But they raced to her side and unbuckled her. One gently helped her to sit up.

"Are you okay?" another asked.

Surprised, she lifted her eyes and saw the concern. Concern for her. She took a deep breath. "I'm okay. I'm okay."

LONDON OPENED HIS eyes to find he was still in the weird altered stated he'd been in when Fern had been ripped from his arms. "Stefan, can you help me out of here?"

A vague form appeared in front of him. Stefan. London sat up. "Is she okay?"

"She's fine. She's here in the hospital. The cops insisted she be checked over."

Stefan reached out his right hand and flicked London on the forehead.

London was ripped back through time and space, his body dissolving and reforming, the sensation eerie, as if he were spinning through time and distance. But, when he opened his eyes again, he was in the same room. The same ceiling. Only it was different. Solid.

His gaze landed on Fern, the beautiful woman he loved, staring down at him. He lifted his hands and stared at them. They were solid.

She grabbed them.

He hauled her into his arms and crushed her against his chest. "Thank God, you're okay. I was so scared."

"So was I," she said, her voice muffled against his chest. "But I survived. Like you ordered."

"You did more than that. You fought back, and you won this time. You won't be a victim ever again."

"And you survived the trip to the in-between."

He stroked her cheek, tilting her face so he could look into her beautiful eyes. "That means we're both alive. For a while there …"

"We're alive and well—hopefully with long lives ahead of us." Her lips brushed over his.

He reached up, cupped her chin and gently tugged her toward him. "Only if you're with me."

And he kissed her. A kiss full of love. A kiss full of hope. A kiss that kept them grounded in today but full of promise for all the tomorrows to come.

EPILOGUE

THE DOORBELL RANG.

Fern sealed up the last packing box and crossed the hallway to open the door.

Reggie stood in front of her. Sick and weak but recovering. He had inhaled some of the poison that had killed his long-time girlfriend and then ran. To the cottage where he and Pam had planned a holiday. He'd been deathly ill but had slowly recovered.

He'd been so ill and in such a remote location, he hadn't contacted anyone as to his whereabouts.

She'd seen him several times since he'd returned, but this visit was special.

He held up the cat carrier and grinned. "It took a bit to catch them as they are skittish, but both are safe and sound. Pam took great care of them. She figured you'd come back one day."

His voice held steady at Pam's name, but his eyes were overly bright.

She threw her arms around him. "I'm so sorry."

She led the way to the kitchen where London and both law enforcement—still not talking about their possible family connection—were hauling out the last of the boxes. She would enjoy watching that relationship unfold in the future. Like most things, it happens in its own time. She whispered a low greeting to her fur babies. When she'd given them away, it had been with the understanding it was forever. But to have them back now …

What an incredible gift. Both cats howled. She grinned in delight as she put the carrier on the floor. "You'll be at our new home soon."

"You done here?" Reggie asked, looking around the bare room. "I think this is one of the best things you could do for yourself. This is definitely a place to leave behind."

He'd heard, as had most of the cops, about her child-hood. The media had her in the headlines for days, but, so far, they'd treated her kindly.

She was good with that.

London walked up behind her and slipped an arm around her shoulders. "We're lucky we found a place and can move in right away. This mausoleum will go on the market, and, when it's sold, she can better assess what she wants to do then. In the meantime we have a lovely home not far from here and a whole new beginning for both of us."

Reggie smiled. "Sounds like a perfect plan."

"Are you joining us at the new barbecue place?" she asked. "Or hiding away again?"

He laughed. "No more hiding for me. Not for a long time."

She grinned. "We'll see about that. Don't forget I know you."

Grant called from the doorway, "We're all done. Are you ready to go?"

After a cheerful spin with Logan, she grabbed his hand and scooped up the cat carrier, racing toward Grant, and cried out, "I sure am."

She looked forward to her future—for once bright and cheerful—with London at her side.

It was perfect.

This concludes Book 11 of Psychic Visions: Seeds of Malice.

Book 12 is available.

Eye of the Falcon

Book 12 of Psychic Visions Series

Buy this book at your favorite vendor.
https://geni.us/dmfalcon

As a young girl, Issa bonded with her pet falcon, was the lookout for her father's smuggling operation in Ireland. After everything blew up one night, and her father and brothers were killed, her mother brought her to America to start over.

Immigrating was hard, but eventually she grows up, pursues a career in environmental sciences and continues to follow her passion for falconry. But she doesn't find the same special bond with another falcon. Until one fateful day when her world explodes again …

Eagle, a former military pilot, has retired to his small

ranch outside Denver, Colorado, where he runs a rescue center for raptors in need. One falcon is acting irrationally. Eagle's only recourse is to euthanize him, but the falcon rips free. Although injured so badly he shouldn't be able to fly, the falcon disappears into the skies.

The next day the falcon returns with a beautiful but seriously injured young woman in tow, carrying a message of death and destruction for both of them ...

Sneak Peek from Eye of the Falcon
Book 12 of the Psychic Visions Series

EAGLE WALKED ONTO the long veranda and stared at the sky. He saw no sign of the falcon who'd taken off on him—the falcon so badly injured it shouldn't have been able to fly.

Out of habit he called out, "Rikker? Come home, boy."

The sky was empty. The falcon long gone.

That didn't stop Eagle from searching the vast blue depths. As always it drew him in like a wounded soldier to the hope something—someone—was out there. He was no stranger to hope. Lying in Afghanistan, waiting for rescue with a bullet-torn body, he'd stared for hours as his hope waned.

He'd woken up in the hospital weeks later, realizing sometime hopes and wishes did come true.

Now he gave homage to the sky on a regular basis, the blue depths having given him the courage to stay alive until the shooting around him had died down and his team could come for him. He'd rebuilt his life outside of the Special Forces unit he'd been in. A life as far away and as unregimented as possible. He had over 120 acres here. Part of it was an inheritance from his grandfather, and the other parcel was purchased as a barrier to keep the rest of the world at bay.

He'd seen enough of what humanity could do to one another. He couldn't stop them anymore, but at least now he didn't have to witness it. Here he worked to save those birds that had always rested at the edge of his heart. Something about the majesty of the raptors just called to him. He hadn't planned on creating a refuge for them, but no doubt that was exactly what he'd done.

A biologist buddy, also a former marine, had found an injured eagle and had brought it to Eagle as he'd been the closest help at the time. The concept snowballed.

And that brought him around to wondering about Rikker and what happened. Something impossible.

Rikker had a badly broken wing, leg and a deep cut on his back. Eagle had found him when out riding several days ago. Instead of panicking when a human approached, the falcon had stayed still and let Eagle pick him up and bring him to the center for treatment. Due to the animal's more docile behavior and, by now, out of habit, Eagle had checked for leg bands, then the local falconry clubs.

No one was missing a falcon. Or no one wanted to own up to it and possibly be handed a bill for the bird's care. Not that Eagle would have done so, but he'd seen how people's behavior shifted once money was involved.

In fact he hadn't expected the raptor to survive the night. He'd managed to stop the bleeding, set the leg and wing and stitch up the injuries, but the bird had been off his food and water and barely holding on his perch. None of which was a good sign. Yesterday morning he'd been even worse. He'd given up the fight to live until he suddenly tried to rip apart Eagle's hands.

When Eagle had taken the falcon outside into the sunshine, thinking it might be a kindness to put the bird down, the raptor had exploded from his arms—as if the falcon had read Eagle's mind and flung himself into the sky in a last attempt at freedom. Except, with his injuries, no way in hell that falcon should've been able to fly. And he was one of the largest that Eagle had ever seen in his life.

But Rikker had taken to the skies with a vengeance and disappeared.

With his rescued dogs, Gunner and Hatter, at his side, Eagle walked to the raptor cages. The two big dogs went a long way to keep a lot of the wildlife back at the fence line where they belonged.

Caring for the large birds brought in a multitude of other prey looking for an easy meal. Although Eagle's property was well fenced, the birds often hurt themselves as they panicked, trying to get away from the threat of predators.

As Eagle approached the pens, he realized something was wrong. He picked up speed and ran the last few yards. Instead of the normal rustling of feathers, calls and chattering among the birds, there was silence. He approached quietly, feeling hundreds of eyes turn his way. And yet not one bird made a sound.

Unnerved, he walked around the perimeter of the multiple pens, looking for the predator that had them all tense. He pulled his gun from his holster and approached the corner cautiously. Glancing to all sides, he could see nothing that would put the birds on full-alert status. Peering around the corner, he saw the same high grass and bushes leading to the tree line farther back. He kept walking. Predators of all kinds had one thing in common. They were sneaky as all hell.

His steps as soundless as his property, he automatically checked the fences, looking for holes. Foxes were notorious for getting inside the fence but were still unable to penetrate the raptor cages. And, if they were smart, they'd stay clear. Coyotes often stayed just off to the side and taunted the birds, letting them know that, given any weakness, they'd be there to tear apart their throats. But the wolves were even more intimidating. They would howl from a distance, knowing the birds were within reach, almost salivating at the luscious meals inside the cages.

And still behind him ... was only silence. Every bird watched his progress. He kept glancing into the pens for any clue. Something was seriously off. A thick dark growl erupted from Gunner's throat. The huge sheepdog ambled forward, his ears up, his back raised. Hatter raced behind with a lesser sense of smell. More concerned with the joys of puppyhood, he pranced and jumped around Gunner, trying to figure out what this new game was all about.

Unfortunately Hatter was no puppy; he was just stunted in growth and seriously stupid.

Eagle walked past, dropping a soothing hand on the back of Gunner's neck. "What is it, boy?"

Gunner hunkered down, even as the hair on the back of his neck rose. Eagle studied the long grass and the thick forest beyond. The air was still, heavy. Nothing moved. Not even the wind.

A negative space was up ahead where the ground cover appeared flattened. A trail of broken and trampled grass led to it, but, unless the animal left the same way, no path exited the hollow. With Gunner at his side, Hatter loping behind, Eagle slowly approached. Reaching the fence line, he stood on the bottom beam and stretched up, hoping to see what was hiding.

Just then something erupted from the long grass.

He watched in amazement as Rikker soared high above,

his cry splitting the air with its piercing screech, only to circle back around again and again and slowly lower himself down. Eagle could see its broken wing, and yet the bird still flew straight. Eagle didn't understand—but he wanted to. He swung a leg over the top of the fence and jumped down on the other side.

He ordered the dogs to stay. Gunner broke into furious barking as if warning Eagle not to go there. But the dog wasn't able to jump this fence easily. With his weapon ready, Eagle slowly parted the long grass. Just as he caught a glimpse of something white on the ground, the falcon rose once again, flapping its big wings in front of him.

"Easy, Rikker. Take it easy now. Let me see what's going on."

Unable to see around the irate bird, Eagle stepped forward, using his arms to brush back the raptor. His gaze dropped to the ground, and he froze, his mind struggling to compute the scene before him.

A nude woman, bloody and scratched to hell, lay collapsed on the ground unconscious—or dead.

"Jesus Christ." He put away his weapon and dropped to her side. Young, with long dark hair half covering her face, skinny to the point of being gaunt. Her bare feet bloody and torn. As if she'd run until she couldn't take one more step …

Instinctively he searched for a pulse, only to have Rikker flap his dangerous large wings in Eagle's face and claw at his hands.

"Stop. I have to help her. Just like I helped you."

With a wary eye on the bird, Eagle was determined to subdue the falcon if he didn't let Eagle check out the woman. He slowly outstretched his arm again. Rikker made a harsh cry but settled onto the woman's shoulder.

Not the best place but it would do for the moment. Eagle found a pulse at her wrist. Slow and steady. He did a quick check for injuries. He ran experienced fingers down her spine, her extremities, looking for breaks. He couldn't find any broken bones, but her right ankle was swollen and her shoulder badly cut. He frowned, his mind racing to identify the wounds and their cause.

Keeping his face and eyes protected from the falcon, still uncertain of the reason for the bird's presence, Eagle searched the woman's back and chest. And found a small hole on the shoulder she lay on. He settled back on his heels. He knew that wound.

She'd been shot by a small caliber handgun at close range. He gently rolled her forward and found no exit wound.

"Goddammit." He glared at Rikker. "What the hell is going on here?"

In a move that shocked Eagle into silence, Rikker slowly lowered his head and stroked the woman's cheek with his beak.

"Well, shit," he whispered. Eagle pulled off his shirt, throwing it across her form. Wishing he had a blanket with him, he glanced at the house and realized it'd be better to pick her up and take her back, but how badly wounded was she? He worried about internal injuries the most. Still she couldn't stay here. That's when he noticed the bright red blood on the grass beside her head. As soon as he probed that side, she moaned. In a gentle voice he whispered, "Take it easy. You're safe now."

Just then she rolled to her back. Her eyes opened, and cloudy midnight-blue irises gazed at him. She seemed to focus only to have her lashes slowly drop again. Her mouth worked, and he could sense the effort behind her need to speak.

"It's okay. You're safe."

Her eyes opened, this time with more clarity. And landed on Rikker. Instead of crying out or screaming in terror, she murmured, "*Mo chara*, you found me." She gently stroked the falcon. He crooned at her touch. Her eyes drifted closed again.

Aware of the time passing, but also aware of something magical happening, Eagle studied her waxy features, his gaze catching sight of the fresh blood on her forehead.

Grim, he slipped his arms under her frail form and lifted her. As if Mother Nature herself was helping, the wind picked up, making the trees bow around him, the branches forming a curtain for him to carry her through. The air held an eeriness, something otherworldly going on. The dust swirled up at his feet, taking away his footprints, even though it had rained just that morning. And then a rumble sounded … as if someone gave them cover to hide the noise Eagle now made.

Unnerved, but understanding an opportunity had presented itself, he cradled her against his chest and strode back to the dogs. He awkwardly made it over the fence and froze. Rikker stood on Gunner's back, both ahead of Eagle as if urging him to move faster, with neither complaining about the odd transportation system. Even Hatter was out in front, for once a serious look in his eye.

Eagle didn't have a clue what was going on, but, whatever it was, it had to do with the injured woman in his arms. He picked up speed, almost running to his house. As he came to the large falcon pens, the silence was suffocating. His heart slammed against his chest, and he could hardly breathe for the tension coiling inside.

As soon as he pounded up the steps to his house and bolted inside, the dogs barked, and the raptors screeched, filling his world with a cacophony of sound—like some invisible command had been released.

He stared down at the frail woman in his arms and asked in a low, shocked voice, "Who are you? And what the fuck just happened to my world?"

Eye of the Falcon

Simon Says... Hide: Kate Morgan (Book #1)

Welcome to a new thriller series from *USA Today* Best-Selling Author Dale Mayer. Set in Vancouver, BC, the team of Detective Kate Morgan and Simon St. Laurant, an unwilling psychic, marries all the elements of Dale's work that you've come to love, plus so much more.

Detective Kate Morgan, newly promoted to the Vancouver PD Homicide Department, stands for the victims in her world. She was once a victim herself, just as her mother had been a victim, and then her brother—an unsolved missing child's case—was yet another victim. She can't stand those who take advantage of others, and the worst ones are those who prey on the hopes of desperate people to line their own pockets.

So, when she finds a connection between more than a half-dozen cold cases to a current case, where a child's life hangs in the balance, Kate would make a deal with the devil himself to find the culprit and to save the child.

Simon St. Laurant's grandmother had the Sight and had warned him that, once he used it, he could never walk away. Until now, her caution had made it easy to avoid that first step. But, when nightmares of his own past are triggered, Simon can't stand back and watch child after child be abused. Not without offering his help to those chasing the monsters.

Even if it means dealing with the cranky and critical Detective Kate Morgan …

Find Simon Says… Hide here!
To find out more visit Dale Mayer's website.
https://geni.us/DMSSHideUniversal

Author's Note

Thank you for reading Seeds of Malice: Psychic Visions,
Book 11! If you enjoyed the book, please take a moment and
leave a short review.

Dear reader,

I love to hear from readers, and you can contact me at my
website: www.dalemayer.com or at my Facebook author
page. To be informed of new releases and special offers, sign
up for my newsletter or follow me on BookBub. And if you
are interested in joining Dale Mayer's Reader Group, here is
the Facebook sign up page.
http://geni.us/DaleMayerFBGroup

Cheers,
Dale Mayer

About the Author

Dale Mayer is a *USA Today* best-selling author, best known for her SEALs military romances, her Psychic Visions series, and her Lovely Lethal Garden cozy series. Her contemporary romances are raw and full of passion and emotion (Broken But ... Mending, Hathaway House series). Her thrillers will keep you guessing (Kate Morgan, By Death series), and her romantic comedies will keep you giggling (*It's a Dog's Life*, a stand-alone novella; and the Broken Protocols series, starring Charming Marvin, the cat).

Dale honors the stories that come to her—and some of them are crazy, break all the rules and cross multiple genres!

To go with her fiction, she also writes nonfiction in many different fields, with books available on résumé writing, companion gardening, and the US mortgage system. All her books are available in print and ebook format.

Connect with Dale Mayer Online

Dale's Website – www.dalemayer.com
Twitter – @DaleMayer
Facebook Page – geni.us/DaleMayerFBFanPage
Facebook Group – geni.us/DaleMayerFBGroup
BookBub – geni.us/DaleMayerBookbub
Instagram – geni.us/DaleMayerInstagram
Goodreads – geni.us/DaleMayerGoodreads
Newsletter – geni.us/DaleNews

Also by Dale Mayer

Published Adult Books:

Shadow Recon

Magnus, Book 1

Rogan, Book 2

Egan, Book 3

Barret, Book 4

Bullard's Battle

Ryland's Reach, Book 1

Cain's Cross, Book 2

Eton's Escape, Book 3

Garret's Gambit, Book 4

Kano's Keep, Book 5

Fallon's Flaw, Book 6

Quinn's Quest, Book 7

Bullard's Beauty, Book 8

Bullard's Best, Book 9

Bullard's Battle, Books 1–2

Bullard's Battle, Books 3–4

Bullard's Battle, Books 5–6

Bullard's Battle, Books 7–8

Terkel's Team

Damon's Deal, Book 1

Wade's War, Book 2

Gage's Goal, Book 3

Calum's Contact, Book 4

Rick's Road, Book 5

Scott's Summit, Book 6

Brody's Beast, Book 7

Terkel's Twist, Book 8

Terkel's Triumph, Book 9

Terk's Guardians

Radar, Book 1

Kate Morgan

Simon Says... Hide, Book 1

Simon Says... Jump, Book 2

Simon Says... Ride, Book 3

Simon Says... Scream, Book 4

Simon Says... Run, Book 5

Simon Says... Walk, Book 6

Simon Says... Forgive, Book 7

Hathaway House

Aaron, Book 1

Brock, Book 2

Cole, Book 3

Denton, Book 4

Elliot, Book 5

The K9 Files

Rowan, Book 10

Caleb, Book 11

Kurt, Book 12

Tucker, Book 13

Harley, Book 14

Kyron, Book 15

Jenner, Book 16

Rhys, Book 17

Landon, Book 18

Harper, Book 19

Kascius, Book 20

Declan, Book 21

The K9 Files, Books 1–2

The K9 Files, Books 3–4

The K9 Files, Books 5–6

The K9 Files, Books 7–8

The K9 Files, Books 9–10

The K9 Files, Books 11–12

Lovely Lethal Gardens

Arsenic in the Azaleas, Book 1

Bones in the Begonias, Book 2

Corpse in the Carnations, Book 3

Daggers in the Dahlias, Book 4

Evidence in the Echinacea, Book 5

Footprints in the Ferns, Book 6

Gun in the Gardenias, Book 7

Handcuffs in the Heather, Book 8

Ice Pick in the Ivy, Book 9

Jewels in the Juniper, Book 10

Killer in the Kiwis, Book 11

Lifeless in the Lilies, Book 12

Murder in the Marigolds, Book 13

Nabbed in the Nasturtiums, Book 14

Offed in the Orchids, Book 15

Poison in the Pansies, Book 16

Quarry in the Quince, Book 17

Revenge in the Roses, Book 18

Silenced in the Sunflowers, Book 19

Toes up in the Tulips, Book 20

Uzi in the Urn, Book 21

Victim in the Violets, Book 22

Lovely Lethal Gardens, Books 1–2

Lovely Lethal Gardens, Books 3–4

Lovely Lethal Gardens, Books 5–6

Lovely Lethal Gardens, Books 7–8

Lovely Lethal Gardens, Books 9–10

Psychic Visions Series

Tuesday's Child

Hide 'n Go Seek

Maddy's Floor

Garden of Sorrow

Knock Knock...

Rare Find

Eyes to the Soul

Now You See Her

Shattered

Into the Abyss
Seeds of Malice
Eye of the Falcon
Itsy-Bitsy Spider
Unmasked
Deep Beneath
From the Ashes
Stroke of Death
Ice Maiden
Snap, Crackle...
What If...
Talking Bones
String of Tears
Inked Forever
Insanity
Psychic Visions Books 1–3
Psychic Visions Books 4–6
Psychic Visions Books 7–9

By Death Series
Touched by Death
Haunted by Death
Chilled by Death
By Death Books 1–3

Broken Protocols – Romantic Comedy Series
Cat's Meow
Cat's Pajamas
Cat's Cradle

Heroes for Hire

Asher, Book 5

Ryker, Book 6

Miles, Book 7

Nico, Book 8

Keane, Book 9

Lennox, Book 10

Gavin, Book 11

Shane, Book 12

Diesel, Book 13

Jerricho, Book 14

Killian, Book 15

Hatch, Book 16

Corbin, Book 17

Aiden, Book 18

The Mavericks, Books 1–2

The Mavericks, Books 3–4

The Mavericks, Books 5–6

The Mavericks, Books 7–8

The Mavericks, Books 9–10

The Mavericks, Books 11–12

Standalone Novellas

It's a Dog's Life

Riana's Revenge

Second Chances

Published Young Adult Books:

Family Blood Ties Series

Vampire in Denial

Vampire in Distress

Vampire in Design

Vampire in Deceit

Vampire in Defiance

Vampire in Conflict

Vampire in Chaos

Vampire in Crisis

Vampire in Control

Vampire in Charge

Family Blood Ties Set 1–3

Family Blood Ties Set 1–5

Family Blood Ties Set 4–6

Family Blood Ties Set 7–9

Sian's Solution, A Family Blood Ties Series Prequel
    Novelette

Design series

Dangerous Designs

Deadly Designs

Darkest Designs

Design Series Trilogy

Standalone

In Cassie's Corner

Gem Stone (a Gemma Stone Mystery)

Time Thieves

Published Non-Fiction Books:

Career Essentials

Career Essentials: The Résumé

Career Essentials: The Cover Letter

Career Essentials: The Interview

Career Essentials: 3 in 1